AGENT DOWN: THE REGION TWO SERIES

BOOK TWO

JANET WALDEN-WEST

JANET WALDEN-WEST

Agent Down: The Region Two Series Book Two

Cover by Black Bird Book Covers

Editor Jenny Lane

ISBN 978-1-7372190-2-6 (ebook)

ISBN 978-1-7372190-3-3 (paperback)

Contact Information: janetwaldenwest@gmail.com

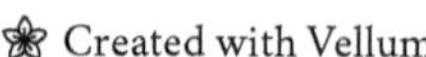 Created with Vellum

PART I

ruce

BRUCE DRIBBLED the basketball between his legs in a smooth move, out of Josh's reach. Then ducked under the taller man's outstretched arm, and took the shot.

"Nothing but net," he crowed as the ball arced, rattled the rim, and sank in. "At least you've got cryptid hunting to fall back on, because your game? Weak."

Josh got the rebound, but tucked it under his arm. Even with the regulation generic fade, and sweaty tank plastered to equally sweaty dark skin, he looked more like some too-pretty movie version of a private trainer than a soldier. "Time to hydrate."

Since there was never a time in Scottsdale cool enough to argue, Bruce joined him, grabbing both of their water bottles.

"Try to catch this one." He tossed a bottle to Josh, then swore and one-handed, hauled his loose basketball shorts up, tightening the drawstring before his pasty white ass flashed the entire compound.

"Bro. We can afford to order you some vertically-challenged sized shorts."

"Shut it. I've been burning it at both ends." Bruce's pop-up restaurant concept, the idea that allowed him to join a semi-nomadic team of agents dedicated to protecting people from not-people, had blown up faster than even his healthy as fuck ego had predicted. Keeping his aggressively public #Bruce-TheBastardNation following and social media commitments up while protecting the anonymity of the team and their parent organization sucked up even more of his time and energy.

"Truth. Desperate restaurant owners for you, and windigos too dumb to remember their own migration patterns for us," Josh said, then drained the mandatory BPA-free bottle in one go.

The team's schedule, specifically Vee's, was the reason Bruce hadn't done the one thing he'd been building up to since he'd installed himself in their world a year ago.

He eyed Josh, Vee's brother and teammate, weighing whether to bring him in on Bruce's plan. He didn't doubt Josh's bravery or loyalty. He had trusted the guy to guard his back while Bruce acted as bait to lure out a Godzilla-wannabe the year before. Josh's inability to keep anything secret from his sisters was another matter—but Bruce needed an insider's opinion.

Bruce stepped a few feet to the side to bring the yard, the expanse of sandy ground between the house and the rest of the team compound, into view. A quick scan showed it and the narrow second story wraparound walkway empty.

Josh stepped beside him, checking Bruce out instead of the landscape. "What's up with you? You've been twitchy as a goat that accidentally wandered into a chupacabra den for the last two days."

If there was a downside to living with a quartet of black ops soldiers—aside from wondering every damn time they drove through the outer gates whether they'd survive to drive back through again—it was the un-fucking-canny observational skills.

"Get back on the court and act like you're only taking a break," Bruce ordered. The court was in the dead-end section at the end of the house, cut off from view on three sides and requiring turning a corner to find on the fourth. Still, agents excelled at being stealthy as fuck and the last thing he needed was Vee or one of her two sisters waltzing in.

"I thought we were taking a break." Josh followed the order though, easygoing as always.

Bruce checked again, then jogged to the bench in the center of the yard, beside an artistic and out of place oasis of bird bath and desert succulents. He snatched the sketchpad case, the only item that was one-hundred-percent private in a world of pathological over sharing, and rejoined Josh.

"Don't make me regret this." Carefully, Bruce untied the case. The stuffed sketchpad bulged, fuller than usual. He flipped it open, revealing a small velvet bag.

Picking up on Bruce's secretive vibe, Josh angled so he could watch the yard and Bruce.

When Bruce emptied the bag onto the book's front page, the sun caught the diamond, refracting light back, the gem coming to life in a hundred tiny facets.

"Is that a wedding—"

Bruce lunged and slapped his free hand over Josh's mouth as Josh's yelped question echoed. "What did I say? What did I. Just. Say?"

"Sorry." The reply came out muffled.

Bruce removed his makeshift gag, wiping his palm against

his shorts. "Are you capable of not blasting the news to the whole Southwest Region?"

"Yeah, I'm good." Josh crowded closer. "So, is it?"

"It's an engagement ring. The wedding band comes after." Assuming Vee said yes.

"Oh, damn. No wonder you've been jumpy."

"I brought it back on my trip." He'd taken a red-eye to New York for a final run-through on a new restaurant he'd consulted on. Which also allowed him to pick up the ring from the jeweler. "My older brother and sister got my grand-mothers' wedding rings. This was an anniversary gift my gramps gave my nona." A diamond celebrating a lifetime lived together felt right for Vee's ring. "A couple of months ago, I took it to a guy in the city who specializes in Neoclas-sical designs, and had a new setting created."

"Can I?"

Bruce tipped the ring into his future brother-in-law's hand.

Like it was as fragile as one of their sister Kimi's origami creations, Josh cradled it and held it to the sun. "This is cool as hell."

"I wanted something different but sleek, and without edges to catch and get in the way." Intellectually, he knew Vee wouldn't be wearing it during mission call-outs. He'd seen firsthand how simple days out held the potential to turn into a fight against a stray cryptid, though.

He flexed his jaw, relaxing it from the automatic clenching that hit every time he thought of the danger Vee and the team faced. "Do you think she'll like it?"

Josh dropped the goofing, a shadow of the analytical, level-headedness that came out once he was sighting through a rifle's scope emerging. "That's a two-part question. She'll love the ring, because you understand her taste and because it's from you, and you'll come up with some wild, romantic fantasy way to ask. Whether she'll accept it and say yes—I don't know, man. That could go either way. Nobody's ever gotten married."

Nobody, as in no Company agent, in the organization's long damn history.

Bruce had run the scenario a million times but he still flinched at hearing his private fear laid out. He hadn't backed down in bucking his white collar family's expectations, in creating his food and fame his way, or in demanding the powerful but invisible Company that created agents also create an unprecedented position for his civilian ass on this team. He wasn't backing down from asking the person he wanted to officially share his life with to marry him, either.

Vee, and every other agent, had been raised to believe they didn't require any emotional attachments outside their team. Or viewing habits aside, that romantic love and permanent relationships were anything but civilian fantasy to fill the hole of not having a team. He'd damned well proven neither of those rules were true.

"Are you waiting until after the Assessor's visit?"

"Yes." He wasn't officially part of the team and allowed to stay until he'd jumped through a shit-ton of red-tape hoops, and proven he was an asset to the team as opposed to a hindrance that could get them killed.

"I want Vee to meet my family, and them meet her, too."

"What if they don't like her or something, like in *The Monster-In-Law?*"

Bruce's eyelid twitched at the reminder that the agents' only outside life experience came from damn movies, usually rom-coms.

"They will. One way or another." Vee wasn't Jewish—the Company was it's own fucked-up religion—but his mother hadn't been at first, either. And Vee handled him and his bluster and ego and attitude. His family wouldn't deter her, not even with the gauntlet every new addition to his family had to run before being adopted into the Kantor mob. His sister-in-law had survived it. His brother-in-law had survived it.

Josh whistled. "You are definitely one of us—brave and crazy. I've got your back."

Bruce slipped the ring into the bag, then the sketchpad, and tied it all closed. And hell if hearing Josh's vocal support didn't ease his anxiety a few degrees.

At least he had one ally.

Now all he needed to tackle was convincing some well-armed lackey of an ultra-secretive agency that a starred chef with a cult social media following belonged on a team of monster-eliminating super-soldiers.

Then convince the woman who held his heart, who'd had instructors and combat classes instead of parents and soccer and a real life, that they belonged together forever.

ee

"THIS CRAP IS GETTING OLD." I patted out the last sparks burning holes through the leg of my cutest cargo pants.

"This is the third time this month." Liv, my sister, broke the seal on a finger-sized canister, dropped it inside the metal dog crate-meets-zoo-animal cage, slapped the cover to temporarily close the front grate, and jumped back out of range.

The gas-based sedative was designed for cold-blooded reptilian cryptids, not humans. It still caused a hangover-grade headache if we accidentally inhaled the fumes.

"Why the heck is a firebug in the middle of a residential area?" I didn't get it. The cryptid species in question was way bigger than a bug, about four times the size of a Gila lizard, but looked a heck of a lot like a cartoon one, all cute-chubby and big eyes. Except for also spitting a substance that ignited when it met oxygen.

"It got lost? Some collector or kid brought one in last night while it was dormant, then it warmed up and escaped? There's no understanding civis." She tossed me a packet of alcohol wipes.

The little lizards also exuded a mildly sedative and euphoric substance that relaxed prey long enough for the pokey firebug to get close enough to toast its dinner.

We both scrubbed our hands just in case, since we'd wrangled our bug into the cage without aid of most of our Company toys. Leaning to use the truck's side-mirror, I checked that the ends of my ponytail hadn't gotten singed in the process, while my sister did the same. She frowned and swiped at a speck of dirt defiling her cheek, same brown as mine, but hers pore-less and perfect thanks to her hydrating mask obsession.

The timer on the canister chimed, the noise muffled by the cage. I tentatively edged the guard back an inch, peering through the mesh. The lizard was sacked out, bumpy square head resting on its stumpy front legs.

I grabbed one end of the crate, my sister the other, and we lifted it into the bed of her truck. Once it was in, I opened the grate fully so that the little pyro had enough oxygen, while Liv punched in a code on her phone and held a thirty-second conversation with our HQ, via the Cleaners, the specialists who sanitized the aftermath of our missions. Although today didn't really qualify. This was more of a shopping trip with an accidental cryptid detour.

"We're good to go. The Labs don't need any bug samples." Liv pocketed her phone.

I slammed the tailgate on her cargo. "I'll do a CYA sweep while you drop Sparky off." Firebugs weren't aggressive or territorial, never went after anything bigger than a roadrunner, and were usually pretty dang shy. They rarely interacted with humanity, so they got a pass from us.

"I'm taking it deeper into the range so we don't have a repeat." She hopped in, cranked the engine and backed out, desert bound.

The range was code for a huge stretch of desert and scrub owned by a Company Asset—someone not born into the Company, but who'd learned about the cryptid world and had a skill useful to our mission of eliminating predatory cryptids and keeping all cryptid's existence secret.

In this case, the Asset was a rancher who was amenable to non-lethal indigenous cryptids doing their thing on her property. The lizard hadn't hurt anyone and I wasn't going to kill it for the heck of it.

Cryptids were just natural animals, with traits that either made them dangerous to humans, or dangerous as weapons in the wrong hands. They all also had the entirely too creepy ability to go unseen if you didn't already know they existed, a defining trait we'd nicknamed the Chameleon Effect.

I double-checked my compact Glock, then replaced it in the bellyband holster hidden under my shirt. In case there was a second firebug, I had another slim gas canister tucked into my pocket, and a handful of zip ties and wipes. Plus my phone, in case the lizard had gotten here via some outdoor enthusiast who might've seen his find wake up and melt its way through a wall.

I swiped my phone screen for any reports of inexplicable wildlife sightings in the last hour since we'd intercepted the police call about a vandal burning a bench in the park. The park was on our way home, and we'd checked the disturbance out, mostly against Liv's better judgment.

She'd voted the call was about a non-cryptid. As lieutenant, her opinion carried weight, but as Commanding Officer of our team, the final say was mine. There had been just enough out of character crap in the last year-plus that I'd decided to check. Thus, another ruined civilian outfit.

There was minimal likelihood the reclusive desert creature had ambled into a well-populated suburb. Liv's idea about a clueless civi hauling it in made sense.

But something still felt off.

We'd had a pair of non-native cryptids show up last year, which we'd attributed to a collector importing them as exotic pets. Then a freakishly large windigo pack led by an uncharacteristically intelligent alpha showed, also in a suburb. This year, the 'digo migration patterns were freaky as heck. Terence, the C.O. of the neighboring Texas team, had seen zero during what was usually their prime breeding time. The canine-ish cryptids, no relation to the *wendigo* of some Indigenous nations, were normally as predictable as they were foul smelling.

Same for ghouls, creepy bipedal scavengers and opportunistic predators. We'd had crazy-high numbers of callouts involving the largely urban but also secretive creatures. As far as I was concerned, that trend began even further back, over two years ago. No one else agreed, but the weirdness nagged at me.

My phone vibrated and I switched from the reports to texts.

> Where the hell are you two?

I grimaced, but we should have been home by now, and late usually meant trouble in our world. At least, it did according to Bruce, my…I still wasn't sure what to call him. Other than the person I'd fallen for during the imported-cryptids-behaving-badly crisis of the year before.

My phone vibrated again.

> B is getting wound up. Bring in contraband carefully.

The two statements only made sense in the mind of my other sister.

I texted Kimi back.

> Delayed by a firebug tag and transport.

Her response was predictable.

> I know. Don't forget the doughnuts.

Of course she'd known. Our intelligence specialist always did, constantly monitoring info via both Company sources and her personal network of contacts.

Although, she also kinda hacked into things for fun. International organizations. Gaming companies to preview new games and skins before their release date. Interesting civilian accounts.

Before switching my phone off for the sweep, I texted Bruce.

> Taking a firebug home. We'll be back as soon as it's snug and happy.

His reply came within seconds.

> Be careful. And don't fucking bring junk food in. I'll damn well know.

I smiled at the mix of care and grump, which summed Bruce up perfectly. He was tyrannical about anything processed or packaged or not all natural, and had zero problem expressing his opinion.

He was also the first person who had ever asked me to be careful. He was the only person who waited up for us to come in from a mission no matter how lengthy, or who demanded we check in when we had a call-out while he was out of town.

It was weird.

It was also awesome.

I put away my phone and stepped back, slipping into the real me, the soldier who didn't worry about cute outfits. I scanned the compact park with its ruined bench. Automatically registering fences, barriers, ingress and egress points in relation to firebug behaviors.

The closest area was part of a neighborhood activity complex. A gazebo and stage in the middle. Soccer and baseball fields on either end. Block buildings side by side with restrooms and a central meeting area between.

The rest of the neighborhood was well-tended streets and homes.

The sun dipped lower, gorgeous multi-colored sunset starting its display. That settled where to begin. After dark, I would stand out, a non-resident prowling their nice streets. So, streets first, relatively secluded and empty park last.

At the last cul-de-sac forty-five minutes later, I was certain our little lizard hadn't torched a house or homeowner's garage. I was also starting to attract attention, wandering around with no pet or child as an excuse for walking every street and peering into yards.

Cutting across the park, I headed toward the super-basic block building. As I stepped from park grass to concrete floor, the sun sank below the horizon in a last pastel show.

The central building's lock gave with only a few seconds of effort on my part. No old smoke or ash signaling a firebug's stay greeted me. I made a circuit then closed the door so it remained innocent looking—and definitely not broken into—at a casual inspection.

I aimed for the restrooms and showers, moving into the narrow walkway, with the set of his and hers restrooms on either side. The back of the meeting building closed the area off into a dead end.

No trace of our cryptid showed here, either. I turned while palming my phone, needing its flashlight as the man-made canyon turned dark.

A pair of molten silver eyes shone from the open end. The feel of absolute wrongness, and evil, saturated the evening air.

The vampire stalked a step closer, blocking my only exit.

The once human face was a skeletal parody, skin stretched tight over bones. Its fangs were visible between blackened lips, and eyes an eerie silver every agent learned to hate. The virus had erased all trace of the person, only leaving this monstrosity. Cryptids were at least part of nature and had a purpose. The virus that ruined people's lives was a disease, one I'd happily eliminate from the earth.

The thing was in full hunting mode. In the middle of an area full of houses with curb appeal, backyard pools, and wooden swing-set forts shaped like pirate ships. And me with no backup, and only one too-small knife, even if it was an alloy infused with our Lab's cryptid and vampire-toxic chem compound.

I had no choice but the gun, always a last resort when collateral damage was a possibility. I ripped the gun free and sighted on its chest.

The vampire grabbed at the wall, claws finding purchase between the cinderblocks. Moving like a giant spider, it climbed in an inhuman, virus-augmented burst of speed. I slammed my back to the opposite wall and dropped to a crouch, aiming up. Just as fangs and backlit eyes materialized directly over me.

I fired and the shot thumped too far left, hitting it in the shoulder. It shrieked and swiped at its injured arm. Then turned the swing into backhand, knocking the gun from my grip. I rolled, claws whistling past where my head had been. The force of its blow accidentally lodged its claws into the concrete, chips flying.

Jamming my knee into the wall, I rolled the other way, further into the dark and the dead-end. The vamp herding me as it wrenched claws free, and threw itself from wall to wall like a ping-pong ball. Coming at me, blocking any chance at dashing past and escape.

I made my stand, going to one knee and braced. It leaped at me in a blur of bone and wrongness, sure of the kill, mouth wide open. As its rotting-meat breath nearly gagged me, I shoved the metal sedative container between its jaws. Moving too fast, going on blind instinct, it bit into the pressurized cartridge. The gas exploded, metal fragmenting.

I ducked, arms thrown across my face, and charged past, aiming for outdoors.

A line of fire opened up across my hip, vamp claw ripping through fabric. Spinning me. I dropped, hand out and searching. Hoping I was in the right spot. My hand wrapped around the familiar textured grip of my lost gun.

I raised it as the enraged vampire landed on top of me. And fired into its ruined face until the gun locked empty.

Dead, its weight crumpled on me in a suffocating load. I got my knees underneath the carcass and heaved it sideways. Enough to scoot free, butt sliding in vampire blood and gunk. I shoved to my feet.

A *scritch* of claw on concrete echoed behind me. I whirled, dropping the useless gun and jerking out my knife. Movement flashed across the walkway opening, silver reflecting, and then vanished, fast. At vampire speed.

I put my back to the wall again, crouching out of decapitation range in case there was another vampire hanging over the entrance, waiting for me.

Crab-walking, I advanced inch by inch. Nothing slashed

where my head would normally be. Nothing dropped from the restroom roof to block my exit. Better to fight in the open than get trapped in here again. I threw myself into a roll, coming out of it with the knife ready. Then jumped to my feet and spun in a circle.

Both sides and roof of the buildings were vampire-free. The park was equally empty, no bird calls, not even the usual tiny bats and bugs flitting around the street lights. I bolted, circling the buildings. Ready for anything.

Back where I'd started, human voices broke the weird silence, panicked people flocking together and shouting questions. I grabbed my phone, calling HQ for an intervention with whatever law enforcement the disturbed residents had undoubtedly called in at hearing the first shot minutes ago.

The firebug hadn't required them, but this, this was *definitely* a job for the Cleaners.

I stationed myself at the entrance to the gore and vampire coated walkway, turning myself into a one-woman blockade, hiding cryptid evidence and keeping civilians out.

CHAPTER 3

ee

I SLID out of Liv's truck into the welcome peace of the compound's extra garage bay, the two small spaces attached to the annex instead of the main garage at the house.

Holding the door to the yard for Liv, I fell in beside her as we walked. The house's upper-level backdoor was already open, light spilling out and merging with the false dawn.

Bruce came down the steps from the narrow elevated walkway circling the house, metal banging under his feet. Liv had already called in, once we had the park scene contained. HQ had activated whatever Company agent or Asset we had stationed in the local law enforcement agency, sending out a false alert about an escaped prisoner. The police had herded civilians out of the area as the Cleaners swept in, dressed as FBI agents from the closest field office.

Bruce still had to see us first-hand, though. Another weird new thing that was also awesome. From behind his glasses, his sharp gaze swept over Liv and me. Arms crossed, his sleeve tattoos were extra colorful under the security lights.

I'd changed in the truck, switching out sweaty, goo-crusted clothes for a set of tactical pants and tee, required extras even in personal vehicles. Bruce took that in as well, as deeply detail oriented as an agent.

"We're good. We both need a shower and food, but reports first," I said.

"Then get started." Bruce blew out a breath, but calmly pointed at the house. He didn't like what we did, as far as the personal danger involved, but he did understand the necessity. He also respected my role as C.O. Even if he angled behind us like he was some kind of compact, tattooed shepherd moving his flock.

At the top of the steps, he veered right for the kitchen, while Liv and I went left for my office.

Kimi met us in the wide hallway and signed, "I switched out drones for the two low-light infrareds and have one over the park neighborhood. The other is working outward in concentric circles, to a five mile radius of the attack."

"Jace said the Cleaners are already back at HQ with the specimen," Josh added from over Kimi's head, appearing and hanging from the corner of the office doorframe, flicking at her long, copper-tinted spirals even though they were nowhere near his face, much less interfering with his view.

Average height and the kind of willowy that hid muscle, adding to her deceptively sweet appearance, Kimi elbowed him in the ribs hard enough he grunted. She wasn't hearing impaired, but had lost her voice in a training exercise gone wrong as cadets.

She signed to him, "Have him message me." She grabbed one of her dozens of tablets, off to monitor law enforcement and city calls, and hit up our street contacts. And apparently,

Jace, Josh's twin. He was stuck at HQ recuperating from a mission that left him the only survivor of his team.

I spun the old leather chair and plopped my butt down. A puff of stale cigar smoke rose, decades after the C.O. responsible had gone. Technically we had enough time to shower and eat before writing and sending the mandatory post-mission report. Reaching over, I pulled my laptop close and opened it, putting everything I'd seen and done into the report. My team wasn't ever going to have to endure what Jace's had.

On the opposite side of the desk, Liv rolled her chair in, doing the same with her report. Standard procedure, and sometimes the dual points of view caught an issue or potential lead the other had missed.

Hers wouldn't say anything about the flash of silver I'd glimpsed. It could have been the rising moon glinting off the soccer net's metal frame. Certainly no other explanation had turned up, no hint of another vampire, despite my and Liv searching and then the Cleaners doing a meticulous sweep.

My gut wasn't sold though, and neither was I.

I dimly registered Liv leaving, and Kimi darting in and out, checking classified items and reports that were only accessible through the link in my office.

My hand was on the laptop lid, finally ready to close it, when a ping sounded. The Lab's pathology report on the vampire popped up, also standard procedure. The file opened, and I fast-scanned it. Then slowed and paid more attention to the summary.

There was a note on the vampire's endocrine system showing signs consistent with disease, or at least signs of alteration. Except once the virus responsible for altering a human into a vampire multiplied and took over, it repaired any damage that would impede the predator in hunting and feeding, its base directive.

Scrolling further, things got weirder. The vampire was seriously underweight. I.E., starving. Again, not hella likely since even a desiccated vampire would reflexively strike at anything warm blooded, the virus' DNA-encoded self-preservation at work.

Sure, the creature had attacked me, but…there had been an entire, active neighborhood available. It had to have already been there, hiding somewhere out of the sun's reach. Meaning it should have gone for a family or jogger whenever it first arrived.

A pair of footnote numbers, no text, were appended at the bottom. Those were marked Level Seven clearance. As a C.O., I was Level Six. Seven and Eight were the top tiers, Assessors and Oversight, respectively.

When I hovered over the links, they opened. I hesitated for a fraction of a second, then began reading. Kimi wasn't the only overly curious member of the team.

The reports were terse, some of the science well beyond my understanding. What the two footnotes boiled down to was the Lab divisions had attempted, repeatedly, to use vampire plasma and blood proteins to help create compounds for healing. They'd experimented with stem cells, too, isolating the regenerative portion of the virus's DNA, without the ugly changes it wrought on a victim. The last had been the most recent, work on blood and proteins tabled to divert all the resources to the stem cell branch.

All of which meant we were looking for more ways to heal wounded agents. I circled my finger round and round on the touchpad, thinking. The Lab division came up with all sorts of useful things. Some cryptids were rare because body parts were coveted in traditional non-Western medicine. Many of the effects attributed to them were accurate, based on our research.

Vampires as useful for anything was such a stretch

though. The virus was natural, but the changes it wreaked on the victim were devastating, and evil, even if it wasn't some kind of supernatural or religious evil.

I exited files, closed the laptop, and stretched, reality returning.

Bruce sat on the giant, weathered sectional sofa lining the front wall of my office. His sketchbook, his way of developing and nailing down ideas, new concepts, restaurant layouts, and menus was open, his pencil scratching over the page.

Without looking up, he said, "I can reheat that."

When I checked, a bowl of veggies and an egg in an artful array sat on my end of the desk, a bottle of water beside it.

We both had our passions. Mine was the Company, his, food and fame. He respected what I had to do. He also couldn't not be near after a mission, and couldn't not show he cared. Food was Bruce's love language.

I took the meal and curled on the couch beside him. Even cold, the veggie and savory tofu ramen was incredible. When I crisscrossed my legs and my knee lodged against his hip, it was like his tension level dropped a degree.

Done, I gathered the bowl and spoon and took them to the industrial-size dishwasher, one of the many upgrades Bruce had insisted on when he joined us. Just like the incredibly fancy stove with mysterious sections and attachments, and the enormous, equally fancy fridge. I raided the latter, full of local produce, and non-GMO milk and cheese from our favorite creamery. My prize was tucked behind a wedge of what we all could now identify as brie.

I closed the fridge, spoonful of pudding in my mouth. The dessert was simple egg custard and vanilla, and what he made when one of us was injured.

Arms crossed, Bruce propped on the wall by the short, two-person eat in bar, watching me.

I scraped the bowl for the last bits of pudding, then added utensil and bowl into the dishwasher.

Silent, Bruce held his hand out, and I took it. Letting him lead us to my room. Now our room, which was a continuing novelty. Still without a word, he flipped on the bathroom light, the private bathroom one of the perks of being C.O. He'd already laid out fluffy towels and lit a candle.

I stripped while he bypassed the shower and filled the freestanding tub, also new and twice the size of the old one. Plus, massage jets.

He turned back for a more detailed inspection now that we were alone, hands balling into fists when he got to my hip. The scratch from the vampire's claw wasn't deep, but it was long. I also had a few new bruises on my forearm, back and ribs.

I slipped into the hot water, tired muscles immediately happier, and watched Bruce strip, subtle highlights from the Arizona sun barely visible in his brown hair and short, neat beard. What he called 'normal people muscles and flaws' I called sexy as heck.

Colorful ink covered both arms in full sleeves, more ink trailing across his toned chest, and connecting the intricate artwork.

The newest design, in the center of his chest, was a vibrant sunflower. My sunflower, according to him. Common, because I baffled him with my love of all things civilian and pop-culture. Bright yellow and vibrant, because he swore I was meant for the sun and the limelight. Green tendrils grew from the stem, the delicate greenery curling around and over his heart.

He laid his glasses and the silver Star of David on the sink, and sank into the water behind me. I wiggled backward until I was between his legs, my back pressed to his chest. His thick arms circled me, wrapping us together.

I felt his sigh, the one that seemed to come from deep in him, and the last of the tension flowing out of him. I sank lower in the heated water, and rested the crown of my head against his chest.

Bruce kneaded my shoulders, working down my spine as far as he could reach. His touch was direct and firm, just shy of painful.

The same way we usually approached sex.

I slid under the water, then reemerged. Bruce sat back, arms propped on the sides of the tub while I shampooed the stink of smoke and dead cryptid out of my hair and pores.

When I resurfaced, rinsed clean, Bruce pulled me back into his lap. He amused himself squeezing water from my hair. Primarily so he could push it over my shoulder, exposing more skin.

He kissed everywhere he'd massaged earlier. His beard burred across my skin, raising goose bumps in its wake. If I turned my head enough to check, my skin would be reddened, Bruce leaving his mark. A different heat built under my navel and spiraled between my thighs.

He pulled me against him, water sloshing, his erection against my ass. Then caught my earlobe, setting teeth against flesh.

At my gasp, he caught my nipple, working it over. Pinching exactly hard enough that I squirmed. I not-so-accidentally rotated my hips, grinding against him.

He growled into the side of my neck, the primal sound vibrating through me and stoking me higher. He gave a last tug, and switched nipples. His unoccupied hand went between my legs. Stroked between my lips, thumb rolling expertly over my clit, spreading the bit of slickness back and forth.

When he slipped two fingers in, thumb still circling, working me inside and out, I arched against him and grabbed, sinking my short nails into his thighs on either side of me.

His turn to groan and swear.

I put more muscle into it, nails leaving crescents, and he increased the speed. My orgasm hit in a rush, as fast and raw as our play. I rode his fingers, thighs squeezed tight.

I let out a breath, grip on Bruce easing.

"Out," he growled against my ear.

I rocked my hips against him first, enjoying his swearing, and rose. He was a second behind me, water sheeting off us both.

I stepped out and grabbed the biggest, fluffiest towel. Bruce grabbed me, turning me toward our room. I tossed the towel on the bed.

Bruce opened the bedside table, finding the bottle of lube by feel, not taking his attention off me. Again by feel, he found our favorite vibrator. I hopped onto the towel, and propped on elbows, heels on the edge of the bed, knees bent and legs spread wide. Showing off.

He stepped in front of me, and squeezed drops of the silky lube on his fingers, making up for what the water had washed away. Then stroking it over my sex.

I stole the toy and circled the flexible ring around the base of his cock. Catching him in a firm grip and taking my time, enjoying the feel of him in my hand. Running my finger over the slit and precum.

Bruce lifted my ankle over his shoulder and slid inside me until the vibrator bumped against my clit. I curled my other leg around his waist, heel digging into his firm ass. Jerking him tighter and locking us together. I flicked the vibrator on.

He caught my hips and set a rough up and down pace. Grinding against the toy, the toy against me, him inside me. I balled the blanket in both hands, watching Bruce, never tired of seeing and feeling him. The way the tattoos seemed to come alive as he thrust, moving and rippling. The muscles flexing and cording in his arms.

Those arms—another orgasm washed over me, the fierceness on Bruce's face proof he understood exactly what he did to me.

His temp increased, the heavy bed frame creaking, his breathing rougher. I levered back up on my elbows, keeping our gazes linked. Telling him that yes, I was alive. We were together. And changing the angle just enough.

His fingers dug into my hips, probably adding another set of bruises. And that visual tipped off another orgasm, legs tightening around Bruce, keeping him with me as he came in one long, wordless rush.

His chest heaving, and my entire body tingling, we both rode the release, and the pure joy of *being*.

Admiring the way his—finally—lightly tanned skin and ink contrasted against my darker copper, I unwound from around his waist.

He turned his face enough to nip the inside of my ankle before easing it off his shoulder. "Stay put."

Fine by me. He pulled out and returned toys to their place while I enjoyed the show. He ducked into the bath, water in the sink running then cutting off, and cleared his throat. Then gave in, coughing, and the water turned on again. The same routine, off and on, for the last few weeks.

He emerged from the bath with his glasses on, silver star glinting against his skin, with a cloth for me, and sipping water. Then he backtracked for more.

I'd tossed the towel, added boy-cut briefs, and was fast-braiding my damp hair out of the way when he returned.

I twisted a band around the end of my braid, and picked up the recycled metal tin from the table, shaking it at him, the locally made all natural honey and mint cough drops rattling inside. "I grabbed them from the farmer's market on our way in yesterday." It was the second batch he'd gone through.

He popped one in, and added boxers. The pair with a dancing baby tree on the crotch, that he hadn't known was on the crotch until they lit up the first time we turned the lights out.

He hadn't been half as amused as my sisters and I were.

"Thanks." He nudged me over, then joined me, reaching to tug me in.

I planted a hand against his chest, keeping us apart. "A doctor. Tomorrow."

He glared at me.

I scooted away and glared back. "Blastomycosis. Valley Fever. Hanta." I held up a finger for each illness common across our region, that we'd all been cautioned about growing up here. All of which Kimi had pointed out to him the first time the cough hit.

He refused to take advantage of the extensive Medical division at HQ, although he did listen to Kimi. She'd taken the same three semesters of basic EMT training we'd all had, then gone on to add the extra semesters to qualify as team medic.

That oh-so-familiar calculating look passed over Bruce's face, and he ran his hand over his beard. "Let's negotiate."

"Doctor. Tomorrow."

"Agreed." He scooted higher on the pillows I kept piled on our bed. "How would you feel about a short, overnight trip next week? Despite my clear as hell directions, the construction team fucked up the bar layout and I need to explain in person."

Overnight was doable, as he knew, although there was always the chance of a last minute call-out or mission, which he also knew.

I had gone with him on an overnight to San Francisco,

because he found out I'd never been. Kimi had gone with him on one when it coincided with a comic-gamer-T.V. convention he'd gotten an apparently highly coveted pass to. Same with Josh and courtside seats when one of Bruce's clients came through on a thank-you bonus.

Liv hadn't gone anywhere, yet, always more conservative when it came to her duty. Sometimes to the extreme. But she'd tentatively agreed when he'd waved passes to some Scottsdale high-end car auction, which, totally did not get that lure, but she'd perked up. As C.O., I'd order her to go if she tried refusing on the grounds that it was her responsibility to never have fun. Only one of us could be away at a time, and it was Liv's turn next.

"New York?" I guessed.

Bruce cleared his throat, although this one didn't sound scratchy. More like…a prelude? "The city that morning. Even worst case, it'll only take half a day. Then to Westchester for dinner with my family. Hear me out. I know that may not sound like the best—"

"Yes."

"Yes?" He repeated it like he hadn't understood me. "Yes, as in you're agreeing to the trip?"

"Definitely." As part of his original debrief and interview, Bruce had been to Southwest HQ, with its town-sized sprawling campus, multitude of divisions, offices, dorms and academy where we'd grown up. No way was I passing up the opportunity to learn all about kid-Bruce.

He took his glasses off, then replaced them. Tone cautious, he said, "Dinner at my parent's. With my brother and sister, and their spouses. In all likelihood, all three nieces as well. That dinner?"

"What should I pack? Is there a standard having-dinner-with-your-boyfriend's-family dress code?" I chewed on my thumbnail. "This is going to require research."

He caught my wrist, like I was going to bail and start checking right now. "Romantic movies aren't research."

"Not true."

"You're really okay with using one of your practically non-fucking-existent nights off to take a red-eye to the opposite coast and meet my entire family? All at once?"

"Of course." I rotated my wrist so our fingers twined together. "I want to see where you grew up, and meet the other people you love. I mean, even if that wasn't the case, you've made so many concessions in order for us to be together. Anything you want, I'm totally in."

"Fuck, Vee." He caught the back of my head, cupping it and leaned in.

Our kiss was as sweet and slow as the sex had been energetic and rough. Equally life affirming, but in a different way.

The sharpness of the cough drop was on my tongue when we stopped. "Doctor," I reminded him.

"Let's go after morning PT and reports, and then we'll check out the new bistro off of the Art District." He relaxed and pulled me into the curve of his arm, that spot that felt like it had been made specifically for me. For us to be us, together.

ruce

BRUCE PULLED into the public parking garage, and snorted. It wasn't the one Vee had hauled him to the night they first met, passing him off as a drunk date when his lack of coordination was really the result of a run-in with a hallucinogen-secreting cryptid. Still, the damn concrete monolith made him smile.

Vee however had a frown when he opened her door. "Are you sure this doctor is qualified? Aren't good civilian doctors always booked up and you have to wait forever for appointments?"

"He did his residency at Cedars-Sinai." And Bruce had already made the appointment over a week earlier, a fact he felt no need to share during their negotiations the night before.

"Ours did theirs at Johns Hopkins."

Hand in the small of her back, he pointed her at the clinic. "Don't be a shit. A friend gave me this recommendation."

The same friend who owned the bistro Bruce had convinced Vee to try.

The one he wanted to get her reaction to, because it had a private outdoor patio in the rear that was elegant as hell. One that would be the ideal place to propose to Vee later, if she liked it today.

A proposal he'd hopefully make after the visit to his family.

The rest of his family harped on 401k's, job security, settling down, plus the usual general nagging, every time he visited. That was old hat. They were a large, loud family full of people with strong opinions and big mouths, him included. For the first time, he had butterflies in his gut when thinking of going home. Asshole butterflies the size of California condors.

He was taking the woman he loved and wanted to spend his life with home to meet his parents.

Unlike becoming a lawyer or investment banker and settling in the Westchester suburbs with the rest of the Kantors, marriage wasn't something he'd ever been opposed to. From a theoretical perspective, at least.

Mostly, it hadn't registered one way or another on his radar. He'd been too occupied, first establishing his reputation, then hopping from high profile gig to high profile gig, to think about it.

There had been a vague sense that if he got involved long-term, it would be with some industry person or maybe someone he met through work related activities, since he hit his share of celebrity-hosted parties, invited by his fans. He'd known it would be someone who enjoyed the same higher-end lifestyle he did, with plenty of traveling, and a public life.

The universe had a hell of a sense of humor.

He held the physician's office door for Vee, then did his thing with the registration desk. He took a seat with the damned never ending paperwork as Vee swept the tastefully done waiting area, seemingly curious about a new place.

Bruce saw her interest for what it was—a security evaluation first, personal curiosity a distant second. Everyone on the team did it, every time they were out, especially in an unknown environment. It was so ingrained, he didn't think they even realized what they were doing.

Which pissed him off all over again. Their lives from the time they'd been able to talk had consisted of brutal physical training that bordered on abuse. Accompanied by non-stop lessons designed to indoctrinate them into the Company's cult-like agenda of seeing themselves only as loyal weapons meant to protect others at any cost. And that damned well *was* psychological abuse.

The worst part was that the people he'd originally assumed were violent, unimaginative assholes with the I.Q. and emotional ability of a cactus were some of the most complex, original, kind souls he'd ever met.

Vee took in his scowl. "Are you reconsidering your potentially second-rate doctor choice? We can go to HQ right now." She whipped her phone out, probably ready to call in one of the Company's med helicopters to land on top of the parking structure.

He put his hand over hers on the phone, and pushed the device down. "Knock it off. Go visit the shops. Take a damn walk. I don't care what you do as long as it isn't getting me chucked out of this office before I've even gotten into an exam room."

Vee fidgeted with the phone, biting the inside of her cheek.

He dialed back his asshole-ness. "If I were Josh or your sisters, you would be hanging out in Medical with them." The team was bonded to an extreme, almost incomprehensible level to most people. He'd lived with them a year and the lack of boundaries and fanatical devotion still occasionally surprised him. "I understand your thought process."

"That's what family does."

"That's what teams do." He pulled on his patience, because this was Vee, and she felt the weight of every member of the team on her shoulders, every day.

"In the real world, a doctor's appointment would be a private event. So go amuse yourself for an hour. There's a patisserie a few blocks over. Buy real pastry and doughnuts. Their pain au chocolate might cure you of ever eating that convenience store trash you call snacks."

"Don't hate on the tiny doughnuts. I'm going, but only because I recognized the word chocolate in your lecture." Vee darted in for a fast kiss, then stood.

He watched her go, and then watched her almost immediately become sidetracked, this time with an older lady and a pocket-sized dog she was pushing around in some god-awful kind of pet stroller.

A smile snuck up on him, another Vee-related hallmark. He loved her openness and curiosity. In truth, he'd have normally been fine with Vee accompanying him into the exam, but he'd already had another plan in place for her today. The patisserie hadn't been a spur of the moment idea.

His goal was a long game. The team wasn't as familiar with this part of town, since it was historically cryptid-free. Tell Vee about a pastry shop, a draw she'd never pass up. On the way to the bakery, there was a bookstore, at least two art galleries specializing in Indigenous art by Indigenous artists, and an upscale body artist's shop. Then there were the shit ton of boutiques as well. New things. New people, with new opinions.

Vee—hell, none of the agents, period—had experienced

any kind of childhood, or opportunity to explore the world and develop outside interests. Somehow, that spark inside them hadn't been suffocated though. He was doing his best to slowly, carefully feed that creativity and inquisitiveness, and foster their originality. Fuck living an invisible life, and being a ghost in society.

He didn't hold much hope that Vee or the other three would really ever turn their backs on the Company. He worked in realism, and the reality was that teams filled a necessary niche. Yes, what they did was vital.

His sticking point revolved around them not being given the tools to make an informed decision. Military, law enforcement, and other first responders also held vital but dangerous jobs. However, they chose those careers because they had all the information on pros and cons, and had weighed the risks.

That didn't mean the team couldn't experience the world. Have some damn fun that wasn't based on a 'hey, we're still alive' party because they'd survived facing a monster. They could see how outside life functioned, and how real, free people lived.

Then, hopefully, learn to value themselves more, as something other than an interchangeable warm body with a gun. Next step, maybe not automatically throwing themselves on every grenade, in some pre-programmed Company mind-fuck. At least look at other options before assuming sacrificing themselves was Plan A.

The idea of Vee sacrificing herself...that scared the hell out of him in a way he had only experienced once, when his grandfather, greatest champion of Bruce's career, became ill. Facing the reality of losing him had knocked Bruce on his ass.

He caught himself touching his chest, right over the spot

where the interlocked stars representing that set of grandparents flowed into Vee's sunflower.

The arrival of the nurse gave him an out from that depressing headspace. He followed her to an exam room. He was ready to check finding an antihistamine for whatever this allergy was off his list, and concentrate on more important matters. Namely, a proposal worthy of Vee.

ee

I TURNED BACK and forth in front of the shop's three-way mirror, checking the rear view of the dress.

"That's your color," the shop owner said, head tilted and studying me, then moving in and twitching the shoulder seams to drape to her satisfaction. "It's also a vintage Pucci. I only got it in yesterday."

I took the vintage part to be a good thing. The dress did fit perfectly, and the colorful geometric pattern had called to me when I glimpsed it in the store window. So had the other two I'd tried on.

The entire store was a treasure chest for grownups, and I'd texted Kimi and Liv about it. It had discoveries in every corner—tiny, round purses and white patent knee high boots in one. Evening gowns that might have been in a black and white movie in another. Even jackets with huge shoulder pads, neon scrunchies, and shell choker necklaces.

"We like it," Liv said from my phone screen. The text had turned into a group video chat.

"You're already planning to borrow it," I accused her. "Both of you."

I was shortest, Kimi in the middle, then Liv. But it really would work on them, too.

"Not until after New York," Kimi signed. "I like the first dress best."

"The second or this one." Liv added her vote.

I checked over my shoulder with the owner, who took stylishly polished to a new level, and was thus our de-facto expert.

"Any of the three are absolutely appropriate."

Once she heard I was looking for a meet the boyfriend's parents look, she had pulled dresses, jackets, and entire outfits for me.

"Okay." I headed to the dressing room. I'd spent longer exploring the racks of treasures than I'd intended. "Gotta go meet B."

"Bakery, then Bruce," Kimi ordered.

"Uh, yeah." I closed our connection and changed back into jeans.

When I came out, the owner asked, "Have you decided?"

"All three dresses, please. Do you mind wrapping them up while I run down the street?"

She smiled and took the dress I'd changed out of, then pulled the other two winners from the rack of try-ons. "They'll be ready by the time you have your pastry boxed—I overheard your sister. Try the pain au chocolate. They are divine."

"So I've heard." I pocketed my phone and wove through the rows of fashion history. I glanced at the street. Then dumped bakeries to the bottom of my priorities.

Many of the shops on this street were older, and had once

had living areas overhead. The tiny areas between the buildings were probably meant for stoops. Most were now either gated off as areas for owners and employees to take breaks, or equipped with a bench for the public.

The niche directly across from me only had a pair of ornate trashcans. Between them, in the shadows cast by the building, silver flashed at human head height.

The unearthly molten quicksilver of a vampire's gaze. Positioned like it meant to catch my attention. Hairs rose along my arms.

I hit the door, the alert chime still tinkling as I stepped from the street into the road. I tried for casual, angling as if I was headed for a gallery to the left. Monitoring the alcove from the corner of my eye.

The silver winked out.

I bolted for the spot, pulling my small back-up Glock from the bellyband holster and keeping the weapon down by my hip. I slowed at the entrance. Took a breath, and back to the wall, eased in. Weapon up, sweeping the narrow alley.

Empty.

The wall at my back was a solid stretch of brick, no doors, no windows. The opposite had a plain metal door, possibly for deliveries. I slid across to it, and tried the crossbar. It rattled, but remained closed, locked from the inside.

Brick scraping my back, I sidled to the end of the alley, and stepped out. A small parking area, holding a couple of cars, greeted me. I dropped into a half-pushup, checking under the cars before approaching into grabbing range in case anything lurked underneath.

All empty.

I stood and checked car windows, gun level. All were as empty as the underneath. Another solid block-long expanse of brick hemmed in the lot, the rear of the shops on the other side of the square.

Hairs on my arms rose. The exact same feeling as at the park, after I ended the vampire in the block building, and glimpsed another flash of the same silver by the exit.

I scanned the roofline of the two buildings in front, then whirled and repeated it on the rear building. Nothing moved. No shadows slanted from the flat roofs to provide a shadowy hiding spot.

Prowling the edges of the lot, I triple checked, then back-tracked. I stopped just inside the alley. Exactly where—whatever it was—had stared out at the eclectic shops and relaxed shoppers.

Swapping the gun for my phone, I punched Liv's number, not waiting for a hello. "Send a drone up now, at my location."

For? Kimi's text popped up.

I answered them both. "Anything larger than a firebug or 'chupe."

Walking as I gave orders, I watched the light crowd that would swell soon as people arrived for lunch. "Text Bruce and tell him to stay inside the office until either I arrive or he hears from one of us. Non-negotiable."

I hung up, and quartered the few remaining blocks of the district. Searching for that eerie sensation as much as for a suspicious figure or an unnatural eddy in foot traffic, humans unconsciously avoiding a cryptid. A door ajar that shouldn't be. A parent glancing around for a kid who wasn't where they'd been a moment before.

Turning up nothing, I branched out, crossing to the private lots, and finally, the parking garage. Weapon out again, I climbed the levels, circling the top deck, surveying the district spread below me. Life continued on, civilians on street corners, talking and waiting for the light to change, dining at outside tables. Oblivious.

I jogged down, barely slowing as I entered the populated

street, dodging around slower groups and into the medical building. Bruce stood as close to the office door as seating allowed, like he could stare a hole through the buildings to where I'd gone.

The hard line of his jaw relaxed when I tilted my head toward the outdoors.

He joined me as I called back. "Anything?"

Liv's tone was collected and precise, completely in lieutenant mode. "Kimi hasn't found anything on visuals or infrared from the drones. I'm monitoring LEO scanners and chatter, but nothing there either."

"Josh?"

"Nothing from our street contacts on his end."

"Same for foot patrol here." I still hesitated, giving the street a last look.

From beside me, Bruce demanded, "What the hell was it?"

That was an excellent question.

* * *

"Silver?" Josh sprawled at the kitchen table, poking at the remaining lettuce leaf in his bowl. According to him, it was weird, frilly lettuce. He wasn't wrong.

Kimi leaned over him and nabbed it with her fork.

From her spot at the eat-in bar, Liv watched me circle and gather everyone's empty bowls, stacking them on my full one.

"Silver. And it wasn't stationary," I repeated for the second time, as much to convince myself as my audience.

"It could've been some civi's drone," Kimi signed. "The cheaper ones aren't coated and can reflect the sun or other light sources."

Her theory was plausible. More so than mine. Plausible or not, it felt wrong.

Doing what a good lieutenant did, Liv correctly read my silence as disagreement. Her fingers drummed out a pattern against the antique counter tile. "Things have been wild, wild west around here."

"Exactly."

"I meant that we've been working more call-outs than we've been sleeping. Adding in the random spate of incidents when we were out socially…" She shrugged.

I didn't miss her emphasis on *random*.

"We're all twitchy. It's normal to be on edge," she finished.

Kimi tapped the table for our attention. "Seriously. I dreamed we had a call-out last night, and had BDU pants on before I completely woke up."

"C'mon, Vee. Vampires are the only entities with silver eyes." Josh jumped firmly on the Vee-is-imagining-it train.

"The alley was in the shade. An old vampire could handle that. Probably."

"Was there any place it could have come from to access that shade?" Liv asked.

She knew there wasn't. We'd both poured over building blueprints and underground city water and sanitation schematics. The only option would have been the building with the locked door. That site turned out to be a very active glass-blowing studio.

Vampires weren't fond of fire, a close cousin to sunlight. The virus created nocturnally adapted predators, period.

I'd still double-checked that their employees were all accounted for, no disappearances, no one calling in sick.

"I'm hitting the gym." Since running through hand-to-hand moves was my go-to stress buster, the announcement was as good as verbally admitting they were right, and I was wrong.

Our room was empty when I went in to change from

street clothes to workout gear. So much for my second favorite stress relief.

After I'd paid for my dresses and thanked the slightly confused shop owner, Bruce had gone straight for the car, cancelling our lunch plan. When I asked about the doctor's visit, he'd flashed a prescription for cough syrup, and jerked the band-aid from the crook of his arm. He had dropped it in the pretty trash receptacle where I'd imagined a sunbathing vampire standing, and barked about yearly blood work.

He grabbed his sketchpad as soon as we got back, and vanished. Which was his as good as verbal request for a few hours of privacy.

I hoped one of the new dresses I'd bought had both impress-the-parents *and* get back in your boyfriend's good graces mojo.

ee

I SMOOTHED MY SKIRT—THE Pucci dress, which I'd looked up and discovered was collectible. I was about to discover if it had the good mojo or not.

Bruce held open the door of our rental car, and I took his hand, stepping out into the suburban Westchester evening. He let go, but immediately put his hand in the small of my back, keeping us connected. He leaned in enough that his breath tickled my ear, his voice rumbling through me. "You are fucking gorgeous, fucking brilliant, and kill monsters as easily as I attract fans."

"Do I look nervous enough for a pep talk?"

"Not one damn bit, and that wasn't a pep talk. It was a statement of fact."

I smiled, which was probably his intent. The driveway in front of his parent's house held two cars, and I assumed the garage held more. We got the last few feet of space.

I wasn't nervous, though. I was excited to finally meet Bruce's family. To see his room, and hear stories about him.

Kimi, Liv, Josh, and I had binged date movies, analyzing the parts with families. I'd also brushed up on notes from our old classes, especially the semester on passing in civilian social situations.

Bruce mostly swore, and walked out. However, he had been in a good mood all day, restaurant snafu corrected, and the drive here event free. While Bruce did his thing that morning, I'd walked the neighborhoods around the restaurant, and video chatted with the team so that they could experience it with me.

I wished I could include them in this adventure, too. Pausing before climbing the steps to the big powder gray and white home, I admired green grass, and trees wider around than Bruce and I combined. The place was landscaped with bright flowers Kimi would have loved.

The way she'd bring an object into focus, I leaned and took in the house. Imagining Bruce coming into it every day after school or a job or whatever civilian kids really did.

When I finished, Bruce was waiting, more patiently than with most side-trips and delays. "Did you get your fill for now?"

"For now." He understood me. "I've never been in someone's home before. I mean, as a guest and not an agent on a cryptid crime scene. Or cryptid related, like when I took you home post-anangoa."

His lips thinned, pressing together. Then he took a deliberate deep breath of the cedar mulch and evergreen scented air, and let whatever had annoyed him go.

He opened the door. The chatter of multiple conversations, and the scent of lemon polish, and cooking beef, invited us in.

"Where's my welcoming party?" He raised his voice over the noise, his specialty.

The light, fast patter of multiple feet on wood sounded, then kids came into view. All three racing down the stairs to our right.

Variations of 'Uncle Rob' hit in a squealing cascade.

"Favorite rugrats." A smile split his face, the kind of pure joy he rarely let people see.

"What did you bring us?" One girl planted herself in front of the other two. Her hair was the same medium brown as Bruce's, and she had that identical *try to impress me* look he automatically directed at people.

Meaning this ringleader had to be Amanda—Mandy—his sister's oldest. I'd created a dossier months before, so I would understand what and who, when he talked about the people that mattered to him.

"I brought me. What else could anyone possibly want?"

"Uncle Rob-Rob." The smallest, Mandy's little sister, threw herself at him, grabbing his leg like they'd done this before.

Miss Ringleader only rolled those expressive brown eyes. "He doesn't mean it, Essie. Duh. Gifts are in the car."

Wow, was she related to Bruce.

"Mandy's right. If you want whatever is locked in my trunk, you're going to have to convince me."

The three girls tackled him, hugs all around.

Happiness came off of Bruce in waves, like heat off a pan. You couldn't necessarily see it as more than a haze, but you felt the impact.

He disentangled himself. "C'mere."

They squished in, ready for whatever came next.

"This is Vee. I like her. So be nice."

Three pairs of eyes drilled into me.

"The *girlfriend*," Mandy said. They shared a moment.

Exactly the way Kimi, Liv, and I did.

"Hi." I ignored the undercurrent of *girlfriend*. His family had discussed me, no surprise. Which? Kind of nice. Almost like I already belonged.

"Why is your name a letter?" Essie, the smallest asked. She was the only one in a dress, and the kind of cute that probably let her get away with lots. Like Josh had.

"Lucky." The older girl, the quietest, who had to be Shoshonna, finally spoke. Her hair was the same deep walnut as the polished floors, one side of her curls clipped back, the way Kimi sometimes did. "You don't have to spell your name out for everyone all the time."

"It's not her name—it's a nickname. Like Rob-Rob isn't Uncle Bruce's name." Mandy re-took her spot as leader.

"True. My name is Victoria." I spoke to Shoshonna. "My sister always has to spell her name for people. She usually goes with Kimi instead of Kimora, because she gets annoyed, too."

Shoshonna's eyes widened. "Whoa. Cool."

"If they're your sisters, why do you all have different last names?" Mandy asked, not giving up her spotlight to anyone else. And obviously having listened to the adults talk, at least once.

She was a mini-Bruce.

"Jesus H Christ," he muttered.

I didn't see the problem. She was curious, and he'd told me to never apologize for wanting to learn. *He* never apologized.

"We just do—it's what we were born with. My brother and his twin have their own last name, too."

"Robert."

The girls and I looked up. We were now in the middle of a double crescent, kids in the closest arc, adults ringing them.

"Marissa." Bruce answered in the same kinda exasperated tone she'd used. "Vee, my sister."

She didn't really resemble Bruce, from her sleek, dark hair to her hazel eyes. Until you got to her expression.

Bruce nodded to the man beside her, the one with the kind of lines that meant he laughed a lot. "My long suffering brother in law, Isaiah. The tall one beside him is my brother Kenneth, and his even longer suffering wife Hannah."

She was the only one to give me a real smile, her hair a longer version of Shoshanna's curls.

I retuned her smile, as Bruce motioned to the last two adults on the end. "My mom, Donna, and dad, Levi." He narrowed his eyes at the distinguished-looking pair, the way he did when warning Josh about contraband sports drinks, and warning me and my sisters not to buy him gifts. We always ignored him.

So did his family.

His sister and brother crowded closer to me. His parents converged on Bruce.

I assumed parents had seniority over siblings when it came to catching up, and turned to my welcome committee with a smile. "It's nice to meet you and put faces to Bruce's stories. He talks about you guys all the time."

His brother and sister shared a look, and his sister grimaced. "I can only imagine. I'm surprised you agreed to visit our den of domestic responsibility."

Since I wasn't sure what that meant, I went with one of the fail-safes Kimi and I had put together in case our social training proved inadequate for extended civilian social interactions.

Rule One—people always enjoyed talking about themselves.

"Bruce was excited about your partnership. Weren't you

one of the youngest lawyers in your firm to make partner?" I asked his brother. "Congratulations."

"Actually, yes I was." He blinked at me. "Thank you."

"He also mentioned you were chairwoman for the charity drive this year. Please don't let me forget—I have a check from my group for you, but I think I left my purse in the car," I said to his sister. I wasn't accustomed to carrying one, and kept misplacing or forgetting it. I should have bought the cute round one when I bought the dresses. It was more toy than bag and I might've kept up with it.

"My charity? The Maimon Home?"

"Yes."

"You aren't Jewish. Are you?"

"No, but, B—sorry, Bruce—told me about it and how it helps kids." The idea of children orphaned, sometimes siblings separated, and all alone...That was the worst fate imaginable, and the whole team had offered to contribute when Bruce had explained.

Shrewdness very like her brother's peered out from Marissa's eyes. "Do you support children's aid groups due to your background?"

"Stop grilling people." Bruce turned to our group with a frown. "You've picked up Mom and Kenny's interrogation habit and you aren't a lawyer."

"Anyone who knows this family expects a mild grilling," Bruce's father said. "They also expect excellent hor d'oeuvres and wine."

When he turned down the hall, the rest of the group followed.

Bruce's mom hung back with us. She eyed Bruce critically, another mannerism Bruce had inherited. "You've lost weight. I don't think I like it."

"Mom, don't feed the Jewish mother stereotype." Bruce reclaimed my hand.

"How am I a stereotype when I'm making a factual observation? You've lost weight since I saw you last, although it's been so long I'm surprised I remembered what you look like."

Bruce groaned, and his brother laughed from somewhere ahead of us. "It's your turn, kid. You may think running all over the country will save you, but it only means you get months worth of guilt compacted into the span of each visit."

I was pretty sure it had only been three months, max, and Bruce glared a hole in his brother's direction.

His brother sing-songed, "I don't need to see you to know what you're thinking."

The rest of the family laughed at that. As we entered the kitchen, which seemed to be the center of family-time, his mother added, "It's stress from all your traveling."

Isaiah held out glasses of wine to us, and I accepted. "Fortify yourself. They get worse."

It took me a second to realize he was talking to me. "I'm sure they're concerned. All families do that."

Although ours was usually way less critical.

Bruce cleared his throat, which turned into a full-blown cough.

I checked, in case he wanted the cough syrup, which seemed to work much better than the cough drops.

He took a swallow of wine and answered my unspoken question. "I'm good."

Both of his parents zeroed in on that, examining Bruce.

His sister beat him to the questioning. "Are you sick? The girls have a recital in two days. They cannot miss that."

"Do you really think I'd purposely risk my nieces' health?"

"You could have picked up something on the plane. All that recycled air, you know it's full of germs," his mom said.

"I did not suddenly turn into a plague vector in the ten hours since boarding a plane."

"How are you feeling, Vee?" His dad looked exactly like Bruce in that moment, or the other way around, I guess. True concern softened his expression. They had the same build, the same firm line to their jaws. His dad's deeper brown hair held silver where Bruce's didn't.

"I'm fine, thank you."

"Vee isn't a plague monkey, either. Where's the food?" Bruce took another healthy gulp of wine.

As his mom and sister beelined to an oven almost as fancy as ours, his sister in law tucked curls behind her ear, and whispered, "Smart move. A brisket is one of the few things that they'll abandon an argument for. I wish there had been one available as distraction the first time I met them. You're doing great though."

"Thank you? Food holds great power in my family, too." I wasn't sure what I was thanking her for, so concentrated on the food part and sipped the light white wine. Hoping no one asked my opinion on it. Bruce was doing his best, but nuances were eluding me. It was all…wine.

"Do you cook?" His dad joined our non-brisket obsessed circle.

"Bruce has informed me microwaving isn't legitimate cooking, so no. He's in charge of our—" I caught my error "—the kitchen."

His dad's salt and pepper eyebrows went up. "Are you two living together?"

When I'd slipped up and said our, I'd meant me and the team. It had been decided that group living situation would raise too many questions though. I hurried to redirect. "Yes. We are. Living together."

Bruce flinched.

"You moved in with someone and didn't tell us? You've had a million opportunities when mentioning Vee." His sister whipped around and pointed, forgetting or not caring she had oven mitts on, although she seemed more…triumphant than shocked?

"I am telling you now. That was part of the reason for our visit."

"Are you married to Uncle Rob-Rob?" Essie looked up from the tablet all three girls had found more interesting than the adult conversation. Until now.

"No." At least I could answer that without stepping on a hidden social landmine.

"You told mommy you lived with each other so that means you're married," Essie informed us.

"Adults can live together without being married," Bruce informed his niece in turn.

His sister glared across the kitchen at him. Looking at least as dangerous as a cornered ghoul.

"Are you getting married?" His mom laid her oven mitt down, in a precise and formal way. Like she'd been waiting for this exact moment. She and his sister traded glances, the way Liv and I did, agreeing on a pre-planned move during a mission.

I had no idea if that was good or bad. Bruce tensed up though.

But when he answered, he looked at me instead of his mom or family. "Vee and I are together."

I didn't know what etiquette was as far as PDAs when in front of parents. I also didn't care at the moment. I leaned in for a kiss, my empty hand splayed on Bruce's chest, and he cupped my cheek, meeting me.

We kept it short and respectable, but something was different. It felt like Bruce had left a question on my lips when we drew apart.

"That wasn't an answer," his brother said, as Hannah rolled her eyes.

"It's the only one you're getting, here and now. This isn't a courtroom and none of you get to cross-examine us." Bruce chose an olive from the elaborate tray of olives, cheeses, and breads taking up most of the formal kitchen island.

He held it out to me. "Try this. They're from a small grove that's been owned by the same family for around three hundred years."

"Has he had this conversation with your family?" Nursing his wine, Bruce's brother looked intrigued.

"My family knows that I care about Bruce. Very much."

"How do they feel about my brother?"

"He's part of our family now. I love Bruce. Bruce loves me. My brothers and sisters would be cool with him just for that, but they know him and love him for himself, too," I said promptly.

Bruce kissed my temple.

"That seems fast," Kenneth—Kenny—said, but with an expression that looked more like he meant something totally different. Kind of victorious-ish.

"They've had a year to get to know me. Plus, people decide whether they love me or hate me quickly," Bruce said. "Sixty seconds, tops."

His brother-in-law laugh-choked on his wine, earning another lethal Bruce-like glare from his wife.

"We should get to know your family, then. Since they aren't here, you'll have to stand in for them all."

"I'm happy to. But they truly would love meeting you guys, too." Josh was Mister Friendly, anything new interested Kimi, and Liv…she loved us all enough to break rules and make the effort.

"And you two met a year ago, at work?" His mom asked.

"You already know we did," Bruce said. He looked at me and sighed. "Get it out of your system."

"Ours really was a work meet-cute." I had *so* always wanted to say that.

"Did he yell at you or throw things?" Kenny asked with a snarky grin.

"There were some—" Bruce glanced at me, then the kids, then back, and I chose my phrasing carefully "—words said. Colorful ones. Loudly." I nudged against Bruce and he snorted, but more relaxed and amused now.

"And this was in front of your employer? At work?" His dad got in on the action, setting his wine to the side.

"We were technically off the clock." Bruce had just stormed out on his job, creating a scene, and the team and I were celebrating a cryptid-free night out. Until Bruce and a cryptid dropped into my karaoke set. "So, instant sparks."

His mom completely abandoned the food, giving Bruce all of her attention. "This employer is?"

"You already know the answer to that, too."

"NDAs." I shrugged. There really was one on Bruce's part, just Company enforced. We had an iron-clad cover story to go with the NDA.

"You should have sent that across your mother's desk before signing," his dad said, like he was speaking for the group, and like they'd already had this conversation.

"I knew what I was signing."

"Silicon Valley tech millionaire? Elon Musk?" His brother guessed. "Actor?"

The rest of the family leaned in, equally fascinated.

"A political figure. It's a political figure, isn't it? Who else needs a private chef and a security detail." His brother pointed an *I-gotcha* finger.

Bruce layered a fragrant bit of cheese on a crostini and passed it to me.

"By definition, political figures have a finite time at their jobs." His sister had also now abandoned the poor roast. "What happens when they no longer have some high profile life and no longer need a chef?"

"At what point did you hear me utter the phrase 'I work for a politician'?"

Like she hadn't even heard him, Marissa crossed her arms, and tried staring Bruce down.

I could've told her that wasn't ever a realistic possibility.

I gave myself points when she broke first. "Whomever you may or may not be currently employed by, have you at least been taking care of your portfolio? That's even more vital if you're talking about adding a mortgage soon."

Bruce seemed to understand her accounting-speak and whatever a mortgage meant. "I have an excellent investment firm, and broker. Never fear."

"The share of inheritance Grampy willed you from his estate won't last forever."

"I never expected it to." Bruce's tone remained even, but I couldn't miss the frustration in the set of his shoulders. Or how his hand had balled into a fist. That was his go-to when he either had nothing at hand to throw, or wasn't in a situation where he could. "That's where the whole having a career comes into play."

"Jumping from job to job doesn't look good on a resume," his dad put in.

Bruce gave an unfunny laugh. "Beat Marissa to it this time, Dad."

"You've been in your current position at least a year haven't you?" Isaiah edged in and helped himself to the cheese board. "That's pretty impressive."

I got the feeling he played some sort of mediator role, and had been in that position long enough for it to become second nature. Putting himself physically between Bruce and the questioners was a classic de-escalation technique.

So was redirecting the focus of conversation.

I shot him a silent thank you on Bruce's behalf, and he winked at me.

Behind Isaiah, his wife kept going. "A year is a start, but it's only notable when you're talking about Bruce, not the rest of the world."

His fingers gripped the wineglass hard enough his skin mottled.

Isaiah wasn't the only person here versed in managing volatile situations. We employed the same techniques defusing jurisdiction disputes when keeping local law enforcement out of cryptid missions or crime scenes.

I stayed cheerful, smiling since it came through in your voice. "Bruce is always busy. That's why this was a combination of family visit and finalizing a new restaurant's concept. I got to see it this morning and it's gorgeous. You should make reservations now—there's so much buzz that the owner said they're pre-booked for the entire first month."

Isaiah couldn't browse the hors d'oeuvres indefinitely and moved, giving everyone on the other side a clear view.

Bruce's mother was frowning. Bruce might physically resemble his father, but his expression and attitude was all mom's.

"That's the point, isn't it?" She said. "It isn't Bruce's restaurant, so he doesn't benefit from reservations or popularity."

His dad was nodding along. "I'm sure you were helpful, but the design firm was responsible for the look. There's no benefit there, either."

The restaurant world process had baffled me too, until Bruce took the time to explain its structure. He wasn't always as willing to educate as he'd been with me though.

"B developed the entire concept. That's what the team worked off of. That's also why he had to fly in today, when there was an issue. His was the final say. Only he or the owner could sign off on it." I finished the bit of cheese, so I could lay fingers over his fist. A physical reminder that I always had his back. Touch had become our shorthand.

"How long will your current employer put up with your side hustle?" His sister waded back into the argument.

"It's a rider in my contract," Bruce said. "The one doesn't interfere with the other."

All true. Company Legal and the delegates that worked with the public looked liked they'd been mauled by a windigo when they'd finally hashed out a contract Bruce agreed to.

What Bruce did also wasn't a side hustle. I waited for him to correct the misconception.

"I really would like to take a look at that contract," his brother said. "You may think you have carte blanche, but that's rarely the case. There are any number of ways they could claim your absence interfered and gave them grounds to terminate you."

Again, I waited for Bruce to explain. He didn't go to law school, but he had a degree and took classes on business and marketing because he said being the best chef in the world did no good if you didn't understand how to keep a business open and solvent.

Plus, aside from interfering with a mission or purposely outing cryptids, the Company, and us, there was no way he could violate his contract.

He'd already passed every written and oral test, the psych eval and interviews, and completed the required basic firearms and EMT training. The only thing left was a working review with an Assessor in the compound for twenty-four hours and a mock call-out exercise, reviewing how we meshed. Which, basically a formality. The Company was all about helping and supporting. Most Assessors joined in the team party afterward, happy to see agents thriving.

A wash of pride and happiness suffused me. Bruce was

awesome. He'd made a role for himself, facing down HQ, all for us. We both had the thing, the career we most needed, and were able to be together.

Bruce stayed silent, refilling his wine glass. He tilted the bottle over mine, but I shook my head.

I'd only taken a sip. We occasionally went all out, usually as a celebration—our annual week off, maybe a birthday or other pivotal event. I never indulged when I wasn't in a secure setting, and with people I trusted though.

Bruce filled the latter requirement, but the former... This didn't feel like what I'd imagined a home with parents would be.

This felt more and more like hostile territory. I quit pretending I wasn't on the verge of slipping into that head-space where I catalogued and evaluated threats to my team. I'd already marked exits, which of the group around us was aggressive, and who they looked to as leader.

None of these people were cryptids or physically dangerous.

This still wasn't a safe situation. I set my mostly-full glass away.

Bruce, who was always tuned in and understood my tics and moods, didn't notice.

"Do you need help with dinner? You don't want the brisket to dry out." Bruce took another drink.

Like Bruce had ever, even once, not made himself at home in a kitchen, or asked anyone's permission.

"Don't try changing the subject. Your brother has an excellent point," His mother said.

His dad got in on the demands, too. "It would be smart to accept Kenny's help."

"No thanks. I'm good."

His sister huffed, like she was dealing with the kids. "If you're serious about a relationship and settling down, finally, you have to look at your career options, and be smart about your choices."

"I'm perfectly happy with my choices."

His sister turned her attention on me. "How do you feel about Bruce's scatter-shot ambitions?"

"Bruce's career is always his decision. I support him in whatever he chooses." I couldn't keep the smile going. Neutral was going to have to be good enough.

"You're part of some family business, correct?"

"Yes. My siblings and I work together. We have since we were old enough." I chose the next part carefully. "Ours is a long-standing family tradition."

"Then how can you be happy with Bruce's lack of commitment?"

"Bruce is all about his career. He has his pick of restaurants for his pop-ups. He turns down as many consulting requests as he accepts."

His mother gave me a level look. The same as when one of our Instructors decided we weren't taking training seriously. "A good marriage is about not just supporting each other, but calling your partner on harmful behavior. It's about cooperatively making choices for the greater good. It's not about fun and avoiding tough decisions."

At least I didn't slip and laugh in her face. She'd never get how tough choices and working cooperatively played out as life or death for us. "I support Bruce."

"You should be encouraging him to do, and be, better instead of enabling."

"Your son has an incredible career."

"I have to question whether you're the person *my* son should consider a future with, and whether you're ready to settle into a real relationship."

"That's enough, Mom. All of you." Bruce glared at each

person in turn, some switch in him suddenly flipped on. "Vee is off limits."

I waited for the part where he also, finally, called them on their crap. And the verbal abuse.

"Dinner," he said firmly instead.

"Well continue this discussion later," his father said. "You need to be realistic."

"Bruce is artistic, and has a temper, but he's far from incompetent. No one can accuse him of being naïve. You should check his social media accounts, and his fan base. He's an incredible businessperson. He's an incredible person, period."

I took a deep breath. "We are also our own people, and I won't stand by while you assassinate his character, belittle his ability and talent, and discount his drive. I'm sure he has his reasons for allowing this behavior. I don't."

I turned to Bruce. "I'm calling a ride and I'll wait outside. I'll see you at the hotel later."

I nodded politely to his family. "Thank you for opening your home to me. I'll leave the charity check in the car for Bruce to give you."

"Bye." Essie looked up from a game, while the other two stayed engrossed.

"Bye. It was nice to meet you." I closed the front door carefully. The air was crisp, but had the feel of moisture to it. So different from our region most of the year.

Breathing in, I enjoyed the novelty as I ordered a car. I took a few photos for my family, especially one of a pair of bright red cardinals in a huge evergreen, like drops of joy on a dark canvas.

Light splashed over me, then the door clicked closed again.

"I can go back in and do one of those apologies that isn't

really an apology if you need me to." I put the phone away. "I won't apologize for being truthful, though."

Bruce rested against a porch column. "Fuck that. I need to stay, but you don't."

"I don't—I don't understand." I paced one end of the porch to the other, not able to process any other way. "How can they not support you? You're doing what you excel at. I mean, you're good at a lot of things, but you're a master in the kitchen and weird as it is, with the public too. It's your passion. Why wouldn't that make them happy? And proud?"

Bruce stepped in front of me and caught my chin. "Maybe this is one place where the Company has it right. You are part of—let's call it a diverse industry—and you choose your specialty, then that decision is supported by everyone around you. The end. For us though? Parents worry. They have pre-conceived ideas about what's right, wrong, safe, you name it. They are usually doing the best they know how to raise and prepare kids. That doesn't end just because the government declares you an adult. It's more intense when the kid is far away, adding another layer of worry."

I chewed my thumbnail. "If I wasn't with Josh and Kimi and Liv... I suppose I'd worry. That would be hard. But I'd trust them. They know what they're doing. I'd trust that they were smart and prepared, and be happy for them."

He wrapped me in a bear hug, another specialty. "Yeah, I know. Sometimes you bunch are too well-adjusted. My family means well. They just have a hard time understanding, especially now that they know we're together."

"It hurts you."

"It frustrates the fuck out of me. Sometimes it pisses me off. I know they love me though. It only looks different on the outside. Inside, it is the same bond as what you share with your brother and sisters."

He loosed me and kissed my forehead, then handed me

the car fob. "Beat it. I'll have Kenny bring me to the hotel after dinner. It'll be his fucking penance."

He gathered up the gifts he'd brought. When he stuck his head in the driver's side window, I handed him the envelope with the check. "I love you."

"I love you too, Victoria Ramirez. Don't fucking eat dinner out of the hotel vending machine. I'll bring you a plate."

CHAPTER 7

ruce

"Gone off to sulk?" His sister gave him a self-righteous smirk.

He saw the *oh shit* lurking underneath. The same as when they were kids, and Marissa went further than she'd meant to, and guilt was already eating at her.

"Vee's never heard of sulking, unlike some people. Table, rugrats." He swept Essie up, high-pitched shrieks and giggles the perfect mood buster.

He sat all three at the table, getting a sympathetic, "Sorry, Robert," from Isaiah as he came in with shatterproof cups.

Mandy immediately demanded a real, grown-up glass one, and Bruce left her to negotiate.

"I didn't intend for her to leave." Marissa stirred a bowl, only looking at him from the corner of her eye. "She seems invested, and obviously cares for you."

"Here." He dropped the check on the island by Vee's abandoned glass. "Her family was pretty damn generous."

He'd accept his sister's apology, but she could squirm a little along the way. Then apologize to Vee. Right after he did.

"She still left it?"

"Of course she did," his dad said. He took the bowl from underneath Marissa's hand and headed for the table and the kids.

Bruce had known Vee's calm practicality would win his dad over.

Hannah, too. "Ken can get Shoshanna ready in the morning. I'd love to have breakfast or coffee with you and Vee before your flight."

"Pick a spot." He gave her a side-hug.

"What does Vee like?"

"She's ridiculously easy." He handed off a platter to her. "She'll be happy with anything."

When he made a move for the brisket, his mom smacked his hand. "Hurry up and sit. You need food before you fall over. Invite Vee for Thanksgiving, and give her my number, too."

"Sure, Mom." The passionate defense Vee mounted on his behalf was the best damn way to win over his mother.

He propped his rear against the island, and crossed his arms. "Your turn, asshole."

"How is it that I'm culpable because your girlfriend overreacted? We weren't that bad. Isaiah had it far rougher when Marissa introduced him to us," his brother said. "You had to know what your bringing a woman in, one you'd mentioned not only to me, but to Mom and Dad, would look like to them. Mom's probably already made an appointment for the two of you to talk to a rabbi."

"First, Vee's family is the gold-standard for supportive

and caring. To her, your actions equate with kicking a kitten. A kitten held by a cute kid. On the kid's *birthday*, you monster. I screwed up too, though. I didn't factor in the extra intensity that Mom and Marissa would hit her with because I've been with her longer than a month." He frowned, and dropped his pose.

"Second, Vee was the model of politeness, and you damn well know it and are trying to avoid admitting she won and you lost this case, counselor. Finally, you're lucky she didn't put you in a shoulder lock." Bruce rotated his. "From first hand experience, those hurt like hell."

"Well…damn."

"Vee doesn't sit by without defending the people she loves. I should have prepared her better for our brand of family love, though. Lucky for you, she isn't capable of holding a grudge."

"You did pretty good, baby brother."

"Fuck you, old man. Of course I did. You're coming for coffee in the morning too, and you're buying."

* * *

"I RESISTED VENDING MACHINE TEMPTATION," Vee said as he walked into their hotel room. She sat in one of the chairs positioned around the tiny desk.

The rest of dinner had gone the way all of their family events did. Loud, full of debate, good food, and kids falling asleep on couches, requiring adults to carry them to the car.

In other words, perfect.

Content and ready to play, he sat the promised plate on the desk, and eyed the room anyway. Tipping the trashcan his way, pretending to check inside. "I see you're still dressed. I find that highly suspicious. Should I check the car for contraband wrappers?"

When Vee bounced out of the chair, protest on her lips, he caught her around the waist and pulled her against him. He found her lips, sweeping in as soon as hers parted. Her lip between his teeth, he pulled away slowly before letting go. "I've waited for that ever since you declared you loved me in front of my whole damn family."

He tilted her head, working his way from her jaw down her neck, mixing kisses and nips, his beard dragging over her skin. Vee's hands dug into his shoulders.

He put his lips against her ear and spoke, relishing her shiver. "Now this I planned to do ever since you stood in my parent's kitchen and gave them hell."

Her grip loosened. "I'm sorry. I didn't mean to ruin your visit. You were so excited about seeing your family. And now there's probably going to be all this weirdness and stress whenever you talk to them because you're with the person who insulted them."

"You were glorious. We're also having breakfast with Hannah, who is pro-Vee, and my brother. In addition, I was told to deliver an invitation from Mom for Thanksgiving. Whether to accept or decline is up to you, and I'm good with whatever decision you make."

"Oh."

"Basically, I've mentioned you to them more than twice, we've been together longer than a couple of months, and I brought you home to meet them. They knew this was about adding a new member to our family. I should have thought of that, and I should have done a better job of warning you, and letting you make up your mind whether to still visit."

"The career thing, and the complaints, and not listening to you?"

"Standard Kantor conduct. Think of it as an initiation. You're one of us now."

She took a second. "Oh! Like when the Region team

they'll be interning with pranks their cadets after the graduation exercise."

Close enough. "Yes."

Vee's expression cleared, his family already forgiven. "I'd like to see a real holiday thing with you. I won't change my reaction if they insult-insult you for real though."

This woman. "I'd never expect or ask you to. I've issued orders not to insult you. As for the rest, we bicker and nag and offer unsolicited advice every other sentence. Meaning you can say what you want, and never be anyone but yourself. Never compromise who you are."

"Really?"

"Really."

His phone buzzed in his pocket and he grabbed it long enough to see it was only an automated notice of his recheck appointment in two days, then dropped it on the desk. He was exercising his lunch rain-check option and getting Vee into that bistro when they went. Nothing was going to stop him from telling Vee what she meant to him, and publicly vowing he'd spend the rest of his life making her as happy as was in his power.

He ran his fingers along the split neckline of her dress. Watching chills race over her skin and Vee lean into his touch. "There's one other item I've planned since you came out in that dress."

"What item?" Her voice was husky, and pupils huge, making her eyes look even darker and more magnetic.

He looped his finger in the tie holding her dress together. Then took it with him as he knelt in front of her. The dress fell open, revealing her in all her glory.

He skimmed his hands up her thighs. "Allow me to show you."

ruce

As soon as he saw the doctor's face, Bruce knew.

Honestly, he'd known from the moment he'd walked in expecting a prescription, and been handed directions to the lab and imaging center, and told he was expected there immediately.

He held the chair in front of the doctor's desk out for Vee, then took the seat beside her.

The diagnosis and doctor's voice came from the end of a tunnel, echoing and distant. *Stage Four* and *treatment options* blending with the voices of his parents when they'd sat him, Kenny, and Marissa down at the kitchen table and broken the news that his grandfather had cancer.

Now, Bruce had the same type. Warm, strong fingers closed around his. Solid and real, Vee's touch banishing ghosts and bringing him back to the present.

She'd scooted so her chair was flush against his. "Do you need a minute?"

He let the velvet of her voice wrap around him, and squeezed her fingers in thanks. "No. Keep going."

The doctor nodded like Bruce had given the right answer. "This is an aggressive cancer so we'll be equally aggressive with your treatment. I've spoken with one of the University's best oncologists, and she has an opening for you day after tomorrow. I'd like to get you in tomorrow for the port to be put in place. It's an outpatient procedure but you'll need a driver."

"He has one. What else do we need to do?" Vee focused on the doctor and his answers with the same singular intensity as when planning a mission.

She left the doctor looking like he'd been the victim of an interrogation, and with a handful of literature. She also had the same set to her shoulders as during a mission.

They stepped outside. Bruce stopped, closing his eyes and lifting his face. Letting the sun beat against his skin and closed lids.

When he opened them, Vee had her phone clutched in the hand not holding his. She hadn't let go of him since the doctor started speaking.

"I can text everyone so you don't have to talk about this. I can tell them to give you space when you get home, too. If you want."

He took in a breath of dry desert air and the tang of cinnamon from the food truck across the street. Naming the ominous rattle in his chest as he did. He concentrated on the feel of the sun and the surety of Vee's grip.

"Or we can go to the condo if you need more privacy."

The condo the Company had set up as part of his cover, a place for family and friends to interact since he couldn't avoid outside relationships like the team had to, and sure as hell couldn't bring people to their compound.

"I won't bother you if you need quiet or time to think. I'll stay in the car. The garage is fine, and I can work from the apartment Wi-Fi."

As much as this was his life and ordeal, it wasn't only his. The family, friends, synagogue and community had all been involved in helping his grandfather. Everyone had made changes to their schedules. It was never a solitary thing—it upended all of their lives.

"I'll talk to them." He squeezed Vee's hand the way she'd done for him, his decision made. He needed Vee and the family. He'd need them even more before this played out. But fucking with the team's schedules didn't mean taking a leave from work or losing sleep. For them, it could mean ending up shredded in a monster's jaws.

He'd do his best to keep things normal, until normal was no longer an option.

"It's fine for them and you to have questions."

"It is?"

"We did when one of my grandparents was diagnosed. I've got some experience here. The plan sounds pretty much the same, and I took him to most of his treatments." He couldn't smile and reassure her—that was beyond him. Instead he brought Vee's knuckles to his lips.

He was hanging on to being in control as fucking long as he could, digging in and fighting for every bit of normalcy. There would be enough shit coming his way that he'd have no choice about.

Who he told, how much he revealed, and how he framed that information was his right. So for the foreseeable future, he'd stay innocuous and low-key with Vee and the team.

His disease, his terms. "We're keeping our lunch plans, then going home. And fuck sitting alone in cars. You'll damn well be where you belong—in the middle of the action, and with me. Got it?"

With her hands occupied, and cuticles unavailable, she resorted to chewing at her lip. "You have been talking about your friend's restaurant for weeks."

He dug out his keys, swallowing past the lump of regret. He wouldn't be using the private patio for any fairy-tale proposal. The ring meant for Vee as a symbol of their future stayed in the box for now. Possibly forever.

When a measure of the worry left Vee's eyes and her shoulders relaxed, instead of adding one more responsibility on her, his plan was fucking worth it.

He'd savor this bit of normalcy and ease all of them, himself included, into the fight he'd landed in the middle of.

CHAPTER 9

ee

THE SUITE DOOR SLAMMED, then our bathroom door. Right on schedule, a few minutes into the dinner prep Bruce insisted on starting. With the same results as the majority of his attempts the last six weeks.

He'd banned me from the bath, not allowing me to hear him getting sick, even though there probably wasn't anything left on his stomach to throw up.

I squashed the urge to pick up the cutting board and neat ramekins of ingredients and hurl them at something. Instead, I emptied the herbs and chicken that had triggered Bruce's non-stop nausea, into the trash, then tied the bag. After putting the few utensils in the dishwasher, I carried the bag out, leaving no trace.

Kimi sat on the bench in the yard, her face reflecting the frustration and helplessness churning inside me. The gate chime sounded as Liv's truck rolled around to the bay beside the armory and annex.

A minute later, Josh loped out and our way, takeaway carton under one arm, a pair of recycled hemp bags Bruce insisted on for groceries in his other hand. Liv followed, carrying another.

Kimi scooted to make room for them as Josh handed out Styrofoam cartons. Bruce tried to act like anyone nuking a frozen burrito or heating a pizza wasn't an issue, but those smells had the same effect as when he tried cooking.

We hadn't needed to discuss it—the microwave moved to the annex, the building outfitted with containment for any captured cryptids HQ might require for cadet training classes or as samples. We'd added a dorm fridge, and breakfast and lunch were cereal and frozen food. We'd survived on them for years until Bruce arrived.

When there was a patrol, whoever was on brought back takeout. Eaten out here, the reason a folding chair had been added beside the bench, so we all had room.

Josh sprawled in it, container on his lap. "Bad?"

"Bad."

Liv handed me her tray, so she was free to run through the bags' contents. One was more cereal for us. "Ginger capsules from the stall that Bruce always said had the best herbs. Refill on the anti-nausea medication and edibles." She dropped each item back in the second bag, and held up sleeves of crackers. "Saltine and plain, but I added rye and rice as well. We haven't tried those yet. More ginger ale."

She replaced the bounty that Bruce could keep down. Sometimes. She nudged the last bag with her foot. "Bone broth from the truck. They added a veggie one to try too, and they'll have another batch for us Monday."

The food truck was a favorite, run by a couple of nice abuelas. When we brought Bruce along the first time, right after he moved in, it turned out they recognized him. They were part of his #BruceTheBastardsNation fan club. He'd been respectful with them, dropping off heritage seeds when he came across any on his trips.

When they found out he was sick, they'd sent broth. It had become one of the only things that he'd consistently been able to eat.

Turned out, most of the world knew more and had more first-hand experience with cancer than any agent. From the Friday pharmacy tech we'd learned about ginger capsules. From our food truck friends, to stock up on fleecy sweatshirts because most patients were cold even on hot days. From the farmer's market vendor, who still wore her crotched pink hat even though her hair had grown back, to take afghans and barf bags along on the chemo days.

We'd also learned that when Bruce painted us a picture of taking treatments, retesting, and the cancer being gone, the experienced tied up neatly, he'd left out parts.

Like the part where there was surgery and worrying about infections from random people who had a cold that only annoyed them but would put Bruce in an emergency room. About nausea and losing weight and feeling awful for days. Days that had begun to stretch into weeks, and lab results that made the doctor frown.

The other things we learned from the oncology nurse, whose sister hadn't gotten better despite multiple treatment rounds. We'd learned what Stage Four really meant from the postal clerk whose wife had gotten clean labs and they'd celebrated, but now all he had was a photo at his desk, because it had returned and there wasn't anything to celebrate that time. Those realities had sent Liv and Kimi on morning runs that lasted hours, and Josh working over the hanging bag in the gym until his knuckles were raw, even with the protective tape.

Those truths sent me first to HQ and our year-mates who had chosen the medical track. Then after talking to them, because Company never lied to Company, no matter how ugly the truth, on sweeps that left every windigo and chupacabra within twenty square miles dead.

My phone buzzed, also on schedule. I opened the video chat, Marissa and Bruce's mom's images greeting me. It turned out that loving Bruce was the only thing necessary for us all to turn into one united family. Bruce had been right about their already adding me to the family. And my brother and sisters.

From beside me, Kimi and Liv waved. Josh leaned in enough to greet them. This was chemo day, so they called an hour into what would have been dinner. Because Bruce tried playing them too, but they'd also known more than we had. Like that Bruce's grandfather had died from the same disease. And that Bruce was stubborn but the scent of food would still only end one way.

Our calls were safe from Bruce's scrutiny for at least an hour every evening.

"How did today go?" Donna asked.

It was always the same question from his mom.

Part of me wanted to yell. To snap at her, mostly for making me put into words the things I didn't want to see or acknowledge. The rest of me ached, failures piling up. She had watched someone in her family go through this, then lost them.

I'd only begun to experience that, and I was so messed up. I didn't want her to have to relive the experience again, and I didn't have a way to prevent this part. The part where Bruce was sick and felt terrible and tried hiding it, and there wasn't any good news for his mom and sister. Or his mom and brother, or his mom and dad. Like Bruce had said, love only looked different on the outside

His family was tight, loved each other, and their brother. They were supporting each other, and I'd realized how wrong I'd been in once accusing Bruce of not having ties and only living for himself and his ego.

So I did the best I could and maybe took a tiny bit of the bad away for them. "Treatment went smooth today, and I think he finished the book series Mandy sent."

Kimi wiggled in so that they had a clearer view of her. Slowly, she signed, "I'll edit the recordings this week, and email them to you in time for Essie's birthday."

His sister smiled, so dang much like Bruce when he was happy-happy. The family had known some ASL from cousins who were part of the deaf community. They'd put in the effort and brushed up so they could easily converse with my sister.

"The girls loved the animation you added to the first series," his sister said.

"I upped my game on this set," Kimi added, her smile as genuine as Marissa's.

It didn't kick me in the chest *at all* that Bruce was reading stories aloud and recording them for his nieces. In case he wasn't around anymore to read them in person, and they needed a reminder of the uncle who had doted on them.

I locked my hand around the edge of the bench, grinding metal against my palm. Holding the fear at bay. Instead, I tilted the phone so they could see the shopping bags and Liv could run through the contents again. His mom could tell us she was overnighting more rugelach, and another set of fluffy socks the girls had picked out, these with dancing vegetables.

There had to be a way to insure three cute kids and these people who added us to their circle didn't have to rely on a video of their favorite uncle and son, the only thing they had left of him.

A way that Bruce was healthy again and in his kitchen and terrorizing line cooks and owners and bringing seed packets to funny grandmas.

And a way that I wouldn't lose him. I just had to be smarter, work harder, and find that loophole.

ruce

A SHAFT of light cut across the dark room, paused a second, then reversed its course.

"Hey." He cleared his throat. Which set off a round of coughing, feeling like sandpaper was grinding against the inside of his chest.

The light on Vee's desk snapped on. Boot heels thumped, disappearing down the hall at a fast clip. Vee was back even faster.

She crouched in front of him and held out the bottle of cough syrup.

Fuck. They'd moved on to the serious stuff. It would stop his cough. It would also make him loopy as hell, and sleepy.

With no better option, he tilted the bottle. They'd left off bothering with tiny measuring cups and exact amounts weeks ago.

Vee took the bottle back and recapped it. In turn, he took

an experimental breath. When nothing rattled loose, he pushed into a sit. Then grabbed for the tablet sliding off the arm of the couch at the shift.

Vee caught it first. "I didn't mean to wake you. If I'd known, I wouldn't have been so loud."

He already knew that. She'd have stealthed by the same way she'd done the last two days, in and out of their room while he was asleep. Which was the whole reason he'd camped in her office.

She'd patrolled every inch of Scottsdale and the sandy expanses of compound acreage. When she ran out of shit to patrol, she hibernated in here. Doing God knew what, but buried in books and notepads, laptop open constantly.

"I can re-start your book." Now that he wasn't hacking up a lung, she'd shifted all her attention to the tablet. Fiddling and not meeting his eyes.

"Look at me."

Since no one would argue with him or tell him no anymore, even when he turned his asshole dial up to eleven, she obeyed.

The lines carved in her forehead, and bloodshot eyes got to him. It was the fear in the back of Vee's eyes that gutted him though.

His Vee had never been scared. She'd shown no fear facing down cryptids that more resembled something that crawled out of a nightmare than any natural-born animal.

Now, that fear was with her all damn day and all damn night.

He scared her.

The discussion hanging over them wasn't going to offer her any damn comfort, either.

"We need to talk. No running out for a mission, no creeping in once I'm asleep. I get it, but you don't run. Ever. Woman up, Commander Ramirez."

She gave a jerky nod.

"C'mere."

She joined him on the giant antique couch. Then compulsively grabbed an afghan, since the compound was drowning in them now. His sister bought and sent them in every care package. Hannah sent them. Hell, Mandy had included one, the crotchet stitches wonky and uneven.

At least Vee wrapped it around both of them, cuddling up against him. He took a minute to enjoy it. The two of them together, Vee's weight against him, hair tickling his cheek.

When he reached, she ducked her head helpfully, letting him work the band free and shake her hair out. He fluffed it to drape over his shoulder. Under the betraying sun-warmed dust that proved she'd been in the desert again, he inhaled the cocoa butter that meant Vee to him. Stealing this moment.

He figured he deserved it. Greedy for as many moments like this as he could pack in. He looped an arm around her, pulling her as fucking close as they could physically get.

He wrapped both arms around her and she burrowed her face into his neck. If she needed not to look this shit in the eye right now, that was fine with him. She was already taking care of everything, and everyone, else. She could fudge this once.

"One treatment left." He let the statement hang in the air.

One treatment left. He didn't need to see labs and scans to know what they were going to say.

"You probably feel so cruddy because it's working. The chemo is killing off the bad. Then, you can start building back up. Keep food down, and, and meds, that's huge. Once you can do that, everything will look better."

Maybe he should've been pissed. Yelled about reality and false hopes, and that he was the sick one, not her or the team or his family.

For probably the first time in his life, he couldn't get mad. It had taken falling in love to knock most of the self-centeredness and arrogance right out of him.

Vee kept going, like she could talk all of it away. "Your mom and dad are talking about a short vacation of some kind."

He gave a soft snort. He wasn't falling for that ingenuous shit. Vee undoubtedly knew where, what time their flights left and arrived, had the number to their resort, and a detailed itinerary.

The whole team was thick as thieves with his family. For special operations soldiers in a secret private organization, they were also shit at subterfuge and lying. Josh dropped a mention of Kenny's courtside playoff seats. Liv carted in a vintage dress from the shop they were all obsessed with, but not in any of their colors, styles, or sizes. Like he didn't know it was going in a box for his sister the next day.

"We need to air out the condo, and put fresh towels and sheets out."

Vee went still against him, but he continued. "I'll send Mom and Dad tickets. See about booking a couple of suites nearby for Marissa and Kenny."

"You wouldn't let them visit before," Vee whispered.

"I know." He'd stomped and bitched, and Vee had backed everyone off, understanding he needed the illusion of normalcy more than being suffocated, even if it was by the people he held dearest. He hadn't been ready then for a full dose of reality.

"They should come out in the next few weeks." His last treatment was tomorrow. A week post-treatment would at least cut out the worst of his nausea.

"B." She quit. Not knowing what else to say, or not wanting to.

"Everything may work out in our favor," he lied. "However, I'm feeling guilty as fuck, so they may as well come out now. This is a good time—it's not hot as balls, so they won't broil their pasty suburban asses."

More like he wanted to see them while he was still himself. Before the vague off-and-on pain turned into a constant, and while they could still look at him and see most of their son and brother.

"Okay." Vee's answer was almost lost in the big room, and the soft darkness enveloping them. "I'll get some of the creosote candles your mom likes, too. And the scotch your dad and Kenny prefer."

Again, she didn't seem to notice she was outing herself and the supposedly secret conversations.

He'd never loved Vee more. He kissed the top of her head, and for tonight, pretended along with her that this was just another night, just one more visit from his family, one more of a string of them stretching into their future.

He rose, tossed the afghan across his shoulder, and offered Vee his hand. "Let's go see what affront to the film industry Josh picked out tonight."

ee

I PUSHED HARDER, boots hitting the downtown ground faster, covering the sound of Josh behind me and the vampire he'd wounded.

Liv split left, gaining on the second vampire, also weakened from rounds to its knee and chest. They kept going, around the corner from our dress shop, and out of sight.

My quarry jetted left in a burst of vampire speed. I followed seconds later, leaping the decorative iron gate, now twisted into a ruined mess from the vampire tearing the obstruction out of its path.

I dodged the matching round table and the scattered chairs, part of the hidey-hole behind a jewelry store where the owner usually had lunch. The courtyard, hemmed in on three sides by building walls too high to scale, was precisely where I'd wanted the creature to go.

It whipped around, eyes blazing like halogen headlights, hissing. Furious at finding a dead end.

I kicked the closest chair at it. Firing while it batted at the distraction. A bullet in the knee and it listed sideways, hiss turning to a shriek before it recovered its balance.

Another round went in the other leg. Missing the knee but still slamming into a thigh.

It took a step toward me, claws gleaming. Then stumbled, its angry hiss rising into a high-pitched whistle. The table and chairs chimed like tuning forks as the volume increased.

My ears ached but I holstered my gun, switching to knives. I *needed t*o kill the thing. We needed information first, though.

I circled, blade constantly moving. Keeping the creature's attention. Keeping it moving too. The chem from the two rounds spreading with every step.

It skittered, slower and favoring its thigh. Hopefully, I'd hit the artery, letting it pump poison with every heartbeat as the thing's body tried to regenerate.

I ducked in, scoring a line along its stomach, other blade blocking its retaliatory swipe, steel vibrating off bone. Then back out. In again under its guard as it stumbled, grabbing the rough brick for balance. Slicing its good thigh as I reversed.

Pain blossomed along my shoulder blade, a claw ripping through fabric. I kicked at its bad knee, rolling out of reach as it lurched. Then back in again, in our dance of knives and claws. Targeting its hands this time, and the lethal claws.

The thing overextended, swiping but missing. It crumpled to its knees, one arm now useless, body barely supported by the other. Claws gouged sandy dirt, searching for purchase.

I stomped on its good hand, the crunch of bones lost under another piercing wail. I slashed wrist to elbow anyway, blood not spraying as far as it should, heart rate already slowing.

It braced on its elbow, snarling and swaying. A trace of its lost human features showed, the blue of its human eye color slowly winning over the inhumane silver.

My kick caught it under the jaw and it flopped to its back.

I chopped, its wrist left dangling by cartilage, then repeated the cut on the other wrist. Careful of a potential hurt-vamp ploy, meant to draw inexperienced fighters in close enough to bite.

Kneeling on its chest, now heaving like a human's, I put the tip of one blade under its chin. "There was another with you today. Where did it go?"

The vampire snarled. Stopped when I dug a fraction harder, drawing blood. More blue shaded its eyes and trace of fullness plumped its lips.

"Where did the other vampire go?"

"I dunno." The words held a sibilant undertone but were understandable.

I nudged with the knife, tip sinking a centimeter deeper.

White ringed its eyes. "Sienna ran. I don't know where. She said *Il Creatore* was coming, and ran."

The vampires Kimi had picked up via drone photos weren't old enough to be a Master, a vampire at least a century old, with the virus mutating again and again during those long years. A vampire couldn't even infect humans until that decade mark. Three of our four newbies tonight had been in freaking University tees. "Where is your nest? Don't bother lying about not having one."

"I can't."

"If you want to leave this courtyard, you will."

Its breath caught, possibly from the toxin spreading, possibly from the hope of an escape. "They're gone."

Whatever it saw on my face, it talked faster. "They left. Felix and the rest vanished months ago."

Fuck.

"Where are the nest's other safe-houses?" All nests had them, a foul echo of our secondary bases.

"We don't know. Felix never took us. Sienna is older than us, but I don't think by much and we all stick together now. We're it."

I sat on the creature's chest, searching its face. The nest offshoot hadn't been discrete. Bodies by a frat house, left in plain sight. The four vampires together the last few nights instead of spreading out to feed. The behavior of stupid, brand-freaking-new vampires without a leader. "I believe you."

I put everything into the shove, punching the blade through its palate, up into its mutated brain. A last twist, and the silver faded, body going limp.

"Bitch!"

I spun at the snarled word.

Sienna hadn't run after all. She crouched in the mouth of the courtyard, my trap turned on me.

I shoved, getting free of the corpse and dropping my extra knife. Pulling my gun. Firing, the angle wrong, brick chips flying. The enraged vampire speeding at me. Young but still fast. Too fast.

Her eyes widened, back arching. Surprise in the line of her body.

I emptied the Glock into her, her face disappearing. She fell inches from me.

Silence backwashed. Broken a heartbeat later by boots pounding my way. Josh pelted in, Liv a stride behind, their weapons drawn.

"Damn." Josh whistled. "A two-fer. Score."

More practical, Liv nudged the splayed vampire while I stood, searching for my dropped knife.

I spotted it by the first vampire's foot. Liv followed me, checking the corpse out.

"Did it knock your gun away?" She eyed the corpse's cuts and butchered arms.

"Mhm." I made a non-committal noise.

"At least you got it back in time to toast this one," Josh said, more willing to take things at face value.

I dug out my phone, making the quick call to the Cleaners, then texting Kimi. Tonight was her turn to sit with Bruce, my text going to her phone in case he was finally asleep.

The last treatment was completed. He'd managed the visit with his family, and they'd left days ago. The visit, the treatment, subsisting on broth and freaking medical drinks, one or all had taken their toll.

He'd visibly lost weight in the last two weeks. He had new, pinched lines around his lips and eyes. Something hurt, and sleep wasn't as easy to come by. We hadn't had our last appointment with the oncologist, Bruce putting it off until his family left.

I wanted to believe we'd get good news.

But I felt Bruce, and my time to figure out some miracle, slipping away.

I bent and jerked my lodged blade free, bone cracking and a bit of gray matter sticking to the knife. I flicked the gunk off, wishing I had more vampires to end. Windigos. A ghoul. Anything.

"You got this one earlier? When did she show between wounding her, you trapping the male, then finishing her?" Liv crouched by the last vampire. Her knife tracked slashes in the fallen creature's shirt. Slashes that went through cloth, skin, and muscle, spine showing pinkish and bare.

The gashes weren't clean enough for a blade, even one of ours.

"Excellent question," I said.

Josh glared at the newest cadaver. "Friggin' vampires. Now you two will have a longer report to detail. Even windigos are sorta useful, eating rats and 'chups and shit. Ghouls eat windigos and dead crap. Vampires aren't good for one damn thing, though."

I froze mid-wipe, blade I was cleaning on the vamp's shirt still. *Useless vampires.* I'd had the same thought. And recently. Memories snapped together. I'd thought it the day I filed the park attack report. Clicking on the footnotes. Notes that linked to the HQ Lab's research with vampire blood proteins and DNA.

I shoved the dirty blade into the sheath, and strode past a frowning Liv. "Let's go. Cleaners are two minutes out. We have reports to file."

And I had a deeper dive to hack.

* * *

I RUBBED GRITTY EYES, and reached for coffee, careful not to dislodge any of my legal pads. I scowled when the cup only held the stain of caffeine long gone.

Running my hand over the filled-up reams of paper, the first spark of hope in months kindled. Tiny, and too easily extinguished, but there.

Someone would face an Oversight hearing if it was ever discovered but the footnotes and brief on virus research led to a virtual backdoor. One that opened straight into archived abstracts, inter-departmental memos, the original tests and results, scientist's notes—virologists, pathologists, a couple of genetics experts, and a whole heck of a lot of emergency medicine experts.

None of those files were from HQ, as I'd first assumed. The screw-up was in Oversight. I'd stumbled into the domain of the Company's leaders, and the Assessors, our ultimate enforcers.

Oversight had conducted—possibly was still conducting because there were levels I couldn't reach—its own research initiative. With its own Labs, under their think-tank. None of which HQ had been informed of. That was Oversight's prerogative.

If they discovered I'd found a flaw and hadn't reported it, I'd be sanctioned.

If they discovered I'd dug and downloaded via plain pen and paper that could be destroyed without leaving a trace, and taken everything available from an Oversight cell far above my clearance level, I'd lose my C.O. position.

If they discovered what I intended to do with the stolen research, I would be the first Company agent ever executed. I'd become the whispered legend, the boogeyman used as a lesson for all cadets.

I wasn't telling Liv, Kimi, or Josh about my plan. Only Bruce. If I was exposed, the worst the Company would do was cut him loose, a civilian asset who wasn't yet a full Company agent and a dying one at that.

Not so with the team.

If they remained ignorant, they'd be safe, their commissions and lives unsullied by my punishment. For the first time in our lives, I was going to lie to my family. Lie to and defy the Company. The two most important things in my life.

The chance at saving Bruce was worth any punishment.

Compulsively, I paged back through labs and reports, stopping finally at the private correspondence between the two lead scientists.

We all understood how vampires were created. The

human needed to have lost blood almost to the point of death, then the missing blood was replaced by infected blood from a vampire at least a decade old.

The virus DNA held a sequence to kick healing into high gear, replenishing blood at an astounding rate. Healing the wounds, repairing the infected host's injuries.

The research teams hadn't been able to isolate the sequence in the alleles or markers within the virus responsible for regeneration. Yet. The research that originally began as an initiative to discover the means to stop the virus from taking hold had shifted to emergency applications. From tests on newly infected subjects to more theoretical work, sequencing codes. I hadn't been able to find a way into those records.

They'd theorized that if an agent had abnormal red and white cells, the virus DNA would immediately target the abnormalities, repairing them. And, theoretically, any associated cellular abnormalities.

They'd pivoted and refocused on wounds and regenerating injuries beyond the help of current medicine, not diseases.

I'd spent all my non-mission time gathering everything I could on cancer, on Bruce's type. Sending questions to our year-mate, and having virtual face-to-faces. She was humoring me out of kindness.

The result? I understood enough about cellular damage, unregulated cellular growth, to grasp that some cancers, like Bruce's, were abnormal blood cells, at their foundation.

If the treatments had done their job and killed most off, virus DNA might push the job over the edge. Right into a solid win.

If the treatment hadn't...I curled my fingers in, nails nothing but bitten back memories. Shoving the raw terror and tears back.

If the chemo hadn't worked, another course and the virus could, theoretically, work together. Kill the bad, let the virus find the few remaining healthy, original cell structures.

The researchers tried blood, tissue, stem cells, saliva. The virus mixed with a carrier. Blood administered as an inhalant. That had been the closest to a success, leading to instructions for setting up an oral testing plan, hopes for an oral form. That was where I'd hit the wall I couldn't hack past.

Oral though—vampire blood taken by mouth—that I could manage.

I exited the files as Liv poked her head in, closed doors a thing of the past. Mine was always open, listening in case Bruce needed me. The rest of the team had followed suit on their own.

"It's nearly eight," Liv said. She came the rest of the way in, and set a cup beside me. I scooped papers up, tapping them into a neat pile.

"Still obsessing over that wounded vampire?" She asked.

"I know I wasn't the one who cut her up. Plus, the newbie I questioned swore the majority of the nest abandoned them, or left fast. He was babbling about *Il Creatore*, but that didn't sound like he was their nest Master." All true. And something was off. I felt it, like another layer of dread, right under the dread of losing Bruce.

"It's almost time for the appointment." Liv's words might as well have been in all-caps.

The Appointment.

Was Bruce getting better.

Or were we going to have a permanent, unfillable hole in the team.

I chugged my coffee, scalding my tongue, and shoved the reports in a drawer. "I'm hitting the shower. Get the travel kit ready?"

"Already done. Fresh bags and wipes and ginger caps, plus cough syrup, are inside."

I hugged my sister, her grip equally strong. We hung onto each other for a moment before separating, because Bruce was her family now too and she loved him in the same way as she did Josh.

ruce

THE COMPOUND GATES slid sideways with a low chime, allowing them back in.

That was the first sound that had intruded on their silence, neither saying anything, after Bruce told the doctor that he would let him know within twenty-four hours if he chose to do a second round of chemo.

He didn't need the gentle discouragement in the specialist's voice to know the oncologist saw little point. Bruce knew the stats by heart. He'd heard how high his virus load was. Higher than when they began.

He also didn't need a professional opinion to know that he hurt. An all-over pain, worse on some days than others, but always present.

Vee's hand was wrapped around his. Just shy of too tight. She'd driven in silence, one hand on the wheel, the other around his. Taking her cue from him.

She met him as he opened his door. Taking his hand again, not able to endure the few feet and few seconds of separation.

He understood. The thought of leaving Vee...he swallowed hard, then rubbed below his collarbone, feeling as if something was lodged there and in the way. Tumors. Unstoppable and multiplying. The Arizona sun danced along his skin, obliviously cheerful.

He tugged Vee's hand when she tried skirting the plantings in the yard, headed for the stairs to the walkway and their common area.

"Sit out here with me for a few minutes." She tensed and he ran his thumb over the back of her hand, aware of her thoughts like they were printed on her forehead for him to read. "I can make the climb. I'm not that tired." Yet.

He sat on the bench, the warmth welcome, taking a second to admire the succulents and flowering cacti, the way Kimi had arranged darker to lighter in a harmonious tapestry. The birdbath sat in the center, like the ruler of the planting.

"Are you okay? Do you need another hoodie?" Vee dug in the damn bag she and her sisters kept stocked with everything they could anticipate him needing.

"Not right now. Vee, I know you don't want to hear this. Hell, I don't want to say it. Neither one of us hide from reality or hard choices though."

"I'm listening." She edged against him, and when he didn't complain, wrapped both arms around him.

"We need to make some decisions. Let me talk without interrupting."

She nodded, cheek sliding against his bare skin. The beard was long gone, shaved at the same time he'd shaved his head, the clumps of hair on his towel that day his warning of what was coming. Josh had pulled out a razor and joined

Bruce, shaving his head alongside, probably breaking bullshit Company rules.

"I can go home to Westchester. Mom is a senior partner—she can take off as long as necessary. Marisa has already lined up her paperwork for a temporary leave. I can also go to an inpatient hospice."

Vee's arms tightened, then relaxed a fraction, like she was fucking afraid she'd break him.

"This isn't what you want to hear, but things will get ugly." He sighed, fucking hating the idea of not having Vee with him, by his side. Of not turning his head and seeing her asleep beside him. Not having her curled around him like she was a fucking shield as they watched shit movies, or read, or just sat together.

Being alone, without the other half of his soul was, to date, the worst, most unbearable thing he had to look forward to. It stole his breath.

He loved her in a way he'd never loved anyone else though, and he'd spare her seeing him die slowly.

"What I'll need—before long, I'll need someone there with me at all times. Not even the way one of you hangs out here when the rest are training or patrolling, but full time. Do you understand?"

She nodded again, short and jerky.

It fucking broke off a piece of his heart, but he said it. "All right. Think about what I've said, then we'll decide."

"Can I talk now?"

"Yes."

"If you want to be with the rest of the family or in hospice near them, I understand." She loosened her hold and pulled away.

Fucking killing a bit of him, but he'd told her the truth, and this was her choice to stay.

"I'd like to go with you though."

"Vee—" Relief and regret swamped him in equal measures.

"Unless you really don't want me there, and forbid it, I'm —I want to go. I've talked to your Mom, and she says we'll always be family, and I can stay with her and your Dad. Marissa said the same. So now you listen." She looked him directly in the eye, for the first time since the doctor visit. "We've already discussed this and talked to support group people and the online forums, and all of us want you here. We will make arrangements to be here and get and do everything you need. *Everything.*"

He tried again. "Do you really want the next few months to be spent seeing awful things? Having to do awful things for me? Those will be your last memories of me, and of us."

She locked gazes, determination blazing off of her. "Yes. I treasure every second we're together. Every heartbeat. We don't run from hard things."

"Fuck, Vee—"

"It's still my turn. I'd like you to consider this last treatment." She swiped at her face. "I know now what I'm asking. Okay, not know-know. It's freaking—it's a heroic effort. It is. And I'm selfish because I'm asking you to make the call tomorrow and say yes anyway. B, there's hope. I need to tell you—"

He touched her lips then ran his fingers over her cheek. "This will impact the team." He touched her shoulder and the damn gash she'd come in with the night before. "It will impact *you.* Lack of sleep alone—"

"I have hope." Her head was already swinging in denial. She glanced around and lowered her voice, leaning in even closer. "B, there's another possibility and—"

He kissed her. Savoring her fierceness and dedication. "You have hope for both of us. That will be your job. Mine will be chemo. I can't do both. This is assuming Kimi, Liv, and Josh even agree. We need to discuss the decision with them because they are impacted, too."

Metal bonged above them. Bruce lifted his gaze to the metal walkway. Fucking *knowing* what he'd see.

"Guys, it's okay," Vee said, no surprise evident. She'd already known this part, as well.

All three rounded the corner into view. Eavesdropping. No, scratch that. They were executing some damned pre-planned maneuver. This—this wasn't just Vee. This was a team op.

They came down the steps and made a circle around him and Vee.

Josh elected himself spokesperson, all trace of his everyday irreverence and laid-back persona gone. "We already talked about all that too. If we need to take a sabbatical and HQ send in a support team for the Region, we'll do that. You're one of us, you are one of the team. We will have your back. We don't let family face monsters alone."

"Jesus F Christ," Bruce half-swore and half tried not to cry. He'd keep fighting, because, yes, he was part of the team. They always grabbed life and fought to hang on no matter how shitty the odds or how high their probability of leaving this world too soon.

He wouldn't be any less brave. Fuck if he was dishonoring them and the contract he'd signed that promised he was in this for life.

He stood and hugged his brother, Vee and his sisters linking arms and pressing in, turning it into a group hug.

His family had grown, and he'd almost missed the miracle.

CHAPTER 13

ee

I PULLED our bed's blanket higher, tucking it around Bruce's shoulders. Careful not to jar him and wake him up.

From the lines marring his forehead, even asleep he didn't escape the pain he'd finally admitted to. A pair of new medications had joined the mini pharmacy on our night-stand. At least they let him sleep.

He'd finally drifted off, head in my lap. A new screen on the opposite wall reflected back a ghost version of us. Sitting through gaming battles or movie nights had stopped, even the lumpy couch too uncomfortable for Bruce.

So Josh had bought and installed the giant screen in our room, maxing out video games, streaming services, movies—anything that might distract Bruce for an hour or two.

Instead of him reading for the kids, Liv sat in here as long as Bruce would allow, reading to him. Kimi kept up with meds, and kept him company. Having their own conversations they kept strictly private.

I pulled out my phone, my newest compulsive habit.

The one freaking time I needed a vampire, they disappeared. In the last three weeks, we'd had dozens of windigos, ghouls, and false starts, and only one vampire call-out. Josh had taken it out from a distance as it attempted to sneak over a rooftop to avoid me and Liv.

I'd finally cobbled together how to keep one alive and put aside. There was a sedative in one of my BDU pant's pockets, chains stashed in the SUV and Liv's truck, and one of our bare-bones tertiary sites ready. It held a cage and more chains.

My shaky extraction plan hinged on lying about HQ requiring a vampire specimen, then telling the team I'd take it to HQ myself. Quietly dropping it at the site, and swearing it had gotten free in the SUV, attacked, and I'd been forced to eliminate it.

Assuming Liv didn't decide to include the incident in her obsessively thorough reports, a quick side-note that would result in questions and a call from HQ. Ditto Kimi and her insatiable curiosity, checking HQ for what the vampire specimen was to be used for, because she had five minutes to kill and was bored.

Now I needed a vampire. Fast.

This round of treatments was so much worse than the last. I smoothed over Bruce's shaved head, and lightly across his face. His cheekbones were stark hollows, eyes looking like he'd been punched. The contrast between the dark circles underneath and his chalky pallor gave him a bruised effect.

He was fighting so hard, because I'd asked him to. He was the one suffering because I was selfish. I couldn't even tell him why I'd asked him to endure this torture. He'd said he needed all of his energy for the treatments. Sometimes, hope really was exhausting. Too much to look at.

A notification flashed on my phone. I prayed the way I'd seen Bruce do, not knowing who I was begging, only that this be our miracle. My street contact's icon filled the screen. I hit the text option, heart hammering.

--Heads up. Talk about a couple of women from one of the camps missing. One a week ago one maybe today. New bad vibe in town.

A rough, general area description followed.

I'd gone behind Kimi's back. Putting out word that all intel and chatter on the streets go through me. This could be my miracle. I eased a pillow under Bruce's head, then carefully slid off the bed.

The crew was in the common room, but the movie volume was way below our usual levels. Part concern about disturbing Bruce, part the air of sadness enveloping the compound. Everything felt muted.

They all came alert at my arrival. The same fear I lived with on their faces. Hands clenching chair arms, muscles tensed, ready to jump up, get Bruce what he needed, get him into the truck and to the E.R..

I tried for matter of fact. "B needs a refill on the nausea meds."

"I can go." Josh started to rise.

"B's asleep. I'll go. I need the air," I lied, feeling like I was betraying Bruce by even pretending to need time away.

Liv popped up and grabbed her tablet from the back of the couch. "I'll stay with him."

"Thanks." I took the SUV keys from their hook in the kitchen and tried not to rush. Pretend this was a normal trip.

I made it through the gates and down our road to the bend where I was out of the compound's sight, then pulled to the shoulder. Nothing but desert, stars, and night creatures surrounded me. I stashed my jeans and shirt, changing to full tactical gear. Weaponing up, I made sure I had the sedative, and dropped the ugly chains that weighed nearly as much as I did to the passenger floorboard.

"Please, please don't let this be another ghoul," I whispered, the serenity of rolling desert and mesas giving way to stoplights and buildings with Greek letters over the entrance. I cruised campus, thinking about the new vampires we'd taken out, most wearing college attire.

Then the disappearances of the homeless women. Besides ratty housing, the strip running through the edge of campus held a ton of bars and hole-in-the-wall dives. There were spots aplenty to hook up if any of the women resorted to off the book sex work.

The area my contact mentioned was a couple of blocks north. I cut left, the campus apartments giving way to duplexes, and houses with as many students as possible splitting the rent. The houses were on a gradient, getting more and more run down until I hit the dead zone. Here, houses sported yellow *condemned* tape, aged and peeling from the doors, the windows long gone.

I parked behind a gas station-car wash combo that hadn't been in use since phone booths were a thing, tucking the truck into a wash stall. Running through weapons, I touched the sedative like it was my good luck charm. Satisfied, I used a defunct vacuum stand and boosted myself enough to catch the edge of the station roof.

I peeked over, gauging structural integrity and checking for other unwanted residents, then climbed onto the roof. I squatted in a corner, blending into the cover of the shadows, and stared out at the neighborhood. Unfocusing and letting that subconscious part take over. Not purposely looking for any one thing. Absorbing the feeling, what belonged, what didn't.

One house had completely fallen in, no way for anything larger than lizards or snakes to fit under the rotted wood.

Then another mostly intact structure, sandwiching the remnants of a house that had burned at some point, charred foundation all that remained, then the last two houses. Both yards were full of tossed out bottles, remnants of plastic sacks and cans, broken glass providing out-of-place glimmers.

My attention kept drifting to the last building.

Hindbrain having done its job, I focused. Gaze going between the last house and the one beside it, a real life spot-the-differences puzzle.

The closer house wasn't as far gone, smaller and with less junk in the yard. The windows were all busted out, gaping holes letting the elements in.

The last house was larger, more overgrown scrub, especially in the rear, where some kind of rickety outbuilding listed sideways. The house's stamp-sized porch had holes, the steps completely gone. Papers, wind blown bags, and more trash had collected in the corners.

And it had windows covered by newish plywood.

I grabbed the edge of the roof and dropped to the ground, bent knees taking the impact.

I slipped from the wash building to the gas pumps, then darted across to the smaller house. Waiting for the dry crunch of a foot on sandy dirt or the pop of clothing catching on scrub and getting jerked free as its owner moved.

Nothing stirred. At all. None of the usual night chorus, no rats scurrying, no bats swooping, disturbed the silence. Like a major predator was prowling, and anything smaller had bolted or hidden.

Creeping around the house, I eyed the next lot. Then darted from my spot to the shelter of the outbuilding. The sick-sweet rot of decomposing meat hit me, an oily miasma attaching itself to my skin and invading my nose. I pulled my shirt over my lower face and breathed through my mouth.

Sliding my gun free, I followed the smell, to a foot with a chunky heeled shoe, sticking out of the open-sided lean-to. Staying low, I peered inside. Our two missing people were now accounted for.

Punctures covered their arms, legs, and neck, clothing ripped carelessly away. A few of the spots had ragged chunks bitten out to get to veins, the tissue scattered around the kills.

I chewed on the curses trying to escape my mouth. These people had been savaged while still alive. The ferocity, and leaving bodies for easy discovery, spoke of young vampires. If it hadn't been so perverse, I'd have prayed for the older vampire that created them to still be around. Anything less than a decade old was useless to me.

I edged around, enough to get an unobstructed view of the nest's house. A screen door hung from one hinge, mesh long gone. The splintered main door behind it wasn't completely closed, harsh light escaping in a narrow line.

I palmed an aerosol sedative cartridge, like what we'd used on the firebug. The amount was only good for contained spaces. If there were multiple vampires inside, use gas to incapacitate them, choose my specimen, and dispatch the rest.

Using the gun barrel, I nudged the door, thumb over the pressure plate on the cartridge.

Bodies slumped over a sawhorse and plywood table in the old kitchen. Blood spattered the trash-filled sink and walls, and kept going, into the hall leading out. Hugging the wall, I eased in, pausing long enough to verify the three bodies had been vampires. Fangs shone from mouths pulled into an O of surprise. One of the heads hung upside down, facing the back wall, only tendon holding it now.

This—the kills had happened so fast the vampires hadn't had time to move. Chills pebbled my covered skin. Whatever had done this wasn't a newbie.

The hall lay in front of me, far narrower than modern houses. A perfect pinch-point trap.

Only one room along it, to the left, where light from the front room shone in, pooling on dirty linoleum, bath bare of shower curtain or vampires.

If there was an older vampire here, my heartbeat was audible to it. I charged in, down low and out of strike range. Slamming my back against the living room wall, gun level.

Bodies piled up here. Literally on top of each other. Thicker by the front door, like they'd tried to flee and bottle-necked. The door was still shut tight, none of the victims successful in escaping.

It looked almost like a contained, murderous bomb had gone off, radiating from the center of the room. Blasting bodies to fall outward.

Nothing moved.

By the light of a halogen lantern in the corner, I watched my chance to save Bruce die. Rotting with the blood already going bad, and the limbs and heads ripped and tossed against ratty chairs and couch.

Numb, I straightened and walked over a vampire with a hole punched through its chest, and into the middle of the bodies. Trying to count torsos. Four, five, six, seven. Seven plus the three in the kitchen.

Ten chances to get rid of the pain gnawing at Bruce from the inside. To stop the tumors, and let him eat something besides meal replacement drinks. All gone.

With no one to hear, I screamed. Putting all the rage and fear and grief into the wordless shriek. I dropped, knees slamming into the filthy floor. Head bent, the tears I couldn't let flow at home or around Bruce and the team dripped off the end of my nose. Splatting into wet spots on the bloody floor, and an arm sticking out from underneath a tangled pile of dead hopes.

Another salty drop hit the open hand, pooling in the rust-brown streaked palm, following the lines crisscrossing the skin.

A finger twitched.

Then another. Curling in like they were cupping my tears. I dropped the canister, switched my gun for a knife, and toppled the body on top of the pile off. Grabbed the feet of the next, hauling it until it slid out of my way.

Underneath, a male lay. Black shirt and jacket, even the zipper darkened, multi-pocket pants, all echoes of our uniforms. Nylon webbing buckled around his legs. Sheaths for the two machetes, one still clasped in his scarred hand, the other peeking from underneath his body. Both stained with blood.

Under coppery skin, he was ashy. His blood pooled around him, exposed skin covered in gashes and bites. He was nearly bled out.

Nearly, but not completely. My knife under his jaw as insurance, I used my free hand, pressing two fingers to the corner where jaw met neck. A second. Another second. Then a thump tapped under my fingertips, with a long pause between another thump. His pulse was slow, but it was there.

Grunting at his solid bulk, I rolled him face down and pulled out the heavy steel cuffs, bolting his wrists together behind his back. Then jerked off sturdy work boots with reinforced toes, ignoring the gray smear of brain on one, and locked his ankles together.

I patted him down, recovering knives of every size, what looked like det cord for explosives plus a lighter, and a small, plain wooden crucifix.

I took it all, jogging to the SUV and dumping it beside the

recycled hemp bag that held all the things Bruce might not need ever again, and drove over curbs and yards to load my cryptid miracle.

A pass through the building with fuel from the small refill container we kept in the truck, and I stood just outside the body-filled living room, and tossed the lit matches in.

I watched the fire ignite and race through the dry building, burning away cryptid evidence that should've been reported as another link in the chain of aberrant vampire behavior. And burning away a part of who I was, an agent, one who put Company and rules first.

I did use one of the extra phones in the SUV console to anonymously call in a fire near campus.

* * *

SNEEZING at the dust still present in the building despite my cleaning efforts weeks earlier, I tested the chem-plated chains, then the chem-lined cuffs now fastened around the vampire's wrists and ankles. Satisfied they'd hold, I ran the chains through the bars of the cage and locked them.

Leaving the vampire spread-eagle on the floor, limbs pulled to their limits. Paranoid, I checked yet again, but its pulse beat a reassuring rhythm against my finger tips, same as when I'd loaded and unloaded him. Before I left the neighborhood and the burning house, I'd given him a half dose of the sedative. Not willing to trust that blood loss alone would keep him unconscious while I drove the hour to the hiding place.

Then I worried the entire drive whether the sedative on top of extreme blood loss had finished him off.

By the time I backed the SUV into the metal building disguised as rental storage units, his pulse had sped up.

Now it was steady, and close to normal-ish, at least for a

vampire. I cut the trashed sleeve of his jacket and shirt underneath away. Then laid the collection tube, syringe, and tourniquet on top of the folded shirt scraps.

Now that all I needed was ready, my vampire source obtained—my lungs felt like someone was reaching inside me and squeezing them. My heart jumped, out of rhythm, then speeding like I was at the end of one of Liv's double-time marathon runs.

I bit the heck out of the inside of my cheek, tasting blood. My body at least recognized the pain plus blood signal, habit and conditioning taking over. Drawing a deep breath of stale air, I scrubbed my damp palms against my pants. Then rolled the tourniquet up the bare arm in front of me, jerking the rubber strap hard.

The vampire's eyes snapped open.

I had the knife under his jaw, tip breaking skin, in a heartbeat.

His nostrils pinched in, taking my scent, and he blinked. "May I hold my crucifix as I die?" His voice rasped, from damage and blood loss. The cadence and accent underneath were familiar, but not. He repeated his request in Spanish, with the same lilt.

His brown eyes blinked again. The square, solid planes of his face remained human.

If I hadn't watched his wounds heal—I would have doubted he was anything but pure human.

I finally answered his question. "Hand you what's basically a weapon with four points so that you can take a shot at stabbing me? Pass."

I couldn't flex his arm to try pumping up blood pressure, forced to wait until enough flowed to the pinched off point as the vampire frowned. Its thick brows bunched. After a moment, the scowl eased, like he'd figured something out.

Then snapped back, frowning harder than ever. "I would

never blaspheme by using the symbol of our Lord in such a fashion."

I ignored him, concentrating on not blowing the vein that finally filled. I eased the needle in, then attached the tube. I had to bite my mangled cheek again as the blood filled the tube, because I wasn't shedding tears of relief in front of a vampire.

I'd brought two tubes and collection sets, one as a backup. Now, I debated whether to fill it.

The Lab's tests had all utilized small amounts. They'd also been able to concentrate their samples, and I didn't have the equipment to replicate that portion of the research. But if Bruce had a crappy reaction…I pulled the tube free and removed the needle and tourniquet.

Reverently, I wrapped the blood in one of the shirt scraps, tucked the extra in another, and placed them in the tiny insulated bag meant for carrying lunch.

Through the entire process the vampire watched me. His eyes stayed human, face as well. He didn't try fighting, not even a twitch. The soft hiss of the bag's zipper echoed.

"I am prepared for my death." He switched to that archaic Spanish, and closed his eyes.

It took a second to translate the last bit he'd uttered. *Strike true, little general.*

I rose with the bag and the jacket remnant. I doubted a swatch of fabric and metal zipper teeth would fashion a weapon, but Company never took risks.

I reset the perimeter and building alarms, redirected weeks ago to only alert to my phone, turned off all the lights except the one blaring down on the vampire, and left.

* * *

"A GHOUL?" Kimi met me as soon as I cleared the decon breezeway between garage and house.

I crushed the internal flinch, and finished off the lie I'd started when I left the compound, then added to when I'd texted about running across a ghoul. Counting on no one here linking my trip out, and the mysterious fire, and coming up with 'Hey, Vee is breaking the code we live by'. All while an unconscious vampire weighed down the rear of the SUV. "Yeah. In the pharmacy dumpster."

"Which is all kinds of wrong," she signed, making a face. "I mean, was it after drugs, or scouting for—" She caught herself, face blanching.

I finished the sentence in my head. *Or was it scouting out terminally ill and dying customers for later.* Like Bruce. I shrugged, tossing the dirty BDUs balled under my arm into the washer, starting the wash cycle immediately. I'd also cleaned the SUV, although there shouldn't be anything to scream 'Vee's lying, it was a vampire, not a ghoul' on the rear cargo matting.

Liv, a few steps behind Kimi, said, "We'll start patrolling there. And two of us with Bruce for appointments may be in order." The savage expression eclipsing her usual collected calm told me how she'd deal with anything targeting Bruce, or any of the people we'd met during treatments and trips. And that she needed to kill something the same as I did, feeling as useless as I also did.

"Bruce?" I'd switched the lunch bag into his carry-all kit, hauling it all in, and it felt as if the blood would burn through any moment.

"Josh and a playoff game," Liv said. They both followed me to our room.

Bruce was still on the bed, something he'd never allowed when others were in the room with him. He had one of Mandy's wobbly-edged afghans over him.

The stupid hoodie hung on him, the purple clashing with the yellow of the pillows he'd propped on, and the paleness of his face.

The second-guessing, a voiceless but vivid montage in my head, intensified. What if instead of helping him or doing nothing, the blood made him worse? I fixated on the Lab reports. Black and white, and tangible evidence the virus DNA was a sound theory.

"Should I ask who's winning?" I raised my voice as I ducked inside our bath, tucking the bag under the sink. Then washing every guilty trace on me away, scrubbing my hands and cuticles where the rust of old blood lingered.

"Bruce's boys are up by two," Josh said, sprawled in one of the two chairs, legs in everyone's way.

I ran my clean hand over his buzzed scalp, a quick, silent thank you. His hand rested on mine for a moment, giving and receiving comfort.

"Catch me up tomorrow on who won." All of Bruce's attention was on me, eyes tired.

Josh's hand clenched around the chair arm. Bruce never bailed on a game, especially when his team was up. Hiding his worry, Josh stretched and grabbed the mostly empty bottle of sports drink, another thing Bruce never would've allowed before, from the floor beside his perch. "Will do, man."

Liv and Kimi followed him out.

"Are you hurt?" Bruce didn't wait for the rest of the team to get out of earshot.

"Not even a little."

"Go change." Which meant shorts and tee and the chance for him to see if I was holding out.

I pulled a sleep set from a drawer and did as he asked. Not wanting him to waste energy worrying about me.

His voice carried into the bath. "I didn't know we were low on prescriptions."

"We were getting there. And I picked up a few shakes." I had made a fast run through the pharmacy, shoring up my cover story. "Hey, it's time for an evening dose."

I pulled out the packet of stupid meal replacement drinks. Chocolate, because they would hide the blood.

I palmed the tube while cracking the seal on a bottle. Holding the tube over it—I caught my reflection in the mirror. More than capturing and caging a vampire, this was the point of no return. If I did this, the Vee looking out at me was gone. If there was such a thing as a bad afterlife or hell, that's where I was headed.

I tipped half of the vial's contents into the bottle. If it saved Bruce, that was a price I'd pay. I hid the tube and shook the bottle, mixing the contents, and grabbed the prescription bag.

"Let me see." Bruce meant, pull my shirt up for inspection.

"Let's negotiate." I handed him meds and the bottle. "You drink, I'll flash you."

I hated that he didn't even grump or argue for show.

"Chocolate?"

"I thought a change might help." When he took a sip, I pulled my shirt off, did a turn as proof, and put it back on. Then crawled onto the bed.

"A ghoul. Alone."

"Didn't even break a sweat," I promised and curled up beside him.

"If you do—"

"I won't." I gentled my tone. "If I'm tired or off, I'll tell the team. That's our deal. They'll do the same to me."

He took another drink, then offered me the bottle, already done.

"A little more?" I coaxed. "Two sips?"

Because he loved me and couldn't tell me no anymore than we could tell him no, he did as I asked. The way his throat worked after the second sip told me pushing any harder would end up with none of it left in his stomach.

I capped the bottle and set it on the nightstand, wrapped myself around Bruce like I was another blanket, and rested my cheek against his.

"Still every heartbeat?" He whispered, voice ragged and exhausted now that there wasn't an audience.

"Every heartbeat. Always," I whispered back.

ee

THE TEAM'S chatter shut off as the house door closed behind me. They were barely back in the yard, but I'd bolted ahead. That dread that dogged my footsteps, tucked just out of sight in my head, wouldn't let me take my time and cool down with my sisters and brother.

We couldn't slack off training, especially now when we were all on edge. Honestly, moving, training, fighting kept me from devolving into a worse mess than I already was. So far, the toxic stew was all still penned safely inside me. Not affecting the team, which was how it had to stay.

But I'd still been away from Bruce for hours. He'd been alone for hours. The fact that it was only in our home, he had told us to go, he had his cell on him…that was logic. Logic and my emotions weren't on speaking terms at the moment.

I had to grab the bar corner, jerking myself to a skidding halt when my brain caught up with my legs, and registered that Bruce was standing in the kitchen. In the kitchen, and at the fridge.

I'd left him in our room with an audiobook, and assumed it would lead to him sleeping, since he'd had pain meds not long before.

"What's wrong?" I let go of the bar and tried to act as if I hadn't charged into the house and bolted down the hall like we'd gotten an emergency call-out.

He frowned at me and my speed. "Do we have any more of the new drinks? The chocolate flavored?"

I'd coaxed him to drink more of the blood-laced shake this morning, pouring a quarter of it out before adding the blood, hoping he'd get more of the doctored mix in him that way. And he'd done better than the night before, getting close to half of the bottle down before handing it back.

It was too soon for even vampire-virus DNA to do crap. I repeated the mantra to myself. Afraid to grab too much hope, too soon. I made my voice come out matter-of-fact. "Yeah, two left in the suite. Guess I forgot to put them in the fridge." One more lie to add to the growing pile. I didn't dare doctor a bottle in the kitchen, where anyone might walk in.

"Maybe room temperature makes the difference. The one last night, and this morning, weren't as bad as usual."

"I'll grab one for you." I spun for our room before he changed his mind and before the nausea returned.

When I came out of the bath, he was already in our room. I shook up the bottle then offered it to him.

"I'll drink, you go shower." He tossed one of my fuzzy pillows onto the bed as a backrest and sat, pulling his tablet from the stand.

One lightening-speed shower later, I leaned against the bath doorway, watching Bruce. The bottle was already back on the damn table, although he had his book going, one earbud in.

Even a few ounces of anything counted, so I'd take his few sips of the shake as a win.

I flipped my head upside down, toweling wet hair. "We have some fresh bone broth, or Liv found a new brand of crackers. Stone-ground something—spelt? Barley?"

"Not right now."

I kept my head down so he wouldn't see my frustration.

"Another shake later might be good, though."

I froze mid-toweling, damp hair dripping onto the floor. "Another?"

"Yes."

I flipped my head up and hair out of my face. Then took the few steps to check for myself and picked up the bottle. It wasn't empty, but it was damn close. It was also more than he'd drunk at once in too long to track. Possibly more than he'd had in a twenty-four-hour period in days.

I knelt by the bed. "Really? No barfing?"

He pushed the wet strands behind my shoulder. "Yes, and no. I feel fine so far."

We both knew not to make blanket statements, and to add qualifiers like 'so far' and 'this time.'

There was every chance today was a one-off. But if it was my job to hope, I was all over this possibility.

My phone pinged, and I tilted it on the nightstand enough to see the caller I.D. "It's your mom."

"Tell her to call my phone."

I messaged, thumbs flying. Happy to give her even a tiny portion of good news for the day.

As her voice came from Bruce's phone, and he opened the video link, I grabbed jeans and shirt, not even checking what I put on and slipped back into the bath. Pulling my hair into a ponytail, I tossed the towel and grabbed the bag holding the unused blood collection tube.

I closed the suite door halfway, and jogged down the hall

in search of any of my siblings. They were all settled in the common room, our den. Josh and Kimi in headphones and gaming with Jace, Josh's twin. Liv watched over them like she was watching over a flock.

We'd never taken each other, and family, for granted. Now though, it was like we all needed the extra time together and that connection.

"I'm going after more shakes. B almost finished one."

All three heads turned my way, Josh and Kimi jerking their headsets off, Kimi accidentally pulling out a few spiral curls in her haste.

"He's also talking to his mom." I wasn't the only one grasping for any shred of hope. All their faces lit up.

"I'll check on them in a few minutes," Liv said. "I wanted to ask how the girls' regional spelling bee shook out anyway." Something almost like guilt shaded her eyes, then was gone.

"I may be a while. I'm going to see what else I can find that B might be able to stomach now." Like more virus-enhanced blood from my vampire.

* * *

I TURNED THE IGNITION OFF, opened my phone app and checked the security feeds, confirming the vampire hadn't done a Houdini, gotten free, and was waiting to attack me the second I walked in.

It wasn't a likely scenario, but then neither was ten dead nest members, all at the claws of one vampire. However old he was or wasn't, he was undisputedly powerful.

The feeds showed him where I'd left him, and fast-forwarding through the last eighteen hours of footage confirmed he hadn't moved.

I flicked more lights on and went straight for the spread-eagled form. He turned his head, watching me while I pulled out my supplies. I'd have called the expression in his deep brown eyes patience in a human.

Even as I inserted the needle, none of the usual vampire reflexes bled through his façade. I finished, storing the precious vial in the cooler bag, then took a minute to really examine him. His chest was crosshatched with lines of old scars.

His new wounds were healed like he'd never been touched. Even the chunked-out bites had filled in. For a vampire that hadn't fed and replenished itself, the healing was freaking impressive.

The Oversight Labs hadn't seemed to factor in age, past the decade marker allowing a vampire to infect and create new vampires, the point where the mutation completed.

If age and ability were a factor—excitement fanned the weak ember that had grown a degree when Bruce finished off a liquid meal today.

"Did you single-handedly kill all of the vampires in that nest?" I squatted and watched his face, searching for a tic, a tell, anything that indicated he lied.

His expression remained composed. "I did."

I wasn't sure why I asked. Not like we were trained to read vampire body language for anything other than combat skills, but still.

"If you won't allow me my crucifix, will you hang it where I may see it as I perish?"

I gathered my bag, re-armed security, and turned the lights brighter.

* * *

OVER THE LAST FORTY-EIGHT-HOURS, Bruce had way exceeded my hopes, more or less finishing off the pack of shakes. All with only a little coaxing and mild bribery. He'd also talked to both his brother and sister.

Then came today's treatment, and the usual horrible nausea and exhaustion, just as bad as after every other appointment.

I held onto the emptied bottles, and the whisper-thin thread of hope they represented.

Once again, the security footage, and real-time peek inside showed me the same deceptively peaceful scene as before. My vampire restrained, and spotlighted like a piece of performance art. I'd added a dose of tranquilizer to my bag today.

As impressive as this specimen was, it had healed itself of major injuries, worked through one dose of sedative, and we were coming up on an entire week without it feeding.

I had the sedative prepped and out when I knelt. We repeated our pattern, the vampire simply watching me until I finished. This time, I filled two vials.

* * *

I SAT IN THE TRUCK, outside my illicit base, and worked up the energy to go drain a vampire again.

We'd had an all-hands call out and all four of us had returned some degree of beat up. This was probably what people called karma. I'd lied about a ghoul, and our call-out had involved a trio. All male, and as mindlessly aggressive as during breeding season, except that was months away.

I'd also discovered that scientists kept crappy notes, at least, the ones available to me. Vampire blood-DNA-virus whatever lost potency or effectiveness around thirty-ish hours. My discovery, not theirs.

My second tube had been a waste. I only hoped that Bruce's waning appetite and nausea were because of expired blood, not the stuff failing to work any longer. By my super non-scientific estimate, the outcome of tonight's spiked drinks would prove whether I'd been deluding myself, or whether it was a matter of the virus having a short shelf life.

Base security feed scanned, my safety review was accomplished. I forced myself to move. My calf twinged, a gift from a ghoul that should've been incapacitated, spine severed, but had still managed to shred tactical pants and spear me with a nasty broken tooth.

I pulled the sedative out in preparation, in no mood for a repeat, this time from a starving vampire.

Tonight, he kept his face to the light, although there was still no feeding frenzy attempt. I shifted on the concrete, knees sore, and my calf banged into a cage bar, waking the stupid puncture up. A trickle of dampness seeped from my leg to dampen my jeans.

Right by a hungry vampire's face. I popped the cap off the sedative too fast, the cap skittering into a corner.

"You have nothing to fear from me."

I froze, needle by his neck, at the soft statement. The vampire sounded as exhausted as I felt. "Yet. I don't have anything to fear from you yet. Don't forget that addendum."

"You have never needed fear me, nor do you now."

"Easy to say at the moment." I flicked a bar, setting off a *ting* of metal chiming.

"You are too fatigued." A frown carved across his forehead, following old lines. He'd apparently been a grump before his human life was ruined and twisted by the virus.

He stared into the ceiling and light. "Fatigue is as dangerous as you believe me to be."

I jerked the tourniquet tight, and drew my one tube allotment, not especially careful about veins or bruises tonight.

"I hadn't thought you cruel." For some reason, it didn't feel like he was referring to my cruddy nurse skills.

"I hadn't thought I was either, but here we are." Having a vampire question my moral compass probably should've been cause to stop and reevaluate. At least feel conflicted about my actions. Instead, I packed up and armed the system, cutting the other lights.

Then backtracked, digging through the junk I'd dumped on a table the night I'd brought the vampire in. Using a strip of cloth ripped from his shirt remnant, I tied the wooden cross to the cage bars above his head.

ee

MY AMATEUR RESEARCHER HYPOTHESIS? Theory? Whichever, had proven accurate. I'd already picked up new shakes, and more vials and syringes. I'd left Bruce and Josh watching Bruce's team advance in the finals.

A night's sleep, where Bruce had also slept a solid eight hours, and a huge coffee shop Americano had jolted my brain cells back into action, snippets of the vampire's speeches whirling and almost clicking together. I had questions, and was about to run a second, very different experiment here.

I set my cup on the worktable, the vampire still ignoring me in favor of his cross.

I spread out everything I'd taken from his pockets and person, finally paying attention to their significance. What I'd assumed was det cord for explosives turned out to be spot on, and a decent brand at that.

Same for the thigh rigs. I held each machete—because these were way too large to be passed off as knives—to the light. They weren't new, edges sharpened again and again from the looks of them, but they were honed and cared for. The handles had hemp crisscrossed along their lengths. An old-school trick, keeping the grips from getting slick when wet, or drenched in blood and fluids.

The shirt had been a tactical style. But the jacket was more akin to a serious motor cross racer's, tight and good quality, the waxed surface keeping it water or goo repellant. With one finger, I tipped the boots my way—they'd been military issue, available from any army surplus place, and as worn as the blades.

I entered the cage, but rested against the bars, watching the vampire. Still as human-seeming as the first night I'd captured him. "Why did you kill your own nest? Assuming you weren't lying about taking on nearly a dozen vampires."

I sorta expected him to continue with his ignore-the-agent routine.

"They were not my nest."

Guess he'd finally gotten bored.

I poked harder. "So you offed them in order to take territory for yourself and your nest."

"I have no nest, and I don't claim or desire to claim territory."

"Are you *Il Creatore*?"

He snorted a soft blast. "Ignorant young vampires. Foolish stories and foolish choices."

"What counts as a smart choice for a vampire?"

"There are none. Once they become vampire, they are damned."

"By you?"

"By God."

My luck to get a coherent but delusional vampire. "Except for you, huh?"

"I am damned as well. We are demons and we have no soul. Because we have no soul, we cannot repent and be forgiven. Only one end awaits us in the pit."

"You were mutated by a virus. Biology, not theology. An illness, I suppose."

"Hell has many forms. Had you lived through smallpox and plagues, you would agree that disease can be evil, a device of the Devil to torture man."

He wasn't looking but I ducked my head, hair shifting and shielding my face. Bruce—maybe I could understand why the vampire believed as he did.

Time for what I came after. Bruce had a treatment the next day. I filled my tube while the vampire went silent. Sulking, for all I knew. I put the blood away, and he resumed talking like there hadn't been a pause.

"Emotions weaken you. They will make you slow, and you'll fall."

If we were getting personal, I had questions too. "Should I thank you for the save in the Art District that night? How about the park before that?" I doubted he knew anything about either, but he might spill intel on other nests and what the heck was going on.

Thick disapproval laced his voice. "Your emotions ruled you in that ambush. It became a trap of your own making." He turned his head my way, scowl back in its full glory. "You indulged, and nearly paid the final price. That was as foolish and indulgent as those new made vampires' decisions. You must stay vigilant."

The reprimand stung, as much as one issued by our trainers in Academy. I opened my mouth to defend myself. To a vampire. With both a religious fixation and a judge-y streak.

But his answer set off some catalyst or chain reaction in my head. Pieces began clicking into place. On my previous visit, he'd said I'd *never had* a reason to fear him, past tense.

He had watched me that night. At least long enough to critique my performance in the field.

Holy—I shoved off the cage bars, rolling to my feet as ice frosted my bones. "That afternoon you *were* between those shops. Where did you hide? Did you compel someone in the glassblower's studio to open and close doors for you?"

He turned away. If I hadn't known better, I'd have said he was embarrassed. He kept his mouth shut.

Fine then. "I guess I'm not the only one who got sloppy. How old are you, to be able to move in shadows during the day?"

"Part of my forefathers were in this land before my other ancestor arrived to conquer it." He gave me his attention again. "As were yours. Why haven't you done your job, *pequeña general*? You have taken many samples for your army's inspection. You are not taking me to be used to train your young ones. There's no reason I should still be alive."

Hairs rose along my arms, in a chill way worse than when he'd admitted to watching me. "You know. *How* do you know about us?"

He didn't answer.

I grabbed under his jaw, jerking his face to me, his neck torqued at an ugly angle. "How many? How many more of you are there?"

Nothing vampire or cryptid could know about us. That was a core tenant second only to protecting humans and concealing cryptid existence. We couldn't allow higher cryptids to know we existed, or—

I grabbed for my phone. Then stalled out. What was I supposed to say to HQ? *Oh, hey, I illegally took and am holding for my own use a vampire, because I hacked Oversight files. And*

I'm dosing my boyfriend with cryptid DNA? But ignore that, because, potential invasion.

I shot off a text to Kimi. *Put every drone out. Plus sweepers on the ground. Run a full scan, city, access road, and compound.*

Then sent an equally terse one to Liv. *Hit every source. Check and crosscheck hits, street chatter, and LEO and hospital records.*

Kimi's response came as I finished Liv's. *Mission critical? Backup estimated ETA?*

Damn it. I couldn't put the base and team at risk—they needed to gear up and prepare. I began the text that would expose my lie, and put them at a different kind of equally deadly risk.

"Be easy." The vampire's tone had gone from disapproving to reassuring. "I am alone, as well as the only of my kind to know of you and your army."

"Bull."

"I have watched you for nigh on two years. As I said, you are in no danger from me."

That he seemed sincere was exactly why I couldn't trust him. "Bull again. I can't verify anything you say, even if I was suicidally stupid enough to listen to you."

"You are faster than your sister, though she loves the obstacles you train on. Your other sister has many admirable qualities—she controls her emotions. You are a poor singer. Very poor."

My fingers stopped mid-typo. "What the hell—"

"Enough cursing! Once I'll tolerate. Twice is undisciplined, and any more dishonors your role as leader." He glared at me, his disapproval crackling in the air between us.

"Did you just—are you freaking kidding me? I did not get language policed, and lectured, by a bloodthirsty killer." Who knew about us. Had known for two *years*. And had stepped in and maybe saved my butt at least once. Maybe.

"Foul language is also beneath you, but it is blasphemy that I won't tolerate. Yes, I am a killer. God has seen fit to use me as His scourge on earth."

ETA? Vee, report!

Liv's message snapped me back to reality. "My team—"

"I have never killed a human. I never will. I will swear to this on the cross. Your secret will die here with me." That sincerity shown from the vampire's eyes. Sincerity or religious zealotry.

Vee!

I did a group text to Kimi and Liv. *Stand down. Another rogue ghoul. Abt 2 dispose of the body. But keep all channels active.*

Evidence of more?

I kept my lie going. *Negative. Gut feeling.*

They would both roll their eyes, but they'd keep surveillance up and follow my orders.

I stood and stared at the vampire.

He lay and stared back.

The crucifix he prized so highly. The God talk.

"I may—may—buy that you think you're some avenging angel on a divine mission to kill cryptids—"

"I am the lowest of the damned, far from an angel's grace. I have no time for animal pests. God has aimed me at only other demons. I kill those as cold and soulless as I became."

"Whatever. You are blowing every bit of credibility with your lies about not killing humans, though."

"I don't lie and I do not touch humans. I defend those still capable of receiving God's grace and forgiveness from Hell's corruption, precisely as your human army does."

Whatever was going on here was threatening to scramble my head.

The vampire was just a delusional monster, with a religious bent. "You are a vampire. You can't survive without blood."

"I do not touch human blood."

I abandoned the cage and took my coffee cup to the sink, dumping the dregs and rinsing. Once it was clean, I slid the tourniquet onto my arm, pulling it tight, then did the fill-a-tube thing. Rolling the strip of rubber off, I bent my arm in place of a band-aid. Using a thumbnail, I removed the vial's rubber stopper and poured the contents into my repurposed cup.

I crossed back to the vampire who couldn't be what he claimed he was, sat the cup by his hand, then triple checked that the cage lock engaged behind me. I loosened the chain to his arm, giving him enough slack to have his snack. Then left to ruin a pair of jeans on the gravel outside while scuffing myself up, to better sell my lies to the team.

Later, when the vampire had to come clean, we could discuss reality and what else he knew.

I'd find some way to get any information that could compromise agents or the Company to HQ, in case Jesus-vampire had accomplices.

One more borderline impossible task to add to my to-do list.

ruce

HAVING ALREADY FOUND her office and the kitchen empty, Bruce walked into the common room in search of Vee. They'd had training earlier, and she'd gone from it straight to a video conference with two other Regional commanders. Even multi-Region conferences didn't go on this long.

The vague uneasiness, left over from whatever shit had really gone down the day before last, which they'd busted their guilty little asses keeping from him, and the still-delayed stomach twisting after effects of a treatment gnawed at him. Leaving him on edge. Jittery, if he'd had enough energy to be jittery.

Vee, though. She'd had enough energy for both of them lately.

He stepped into the room that was their catch-all game haven and hang out site.

Today, it served as an illicit dining room.

Josh stopped, spoon halfway between his bowl and his mouth. Whatever had been destined for the latter now dripped on his shorts.

Vee froze with a spoon at least in her mouth. She spit the utensil out, her face blanching, while Josh bounced up, reaching for her container. Liv and Kimi snatched a bag from the floor, dumping their unopened portions and plastic ware inside.

"Fuck, man. I'm sorry," Josh said as he reached for the bag next. "It was windy as hell outside, dust everywhere, and we didn't think there was any smell to this or I'd never have brought it inside."

Bruce checked with his stomach—which remained un-fucking-nervingly settled. And when the hell had *not* wanting to puke his stomach lining up become the oddity and cause for concern? "Sit back down. It's fine."

Vee looked like she wanted to call him on his bullshit, but again, no one was doing that anymore. She resorted to shredding a cuticle instead.

He sat beside her. "Food goes in your mouth, not fingers. Essie mastered that before she was two."

Vee angled the food away from him but he was close enough now to catch a whiff of rice, vanilla, and cinnamon. He tensed, tired muscles slow to respond, ready to retreat out of the room.

And nothing happened. He waited another beat, then relaxed onto the ugliest couch in the history of design— which also happened to be the most comfortable.

His stomach came to life, but only to growl. Even then, it took him a half-dozen heartbeats to remember what the noise meant, and another beat before he realized it was coming from him.

He leaned and tipped Vee's cup enough to read the scribbled handwriting on the outside. "The abuelas made rice pudding?"

"It's a new try-out on their truck. They sent it with me when I picked up our broth order," Josh said.

Bruce weighed his allegedly hungry stomach versus upchucking and his already aching bones kneeling on the cold bathroom tile. His stomach rumbled again, loud enough the whole team heard it. "How about sharing a bite?"

The echo of his question hadn't faded when Vee grabbed an extra spoon, scooped up pudding, and offered it to him.

His taste buds had lost their finesse, not picking up nuances. The simple dish didn't depend on nuance though. Honest, straightforward, made by someone else's grandmother, but still a grandmother.

"Yes or no on a refill?" Vee asked, offering him her entire cup.

Who the hell knew if it was a good idea or not, but when he dipped up the second bite, then cleaned out the container by finishing off the last third, the happiness on Vee's face was worth the risk.

"There's more." Liv had the bag in her lap, offering him her and Kimi's untouched cups.

"I'm good for now."

"Want to watch *Hamilton*? It dropped a few weeks ago," Kimi signed.

He'd seen it twice on Broadway, and wanted to introduce the other four to it. A video version might be the only chance for that now.

"Is 'It dropped' Company code for secret private armies get copies directly from Lin Manuel Miranda, or Kimi code for 'Let's bend the definition of legal'?"

"Does it matter? *Hamilton*." Vee picked up a remote and waggled it at him.

"We need to have a refresher conversation regarding legal

versus illegal, and artist's rights," he grumbled but took the remote from Vee and tossed it to Kimi to do her thing.

He also nabbed a pillow from the mismatched pile on the floor and gave it to Vee with a hard look at her newly skinned up arm. Another result of the incident they were hiding.

Meekly, she took it and propped her arm on it. "I'm fine, for real."

Neither one of them were anywhere near *fine.* This would work for now, though. He pulled Vee's relatively uninjured hand into his lap and twined their fingers together.

He only made it through the first act, normal sleepiness taking over. Vee snuggled into the bed, spooned against his chest. He drifted to sleep with her warm and soft in his arms.

When he woke, clock showing it was still night, he was holding a pillow.

Vee had switched it out in her place, and if he got up, he'd discover she was gone, with some line to Liv or Kimi about a supply pit stop that took hours. Or a fucking lone patrol that gave Liv reason to pinch the bridge of her nose, fighting off a stress headache, because her C.O. was going dangerously off-book.

Vee's behavior wasn't something he and Liv directly addressed, on any of the occasions when it was Liv's turn to sit with him. Just like they didn't directly discuss the access code and thumb drive he'd entrusted to her. He'd gotten a vow that she'd never open it, unless he was gone, and the team was in trouble.

If his death distracted Vee, any of his new family, if it was a matter of leaving the Company, or one or all of them falling, the thumb drive full of incriminating videos, Company reports, and photos was their way to safety and a new life. He didn't use the word *blackmail*, but Liv was far from stupid.

Now, he laid there until his phone chimed a notice that it

was time for yet another round of drugs from the pharmacy on their nightstand.

He shoved the pillow to the empty side of their bed, and spent the rest of the night wondering if this was it. Whether he'd hit the point where he was a burden, and that was all Vee would remember about him, or their lives together.

ee

I STARED at the cheap coffee cup, simple plastic and cardboard, which shouldn't have freaked me right the heck out. But the congealed blood inside did.

At the end of my last visit, I'd drawn a few ounces of my blood, squirted it into the repurposed cup, and left it in vampire reach.

I bit my thumbnail, studying him. He had an eerie resemblance to Bruce, his face thinner and skin that dehydrated rough-dry, cheekbones prominent, and dark crescents under his eyes. His collarbone stood out like a relief map. All the signs of starvation.

Yet he hadn't touched the blood. I'd even tested a drop with the base's I.D. kit, suspecting he'd drank mine, then replaced the contents with his blood, to fool me. But nope, all human.

I knelt in the cage, and sliced a fingertip. Fresh today

should have an effect, even if it hadn't a day before. Thirty-six hours without food or water made a lot of difference in my experience. Blood welled and ran down my finger.

I held it under the vampire's nose.

He turned his face away. I followed, a drop splatting onto his face.

I jumped when he shook his head hard enough that the chains rattled, then brutally scrubbed his cheek on the floor, scouring the drop off.

Giving up, I spun the extra collection tube in an aimless circle, thinking.

Like he was patched directly into my head, the vampire sighed and said, "Please don't bleed yourself again. It won't be of any use to me, and it may weaken you, something you can't afford in these unsettled days."

We rested in one of what was becoming our trademark silences.

I shored up my pride by rationalizing a vampire had way more practice at being patient. "You have to eat something."

Which sounded a lot like Bruce's mom talking to him. To his sister, to the girls, to all of us. I rephrased. "What do you survive on? Do not try to sell me on that living off of animals fantasy. We learned that was a myth as first year cadets."

"Do you intend to see to your hand?"

"Nope."

He sighed again. "What did you discover when you returned to the marketplace where I stood in the shadows that afternoon?"

"You are enough to make people believe in those stupid movie vampires who can read minds," I muttered.

"What did you discover?"

So, yes. I had retraced every step earlier today, invited myself into buildings, and even pulled up the video and stills Kimi's drones had from that day. "There seems to be no route that would've allowed you to remain sheltered from the sun."

"Why did you return to the location today instead of yesterday?"

I spun the vial faster, facets picking up the unforgiving lights and reflecting over the pitted concrete.

"Why?"

"Yesterday was cloudy," I burst out. Which he likely already knew, getting a good look out the open door whenever I came and went. "Today was full sun, the exact same weather conditions as the day I saw you."

He gave a satisfied grunt, but kept poking. "Why else? Finish your observations to their conclusion."

"There was no way. None. Any shelter or shade was far enough apart that even in a fully-fed state a vampire would have burned, giving off a flare of smoke easily observable. It isn't possible."

"Therefore?"

The only answer had rattled around in my head until I couldn't stand it any longer. Except, not possible. Because if a vampire walked unharmed under a noon sun, giving no visible warning that it wasn't human? We were all so, so screwed. "No."

"The afternoon in the park, you and your sister were unusually gentle with the fire lizard."

I jerked my gaze to his. There was only one way he could know that.

"Do not blaspheme," he ordered me, more of his weird vocabulary rules.

The word-policing vampire who'd been following us, who strolled through lunch crowds, a playground, was doing the exact same thing as our Instructors used to. Forcing me to stop, observe, then create and follow a chain of facts to their logical end.

"You can go in the sun, duration of safe exposure unknown. Fact. This ability has something to do with what you feed on or you'd never have gone down this rabbit hole when I asked about feeding. We've eliminated humans and animals, cryptid or otherwise."

This time, he all but patted me on the head, praise all in Spanish. "My continued existence is made possible by the blood of those as damned as I am."

It was true. Everything he'd said resonated in my bones, like they were lie detectors.

"The first time was by accident, not by design. Once I understood what I had become, there was only one course. To save the people who hadn't fallen to the demons as my family and workers had. I couldn't stay in my hacienda or valley. I sought the demons, determined to kill them and die in combat—a small penance." His gaze fastened on the cross. "I kept the first part of my vow."

"But not the second."

"I will one day fall and fulfill that promise as well. The Lord's hand was at work, showing me my duty and means to carry it out."

Since he was touchy about language, and I was in no place to waste time on another lecture, I went with "How long? How long have you been feeding off your own kind and killing them?"

"They aren't my kind. As for time, my grandmother was daughter of a conquistador."

"Holy cr—" I caught myself as his thick brows scrunched into the start of an offended moment. "Wow." My first thought was Bruce. A four-hundred plus year old vampire had to have the power to help him.

My second thought was my duty. "Why? Why haven't vampires been at open war with humanity, and us?" How had they not at least targeted the Company?

"Few know. Fewer survive to keep and exploit that knowledge." His icy tone changed back to the earlier lecture mode, and I had to stop myself from coming to attention as he continued. "Feeding off of vampires offers no benefit once a new vampire has desecrated a human. Only those that drink their first blood of another vampire can become one that tolerates the rays of the sun. God's hand shows in that as well."

It sounded more like there was some additional mutation going on but I needed actionable information. "That doesn't answer why there hasn't been an army of cannibalistic vampires at our doors. It's not like vampires have a moral compass keeping them from exploiting their own."

If a vampire could look downright pleased, this one did. "You grasp this quickly. One who was brought into this world of the damned with another vampire's blood has the potential to walk in the sun, as well as having an advantage in strength. What a vampire first consumes becomes their—" he seemed to search for words "—their preference. What one who drinks a vampire's blood feels is far stronger—it is all they will ever want, no matter the risks nor cost."

"Addiction? You're saying vampire blood is *addictive?*"

"Now you understand why there is no vampire army. The few ancients who know this secret pledged never to let it become known. Any that stumble on it by accident aren't allowed to survive."

"Yet you're right here, in my Region, in my cage."

"Any vampire I find dies. None walk away. For those few ancient Masters who keep the secret, the potential for an uprising and mass cleansing far outweighs any possible benefits." He gave a *been there—done that* shrug. "A new vampire's inability to move in the light is of benefit to Masters. The necessity to be cloistered in the day, to learn to wake, to stay up longer and longer over the decades, is an imperative in order to train new vampires who otherwise are reckless and foolish, bringing attention to their kind, and death to a Master who allows such infractions. This ruling was made far, far before my time."

"Then—"

"None can live to tell of me, even if my duty wasn't to eliminate the scourge. I do not exist."

I mouthed *holy crap*, skirting his blasphemy rule. No agent knew any of this either.

But living four hundred years alone, as basically a ghost—I couldn't comprehend that existence. Lonely. Empty.

The vampire twitched. "Why do you feel sadness?"

"We are re-visiting the mind reading, right now."

"Though we have none of our own as is befitting a demon, part of our punishment is to sometimes feel a human's emotions. My condition…I always feel them. Humans are loud. *You* are especially loud."

More like he was a hermit, and way over-sensitive. Or out of practice. Probably both.

The information about sensing emotion though, that was a goldmine. We'd always assumed it was superior hearing when one managed to attack before we were in place on a mission.

Back to business. "Why were you following us? Honestly, why are you even telling me this?" I waved a loopy circle in his direction. "You're adept at the whole stoic deal. Pretty sure you wouldn't talk no matter the pressure I applied, so you aren't trying to avoid a painful interrogation by being forthcoming."

"I have known of your people for hundreds of years." He switched topics between blinks. "There are more and more vampires. The ranks swell at a pace I have never seen before. They have also begun acting—"

"Like super-murderous jerks?"

The hairy eyeball look he shot me spoke volumes about his lack of a sense of humor and his dislike of cheeky agents and their interruptions. "They are that, yes. Vampires are without any emotion that isn't of violence, greed, and survival. Young vampires are without a sense of restraint, but they are born with a base sense of survival. Now, they act against their own best interests."

"Like leaving corpses pretty much out in the open to be discovered, and doing it right where they nest during the day. Oh, and doing crazy things like congregating in nests too big for an area to support, thus risking exposure."

He nodded his agreement. "Four hundred years and this is—not right."

"Unprecedented."

"Unprecedented." He tried the concept out. "This exactly."

A-plus for me on tonight's lesson.

It also tallied with my gut feeling that things were weird. And weird never boded well for humans. "Is there some link between vampires, ghouls, and windigos that's similarly need-to-know information? Or vampires and other sentient cryptids in other biomes?" Vampires were a virus mutation, and cryptids were natural animals, but still.

He frowned, and after hearing his hermit story, I was betting my vocabulary confused him.

He finally translated though. Offense replaced his confusion. Loads of offense.

He schooled me, tone snippy. "Vampires have no use for pests, nor do I waste the Lord's time on such minor vermin."

Since most of my vocabulary was off limits, I stuck with rolling my eyes. He was a little more elitist vampire than he'd admit.

"I have given you a secret. Honor requires you do the same. Why do you keep me here, take my blood, yet no others of your group come nor do you take me to your army grounds."

There was negative zero reason for me to answer him.

"You are strong, smart, an honorable leader your people follow gladly. This action—I don't understand it."

"Neither do I." The dam that had held back the fear and desperation—the anger and guilt, not letting any leak onto my brother and sisters to add a selfish level of doubt and stress for them, and definitely never ever, ever giving Bruce more of a burden—disintegrated. Finally crushed under months of terror and responsibility and grief.

"Someone I love very much is sick. And okay, yes, wow were you right about viruses and evil, and I'm kind of hazy on hell and religion, but hell sounds exactly apt for what's killing him. And nothing, not the doctors and specialists and their treatments, and not the Company and all our knowledge and resources, can save him or relieve his pain. Nothing. But you might. The DNA in the virus that mutated you, that might, which is totally messed up. Everything is messed up. I'm lying to my team, my family, and to the Company. I'm breaking rules and mandates I swore to uphold, that mean everything to me. And you're a vampire, but you were human once and I don't relish basically torturing you. You are an abomination and should die, but as quickly and relatively mercifully as possible. What happened to you was horrific and I'm sorry you were infected and your life and future taken. Instead—this. So no, I don't understand either, okay? That's it. All I've got. My not-an-explanation explanation."

My voice had risen with my emotions. Now my stream of confusion echoed off cage bars, rolls of chains, and easily cleaned metal and concrete surfaces before being swallowed by the darkness above us.

The air...crackled. Cold and electric. For the first time, I saw the vampire under the mask of a four-hundred-year-old Spanish-Azteca noble. His already malnourished face thinned, ashy brown skin nearly translucent like the virus wanted free of flesh and bone to attack. Fangs snapped into existence. His eyes swirled quicksilver, turning to the ones I'd glimpsed in the shadows the night of the park attack.

His voice felt like it left an ice rime on my skin. "I will never damn another. We will both die in this cage before I break my vow and betray the duty laid on me by God himself."

When I breathed, the frigid air burned, my lungs aching. I got out, "I'd end Bruce's suffering myself before letting him turn into one of you. Cryptids are only animals. You—vampires—are a walking disease that isn't supposed to exist in the world."

Gradually, the skin-blistering static dissipated and the air turned the warm and dry of my desert. The vampires face reformed, only a line of silver fire encircling the brown in his eyes. "Speak to me of this."

Because I needed to offload some of my guilt, and the only way and only audience that wouldn't be hurt by my—sins, definitely sins—was this vampire, I did.

"The Company, my people? It is always working to take care of us. Our scientists and doctors have researched using parts of the virus to help agents. Like healing wounds faster, saving lives. Keep agents human but get them back into the fight."

"They have discovered this? This medicine?"

"No. Not exactly," I admitted. "They're still trying. But my friend isn't wounded. Something in his own body is killing him. Vampires heal quickly because one tiny sequence, somewhere in the virus' code, returns you to whatever your original ideal form was. It might do that for him—return his confused cells to normal, helped along with the boost from our other medicine."

I slumped against the bars. And rested the crown of my head against the still-chilled metal. Hating the desperation in my voice, hating how desperate my plan sounded aloud. No normal mission would ever get green-lighted with so many unknowns, such a slim margin for error, and even slimmer probability of success.

"I have never heard of such a thing," he finally said, deep voice thoughtful.

"That makes two of us. I mean, neither have I. But it's all that's left, and I have to try."

I huffed a not-funny laugh. "You might even approve. My friend is very committed and religious, in his own way. So is his family. He isn't like us—the Company, my people. He believes."

Chain scratched across concrete. And I was too tired to fight. My entire body felt filled with sand—too heavy to move, too unstable if I tried.

I dropped my head and faced the vampire who, vows aside, was probably attempting to kill me in order to escape.

He stretched his arm as far my way as his bonds allowed. "I don't truly understand your science, nor do I know if what you desire is possible. However, I am honored to be of aid. If it's God's will I be here, perhaps it's his will that heals your friend."

He rolled his arm, exposing the vulnerable underside and the veins.

I retrieved my kit and took him up on the reason I'd come. One of the reasons.

After I tucked the blood away in my bag, I worked the bolts under the worktable and loosened the length of the two chains on his wrists. Just enough for him to scratch an itch. Or pray, if he did it the way Bruce did.

I faced the cage. "I'm Vee. I know what you said, but Scourge of the Lord is kind of a mouthful. Help me out?"

For a beat, nothing in the building stirred, human or vampire. Maybe him processing my slang, me accepting that he'd gone from an amorphous thing to a person.

"Stavros. I am—you may call me Stavros."

I turned the light over his cage to comfortable night-light level and armed my alarms. "Good night, Stavros."

"Vaya con Dios, pequeña general."

I had no idea if his God went with me, but maybe the blood of a devout four-hundred-year-old was close enough.

ee

WE STREAMED into the yard as the sun cleared the mountains, drenching the yard in gold and pink light. Charged up from our morning run, Josh jogged circles around Kimi, taunting her.

"Too slow. Too short. So sad." He swept his arm back and forth over her head with each pass. The same stuff he did when we were kids.

Kimi smiled, and Josh hesitated. Then in a burst of speed, our sister ducked under his arm, grabbed the hem of his shorts, and pantsed him.

His yelp scared the crows from their perch along the fence, cawing their disapproval.

"I'm glad I already ate, because that shit has killed my appetite indefinitely," Bruce grumbled as Josh hauled his shorts up.

This was the second morning Bruce had come out once

the sun rose, and sat on Kimi's bench, now padded with turquoise canvas pillows from her shopping spree at the outdoor store.

Evidence of Josh's spree sat on the end of the bench, in the form a glass jar from the farmer's market. Specifically, from the organic dairy creamery stall. The day after Bruce had finished my pudding, Josh had brought in the rice pudding from the food truck, more from the all-natural grocer, and the creamery.

Then he'd expanded out to anything pudding-ish and dairy.

Bruce had glared at the fridge, three of the four shelves jammed with cups, jars, and tiny bowls. But that afternoon, he'd also ventured into riffling through it for whatever interested him.

Today's choice was some kind live culture Greek yogurt, the only thing Josh bought that came in jars.

Eight weeks into the treatment. Six weeks into my capture-a-vampire plan. Four weeks from the earth-shattering conversation with Stavros. That was how I counted time now.

The treatments still sucked. But on non-treatment days Bruce's nausea was mild. He found more things he could keep down, thanks to Josh and Liv's constant shopping.

Even better, Bruce was hungry. Not normal hungry, but a thousand times better than before the grueling treatment and the sip of liquid now and then, and him only trying because he wanted us to worry less.

He slept better, too. The pain meds were only an occasional thing, not wearing off and making the time until it was safe to take more pure torture.

Now, he'd sat outside two days in a row. When I'd spotted the sketchbook in his lap the day before…I blamed my stupid weepy response on Josh goofing and kicking up grit in my eyes.

The sketchbook hadn't been out, much less open, since midway through Bruce's first treatment. Him not touching it, not sketching ideas and menus and theoretical plans, felt like he'd given up on our future.

Yesterday felt like the opposite.

Bruce said he wasn't up to diverting energy into something as nebulous and potentially heart breaking as hope. I thought I'd understood before but in the last six weeks, I'd seen how it took everything in him to make it through a day. Okay, I'd seen it from the outside. What was really required, what that looked and felt like inside for Bruce, I'd never fully understand.

"Plenty of people admire my butt." Josh struck a pose. His relief translated into basically bouncing like the puppy Hannah and Ken had brought home for Shoshonna.

"I am not one of them." Bruce drew intersecting circles on a page, writing labels I was too far away to make out without leaning over him, and I was way too sweaty-gross for that. Cereal first, then showers.

I whistled, breaking up Josh Never Learns, Part Two, and pointed to the annex. "Double time."

"CoCo Snaps, here I come." Josh darted ahead of us.

Kimi launched after him, the two in a race for the last of what amounted to sugar and chocolate in a cereal bowl.

Bruce gathered his notebook and stood. "Eat in the damn house like civilized humans. You're beginning to act like starving chupacabras."

Josh stopped, as fast as one of his bullets. A step behind him, Kimi bounced off him. He grabbed her shoulders, keeping her from landing in the dirt.

Liv hesitated, bent in half and touching her toes in a cool-down stretch. She looked at me through the ponytail flipped over face. Josh and Kimi did the same, minus the flippy hair.

"The annex is fine—chairs, a tiny fridge, cereal—we've got it all." I fidgeted, stuck between team and Bruce. Being C.O. but trying to soften a decision.

"The annex is an interrogation unit, no matter how many boxes of cereal you stock in it."

"Are you sure?" My question blended with the soft rustle of the crows alighting.

Bruce rubbed his hand over his chin, forgetting there was no beard, then frowning at the reminder. "No, I'm not sure. None of us have the luxury of blind confidence. Am I willing to risk it in order to have all of you inside for a meal? Yes."

His grumble was a thin veneer, too new and delicate. Like fresh paint, easily scratched and showing the truth underneath.

It felt like there was some screwed up inverse equation in play. The more Bruce improved physically, the more...questions he wouldn't ask or some kind of doubt lurked in the back of his eyes. I wasn't sure what to call the quiet new thing when he looked at me.

Maybe my sins were written on my skin. Not completely legible, but enough that Bruce sensed them.

According to Stavros, that's how sin worked. Some action or thought that you knew was wrong, and the deeper you tried to hide it, the stronger it became.

He had a propensity to lecture, and I was getting over four-hundred-year's worth, in every other day chunks.

For now, I avoided the entire subject. "I'll haul in cereal, the rest of you—" I plucked my damp tee an inch off me in demonstration.

Liv gave a barely discernable nod, and herded the group toward showers.

Instead of following them in, Bruce watched me. It was

like being back at the beginning when we'd first met, and I had no idea what he was thinking. And when I tried guessing, usually made a mess of the situation.

"Did you change your mind? Once they're showered I'll tell everyone we are eating out here." Tentatively, I felt Bruce out.

"Eat indoors, in the room intended for that purpose, on the table intended solely for that purpose."

I took a step closer, then stopped because everything from sweat to lotion had triggered his nausea, and I didn't know how much of this morning was real, and how much was a brave face. "You don't have to prove anything to us, okay? It's no big deal to take five minutes for cereal or toast in another building."

That strange shadow pooled in his eyes. He sighed. "Eat in the kitchen today. Please."

I dipped my head and went after food.

Popping open the dorm fridge for the milk, I slapped my other hand over the freezer section as frozen burritos threatened to avalanche out of the tiny cubby, stuffed to its limits.

I slammed the door, the entire unit skidding sideways.

We had plenty of food options. Bruce's were a constant juggling act, getting enough of anything in him to keep his energy from bottoming out and God only knew what organs from shutting down, but he had a fridge's worth of choices.

Stavros—Stavros was slowly starving. The term emaciated flirted with my other descriptions of the stoic, dedicated vampire, needing added to my list.

Yet he willingly held his arm through the bars for me to drain him of a bit more blood every visit. He spent the time I was there alternating between sharing facts about vampires, thing's he'd discovered over centuries and from traveling all over the Americas. Teaching me to better anticipate and fight them.

The rest of the time was me sharing bits of my life—the thoughts on the changes I was seeing in cryptid behaviors, collating them with the vampire oddness, even if he only humored me, not classifying cryptids as the same threat as vampires.

Both of us eventually let personal topics drop into the conversation. I'd learned about his wife, son, and daughters, victims of the attack he more or less survived. About life on a hacienda, in a world still reeling from invasion and colonization.

In turn, he got to hear about Josh's sniper skills and sneaker obsession, both evident from childhood.

I talked about growing up Company, how amazing it had been.

He reminisced on his home, the small vineyard, and American wines.

Ours was a symbiotic relationship, not even taking into account my literally draining his blood.

I was the only creature he'd spoken to in hundreds of years. The only person who knew his name, because his existence was hidden, a ghost in both the human and vampire world.

He was the only person—because it was becoming more and more difficult to think of him as a non-person, a collection of virus mutations, even as his being vampire was never in doubt—who I didn't have to perform for.

In the cruddy, third-rate base, I wasn't Vee the C.O., Vee the good agent, Vee the sister, Vee the go-between for Bruce and his family, Vee the girlfriend, the person who lay there too many nights listening for Bruce's next breath, scared there might be a time when the next didn't come.

I could just...be. Tired. Angry. Hurting. Confused.

And well fed, while the being who was possibly saving Bruce's life starved painfully because of me.

Arms full of boxes, I closed and locked the door behind me. Taking a second, face to the sky, eyes closed, to rid myself of anything but the C.O. and prepared partner roles I needed to be when I climbed the steps into the house.

My tune blaring from the inner pocket of my shorts was almost a relief. I dumped boxes on the bench, grabbing the phone. I jogged for the house, the door opening and Liv leaning out. Her, Kimi, and Josh's phones chimed in the background.

We had an official mission call-out.

I was dressed and weaponed-up before the rest of the team. I came out of my office, tightening the band around my hair.

Bruce sat at the kitchen table, a paler, more wan version of how he'd spent his time during our first mission after his arrival.

A compact plug-in cooler sat on the bar. I lifted the lid. Cups of the slightly gross but high protein yogurt were nestled inside, along with spoons. "These are for you. You need them."

"What I fucking need—" Bruce took a deep breath and started over. "There are plenty here for me, and if by some miracle I do empty the fridge, Josh will buy the dairy's entire inventory as replacement as soon as he gets back and realizes. None of you have eaten in ten hours. I *need* you to not go into a mission with a calorie deficit. Can you fucking do that?"

I gathered up the cooler, put it between the back seats, and had the SUV cranked when the team joined me.

Liv eyed my position in the driver's seat, her usual spot. "Bruce?"

"This seemed the smarter option than waiting inside and having an argument with him, when I have no idea what we're arguing about."

"I call an argument refreshingly normal," Josh said, digging into the stupid cooler and passing around the equally stupid yogurt. "Fighting is Bruce's thing."

It didn't feel like our kind of fight though.

* * *

AT LEAST THE windigo fight was our kind and gave me an outlet.

The pack had split and run when three of the leaders in the front of the attack went down. Typical 'digo behavior for once. We'd each chosen directions, and spent the last hour tracking the remnants of the horde.

I put a shot through the last of mine's head, the stink immediately increasing. The only thing grosser than a live windigo was a dead and decaying one.

A claw scratched over the metal of the landfill's cattle-guard style weight platform, where people dropping off trash had to weigh their load and pay accordingly.

I stepped over the dead cryptid and approached the one gasping its last, lips drawn back over sharp, yellowed teeth. Blood pumped from the wound in its chest, where I'd hit it right behind the front leg.

Blood would keep running, until its vicious heart stopped.

It wasn't vampire blood. But it also wasn't forbidden human blood. I slipped to the corner of the platform and checked. Josh and Kimi had reported all clear on their end and were already by the SUV at the entrance, judging by the truck's headlights flicking on.

On the other side of the dirt roadway bisecting the dump, Liv sighted on her last pest, a sharp pop marking its end.

I pivoted back to the dying monster. Then dug into my tactical pant's pocket, pulled out the collapsible water bottle, and holstered my weapon. I grabbed the blade from my thigh, knelt by the reeking predator, made a neat slit in its carotid artery and held the bottle's top squished over the cut.

Counting seconds as more blood hit the air than went into the bottle, the level inside rising but slowly. Counting my time by how long it took Liv to meticulously assure her cryptids were dead, note body condition and sex, switch out guns, and come see why I wasn't back at the truck.

I hadn't consciously planned on collecting blood for Stavros. I also rarely included the bottle unless it was a mission that might prove lengthy. 'Digo missions were never lengthy.

The clunk of a boot on the metal grid sent my guilty heart into my throat. I capped the bottle, hastily shoving it into a pocket, and stood.

Liv stopped, nose wrinkling. "What happened?"

"I only nicked it. I turned around from the last, and this one charged. Slow, but still. No time to switch to a new clip." I shrugged, getting more and more adept at lying on the fly.

Cutting off any further conversation, I pulled my phone out and made the Cleaners call, walking as I spoke. No need for Liv to get a better look at my diced-up 'digo. Sweat trickled down my spine, the product of pure guilt, not from exertion.

Once I got close, the usual post-mission high-five was off the table. Kimi actually backed away from me, and Josh pulled his shirt up over his nose.

His voice came out muffled. "Did one explode on you?"

"I had one who took extreme objection to dying. Trust me, I do *not* care for how I smell either."

"Fresh clothes won't help," Kimi signed.

I ended up in the last row of seats, windows down. The bottle feeling like it had a glowing arrow over it, pointing to my pocket.

"Let me out here," I said as soon as the compound gate rolled shut behind us. "I'll shower in the gym and toss these in the disposal unit."

"Bruce may flip," Josh said.

"I'm texting as we speak. Better yelling at me than throwing up whatever he managed to eat today."

I bailed and slammed the door on any counter arguments, avoiding looking Liv in the eye and the assessing stare I felt drilling between my shoulder blades.

When the SUV disappeared into the house garage, I darted for the annex. After wrapping it in layers of plastic, I transferred the bottle to one of the insulated cooler bags we kept for the occasional sample HQ requested.

Time still ticked away in my head. Waiting for someone to wander in, stumble over the bag, and for my plan to detonate. But de-windigo-ing wasn't something I could skimp on, and I hit the shower.

Hair still dripping on my clean shirt, I collected the cooler bag, came inside via the door at the corner of the garage, and hid the blood in the back of the SUV, under a couple of shopping totes.

Having escaped being windigo scented, everyone else was already finished, and the sounds of a bubbly movie track came from the common room.

I headed for our suite, expecting Bruce to be tired and inside since naps were his current routine even on slow days. He'd been outside this morning, then either stressed or angry about the mission, using up more energy than usual.

The room was empty, bed untouched.

I whirled to backtrack, aware I was panicking, and aware that if Bruce hadn't been okay, Liv would've called or Kimi would've grabbed me from the showers.

I skidded to a halt, banging my knee on the dresser and just managed not to plow over Bruce, now silhouetted in our doorway. I wanted to pull him inside, get my hands on him, and make sure he was all right.

But the morning's argument popped up, fresh as if it'd just occurred. I hadn't understood what was wrong then, I still didn't now, and didn't know how to ask or not upset him again.

All I came up with was, *"Legally Blonde?"*

"Josh picked tonight."

"I didn't get hurt. Not even a scratch. Only ooked on."

"So Liv said."

"Do you—do you want to go watch?"

Difficult to tell from his outline, details lost in the low light, but his posture seemed to relax. "The cereal is inside where it belongs. Fix a bowl and lets watch patently impossible law school plots," he ordered.

The idea of joining my family, and cuddling on the couch with Bruce tugged at me, sinking hooks in. Nothing had ever sounded better.

I killed off another tiny bit of myself when instead of agreeing, I grabbed my wristlet. "I have to go de-windigo the SUV."

Frustration laced Bruce's voice. "Let the truck go until tomorrow."

"I can't. The smell will set in permanently. It'll eventually reach into the kitchen and med bay, too. You know it will."

"Vee."

"I'm the one who smeared windigo all over it."

Without saying anything, Bruce stepped aside, letting me slither past him.

"I'll hurry," I squeezed out of a throat that felt suspiciously like it was clogged with half-truths and tears.

Bruce didn't bother replying.

ee

STAVROS ROSE from his seat on the bare concrete as soon as I raised the base's lights to our usual comfortable level.

"Hola, Victoria."

We'd gotten past the *little general* title weeks ago. Other things though—those were works in progress. Like the sleeping bag I'd shoved into the cage, the same night that I'd tossed him the key to unlock his arms and legs.

The *'We are demons, never falter'* lecture that'd followed had been epic.

At least he'd accepted the shirt and tactical pants from the base's stash with better grace.

The stink on his pants, of decaying vampire blood and ick from the pile of corpses I'd originally dragged him from under, had gagged both of us.

The Christian bible I'd brought next had been met with

thanks all out of proportion to a book, but it made him happy.

As happy as he got, which, also a work in progress.

I gave the bedroll a pointed look. "Do I need to revisit the definition of basic necessities again?"

"Those things that are necessities to humans are luxuries to vampires. Demon's don't deserve luxury."

He was gonna love this. I girded myself for another battle.

I'd caffeine-loaded at the gas station after detailing the SUV. That truly had been necessary. One less lie to weigh me down. Then I'd made one extra stop.

I held up the bottle of blood. Then handed it through the bars.

Correction—attempted to hand it through the bars.

Stavros was standing on the other side of the cage before I blinked, as much distance between us as possible.

"After all the lessons on strategy and out thinking opponents, you're wasting energy zooming around like a skittish roadrunner?"

"I had thought better of you, Victoria."

"Remind me to introduce you to the concept of drama llamas." I waggled the bottle at him. "It isn't human."

His nostrils pinched, sampling scents.

The 'digo funk was already leaking through the plastic, even to my human senses. "See?"

He inclined his head in a regal acknowledgement. "My apologies. I had no reason to doubt your integrity."

I waggled the bottle again.

"This remains an unacceptable luxury."

"Necessity."

"I have no need of such."

"You're starving. Like, legitimately starving."

He did that freaking regal thing again.

"I'm pretty sure what you're doing is defined as martyrdom."

"I have no right to Earthly comforts."

I got it out through gritted teeth. "You. Are. Starving. You can't let that happen. I need you to continue doing what we've been doing. That's going to be difficult if you *freaking starve to death.*"

I took a deep, hopefully cleansing, breath. I didn't respect loss of control, and neither did Stavros. If I lost even one ounce, I didn't think I could stop my implosion.

"This healing is occurring?" Question asked from his position still a cage-length away.

"Maybe? Something, between the virus from your blood and the medical treatments, is helping. There's less pain anyway. A lot less."

Stavros walked to my side of the cage and offered me his arm.

I offered him the bottle.

"It will take me a very long time to starve, in the human sense."

"I can't do another argument today about something vital." I closed my eyes and rested my forehead on the chilly bars. "I mean, I can, because what's the other option? You have to do this, and whatever it takes, I will make that happen."

Cool fingers touched mine for an instant. When I opened my eyes, Stavros had put a pace between us.

He'd tried to give comfort, even while he denied it to himself.

I pivoted, changing tactics. "I have no idea how long treatment will take. This is the definition of experimental. You can't become so—whatever the vampire equivalent of dehydrated is. When that happens it becomes extremely difficult to find and tap a vein. Possibly beyond my skill and equipment level. I also have no idea when the next opportunity to acquire cryptid blood will come around."

Indecision tilted his shoulders my way. Liv always shifted her weight incrementally on one leg when about to commit, while Kimi angled her hip, and Josh's eyes gave him away, a quick flick in the direction he intended to move. Stavros did it shoulders first.

Time to seal the deal. "Will it mollify you if I tell you that I will indeed definitely and totally kill you as planned once this experiment ends?" There wasn't any other option.

A vampire couldn't leave here with Company secrets.

Stavros himself had hammered in how that would end. Repeatedly.

"That you will stay the course does mollify me."

I caught the exasperation in the way he hit *mollify*. "You are even more messed up than I am. Nice use of sarcasm though."

I pulled out the second bottle—the objective of my last stop before arriving here. I'd decanted and poured my purchase into an emptied plastic water bottle. "A decent wine vintage. You're going to need it to wash away the taste of windigo. That's pure necessity."

Stavros' short, uninhibited laugh startled us both.

ruce

THE GATE ALARM CHIMED, alerting Bruce that the team was back from their supply trip into Scottsdale, picking up mail and packages from the box they kept. And for Josh to execute another dairy and food truck buy-out.

It had taken a miracle, i.e. him flipping Vee's technique on her, nagging the hell out of her, but he'd gotten Vee and her sisters to go as well. Kimi was on his side immediately, understanding how suffocating even well intentioned help could be, and assuming he needed time to himself.

He took a last look at the counters and the plates and utensils arranged along the top. He'd needed privacy, but for a different reason.

He'd done it. Taken his damn kitchen back. He'd been sure—mostly—that he was ready, not having gotten sick in well over a week. Closer to two, once he counted.

He'd needed to be alone in case he was wrong.

"Hurry up," he barked, once the chatter of conversation filtered in, the team clearing the disinfecting breezeway between garage and house.

One set of steps picked up, and Vee burst into the room.

He needed to kick his own ass. He hadn't thought how she'd take *'hurry'* coming from him.

"Put away whatever inappropriate as hell shit you bought my brother for his birthday. No, I don't want to know what it is in advance." He did a clumsy, half-assed job of reassuring Vee.

Same for preventing a bottleneck as the team jammed together at the entrance.

"B?"

He purposely misconstrued Vee's question. "If I don't know what you bunch picked out, I have deniability. In addition to my getting to see his face as he unwraps whatever you three cooked up." He used the salad tong, pointing at them. "Move. Lunch is ready."

Vee shoved her bag behind her, not even checking to see who caught it. The rest of the team scattered.

With only Vee watching, self-consciousness dropped on him like a thousand pound weight. He hadn't hesitated at shaving his head. He hadn't paid loosing weight and muscle any attention in the context of what he looked like.

This though was more fundamental to who he was, as a person, than appearance ever could be.

He opened the fridge, and hidden by the door, cleared his throat. "It's only grilled chicken and greens."

Hard to get more basic. His sense of taste, even of smell, wasn't back to where it should be. Hell, it might never be.

When he closed the fridge, Vee was there, inches away. "Holy crap, B."

In those three simple words, he heard his worry and her understanding immediately, what even a five minute piece of chicken meant.

He set the cold, diced chicken by the plates.

Then Vee's arms were around his neck, cheek against his. "You did it."

Voice gruff, he choked out, "I did. I did it."

By the time the rest of the team found their way back, he'd gotten his shit together. With Vee as his assistant, plates were centered at each seat.

Lunch was loud and unruly enough he'd normally have threatened loss of a basketball hoop and every board game in the den if they didn't start acting like they'd been raised indoors, even if it was in barracks, as opposed to a feral dog's den.

Today, he soaked in the noise. And the chaos, Kimi sneaking food off Josh's plate, while Liv snuck so called fancy lettuce into the newly empty spot.

Vee sat beside him, and when he edged close, scooted her seat tight against his. His leg pressed against hers from the knee down. Warm, and alive, and affirming.

When he finished his portion, she caught his hand under the table. He played over the back of her hand, thumb sketching swirls, an excuse to touch her and feel skin on skin.

The team's antics finally edged back into normal territory. He stood, keeping Vee's hand and bringing her up with him.

"I'll take cleanup." Josh stretched, and by the magic of unfairly long arms, took and stacked plates without needing to rise.

"Damn right you will. Don't neglect to wipe down the fridge and oven doors, and don't think I won't know," Bruce ordered.

"You didn't use the oven."

"Do it anyway."

Once they were out of the crowded kitchen, he tilted his head at their room. "There's something good I want to show you." He made damn sure to add the positive qualifier, and not freak her the fuck out again.

He closed their door, then tugged her into the bath and under the strip of vanity lights added during his renovation. "Check this out."

He opened her hand and ran her palm over the top of his head, then his chin.

Vee's eyes widened. "Seriously?"

She added her other palm, stroking over the new stubble, tilting his head so the new, darker brown hairs were visible. "You haven't even finished the treatment course yet. This is way early to happen."

He turned his face into her touch, craving the easy intimacy. "It came in a couple of weeks ago, but was patchy so I kept shaving. This week, no bare patches."

"You're a hair growth prodigy."

"The final treatment is tomorrow."

Vee's hands stilled, the memory of the last time they had this conversation hanging over them both like a vulture waiting over prey.

"You cooked," Vee whispered. "And you've had more than broth and yogurt. And your hair—"

Fucking hell, he kept screwing this up. "I'm saying, last treatment and I feel good," he cut her off, rubbing his cheek along her hand and coaxing her to resume. As much to give her something else to do as to sooth them both.

"Really? I mean, I thought so. But then you try to make us —me—feel better, which is a nice way of saying you kinda hide when you feel bad or tired and I wasn't sure what was real and what was you protecting me."

He gave a dry laugh. "We've had this pot-kettle discussion before."

Something other than getting called out on her shitty subterfuge skills and protectiveness tightened her shoulders. She started for a damn cuticle to shred.

He put her hand back where it belonged, on him, then laid his over it, keeping them connected. "That is not a criticism, Vee. I knew that about you when I entered into this relationship. Sometimes it irritates the fuck out of me, but even then I also love it about you."

"Then what does all this mean? What's happening here?"

He heard the soft plea under her factual delivery. "It means, I feel good. Not perfect or one-hundred-percent, but some of that is building my stamina back up and adding more protein and probiotics. I'm not in pain."

He moved one of her palms to his chest. "Nothing hurts here. I don't pretend to have any idea of what the scan and labs will show, but that's where I'm at."

"You have hope?"

"I have hope now."

Vee made a noise, and was pressed against him like she was trying to meld them together. No, like she needed him and wasn't afraid to go there with him again. Like maybe they were back on equal footing as partners.

He wrapped her up, fitting her against him. She burrowed in, not holding back and not terrified she'd hit something that would hurt him or like she might break him.

He breathed in the cocoa butter and plain soap that meant Vee to him, relearning how she felt in his arms.

She'd kept up the odd absences, true. When she was here, she still played caretaker first. She'd made it a point to bring him his first drink or broth of the day, and before bed. Once he'd moved on to tea again, she'd even bought a black tea blend, and smoothie and protein mix that she'd researched on her own, and claimed contained more antioxidants than his usual green tea.

Those moments felt different than any check to make sure meds were on schedule, or that he stayed hydrated, or obsessed over getting calories in him.

Vee never rushed. She ignored schedules, not allowing anything outside their bubble to interfere. It was like that was their time, and sacred.

The interludes made her solitary trips and extended errands bearable now. If Vee needed time to herself, away from family and him, hell, he understood. He wasn't confronting her, and tossing guilt on her for needing a mental health break.

He shifted her against him so he could burrow a hand into her hair, hanging loose and wavy the same way as when he'd first met her, massaging her scalp. When she leaned into his touch, he kept going, trailing fingers down the nape of her neck.

Her shiver was like tossing water on a grease fire, his libido finally waking up over the last few days. He drew his finger along the edge of her jaw, using it to angle her face up.

Vee's lips parted, her expectation shooting desire straight to his cock.

He caught her lower lip in his teeth, imprinting a promise. Her breath hitched and she wrapped his shirt in her fist.

The ringtone coming from her pocket blew the moment all to hell, and he swore.

"Are you even kidding me?" Vee groaned and her obvious reluctance was enough on its own to give him blue balls.

When the tone echoed back from three other phones, he set her away from him. "Go get ready."

She nodded, fingers slow to turn loose of his shirt.

Vee could go do what she excelled at.

Then tonight, they were revisiting this, no call-outs and no clothes getting in the way.

ee

I GLARED at Stavros from my side of the cage.

He glared back from his side.

The new bottle of ghoul blood at least hadn't been the point of contention this time. Which was a really dang good decision on his part, since I'd once again bailed on Bruce to stealth over here with the bottle I'd nearly gotten caught filling during today's call-out.

I now had a dumpster-edge shaped bruise on my stomach where I'd tossed the bottle inside two seconds before Kimi found me, then had to hang over the side of the crusty thing to retrieve it after I left the compound on a made-up snack run.

And the shower here? The hot water unit had died at some point, so cold shower on top of gross dumpster indignity.

That was another pair of cute pants and a logo tee consigned to the trash.

"I cannot believe we are arguing about this crap." Or that I was missing time with Bruce. A happy, healing Bruce. The happiness and relief from him admitting that he had hope now swam in my bloodstream, like tiny, excited bubbles.

"We argue because you don't *listen.*"

"My listening has negative zero correlation to my thanking you and saying 'Hey, you're not all bad'."

Stavros turned his head, gazing at the crucifix again. He seemed fine with it staying where I'd fastened it, always seated and gazing at it when I arrived.

He turned back, expression graver than ever. "I have compounded my sins in the most vile way. When I hoped I was teaching you, I failed. I inadvertently taught you the wrong lesson, one based on the greatest lie. You now see vampires as something other than the festering evil that we are. You will falter as a general in a moment brought on by your compassion as a human. Then you and those you're sworn to lead will die."

Biggest. Buzzkill. Ever.

"I've listened, and I've incorporated your information on vampire behavior, strategy, and fighting technique into my Company training plus what I've learned in the field. You've broadened my, and by default, the Company's knowledge base."

He started to lecture but I kept talking. "I'm well aware of what vampires are. You however—you have willingly offered me advice and information. You've offered your blood, no strings attached, even when you were starving, and it's not like you're well fed even now. You have been—" I tried for a word that wouldn't set him off again "—decent."

"There is no decency in vampire kind. Only those wily

enough to embrace discretion and not draw attention. That is merely survival instinct."

My temper notched up, a mix of guilt, anger with myself, shame for lying to the team, frustration—and the newest. Guilt at using Stavros then ending his life. He was basically me, only alone, no friends, no Company, no family. Working in solitary to save people who'd never know his role or thank him.

"We are not talking about vampires in the plural. We've covered the part where I've studied them since I was nine, and eliminated them ever since. We are talking about *you*. You are good. Every time I come here, that fact becomes clearer and clearer."

"Fool," He thundered, voice filling up the space around us and ringing back from the walls. "Vampires are incapable. We have lost our souls. That is why we revel in pain and fear. Every urge we have is based on those two desires, and you refuse to hear me. I have divested myself as best I can of those insidious drives."

"That's what I'm—"

"*Be. Silent.* I sit here in prayer every day, as I did when free, repeating the Commandments, Hail Mary's, and my vow so I do not forget who I wish to be. I must repeat this every day, again and again, or I will slip."

His voice turned icy, hitting like hail on a roof. "How often must I repeat that vampires have no soul? I have no soul. All that's left are fading memories of my human emotions. Because we have no soul, love, or hope. I have lost all of those. Only the words, the definitions, remain. This— this is why I have no luxuries. If I weaken and succumb to one, it opens the door to the only two desires I truly have. That ends only one way. Amid blood and death."

More like the virus retooling brains. The amygdala, where urges originated.

Like he saw my thoughts, Stavros slapped the bars. "This is what I am. There is no *good*."

Echo of his claim still hanging in the air, he slammed into the cage bars, the cage shifting an impossible inch. His eyes swirled silver, like riptides pulling me under. He was only a skull now, fangs the size of my thumbs, thick ivory, lips black of death and rot.

My skin itched and pebbled and my hair blew back, from the speed and force of his rush, or some sonic blowback we'd never seen before.

Stavros snarled. My mundane theories fled, and a wave of primal fear rolled over me. My heart jackhammered hard enough I felt dizzy.

As quickly as he changed, Stavros was once again human-seeming, his voice measured and deep. "This is a vampire. We are incapable of living, only existing to bring pain and destruction on those who can."

He turned his back to me, removing me from his plane of existence.

I left, the happiness I'd arrived with turned to horror. And to a new grief to add to the old. I couldn't give Stavros the things that had been taken from him.

He saved one of the people I loved, but I couldn't save him.

I sat, forehead against the steering wheel. Forcing all my emotions down, stuffing them in the small and already over-flowing container inside me. I might've saved one life, but I had to do it at the expense of another.

When I was sure the tears weren't breaking free and leaving me to explain bloodshot eyes, I turned the SUV toward home.

Bruce would be long in bed by now. I'd come up short on both the professional and personal levels tonight.

 ruce

BRUCE'S PALM SWEATED, vised around Vee's, her other hand on top of his. The rest of him was clammy-cold. His hand shook, his body not sure if it was terrified or excited.

He scrubbed his free hand on his pants but left the other sandwiched between Vee's. She didn't give a damn about flop-sweat and they both needed the comfort.

When the doctor walked in with a file, Bruce's grip tightened enough he felt bones move in Vee's and forced himself to ease up.

The last treatment was weeks in the past. He'd had labs and the scan done Monday. Today was Friday and a week had never been so damn long. He cycled relentlessly between optimistic and scared as hell.

More so than when he'd been at rock bottom, prepared for end of life talks. He'd accepted what was going to happen and the pain had made an end at least not the worst thing waiting for him.

It turned out that hope really was more exhausting.

He'd watched Vee and the team going through the same cycle of hope and fear. More familiar with life and death, they grasped the situation even better than his family.

"Mister Kantor. Miss." The doctor pulled out his chair, the castors still in need of oil and squeaking.

Bruce flinched, the sound dropping him without warning into the first time he sat in this office.

"Breathe with me." A firm command penetrated his panic. Vee knelt in front of him. She rubbed over the backs of his hands, easing them from their bruising grip on each of his legs. He didn't remember moving or letting go of her.

He concentrated on Vee and the feel of her. Her touch and voice his lifeline.

The doctor half-rose from his seat. "Mister Kantor, do you need—"

He let out a breath, slowed back to normal again. "I'm fine now." Vee had given him everything he needed to fight back with. Whatever the verdict might be, he wasn't in the battle alone.

He brought her hand up and kissed the back of it in thanks. She tilted her head, a wordless question. He nodded and Vee retook her seat.

"Go ahead." He addressed the doctor, not one damn bit sorry for or embarrassed by his reaction.

The physician laid Bruce's file on the desk and rested his elbows on top, fingers steepled.

If the guy didn't start talking in the next five seconds, Bruce was turning Vee loose on the doctor. Her stare was already inching toward deadly and promising terrible things.

"Mister Kantor, I'm a little taken aback but very pleased

to give you more positive news than at any of our other checkups."

"My virus load is down?" Just fucking spit it out already.

"Better than that. You don't have any detectable cancer cells present anywhere in your body at the moment."

His lips were numb but Bruce got out, "The new tumors?"

"They are gone."

"You're saying—" He couldn't finish the question.

"I'm saying that you are officially in remission."

"Could you repeat that?" Bruce had expected, fucking prayed, that the treatments were working. But this…

The doctor finally smiled. "You are cancer free at the moment. We'll continue screenings every three months, then six. There are—"

Bruce didn't hear anything else.

He was in remission.

When he finally tuned back in, Vee had what looked like his report, the back of one page filled with notes in her tight handwriting.

When the doctor stood and offered his hand, Bruce took it on autopilot. The same way he followed the nurse out past reception, a vague wave of guilt registering for a second as they passed other patients who might not get the same reprieve he had.

When the mid-day sun bounced off his glasses, he stopped. Closing his eyes, he lifted his face to the sky, same as they day he'd been diagnosed, but for a different reason this time. He held his arm out sideways, and Vee was there. Head leaned against his, arms around his waist.

By the time he brought his face down, his tears had dried to itchy tracks. He kept Vee under one arm, and removed his glasses, continuing down over his newly grown beard.

He replaced his glasses and exhaled. Letting go of the fear, pain, and exhaustion of the last year.

Then he shifted Vee in front of him and kissed her. His hands buried in her hair, he thanked her for always being there, holding him when he needed a rock, standing by when he needed to be with his thoughts, and having hope for both of them.

He drew away, because now they'd have a tomorrow to kiss again. "I fucking love you. You call the team, and I'll call Mom and Dad." He'd assured them he'd call after his appointment but he knew them well enough that they'd have the whole family there as well, waiting all day and evening if necessary.

Vee pointed them at a hidden niche between businesses, some gem she'd discovered while she and her sisters explored. She left him on a bench talking to his parents, and stepped across the street to tell their family the news. Fucking teamwork at its finest.

* * *

THE FAMILY CALL had taken a damn long time. Hannah leaving in the middle, picking up all three girls and bringing them back to share in the joy, even if they didn't quite grasp what it was about.

A damn long time translated into enough for Josh, Kimi, and Liv to string a glitter-foil congratulations banner across the hall, and fill the house with enough balloons, party hats, cheap-assed liquor, and expensive bakery cake to do Mardi Gras proud.

He gave in, celebrating with the brother and sisters who had also stood by him. Every one of them relishing getting a hard-earned win.

Pure joy, and tequila, worked their magic. His body wasn't accustomed to either anymore, and when he grabbed a bottle of champagne and pair of glasses and pointed Vee to their room, she followed.

She promptly relieved him of the bottle and flutes, sitting them on the dresser amid her jewelry display.

"You have something else in mind, Ramirez?"

He held his arms out wide and flop-landed on his back on the bed. The room tilted, then righted itself. He propped on his elbows, the better to see Vee. Hopefully, Vee tossing all her clothes.

He was sure as hell ready, their damn nights interrupted by missions and Vee's obsessive patrols. Now it was time to cash the rain check on the scorching kiss's promise, written weeks earlier.

Vee climbed on the bed, and he nabbed her and pulled her close. Coordination shitty, he ended knocked flat with her half-draped across him instead. And him laughing for no clear reason.

She wiggled off him. He grabbed and missed, but then she was back and snuggled against his side anyway.

"I like how you think, B." Her fingers combed through his hair. "However, in about three minutes you are going to be snoring, Mister Light Weight."

"Nu-uh." His head dipped, and he jerked it back up.

"You argue a lot."

"The hell I do."

Vee's laugh and her soothing touch on his scalp was the last thing he remembered.

ruce

BRUCE BLINKED, head unaccountably fuzzy. The room finally came into focus, a champagne bottle the dresser's newest addition. The previous day and evening's events surfaced.

In remission.

Cancer-fucking-free.

He took a minute to soak in the words, and the pure luxury of not having treatments and days spent bracing himself for shitty news hanging over him.

He could be himself again, #BruceTheBastard, the asshole chef, a son, an uncle, a man in love. Vee's partner.

He rolled on his side, sober and awake and ready to finish the celebration with Vee.

The bed was empty, a Vee shaped depression in the pillow. The patter of water from the shower, the bathroom door cracked open, told him where she'd gone.

Even better. He'd installed the separate slate shower with

the multiple shower heads. Partially because it was a basic fucking necessity for him and another step in teaching Vee and the team that there was more out there, things they hadn't yet experienced, and that they didn't have to settle for subsistence-level living.

The other reason he'd installed it was both of their appreciation for shower sex. His cock cheered that idea on. He rolled the rest of the way out of bed, with a fierce satisfaction at performing the previously taken for granted action, without worrying about anything hurting again.

He finished the undressing Vee had obviously started once he'd passed out, leaving a trail of clothing as he went. He tossed his boxers more or less at the laundry bag the same time he stepped into the bath.

Vee stood just out of spray range, head upside down and twisting her hair to get water out, her shower complete.

The urge to be with her turned into an all-encompassing *need.* They had been apart too long. Now, he needed to thank her in a different way. Give her something after her bearing the load of caregiver, and all too often, recipient of his frustration-fueled temper.

In the same way he needed his art, he also needed to erase the last memories of the illness, and reclaim them—him and Vee.

"Don't turn the water off." He stepped into the steamy warmth, aiming for the jetting shower heads and Vee's fucking amazing nudity, his cock pointing the way.

"All sobered up, huh? That drunk alley lesson didn't stick after all." Vee teased him with the alleged circumstances of their first meeting.

He fucking loved that she could already go there, back to teasing and playing instead of giving him the fragile, white glove treatment.

"Very fucking funny," he growled. And because she'd

always loved his ego, he posed under the jets, back to the spray and letting water run down his chest and stomach, right to his impossible-to-miss erection.

She gave her hair a last shake and raised her head, wet strands flipping back. "I'll put your tea on the counter, okay?"

"Or you could deliver it to me personally, right here, right now." He skated his hand over her hip.

She leaned in. And kissed—more or less—his cheek. "Today is crazy. I have to get everyone in gear so I can take care of a couple of issues I've put off too long."

Then she walked past him. Out of the shower.

He left wet footprints, stopping bare-assed naked and framed by the open door. "Vee?"

She stepped into tactical pants, zipping them as she looked over her shoulder. "Did you need something? I can bring the tea in here instead."

He finally got his tongue working. "No. No tea."

"'K. See you at lunch."

Then she was gone, pulling a tee on and leaving without a backward glance.

He retreated to the solitary shower. Time for a plan. Whatever was going on with Vee or whatever was coming between them, that shit was about to meet Bruce the Bastard.

He'd kicked cancer's ass, at least for now, and he'd be equally ruthless in fixing him and Vee.

* * *

Hours later, having had plenty of damn time on his hands since lunch had been a no-show on Vee's part, he took a last glance at the plan he'd detailed. The velvet bag he'd tucked away nearly a year before sat in the middle of his sketches.

He and Vee were solid. More so now than when he'd commissioned the ring. They'd been through hell and come out the other side still together. Even if the cancer returned, he knew now that Vee wouldn't run. The same as he'd never leave no matter how bloody and violent her life as an agent became.

However long they had in this world, six months or sixty years, he intended they live it together.

He paced the area of the roof deck, the spot where he'd slammed head first into the realization that the all muscle-no brain, imagination-free grunts he'd gotten stuck with were anything but. The spot where he and Vee had burned up a hot Arizona day with even more scorching sex and he'd fallen for her, even if he hadn't acknowledged it to himself.

This oasis of platform swing, bright pillows, and candles was the team's refuge even more so than the busy common room.

So this was where he'd ask Vee to officially share her life with him, surrounded by her brother and sisters, already also his siblings now no matter what Vee's answer was.

He'd turn the rooftop into a romantic fantasy under the stars.

He closed the sketchbook, looping the tie around and tucking it and his proposal shopping list under his arm.

He descended inside, then knocked once on Vee's door before letting himself in.

She'd gotten stuck in here, missing lunch for a meeting between the Regions's neighboring Division C.O.'s. One that from the way her foot was tapping out a hard rhythm against the desk leg, wasn't going well.

She'd been on a trail of small changes and seemingly random inconsistencies that she felt were leading to a pattern, possibly heralding long-term changes in cryptid behavior. Vee paid attention when others didn't. Not even other agents, people conditioned to be hyper vigilante and detail oriented. Her brain made connections that made no sense at the onset but that added up once the last details were fitted in.

Terence, the Texas C.O., plus the C.O. for New Mexico weren't convinced but respected Vee enough to at least listen.

Now, a frown cut lines in her forehead. The way her lips pressed together boded ill for whoever or whatever had crossed her line.

Sticking to ASL as the volume increased in whatever debate raged between two of the C.O.'s to their north, neither of whom paid a damn bit of attention to Vee's theories, he signed, "I'm going out."

Vee went ramrod stiff, all her focus switched to him. She signed fast, "What's wrong?" Then jumped straight to, "Wait for me. Two minutes."

She'd hidden it too damn well, but Vee was past simply being on edge. Even he'd missed it until now. Whether it was only his illness, the bullshit with the other C.O.'s, the escalating cryptid oddness, or a toxic combination of all three—he was here and fully present now.

His next project was discovering what Vee needed to level back out, and making it happen.

He hurried to mitigate his fuck up. "I'm fine. The team's fine. Scottsdale is fucking fine. I've had enough of Josh's version of food shopping. I'm taking back over. I might even get a haircut."

For added verisimilitude, he threw in the most mundane task he could think of, one that also always made her perk up. "Want me to pick up ice cream?"

After a second, some of the rigidness left her. "From the happy cows?"

"Like I'd bring any of that antibiotic-laden store shit in." He added a derisive snort.

When her tap-tapping signaled she'd shifted back to C.O.

mode, he eased out and left her to deal with dumbasses and cryptid policing b.s.

* * *

WHEN HE RETURNED, her door remained closed. Part of Bruce was ready to knock agent heads together. The other half took this as God smiling on his plan. Same thing for the rest of the team, all eyebrows deep in a gamer throw-down with a rival team, even Liv sucked into the contest and trash talking. Finally letting go of some of her rabid vigilance, and relaxing.

As added insurance he barked at full volume, "Stay the fuck out of my kitchen while I'm repairing the damn damage you four have done over the last six months."

He brought food in fast, then grabbed everything else, relieved he wasn't stuck relying on his backup plan of utilizing Josh and his third-rate subterfuge skills to sneak his purchases past the three women.

When his lightning-speed decorating spree was completed, even he couldn't find fault. Candles tucked into reproduction glass and brass streetlights, identical to those in the Art District that fascinated Vee, illuminated the vases of live flowers of every type that ringed the outdoor space.

His design wasn't elegant or restrained, because Vee wasn't either of those things. He'd chosen based on color, a lively, vibrant display that evoked the same unrestrained joy that characterized everything Vee did. Life and color to honor her.

Top shelf champagne, as opposed to the cheap bottle from the previous night, was in a bucket hidden behind the flowers, along with five flutes. If Vee accepted his proposal, it would be their celebratory toast. If not, as long as Vee didn't evict his ass from the compound, he'd deal. He was alive, Vee was alive, they were together, and that was what mattered the most.

He used some of the stealth he'd picked up from the team and closed the hatch carefully, then made plenty of noise in the kitchen, reminding everyone to stay off his turf. And also starting the meal he'd designed just for tonight. Vee understood that he expressed himself with food even more eloquently than with words. She'd feel the love and fresh start in what he served tonight.

Finally, he closed the suite door, opened his last purchases, and showered again. This time with his favorite products—and Vee's—that he'd had to forego when every scent risked turning his stomach inside out. He added cologne and dressed in the new fitted shirt and tailored pants he'd bought, since his old clothes were too baggy. For now.

He took a deep breath, a different brand of nerves dancing somewhere in the region between his stomach and heart. Finally, he dared a real, full-on look at himself in the mirror.

Tonight was about breaking the subconscious image Vee was unknowingly holding on to. She hadn't really seen him last night or this morning as sexual because her view of him as a patient was still in the way.

He was doing his damnedest to banish that image.

The new clothes fit, highlighting the muscle he had put on instead of reminding of what he hadn't gotten back yet. The coral of the shirt, a shade Vee loved on him, brought out the color he'd picked up from working outside the last few weeks. Fuck invalid-pale, and shapeless hoodies.

The uneven beard and hair were gone. The new style was shorter than his old one, but it worked, sleek and intentional. The sharp, precise lines of his goatee now replaced the shapeless beard growth, and revealed that the gauntness in his face had vanished.

He had done all he could to look like Bruce 2.0.

Leaving the mirror behind, he checked on the lamb in the oven. The whole house smelled of rosemary and organic lamb, a dish none of the team had experienced until he prepared it for their last Easter. Now, they couldn't get enough of it.

He had brought in Vee's ice cream. He'd also picked up a patisserie chocolate ganache cake he'd paid double for as a rush order. The thing was shaped like a heart, with edible gold around the edges, the sort of cheesy thing Vee, Kimi, and Liv would lose it over. Hell, Josh too.

As he closed the oven, the creak of Vee's door opening echoed up the hall, followed by her footsteps.

She paused in the entry and blinked hard a couple of times. "Whoa."

"I'm going to translate 'whoa' for you," he said, voice dry to hide the way his heart was skittering and rolling in his chest. "'Whoa, Bruce, you are a fucking culinary genius'." Then, heart going faster, added, "'Whoa, Bruce, you are the hottest man I've ever seen in a kitchen, and I'd like to do positively filthy things with you on every horizontal surface in this compound'."

The whole time praying Vee didn't humor him, still not seeing what was really right in front of her—him, healthy, ready to get on with their life.

"That. Definitely. Yes." Her eyes did that thing, widening like a real life anime character's. Too fucking sexy and she didn't even realize.

Some of the pressure in his chest eased.

Until he noticed the key fob in her hand.

She followed his gaze, worrying at her lip. "The C.O. meeting went long. Way too long. I need to patrol. Not a long one, I swear. I just—I can't sit here and not, especially after the Regional discussion."

Her answer didn't feel like the whole truth.

He wasn't starting this evening with a fight though. He took a breath, let it out, and went with, "Damn right it will be quick. Dinner is at eight. Don't even think of rolling back in here even one minute late."

"Right. Lamb doesn't rest well," she repeated from one of his lectures, nodding like a bobble-head doll now. She bolted down the hall to the garage, then yelled back, "Don't let Josh even *look* in that oven before I get back."

He took her haste and heartfelt food-protection plea as a positive. "Get your ass back here by seven fifty-nine or all bets are off."

The garage door closed on whatever Vee replied.

 ee

TWO HOURS, give or take. I had less than two hours to get to Stavros and do what my morals demanded. Not what the Company said was right, but what I knew, bone and heart deep, was just and good.

I'd spent too long mired in death, like a gray shroud wrapped around the compound and me.

Yesterday in the oncologist's office, that shroud had loosened, letting hope and life back in. Now I was tossing it for good.

The stupidly non-productive Regional meeting had thrown me half a day behind. And I was not disappointing Bruce again. They way he'd looked in the kitchen—wholly in control. *In charge.* More than a little arrogant. The way he'd looked at me as he described what he intended to do with me —heat had built south of my belly button. And that ember had only gotten higher on the drive.

At the same time, a drop of some kind of moisture slid down my chin and dripped on my shirt.

I swiped at my face and brought it up to examine at eye level. Tears.

Okay. They had to be mine, since I was the only person in the SUV. Logically, it followed that I was crying, for some undetermined reason.

I made it to the base's parking lot as the view of sand, gravel, and bland metal building wavered dangerously, like looking through the windshield during a rare downpour.

Then my chest was heaving, sobs pouring out the same way the tears were.

With no one watching, I let go. Ugly crying, done holding in the emotions I'd stuffed in boxes for months, done holding myself together.

I finally ran dry, probably because there was no extra moisture left in my body, and relax-collapsed in the seat, the whiff of skunky wet dog that wouldn't ever go completely away reminding me of where I was, and what I needed to wrap up.

I used a handful of forgotten napkins printed with our favorite twenty-four hour pizza place's logo and de-snotted myself. Then dampened another with water from one of the bottles scattered everywhere in the truck and cleaned the rest of my face, draining the leftover liquid and replacing lost tears.

Glancing at the dash, I'd lost more time to my cathartic sob-fest. I slammed the truck door, the weight of the gun in my thigh holster a reminder of my mission with every step, and keyed myself into the base.

I brought the lights up to full brightness, needing a clear view for what came next.

"Holá, Victoria." Stavros stood, giving me our usual greeting, as if the last visit never happened.

Then he stilled, scenting the difference or maybe feeling my emotions the way he'd claimed he could.

His shoulders squared, the way ours had as cadets in the presence of an Instructor or C.O. His voice held a richness, like he'd accessed some level that hadn't been present before. "I have had the occasion over the years to observe many of the soldiers your army trained. You are among the finest I have encountered. It has been an honor to know and aid you, *pequeña general.*"

His head dipped in a nod-salute, strands of silver at his temples catching the light. "May I hold my cross as—"

I shot him in the heart before he finished.

I HUNG up my voicemail to Bruce letting him know I'd be late but that I'd be on my way home soon. Or soon-ish, not especially proud over my relief at him obviously being too engrossed in dinner prep or yelling at someone other than me to pick up his phone. I patted the SUV's dash in thanks for its four-wheel drive, since we had left anything close to civilization behind half an hour ago.

Now it was only me, the desert, and the body in the passenger seat.

Said body's finger twitched. Then its hand. Okay, the hand not cuffed to the door. Metal rattled and plastic gave an ominous creak.

"Please don't jerk the armrest off—or the entire door. Those are hard to replace or explain." Quickly, I added, "It's only a blindfold."

"Victoria?" Stavros sounded out of it from the sedative. I'd tripled the Lab recommended dose. Stavros' lectures on vampire physiology and fighting tips had come in handy.

"Yeah, it's me. I'd also appreciate if you didn't express

your displeasure at still being in the land of the living, also known as BFE nowhere, in a violent physical manner. If I wreck out here? No roadside assistance."

A very nonverbal noise filled the truck. Pretty sure I'd just discovered vampires, or at least my vampire, ground their teeth exactly like Liv when someone, also known as me, went rogue.

"Victoria." The temperature in the truck dropped.

Guess the loopy phase had worn off. "Might as well take the blindfold off. It was only to get you out here without leaving a visual trail back to base. I mean, you can undoubtedly figure out where it is, if you don't already know, but why make it easy, right? Plus, no blindfold will make it easier to use this." I fished the handcuff key out of the cup holder in the console, and tossed it to land in his lap.

"We spoke of this, of you not faltering."

"No, *you* spoke."

"Vict—"

"*Be. Silent.*" I used his high-handed order on him. "I get to talk now. You told me to uphold my values, to be moral. So, I am. I'm telling B—my friend, I mean—what I've done. All of it. I'm not keeping any secrets from him. Then, I'm going to find some way to plant the idea of virus DNA and cancer and the whole treatment concept in a medical agent's ear. Or their files. Haven't completely worked the details out yet."

We, Bruce and I, were figuring out a way to help all those people we'd met during his treatments.

I practically felt Stavros readying a counter-argument, and preempted him. "I'm not done. Don't say one word. When, because it will happen eventually, the Company decodes how to replicate what saved my friend, the hunt for vampires will be a modern extinction event. You should take all this as your god's plan—me, you, a new war on vampires. A long game one, but whatever."

"Then by your reasoning, I am already dead. Thus you lose nothing by speeding up my inevitable demise now."

My turn to grind teeth. But, the guy was predictable. I'd planned for this too.

"Sorry," I said. "That would be betraying my ideals. We help good people, and no, I don't have a ton of centuries of gathering data, but I'm trained to trust a mix of my instincts and my reasoning. They tell me that whatever you may be, you aren't a demon. You haven't done anything a few more all day prayers and those Hail Mary things won't take care of."

I snapped my fingers before I forgot. "Oh, your cross is in your right thigh pocket, while I'm thinking of it." I got back on track, i.e. convincing Stavros. "Although, I haven't seen or heard you do anything apology-prayer worthy. You should look into trying out a minor bad habit. Just one. But not like littering or jaywalking. Something fun. Which leads me to point three. Point four? "

I hurried to finish before Stavros quit acting relatively patient and obliging. "The point is, don't condemn yourself to a joyless existence. You can be a soldier and still *live*. Maybe—maybe if you work hard on those emotional memory things you talked about? They could become real again."

"Your army would never allow you to live for breaching the security of the main organization, nor of your fellows. This is treason of the highest order, and they will deal with you in the same manner as in my day. Swiftly and without mercy."

I rolled my eyes. Pointless since he hadn't removed the blindfold or cuff. "No one will ever be able to extract our secrets from you. Admit it. You're unsettlingly torture-proof. You'll happily die first."

He turned his head away, like he could see out of the side window.

I called that my being right.

"Your plan is what?" He spoke to the window.

"Um, I thought that was self-explanatory. Drop you off out here in no man's land so you can go your own way, to do your thing. Resume scourging and all. I also packed you a duffle with basics like a change of clothes and one of those luxurious sleeping bags. Only because you aren't up to fighting strength yet. There are a ton of chupacabra out here to get you through until your next vampire meal and power-up. The rancher who owns all this would thank you for cleaning the dens out. If she knew."

"You will not be dissuaded." He didn't make it a question.

"I—" A shape darted across the literal cattle trail in front of us. This really was chupacabra heaven, but...I slowed our already sedate speed.

Stars winked brighter and closer. Except even in a light-pollution free desert, they'd never appeared this close.

Or at head level.

The silver glow wasn't starlight but vampire silver. The crimson of windigos appeared between the sets of vampires.

"Your machetes are in the floor." I stomped on the gas as a growl rose from Stavros.

The truck bumped, hit rock, and went airborne.

The sharp pop of gunfire penetrated even through the SUV's closed windows. The red-gold flash of the bullet came a millisecond later.

An explosive snap marked a tire going, rubber *whapping* against the undercarriage.

We came down hard, shocks bouncing my head into the ceiling, the truck listing sideways. Another pop and bullet, and another tire blew.

I stood on the brakes, stopping us before we rolled the truck.

The silver and red eyes of vampires and hunt-frenzied windigos formed a wall in front of us. Three deep, at least. I jerked my gaze to the rearview mirror.

Red and silver closed in a circle behind the taillights. Surrounding us.

Fabric split, Stavros tearing the blindfold off. I jerked the tranq gun from the holster with one hand. Shoving the seat back and going for my ankle knife with the other.

My door vanished in a shriek of metal. The pong of gas and windigo flowed in.

Something landed on the hood, crunching it in, the truck's nose dipping like a bucking horse.

Through my opened doorway, claws flashed at my face. I fired, the report lost under Stavros' bass growl. Deep enough to momentarily drown out the baying of windigos.

The roof sheared off, the baying rising to a mad wail. The signal a pack had found their prey.

The night erupted in snarls, gunshots, and the wet spray of blood.

ruce

BRUCE PACED the length of the house, from the garage breezeway entrance to the door leading to the walkway and outdoors.

As if that would somehow magically bring Vee sailing in one or the other. She wasn't late.

Late was her text, which he'd missed while pulling the lamb out, and the promise she'd be in ASAP.

Late was eight-o-one, after he'd warned her not to be one second later than seven-fifty-nine.

Late was eight-forty-five, when the rack of lamb was officially over-fucking-cooked from resting too long.

Which Vee damn well knew, connoisseurs this bunch had become.

As he passed the common room for the latest in who knew how many times, Kimi sent Liv a *look*. One of those secret-code sister looks that they'd been born knowing, because he and Josh still hadn't cracked the code.

Bruce kept going, and grabbed his tumbler of tea, filled with the new black tea blend Vee had picked out. The same tea she'd left on the kitchen's bar, in too big a rush this morning to notice him naked and wet in their shower.

She'd damn well *seen* him tonight. He knew she had, that he hadn't imagined her wide-eyed surprise.

She'd know from that one look, even if the lamb hadn't registered, that this wasn't simply a routine dinner. He and Vee read each other, constantly, more nuanced than even the unspoken shorthand she, Kimi, and Liv used.

Things had been ass-over-teakettle the last year, sure. But the two of them had never had any trouble communicating, not verbally, not with touch, not with sex.

Except every evening for months had consisted of one missed connection after another.

He took a swallow of cold tea, gone bitter from sitting so long. Attempting to drown out the insidious little voice.

Vee knew something special was on for tonight.

Now, she was four hours late.

Vee, observant, intuitive, detail-oriented Vee was late.

That voice upped its volume. *She'd looked at him, looked at tonight's menu, and put the pieces together.* She had guessed that he was proposing tonight. Then she'd bolted, unable to deal with the idea.

Tempered safety glass creaked, jarring him. He looked down at the phone he didn't recall picking back up, the screen now spider-webbed with cracks. He'd texted. Texted again. Called twice, more demanding with each, and gotten no answer.

Fuck this. He threw the mug in the sink, steel rolling to a rattling stop, and strode into the common room. Kimi, Liv, and Josh's attention snapped his way.

"Has Vee texted or called any of you? Answered any of your texts?" He planted himself in front of Josh, the most inept liar of the bunch, using him as the canary in the coal mine, while waiting for answers from all three.

"None of us have heard from here," Liv said.

Bruce's gut pitched like right after a treatment. Even if she was freaked or pissed at him, she wouldn't ignore her sisters. Hell, they were all each other's go-to.

"Call her. Right now."

Instead of arguing or hesitating, Liv hit Vee's number, her speed telling him as clearly as a confession that Liv wasn't okay with Vee's vanishing act tonight either.

The phone rang then went to voice mail. Liv hung up and dialed again with the same results. She texted nine-one-one, the all-hell-is-breaking-loose code that no agent ever, ever ignored. With zero response.

"She took the SUV." Josh was on his feet and at Bruce's elbow in one lunge.

Liv unfurled from the couch and swept by them both. They spun and followed her, Kimi veering off.

Liv threw open the office door and slid her laptop over and open in one compact move. Keys danced under her touch.

A monochrome gray and black map came up. Liv had pulled up the tracker Company vehicles contained. He pushed close, checking where in Scottsdale Vee was.

The map blipped and shrank. Searching, not finding the target, and expanding to Phoenix. Expanding again, and again.

Josh swore, nearly as creatively as Bruce.

Kimi elbowed in, one of her tablets open, doing a different search on her own. Kimi tapped the screen and Liv looked from her map to the scrolling list of numbers Kimi pointed at.

"Why has she been there?" Liv muttered, and left off the map, finger swiping over Kimi's screen. Sending another long damn list whirling across the screen.

Bruce picked out that they were scanning abbreviations for Company holdings, including bases. Only one repeated, for a base, but damned if he knew which one. The same destination every other day or better.

The map chimed its success, and Liv jerked her laptop closer. It resolved into—

"The desert out by our ranch Asset? What the fuck?" Going for a closer look, Josh leaned over their heads, like he doubted his own conclusion.

The green dot representing the SUV was well past the edge of the rancher's property, the hell and away from a town, the rancher's house, any roads. If Bruce was reading it correctly—the truck hadn't moved in an hour.

"Gear up." Liv turned to Bruce. "We'll call you once we find out what's going on."

Whatever was at the end of their search, he was going to be there when they discovered what or who it was.

When the team finished preparing and filed into the garage off the annex, Bruce was already in Liv's truck's passenger seat.

"I'm treating this as a mission." Liv braced in her open driver's door, head poked inside. "Agents only due to assumed cryptid presence.

"One of you can physically drag me out of this truck, but then I'll get in my damn car and follow you."

Liv motioned, and her brother and sister climbed into the back. Josh dropped one of the kitbags that held extra weapons between their seats, then angled his sniper case in.

"Clear us a path," Liv said.

The glow of one of Kimi's screens cast the rear of the truck in a sickly wash of blue as she activated Company

Assets or agents—local LEO, State, Homeland, who the fuck knew—so they wouldn't be stopped. Emergency lights activated on the outside of Liv's truck, giving them legitimacy.

Once the compound gate opened, speed limits and stoplights meant nothing to Liv.

The metallic hiss of Josh unzipping the bag was background noise as a mechanical voice announced, "I've alerted HQ and the med chopper is on active standby."

Bruce flinched, not at the text to voice program Kimi used to speak while in the dark and with Josh and Liv occupied with tasks they couldn't look away from, but at the assumption Vee was injured. And the subtext, that those injuries were more than Kimi and the compound med bay could handle.

Josh snapped his fingers at Bruce, and butt first, held out a compact nine mil and shoulder harness.

Arizona didn't require classes or permits but drilled by Josh, Bruce had practiced enough to satisfy the agent. Bruce still hated the damn gun and all it represented.

He accepted the harness, shrugging into and adjusting it, then took and holstered the weapon.

Miles and county line signs blew past in a blur. His Star of David dug into Bruce's closed palm and a prayer in Hebrew flowed on a non-stop loop in his head. He blocked out everything else, putting his intent into the plea.

Kimi giving directions, Liv barely slowed once blacktop gave way to packed dirt and sand, the truck bouncing and swerving, Liv avoiding rocks and cactus revealed in the truck's halogen headlights at the last minute.

"A thousand yards and closing, northeast," Kimi reported.

Liv jounced them over a rise, the shocks protesting. The headlights shone over desert scrub. Halogen glare reflecting back from glass ahead of the truck.

Liv jerked the wheel at the same time she hit the brakes.

The truck slewed to a stop, dust plume blowing, the individual grains suspend in the light like gold dust.

The headlights also spotlighted the SUV in high-definition clarity.

The vehicle tilted sideways, only wheel rims left on one side. Glass littered the ground around the SUV, winking back like diamonds, the back windows shattered out.

Driver and passenger doors gone, lost somewhere in the dark, leaving empty black caverns into the truck.

He was out of the truck and moving before the dust motes settled. Kimi and Liv passed him, guns out. Splitting and each taking a side.

A weight jerked Bruce to a stop. He rounded on Josh, fists flying.

The agent ducked and shook Bruce like a terrier with a rat. "Don't cross my sight line. We can't work like this, because if you get hurt it'll slow us finding Vee," he yelled.

Only because he couldn't shake the heavier man off, Bruce nodded. He whirled back to the wrecked mess, adrenalin flooding his system, demanding he move, get to Vee.

Glass and sand crunched under boot soles, the only sound other than the wind. The air flow brought the stink of windigo, mixed with the sickly-sweet punch of perforated stomachs and spilled intestines.

Just windigos. Gutted windigos, not Vee. He kept the mantra going on a loop in his head. Like that magical thinking would make it true.

"Clear," Liv barked. With Josh guarding their backs, Bruce ran.

Despite its after market reinforcements and bullet proof glass, the SUV looked worse close-up. The hood crumpled, roof gone. Gouges and claw marks raked down the sides, the rear bumper broken in half.

He grabbed the frame where the driver's door should've been, jagged metal cutting his hands.

"Vee!" He crawled inside. Seats squishy, knees scooting through wet-tacky upholstery.

He slithered through the middle, then the rear. As if Vee could be hiding somewhere between the rows of seats. Safety glass ground into his palms and knees.

Pulse hammering a primal warning in his ears, he kept going, half falling out of the open back.

He spun in place. "Vee! Answer me, damn it!"

Getting no answer he sprinted, circling the truck. Venturing further and further out with each circuit.

Hands locked onto both of his wrists. He jerked and fought whatever was keeping him from Vee.

He only stopped when eyes so damn like Vee's materialized, inches from his face. They resolved into Liv, face to face with him, her hands fanned along either side of his head like blinders. Her voice raised from trying to get through to him. "Bruce. Stop. You have to stop. Listen to me."

In the moment her voice was also enough like Vee's that his body automatically responded.

The dragging weights vised around either arm turned into people, Kimi on one side, Josh on the other.

"We can't charge out there." Liv stepped sideways, hands angling his head enough. Forcing him to focus out, at the endless expanse of desert.

"We've called in air support and Cleaners to search. Terrence and Jasa activated the emergency flights and are already on their way with their teams too," Liv said. Perfectly reasonable and collected but the stark worry shadowing her words giving her away.

"Vee—" He didn't know how to finish, what he was asking or begging for.

"I know. I know."

"What happened?" Meaning where the hell is she? Why was this happening? Why now, after the hell they'd already fought through

"Windigos, definitely. I'd bet my last knife on vampires, too," she answered. "No bodies on site, only biological remnants, but there are multiple shoe prints, from a number of different individuals."

He finally looked, paying attention. There were gray and black bits. And pink, those too. Parts of—he quit, not going there. There were no damn bodies though. That had to mean something.

"She fought." Josh's voice came from above Bruce, vicious, angry in a way Bruce had never heard. "There are casings all around the driver's side. Fucking trank cartridges. I don't get it. Why would she have tranqs loaded?"

Bruce tried seeing it the way Josh did. Concentrating not on the sheer carnage, but on details. Linking those details together until they fit.

He grabbed his glasses, to clean them off, be sure he didn't miss anything, no matter how small. Something cool and wet smeared across his check and temple as he lifted their frame.

He looked down. His hands were cut, fresh blood oozing though he didn't feel the sting. But the edge of his shirt he'd meant to wipe lenses with was stuck to him. His pants, the same.

Saturated and clinging to his skin. Soaked in older blood. The greenish-red of windigos.

The pure red of human.

Enough human to soak truck seats and carpeting. Wet even after the hours the truck had sat and the time it took them to get here.

More blood than any one wound could account for.

Kimi—who had let go of him at some point—held gauze

and a hand-sized device out to Liv. A biometric reader, a portable version of the one that scanned their DNA every time they went in and out of the compound.

Reading the results of Kimi swiping gauze through the blood in the SUV, listed on the device's screen, Liv's face lost color. "Windigo. Vampire. Vee's."

Bruce held his hands out. Away. Hands and clothes and shoes drenched in Vee's blood. His legs gave and his knees hit cold desert sand, Vee's name on his lips, torn from his soul.

They had thought they won, healthy and together.

Instead, he'd lost everything.

PART II

ruce

BRUCE LET the truck door click behind him and thumbed the silent locking mechanism. Liv eyed him from her spot by the warehouse wall, between him and the rest of the team. He ignored her, double-checking weapons. She'd said her piece about him joining missions as a driver, well over a year ago.

He'd sat his ass in the driver's seat on the next mission, letting that serve as his reply. He didn't have the woman he'd loved. He didn't have his career, that spark to create gone. He barely had his family, not able to confide in them what really happened.

He did have the ability to fight, to rain some of his pain on the monsters responsible for his loss. For the team's loss and heartache.

The warm night air swirled around them and he finished his last equipment run-through, sweeping his thumb over the tiny silver Star of David, then tucking it back under the regulation urban camo tee.

Liv lifted her hand and they all fell in. She took point, he and Josh in the middle, Kimi protecting the rear. Quartering the shitty industrial park between Phoenix and Tucson, following the grid pattern they'd done so many nights, one equally shitty town on their beat blurring into the other, one more routine patrol.

Except nothing was routine anymore, because the routine he'd finally chosen to be part of meant his restaurant pop-ups following the team's rotation through their territory. Routine meant Vee bridging the gap between their two worlds. Vee being the center of the world—at least of his.

But Vee was fucking gone. Dead, no body to mourn over. The most alive person he'd ever known—ripped from this world. So in turn, he was leaving as many monster bodies as he could dead and broken, to start to even the score and begin paying for Vee. If he killed them all, it would never balance the ledger. It had been days since the last run-in with hostiles or a call-out and without the outlet of a fight, his skin was too tight. Rage collecting, with no way to escape.

Like the universe heard and agreed, the urban night exploded. Forms streaked toward them at supernatural speed. Shrill, high-pitched laughter following behind.

He split left, his back to the rest of the team, trusting Josh to go right. The bark of guns picking off targets almost covered the unholy laughter of vamps on a hunting spree. Kimi and Liv trusting the guys and the chem-filled rounds to keep hostiles off their backs while the two took out the smarter—or luckier—vamps who avoided the bullets.

Vampires smart enough to duck, not smart enough to leave though.

Knife blades flashed. Vampire blood arced every time Liv and Kimi struck.

Bodies dropped but more poured in, taking the dead's place. Wave after wave. More than the team's informant had reported as possible, even with the fucking population explosion the teams had been fighting to keep up with in the last two years. More than should be in one town, never mind in one nest. Blood-suckers coming at them like they had a death wish, turning into satisfying heaps of dead evil nearly as fast.

Sweat ran down his face. He lost count, the world narrowing to the number of shots left in the rifle.

The by now reflex of dropping the empty, and slapping in a fresh clip.

The grunts of the women as they hacked through dead flesh.

A warm shape bumped his back and stayed, a quick three-tap on his hip letting him know it was Josh.

Bruce's last bullet left the barrel of the gun. His searching fingers bumped over the saddle on the stock. He came up empty.

Liv and Kimi fit tight on his other side, covered in other creature's blood.

Silver eyes glowed from all four sides. Surrounding the team. Another wave of fresh vampires, while they were out-gunned and exhausted. This was it. Same ending as Vee's. Their blood splashed over some random road in the middle of the night.

Instead of terror, fury washed over him. He'd been chasing this ending since Vee died. But he hadn't killed enough of the monsters. Hadn't made them pay enough. He dropped the rifle, sling pulling it out of his way, and palmed the longer knife from his thigh. He'd take one last vampire with him when he went.

A vamp lunged, saliva dripping from its fangs, more like a

hungry dog's when it scented a meal. Its flat eyes fixed on his throat. Bruce surged to meet it.

And sliced empty air instead.

The vamp was— gone. Too fast, even for an old one in peak condition. He whirled waiting for claws in his back but didn't find a monster behind him. He caught a glimpse of another vamp, landing on top of Josh, claws wrapping in his rifle sling.

Then vanishing off the agent, gone between heartbeats, jerked away by an unseen force. Josh's rifle sling snapping and flying loose, where the vampire's claws had been ripped free.

Bruce whirled again, checking for Kimi and Liv. Liv's knife arced, and imbedded to the hilt in a huge male's neck. Instead of falling, the creature's razor-edged claws slashed at her face. Liv bending backward so far and fast Bruce half expected her spine to snap. His gut knotted, already knowing as fucking good as she was, she was that hair too slow this time. He'd lost her sister, and now he was going to lose Liv.

Something made of darkness blacker than the night dropped straight down from the sky. Then was gone as quickly, taking Liv's vamp with it.

Liv swore, shaking her hand out. Whatever snatched the monster away had done it fast enough her knife went along, ripping the hilt out of her grip. "Fall in," she barked.

The four of them went back to back, covering each other's vulnerable sides.

Cryptid death shrieks replaced the oily laughter, the terrified wails climbing high enough his ears ached. Then cut off, and blood splashed over a wall to his left. Another scattering of drops splatted from the warehouse roof.

Then…nothing. The alley empty except for their breathing.

Silence backwashed. They all tensed, searching the four

directions for a warning of where the next attack would come from. Bruce strained for anything—a whisper of sound, the betraying *skritch* of claw on pavement. He counted heartbeats by one-Mississippi's and got to twenty, still alive.

Nothing moved. Nothing rushed them from the dark. The dead vampires they'd killed stayed where they'd dropped.

Soft twin thumps sounded, directly ahead of the team.

"Steady." Liv's low command held them, knives out, waiting for whatever godforsaken monster that was capable of annihilating a nest of vampires in seconds.

Light flared, blinding them. Tears blurred Bruce's vision and he blinked hard. Like hell he was dying without seeing what killed him.

His vision cleared, enough to see the warehouse loading bay door was up, where it'd been closed a second before. The fluorescent light from inside spilled out in a rough, unforgiving oval, the source of the brilliant illumination.

Between blinks, two figures stood centered in the middle of the illuminated patch, like it was their personal spotlight. He squinted harder, and made out tight black jackets, and pants tucked into high boots. The hilts of huge-assed knives rose from thigh rigs on both. Fucked up costumes of some kind, a damn mockery of Company uniforms.

Bruce concentrated on the taller figure, and finally made out a copper brown face, short-cropped black hair instead of what he'd first assumed was a stocking cap, definitely male. The other—a smaller figure—took another step, stopping level with the first.

That few inches closer was all he needed. Bruce couldn't miss dark hair, pulled into a severe tail and folded over, instead of wrapped in her usual bun. Skin that he'd spent hundreds of hours exploring, so familiar that one glimpse and the ghost sensation of it warm from a shared shower and silky from her cocoa butter rose under his fingertips.

If anyone spoke, the roar in his ears, made up of his heart and pulse going wild, drowned out the conversation. The rush of adrenaline and hope, the thing he'd been without for over a year, swirled into a blend that had his vision going blurry for a handful of heartbeats.

Because if he looked, and the face looking back wasn't hers…he couldn't survive losing her again, even if she'd only every really been here in his imagination.

He raised his eyes the final bit, to hers, to where striated brown meet the nearly black outer band like a perfect starburst. Eyes he'd never gotten tired of looking into. Never would, no matter how many years he woke up to them, her already awake and watching him. Never got tired of all their expressions. Intense while laying out a mission plan. Determined as fuck and leaving no doubt of her first priority when looking at her family. Crinkling in delight while she laughed at some joke she'd pulled off. Hell, smiling at one of his tirades, immune to his grump and loving that part of him as much as other people hated it.

Now those fucking perfect eyes studied the team. *Her* team.

No sign she was happy to see her brother and sisters. Vee, whose emotions were the biggest things about her, and who was shit at hiding her feelings, most especially from him. Vee, who'd never been away from the crew for more than one night. Who couldn't go two-and-a-half hours without texting and calling at least one of them.

Now, her eyes were eerily flat, not one damn emotion he could detect. Same for her expression, a sturdier version of the flimsy mask she wore when making hard decisions and pretending everything was fucking fine, to spare her family the stress, when *fine* was the last adjective he'd use.

Vee also hid injuries, their severity, behind a false front, too.

She was *here*, though. A true miracle. Anything else, they, him and Vee, would figure out together. If her damn precious Company didn't have the right resources to help her, he'd leverage every fucking bit of prestige he had left, every contact and favor, to discover what hurt she was hiding, who or what had taken and kept her for so long, then fix it. He'd spend the rest of his life helping her recover, if that was what it took.

The ground under him stabilized. Right. She'd just faced off against a nest of vampires, and was in shock from some damn wound they couldn't see in the shit lighting, on top of fuck only knew what trauma and damage she'd had going into tonight's fight.

The thought, the instinctive need to get his hands on her and get her what she needed propelled him forward a step. Separating himself from the group. Hell, Vee wouldn't have expected him to be on a mission. He was dressed in the same camo as the team, blending in with them. The combination had to be confusing her, her attention accidentally skipping over him.

"You're all clear. Threat neutralized." Vee's old command, in Vee's voice, flowed over them. A voice he'd heard every damn night, as he replayed the last voice mail she'd left him, listening to Vee tell him not to let Josh touch her share of dinner, that she'd be on her way soon. Again, and again and again. Except she had never gotten home.

Now her gaze skimmed past him again, before going back to Liv.

He had to get closer, let her see he was here, and she wasn't alone anymore.

"Holy fucking—Vee?" Josh's whispered question rumbled from behind Bruce. Amazement and hope colored her name, a brother looking for his sister. Bruce caught fingers moving in his peripheral vision. Kimi signing the same question to her sister.

They were *all* here for her.

"Yes, it's me. We need to have a conversation."

At the soft confirmation, Bruce charged toward her. Then slowed, fighting the wild joy coursing through him, trying to keep his voice soothing. Not spook her, and sure as hell someone bolting at her out of the dark, minutes after a brutal fight, would. "It's okay. It's okay, Vee. We've got you now—c'mere. We need to get to the med bay. Or a med flight to HQ. Kimi will call one in and we'll talk on the way."

He held out his hand, coaxing. There was every damn chance she was in shock, wasn't thinking clearly, with the pain and fight-adrenaline still in control. Hell, the emotional cocktail was probably the only thing keeping her on her feet.

"Not you." Vee barely glanced at him, waving him back. "Our business is with agents."

It was worse than he'd imagined. She was at that functionally delirious point, from injury and blood loss, psychological trauma, or plain pain. The black uniform she wore all too easily hid blood, not giving him a hint where wounds were.

He tried again, sheathing the knife he no longer needed. For all he knew, she was only seeing a weapon and threat when she looked at him, instead of family and safety.

He showed her his empty hands. "Look—no knife, no gun. We aren't a threat. Vee, it's me. Bruce. Just—come here. Or let me come to you. Okay?" He inched forward.

"I'm aware it's you, Bruce."

That was at least a start. "Good. That's good. You're hurt, understand? You aren't thinking clearly." He name dropped, the trauma physician year-mate they were especially close with, the one he knew Vee had consulted repeatedly when he was first diagnosed. "Let's get you to Nandi. She'll check you out, and get you whatever help you need."

"The only thing I need is for you to stop demanding attention. Our business is with the C.O. and Lieutenant." Her gaze landed on him. Looking right at him, her expression never altering.

Then swept past him.

Vee *knew.*

She recognized it was him. Right the hell in front of her.

And didn't give a damn. There was no mistaking the chill in her tone when she said the titles, the first glimpse of emotion she'd shown, and it was about the fucking chain of command. Not about her family, not about him.

The world shifted. Ground cut out from underneath Bruce. Vee's love, the one thing that had been a certainty, a pillar of his life, gone. Vee hadn't come back to him. She hadn't missed him. Wherever she'd been, whatever she'd been engaged in, somehow it equaled out to her not giving a single fuck, not about him or the team.

Oblivious, Josh spoke up, over the mantra of betrayal pounding through Bruce's head. "Yeah, we're all here. C'mon, Vee." Josh broke formation, the joy of a brother seeing his sister plastered all over his too-mobile face.

Bruce latched onto Josh's belt and hauled on it. Stopping Josh, the difference in their seven inches of height and twenty pounds of muscle not mattering for once.

Pure rage gave Bruce strength, all the hurt and pain following a familiar path, flipping over to fury.

He held on, belt webbing scoring his palm, anchoring himself there as much as keeping Josh planted.

Bruce's voice slashed the air. "That isn't Vee."

His voice rose, volume climbing with each accusation. "*That's not Vee.* Because no force on earth would keep Vee away from us. Because if she was alive, if she had one drop of blood left, one breath left, *nothing*, not one goddamn thing on this earth, would keep Vee away for fifteen. Fucking. Months." His bellow bounced from wall to wall. "That isn't human and it sure as hell isn't your sister."

He couldn't tell if the vibration rocking him from head to toe was Josh trying to shove loose, or Josh fighting to hold Bruce back.

She—it—the thing wearing Vee's face, tipped its head. The action all Vee's. Except still perfectly neutral, no joy, no anger, the exact opposite of Vee. "It is me. But yeah, not human."

In a heartbeat, those eyes that always saw straight through his bluster and bullshit changed. Flared from brown starbursts to solid, inhuman silver.

Infected. Vampire silver.

"Fall in!" Liv's command hit, hard and fast.

A blade sailed past Bruce's face, one of Kimi's compact throwing knives let loose, trying for a standard distraction so he and Josh had time to rejoin the formation.

Josh let go of him, going for his backup piece at his ankle.

Between blinks, the arc of illuminated alley was empty again.

The light shone on dirty asphalt, shimmering off Kimi's blade still spinning where it'd hit the wall and bounced.

Vee's—its—the damn vamp's—voice came from behind them. "It is me. Victoria Ramirez. Company Region code SW-five-nine-zero-six. Personal code one-one-seven-four-three. Commanding officer for Southwest Region Two, Division Two. Lover of questionable reality TV. I'm still Vee."

Now the voice came from behind them, and the team spun like a single organism, following the voice. "We are also vampires. You're in no danger from us. Neither of us has ever touched human blood."

"Bullshit," Bruce yelled before Liv could. "Fucking bullshit. You parasites can't survive a week without human blood." This wasn't Vee. It couldn't be. He'd lost Vee in a shit patch of blood-soaked desert, only the moon and saguaro witness to her last minutes.

"Without blood, no. But not human blood, I swear." Now the voice spoke from above him, and Josh crouched, sighting up, gun steady.

"This is what we survive on." A pair of hard wet thumps hit. Two bodies. The vampire that'd gone for him, and the big one after Liv, her knife still in its lifeless chest. Both corpses with throats torn out. No blood oozed from either.

"Go ahead and check, Liv. They're drained. That's what we survive on, and only that. We've never drunk from, much less killed, any human."

Kimi and Josh looked to Liv, waiting for orders.

"Hold," she signed. Then eased past the others, taking point and the potential hit like the C.O. she was now. She eluded Bruce's frantic grab for her arm, slipping past him without looking, quicksilver smooth. Entertaining this insane fucking charade.

Josh flowed out, opposite her, keeping sights on the un-fucking-believable scene.

Bruce gritted his teeth as Liv bent, her last knife out, flicking fabric away from first one body, then the next. She didn't hurry, inspecting both clinically, because Liv didn't jump to conclusions.

She finally rose, and spoke to the sky. "Wounds are consistent with damage from a vampire feeding. However, with you playing hide and seek, it's difficult to have a conversation, Vee. You also haven't introduced your new friend." Liv's voice stayed professional and cool. Liv at her most dangerous.

"This is Stavros," Vee answered without reappearing.

"Ah. Source of your infection, and now your Master."

The two talking like this—like Vee being here, and being a fucking vampire was just another debrief, was one clusterfuck too many. Bruce's temper red-lined. Knowing him too well, Josh reached back and grabbed Bruce's wrist.

Bruce shook Josh's hand off. "Even if, *if,* we consider listening to you, why the fuck should we trust this guy? He's just another piece of shit murdering vampire," he yelled at the roof, not even half what he really wanted to say. *Where have you been? Why is that thing by your side, instead of us, your family? Why didn't you contact Liv or Kimi or Josh? Why the fuck didn't you come to* me, *Vee? Why aren't you with me now, when I'm right the fuck in front of you?*

Not bothering with a warning this time, Vee stepped into the light. Hands held sideways and out, away from the fucking huge knives. "He's not a murderer. He's the vampire I captured, and bled three times a week, over the course of your entire second round of chemo. The one whose blood I slipped into your protein drinks. That's why I switched to the chocolate ones. They camouflaged the color and taste better."

"The fuck?" Josh muttered, Bruce feeling her brother's shock and confusion like a slap.

Vee only stood there, waiting.

Too many conflicting emotions to hack apart swarmed Bruce. Horror at the idea of ingesting vampire blood. Hope, because even if it meant he'd been dosed, it also meant this was Vee. He tore his gaze away from her, to Liv. One glance, and he knew it was some-fucking-how true when Liv only closed her eyes for a moment. Then, because Liv never shirked her duty, opened her eyes and nodded.

"The fuck?" Josh repeated.

Kimi shoved hard enough Bruce and Josh stumbled, pushing through between them and into sight, signing furiously. "There are Labs in HQ, and *I* haven't ever heard of this.

Vampire blood as…what? Regenerative? Some type of stem cells?"

"Oversight has their own Labs. Only level fives and above are aware and only seven's and above are cleared," Liv said, and took her attention off Vee long enough to give Kimi that look, the one that went beyond sister-speak straight into C.O.. "Don't—do not—try locating and hacking them. Oversight is deadly serious about security in a way even HQ isn't."

"You knew?" Bruce got it out, not certain it was from his lips, because he couldn't feel them. Couldn't feel any part of his body. Because if Liv had also been aware of this, of Vee living some other life, if they'd done their private sister thing, and shared this secret too…

"I knew about Oversight's theoretical research," Liv admitted. "They're constantly working on weapons. Next gen bio-agents. Searching to isolate compounds to help operatives heal is high on the priority list. All of that, yes, but not the part where Vee was dosing you. I should've guessed though."

"She really didn't know. That was all me," Vee butted in. But not looking at him, not sounding apologetic, or stubbornly defending her actions because she was a thousand-percent sure she was right, all things real Vee would've done. Instead, she said it like she didn't have any emotional investment.

He whirled on her, pointing his finger. "If I'm going to believe anybody, it's Liv. You—you have zero fucking credibility, you hear me?"

"Santa Fe on the corner?" Liv spoke over him. "I knew someone was watching us.

"Yes," Vee answered.

"Taos? Josh swore someone had been in that safe-house."

Vee shrugged. "I needed a few things only the Company can supply."

Kimi and Josh's attention ping-ponged between the two, between the fucking conversation that meant something more than the damn sister shorthand he and Josh couldn't decipher.

Then it hit him. He figured out their subtext. Liv had accepted the story was true. That this truly was Vee. Tonight, this alley, it wasn't some godforsaken hallucination, a product of a nightmare or a desperate dream—Bruce didn't know which he'd have picked.

Liv cocked her head. "Those were all in daylight. So, that's true too, then. You weren't imagining things that afternoon in the Arts District."

Kimi snapped her fingers, getting their attention. Her face as furious as he felt. "You two better talk. Now!"

"Kimi?" Josh's gun wavered.

"Sun-tolerant vampires." Kimi clued her brother in.

"That's crap that our trainers told kids as bedtime stories," Josh blurted.

Bruce twitched, then prioritized—he'd worry about the deeply horrific revelation that the four of them thought stories of humans lost to a virus that altered them into a blood sucking monster qualified as fucking children's bedtime stories, yet another black mark against the damn Company, later.

"Fucking Oversight again?" Bruce gritted out. "More research they hid from you, because, hell, all operatives are good for is fighting and dying, right?"

Instead of an answer, the whole team came alert. The other vamp did that appear-out-of-nowhere bullshit, right by Vee's side. Close enough that if she curled her hand, the two would touch.

"Victoria, your Company knows of this?" The vamp's voice was rich. A baritone with an accent that stumped Bruce, formal like he was from a damn BBC period piece.

Just as clearly, no form of English was his original language. Rolling his S's, emphasis on syllables different.

And as comfortable with Vee as Liv and Kimi, her damn sisters, were.

Bruce wanted to run him through a meat grinder.

Vee angled in front, protecting the damn pompous monster, and answering its question. "It's only highly theoretical speculation on the think-tank division's part. The equivalent of dark matter and time travel, or whatever civilian physicist's actually study."

"Victoria." Exasperation colored the creature's tone.

"Let me point out, Santa Fe wasn't me." Vee eyed the vampire.

Who cleared his throat, fucking embarrassed. Like they were discussing every day shit. Who finished off the last of the milk and neglected to add it to the grocery list.

"Watching us? You're hunting us?" Josh's gun was leveled again, although not at Vee so much as her companion. Who only shook his head and sighed, like they'd had this conversation before.

"We were helping, not hunting," Vee said.

"Bullshit," exploded out of Bruce. "Fucking bullshit, all of this."

"What do you think happened to the vampire nest in Taos you were targeting? But, somehow, when you hit it that night it had already mysteriously burned to the ground. Same for that huge nest of newbie vampires you pulled Terence's team in on, but the building blew first? A meth explosion? Really?" Vee rolled her eyes.

"I knew vamps weren't cooking," Josh muttered.

"The trafficking ring last week?" Liv's voice was even. "Why were all the women waiting outside for us?"

For the first time, Vee's expression changed. A flicker of irritation showed. "You guys didn't come close to obeying speed limits. You got there way before you should've been able to."

Probably because it'd been his and Vee's anniversary. The anniversary of their first meeting, when she'd sung the worst karaoke he'd ever heard, then topped it off by blowing into his life, saving him from a creature that shouldn't exist, and stealing his damn heart. He'd needed to kill something, anything, and hadn't given a fuck about speed limits or police once Liv got the go ahead for a mission.

"You almost burst in on us. So we sent the women out as a distraction." Vee shrugged again. Casual, no biggie. Like that meant he and Vee hadn't been yards apart. Separated only by a parking lot and a shitty storage building. She'd been that close, knew he was there, and walked away.

He must've made a noise because Kimi was there, hand on his arm. Mouthing, "Don't."

He raised his eyes, not even knowing what he was about to say.

The circle of light was empty.

Vee's voice flowed from overhead again. "Go process. I realize this is a lot. Think it through logically. I've been a vampire for well over a year, and we haven't blown up safe-houses, raided the other teams, ambushed agents or Assets, or ratted out the Company's existence. We'll talk later."

"Fuck that." He spun in a circle, searching for more than a damn disembodied voice. Equal parts enraged and terrified. That he'd lose even this fucked up version of Vee, which was still better than no Vee. Because he'd also accepted this was her, agent and sister and the love of his life. "Dump that vampire, and we'll damn well talk tonight. Get your ass down here. Right. The fuck. Now. We are going home."

"We're a package deal. I'll be in touch in a few days."

Bruce felt it in his bones when she left, and left him standing in another damn alley. Vee was gone, and she hadn't bothered to talk to him. Hadn't willingly addressed him once, before fucking bailing, off into the night with a vampire.

Vee had walked away from him, of her own volition. Again.

He hated himself for the slideshow suddenly playing in his head. The evenings she'd left on solo patrols and been gone most of the night. The patrols that had gone from sporadic, to frequent, and then to bailing on normally cherished time with her family, and time with him. Nights where he'd gone to sleep with her beside him, but woke to only a cold spot where she should've been.

How many times had she walked away before, when they were together, and he hadn't even known? And were those solo trips why she was a vampire now?

ee

"I QUESTION my wisdom in choosing this revelatory course of action for you."

Even after fifteen months, it took me a nanosecond to pick my—commanding officer's? Instructor's? Master because he acted on impulse and now regretted it?—Whatever Stavros was, because we hadn't agreed on a name for it, it still took effort to pick him out of the thicker curtain of shadows where warehouse roof met the taller building next door. Then another beat to distill his archaic syntax into real speak.

"We're both positive that the cryptid situation requires the Company and us to forge a policing agreement. Tonight should have been proof of the need." That the nest tonight shouldn't exist, but did, and was becoming the norm instead of the oddity, couldn't escape the Company much longer.

This batch was four times the normal size. Far too large

to be sustained without hunting an area dry, even in a city the size of Tucson. Too large to prevent notice, which was, or had been, Vampire Survival: Rule Number One.

Stavros gave one of his melodramatic sighs. "Victoria."

Sigh plus my name? I braced for the incoming lecture, frantically grabbing for facts to counter his argument. Facts and logic were the basis of Stavros' existence, and now, mine too.

"You are very aware that I'm speaking of proximity to this team as your final testing."

"They are a direct route to HQ, then to Oversight. If we win the team over, that's our first step."

Nothing gave away Stavros' move, not the whisper of displaced air, not the swish of fabric against fabric. Nothing a human could detect. But, I wasn't human anymore. I felt him by my side. The same way I felt him when I woke, before I slept, during a fight.

"There are other means of forging an alliance. Other teams as well, should we pursue this plan."

"You agreed we can't keep up with this population explosion alone."

"Again, you purposely misunderstand." He didn't push though, not calling me out on my evasion. Yet. Stavros was more exacting and brutal a trainer than any Academy Instructor. He expected perfection. His rules were also ironclad, and the penalty for breaking them was swift and lethal.

Since breaking a rule, any rule, meant a human dying by my hand, his punishment was only fair.

I watched as the team fell back toward the truck in a perfectly synchronized formation. Josh covering the space above their heads. Kimi and Liv at opposite corners, Kimi with a knife in each hand. Liv with her second favorite close-combat blade.

She'd tossed her last-last-ditch backup piece, the small H and K, to Bruce. He watched the ground, barrel steady.

Bruce, who hated this side of team life. Who shouldn't have his own custom fit holster and favorite blade or rifle. Who shouldn't *ever* be doing patrols. Who should instead be in some high-end kitchen in some starred restaurant making sous and line-cooks lives miserable, and delighting diners.

"Control."

I flinched at Stavros' reminder and crushed down on my emotions. Emotion-ghosts, because they weren't real anymore. Only leftovers from when I was human, that would eventually fade away. Dimming eyes I hadn't realized had begun to glow, the first step to falling into hunting mode, retreating back into that hard-won place of detached calm. The place where no trace of the virus' work, of vampire lusts —blood lust, lust for violence, or lust for inflicting pain—was left. I pulled the calm over me like a second skin.

For a breath, Stavros' hand rested on my shoulder, his version of an extreme PDA. "¿Es esto realmente posible?"

What he meant was, was it possible for *me* to maintain my detachment. Leave all emotion out of my decisions and behavior. It had taken almost a year of training with Stavros and his pitiless methods to achieve this level of control.

My new training had weathered fighting ghouls, windigos, and vampires. Getting shredded and going back for more, pushing the limits of starvation and remaining objective while never touching a human we were aiding. Emotions led to opening the door to Vampire Brain. All id, all lust, no ego to restrain the urges. Which led to killing the people I'd sworn to protect.

I'd been right when I'd told him once, while he was still in my cage, that there was no magic or religious demons responsible for the virus' changes. That it basically retooled brain function. It cranked the amygdala up to full-throttle.

The ugly, primal part of us that only cared about what we wanted. At the same time, the part that created the urges to consider others, to help, to embrace selflessness and kindness was shut down. All the good emotions were gone. The virus was all about turning its host into the perfect predator and ensuring its survival, no matter the cost to others.

My old vows didn't disappear just because I wasn't human anymore or couldn't feel, though. Once the team saw we weren't a threat or liability, Liv would approach HQ. Then when the Company saw that Stavros and I were safe, that I still upheld my duty, they would listen, too. They always, always worked to better equip and protect agents. What we could offer would save civilians and agents.

"I'm ready. I can do this," I said, as much to remind myself as to answer Stavros.

Those ancient, cool eyes looked me over, the faintest scrunching of his forehead the only sign that he was concerned. That he wanted me to pass this last test.

As the faint thump of boots on concrete carried up to us, I focused on the here and now.

The team slid into the truck, the door slamming with frame-shaking force. Tires screeched as Bruce reversed out of the alley and took all of his temper out on the machinery.

I prayed I wasn't lying about what was possible. I had to immunize myself against ties and emotions that no longer had anything to do with vampire me, ASAP, before I harmed the people I'd loved most intensely.

One meeting, where we'd been yards apart, where I'd had to keep my gaze on anyone but Bruce, and now I'd let my eyes slip. Something that hadn't happened since I graduated from training and sleeping caged, to being trusted to serve with Stavros on missions.

Maintaining the discipline to potentially work with my family was the last hurdle. The last test I had to pass, ensuring I was safe to move among humanity. Stavros decreed that I be immersed with my old team, my family, and face all those ghosts of emotion associated with them. If I could maintain my objectivity and logic with them, grind down until those triggers no longer had any impact, then I'd be able to do the same in any situation.

If Stavros decided I'd failed, he stopped the trial and admitted he'd erred in ever giving in to pity and saving me.

And he would kill me on the spot. The agreement we'd come to, when he opened my cage door.

I followed Stavros down the side of the building to our ride, to my new version of home, and a team made up of Stavros and I.

The outcast vampires who hunted other vampires.

ruce

"Mother fucker." Bruce hurled the big copper stockpot, the one Vee had bought to replace the shit aluminum one, when Bruce decided to officially sign on with the Company.

The pot whirled across the kitchen and smashed against the subzero fridge, denting both, and ricocheting off. Causing Josh, the last person in the house, to duck.

"For fucking real, man?" Josh dodged the still-spinning projectile.

"I need quiet." Liv slid out the hidden panel under the eat-in bar, pulling up the perimeter feed, and triple checking the security cameras. Then checking the drones she had ordered launched the second they'd hit the car. The machines flew above even vampire reach, scanning to make sure nothing had followed them.

To make sure that Vee hadn't followed them. That a horde of vampires weren't waiting in the compound, given access codes by Vee, to take them out. Satisfied, or satisfied as any of them could be considering this clusterfuck, Liv closed the panel and turned.

"Team meeting." She folded her arms, those eyes so like her sister's freezing them all in place. "Protocol is to notify HQ immediately of this breach and level one threat."

"Hold up." Josh straightened, battered pot in hand.

Kimi signed over him. "This is Vee. Our sister."

"She's a fucking vampire." Bruce slammed a fist on the counter hard enough the pots suspended overhead rattled and chimed. Maybe if he said it often enough and loud enough, the phrase would make some sense to him. Kill off the hope that this was his Vee. That they would see her again, and she'd pull one of her usual greetings when he walked in after a pop-up event or visit to his family, launching at him and wrapping her arms around his neck like she hadn't seen him in months, not the few days he'd really been away.

"However—" Liv raised her voice one notch, all it took to regain everyone's attention "—this is unprecedented."

"Don't fucking go soft on me. Not you." He glared at Liv. She lived by the rules. Rules he'd always chaffed at. Right now, though, rules were all the hell he had to hang on to.

He got a raised brow from Liv that pissed him off at the same time it shut him up.

"As I was saying, Vee had access to everything we do. I have to consider the possibility she has somehow bugged or is otherwise monitoring our coms. As well as the chance our contacting HQ is exactly what she wants, maybe part of some larger plan to gain entrance."

"On it," Kimi signed. Meaning she was doing some damn illegal-even-by-Company-standards shit, and checking to see if they'd been hacked.

"We need to do a deep-dive on any Southwest oddities, specifically potential ops that took care of themselves like

Santa Fe," Liv added, as the two women split off, Kimi for her screens and tablets, Liv for her office. "Also set up a search for vampires meeting the male's description, starting with the Stavros alias—history, old ops, other potential aliases, mythology. Concentrate on anything South and Central American, and I'll be doing the same."

Red hazed Bruce's vision, tinting aged walls, faded Mexican tile flooring, and new kitchen appliances. *Stavros.* The walking virus factory that had stood there talking to Vee like it knew her. The thing that had, at some point, ripped a hole in her, hurt her, and turned her into something and someone else.

He swept his arm down the counter, glass containers and knives flying. An arm locked around his chest, pinning Bruce's arms, another arm around his throat, controlling his head. He still bucked against Josh's hold, managing to stomp a heel into the bigger agent's instep.

Josh grunted and hauled Bruce from the kitchen, past the game room, and outside. He didn't turn loose until the door swished behind them, leaving them on the narrow walkway circling the back of the building. "Let's go. Gym."

Bruce took a hard breath of air already warming from the sun peeking over the mountains behind the compound. The breeze, full of desert creosote and his herb plantings, swirled around him. Breathing the scents of his adopted home sent a shaft of mixed pain and fever swirling through him. Home had always really meant Vee.

Josh stayed behind him, down the metal steps and across the yard to the gym, like he thought Bruce would bolt, storm the armory, fire up the truck, and make another trip out.

If Bruce thought he'd have a chance in hell of finding Vee and that smarmy vampire who had turned her into the kind of monster that stood and looked at them like they weren't family, like there wasn't blood, tears, promises, and nights in each other's arms between them—he would have already weaponed up. Dragged Vee back here, to her compound and her family and their bed, so she'd remember who she really was.

The lights flared on automatically, revealing matted floors, machines, weights, and bags. Bruce stalked straight to the biggest hanging bag in the back of the gym.

"Rules, man."

He gritted his teeth at Josh's reminder, muscles in his jaw popping. Bruce still held both hands out and let the anger build as Josh taped up his knuckles.

Bruce spun for the bag before Josh's hands fully cleared Bruce's fist, an edge of tape fluttering. He laid into the bag, barely hearing Josh's staccato commands over the shit banging around in his head.

"Upper Cut."

"Left."

"Right-left combo."

Bruce let the thuds, his grunts, and the burn in his arms, core, and knuckles carry him. Time lost any meaning, world narrowed to impact.

"I'm calling it." Josh braced the bag. "Enough."

Bruce couldn't actually hear him over his breath, wheezing in and out, only read Josh's lips. He shoved off two steps, his back hitting the wall, and sliding down it. Arms hanging over his bent knees. He finally let his head fall back, crown against the cooler metal wall. Josh sat beside him and handed him a bottle of water.

Their routine for the last fifteen months. Four-hundred-and-ninety-five nights. It had been fifteen months and three days since they had drove up on the empty patch of desert. Where they found the truck, but no body to hold one last time, or to bury and sit Shiva and mourn over.

Because Vee wasn't fucking dead after all. Not really.

Instead, she had turned into a vampire. Then she'd chosen to abandon them.

He must've said the last out loud. He tasted the words on his tongue, as Josh let his head thump back, mirroring Bruce's with a, "Fuck man, I know. I was freaking standing there too. Vee's a vampire," but it lacked oomph.

Bruce was suddenly tired, soul deep. "She's a monster."

Only a monster would let him and her family suffer for so damn long. Then pull some fucked up reveal and return like this without giving a shit about the shock and devastation she'd dropped on them.

Bruce was messed up, to a degree that probably didn't even have a psychiatric definition. He was self-aware enough to realize that.

He'd almost completely cut his parents and Marissa and Kenny out of his life, at least emotionally, because he couldn't tell them what really happened to Vee, or was still happening to him. That him not giving a fuck about creating and his career, aside from a few cancer charity events, was a warning sign.

That yes, he probably hadn't dealt with his diagnosis or remission, Vee dying on the heels of the good news, shoving anything else to the sidelines. His refusing to see any of the Company therapists, or a private one or speak to a rabbi, was only one more sign of a problem.

He was also aware that Liv at least had guessed why. That if the cancer returned, he'd make sure he went down on his terms, on a mission. That even if he stayed in remission, he was still heading for that same ending.

Josh straightened. "She said they hunt vampires, the same as she did before. And that they don't touch humans."

"You believe that fairy tale?" Bruce cracked the lid on the water and drank, trying to wash the taste of her name off his lips.

"Hell. I shouldn't. But she saved our asses tonight. We were out of ammo, except for five rounds in my backup piece, and three in Liv's. There were still over a dozen vamps out there. Vee saved us the way she always has. She put us first. She put humans first—Company motto, all the way."

"She's a monster."

"All I'm saying is maybe there's something here. Maybe a part of Vee is still alive. I'm voting for not targeting her, at least not until we know. Until we really know whether she's legit." Heedless of the sweat coating Bruce, Josh grabbed Bruce's shoulder.

"She made her choice and it wasn't us." He shoved Josh off and left, letting the gym door slam between them.

He headed straight for his and Vee's room. His room, singular, now. He didn't bother with the light, easily finding his cell on the dresser where he'd left it hours ago. As he stalked to the bed, he deleted the voice mail, cutting off Vee's false promise mid-lie. Jerking the pillow off the bed, he grabbed the plain gray tee that had been Vee's favorite sleep shirt. The one he had slept with the last four-hundred and ninety-five nights. The one he had almost had a fucking panic attack over when her scent started to fade from the fabric. He balled the shirt into a wad and dropped it in the trash.

Josh thought he meant Vee was a monster because of some fucked-up virus that turned her vampire. Despite Josh's lifetime of Company training and thousands of hours devoted to cryptid homework, Josh was wrong this time.

Vee was a monster because she didn't have a heart. At least, not one that included them any longer.

 ee

STAVROS PROWLED around me as I set up the video call and all the illegal blockers Kimi ever taught me, as agitated as I'd ever seen him. Without stopping I said, "You're giving me anxiety. Chill. Please."

He stopped, but going by the lines drawing his heavy brows together he was the opposite of chill. "This is unwise."

"They already know we're up and about during the day."

"That was a tactical error we could not afford." He shifted the blame onto himself. "My error."

"We'd already agreed to tell them how we fed in order to build trust. Being frank about our other abilities does the same. It's way better they know from the beginning. Holding back would've been a real tactical error. One they'd have discovered later, and probably at the worst possible time," I muttered, deleting and re-starting. My typing speed had improved thanks to virus-enhanced reflexes. My accuracy, less so. "The truth wasn't an error."

"This *thing* may be a true error." He gestured at the laptop. Like it was made of our chem and preparing to jump off the table and attack him.

"Adapt or die, Stav." So maybe I enjoyed his apprehension of tech a little too much.

Same for nicknames. "Stavros, Victoria. As I've reminded you numerous times."

I mouthed his reply in time with him. My grin mirrored back at me from the screen. The smile disappeared as fast as it had come. Going too far with any emotional trigger from my old life risked opening the wrong behavioral doors now.

Reading me the way only a four-hundredish-year-old anything could, Stavros' voice gentled. "Be easy, Victoria. You did well last night. I am pleased with your handling of the encounter."

"We need to practice after this. Or, there's that chupacabra infestation."

"Our practicing is welcome but unnecessary. As is wasting our energy on desert dwelling scavenger pests." He didn't hide his distaste.

And, okay, maybe chupacabra were only a danger to sick livestock. But sitting still was no easier as a vampire than it had been as a human. Plus, I'd fought too hard to be safe enough to walk among humans. I couldn't get lazy-complacent and risk slipping, either. I'd also learned that not having the outlet of hunting and staying in motion made controlling my anger hella harder.

Understanding where my head was again, part of the reason I'd become okay enough to get out of a cage and Stavros' sight, he spoke. "The vampires we consumed last night were young. Little older than you. We cannot burn that small amount we gained from them dispatching vermin."

He frowned again. "Not with these Company agents and your training as our agenda. We must have reserves."

Translated, reserves in case they came at us to burn us out and kill us during the day. Or I screwed up, Stavros had to end me, and him get away during the day.

He resumed glaring at the laptop. "You are confident they cannot track us through this machine?"

I crossed my fingers under the table. "We're good."

He took a beat to translate my response. Despite our previous cage time, I was kind of a live a language immersion course for him. His progress was slower as much from adjusting to having another creature to speak to, as it was from parsing twenty-first century slang.

That isolation was par for the course if you were supposed to not-exist among your kind. Be a ghost.

The one thing I had to hang onto, the thing Stavros had thrown back at me time and time again as a lifeline as I tried to goad him into killing me those first months, was my training and the vow—that I, Victoria Ramirez, protected people. Always.

It was all I had left.

I shook the doubts off and stood, then flicked on the lamp, powered by the electricity we'd kind of pirated for the loft. Stavros had not been exaggerating about abstaining from any form of material comforts. *Had* being the key word.

He'd kinda eased up on the idea of what constituted an unacceptable luxury. I'd proven that having an actual chair and cots instead of a pallet on the floor didn't send me out on a killing spree. He still grumbled about frivolous distractions from our *holy cause*.

His words, not mine. He'd decided I was also now a divine weapon, existing to eliminate our kind. I agreed on the eliminating part. And by the whole agreeing thing, I meant I nodded along to avoid more lengthy sermons. More of that restraint I'd now been forced to embrace.

Satisfied that when Liv answered my call, because she would, even if I'd miscalculated and she had also informed HQ, we'd look more relatable with basic furniture and ugly lamps. I told myself it was to help build the trust we needed to work together. Not so they'd see me as human enough to still be Vee, not an infected abomination.

Stavros finally seated himself, close enough a twitch would put him in-frame. Legs crossed, his stiff formality so at odds with what we were and what we did.

"We must be circumspect with these Company agents." He tipped his chin at the laptop.

I curled my fingers into fists, nails turning sharp enough to prick my palms. There was *us* and then there were agents. Another reminder of what I wasn't and would never be again.

I dragged a bag from behind me, rummaging amid a crinkle of plastic, and pulled out my prize. Stavros side-eyed me, even if he didn't have a clue that's what it was called. I slit the plastic and popped an entire tiny donut from the equally tiny pack in my mouth, and swallowed. Finishing by licking the waxy chocolate off my finger. Stress eating was a thing, even now.

I'd almost have killed for coffee to go along with the doughnuts, but I was already pushing Stavros' tolerance, stopping for these on our way in. His guilt for infecting me translated into humoring me, allowing me to keep a few things from my human life.

"Does this—" he flicked a finger at my vending machine loot "—mean we need not sit through a dinner this week?"

"It does not. This is a snack. Dinner is a meal."

"We gain nothing from these meals."

I did. Comfort only, but I'd take it. "You're the one who let it slip we could eat actual food, mister wine connoisseur."

"That is a decision I regret. One of many. Let it be a lesson to you on the dangers of succumbing to frivolous material things and how such things impair our judgment." He glanced around the room, scowl deepening.

"Regrettable decisions like turning me?" I wanted to take the question back the moment it slipped free. "Never mind."

Stavros was kneeling beside me, way faster than me, blocking my escape route. He caught my chin, forcing me to meet his gaze. "You are my moment of weakness and I will answer on judgment day for corrupting you. That's my sin, not yours. A sin compounded by my lack of contrition. I should regret condemning you to this shadow life but I can't pretend that I do."

In four-plus centuries, I was the only person he'd ever turned.

"You are…kind not to castigate me every moment." He let me go and was back in his seat.

"I don't hate you. Not anymore." I had at first. Every part of me not consumed with hunger regretted not sticking to my plan and beheading him the minute Bruce's chemo labs came back clear.

I couldn't believe in divine fate the way Stavros did, a relic of his devout seventeenth-century Catholic upbringing, or even the way Bruce did. However, the weirdness I'd felt out there before I was infected, that was real. Whatever was causing vampires to spread their virus far and wide with no discrimination, no Master in evidence, and ignore basic rules of survival, and real cryptid migration patterns to shift, was somehow part of how a mixed horde of vampires, controlling freaking windigos, knew where we'd be the night I went to set Stavros free.

Whatever was changing in the cryptid world? A vampire trained by the Company was a perfect response.

I felt the weight of Starves' gaze on me. He couldn't really read my mind, but like time in a foxhole bred familiarity, time caged—first him as my breathing pharmaceutical source, then me as a raging baby vampire—the forced proximity and hunting packed years, maybe decades, of learning and bonding into months. We were as close as the old Vee had been with the team.

Stavros' voice was a velvet-soft whisper, more despair than pride. "Your heart is still too good. Far too kind, holding on to your human patterns."

From the way he'd stared at me, I doubted Bruce would agree.

Oblivious this once, Stavros continued. "You must be guarded in this conversation. Don't allow residual fondness, nor their potential taunting to affect you. We've lost the battle of not letting this team know of our daylight ability. We must never falter and reveal the vile mechanics behind how we perform this feat. We can't lose that war."

"I know." I had no intention of putting the team in harm's way. If nest Masters found out the team knew the secret of vampires feeding from vamps, they would take out Bruce and the team a minute after banding together and destroying us.

I also knew my sister. Liv wouldn't let the puzzle of how Stavros and I moved during the day go. Neither would Kimi, although this once she was at a disadvantage since there was nothing written or visually recorded about how we were created available for her to hack.

Liv though—she was my match in relentless. She'd had level five coverage before. Now as C.O. she had level six. She'd play with the research abstracts. She'd watch us. And she'd figure the answer out. Hopefully not until we established a détente though.

Assuming an Oversight strike team wasn't already on the way to end us.

"Fuck it." I tapped the icon to put my call through. Ignoring Stavros' sharp disapproval of my language. We'd negotiated a truce—he considered general mild swearing beneath me but not actually blasphemous.

Liv's face appeared on the screen, seated behind the imposing desk in the chair that still reeked of smoke even years after the C.O. with a thing for cigars retired. My chair and my desk. Once.

I put an imaginary hand on the new thing inside me, the one pissed over anyone usurping my power, and pressed like I was holding down a struggling chupacabra, grinding the vicious urge until it was flattened.

Liv laced her fingers together, elbows on the desk and didn't speak.

Neither did I.

We'd always been too competitive.

Sub-vocal, for sensitive ears only, Stavros said, "You are the leader in forging this agreement. Cease this petty behavior. If you cannot rule your base urges, this experiment is doomed."

Blood I needed for other things flushed my cheeks at the reprimand. "Liv. Called in Oversight yet?"

"Vee. Alerted every monster in the Metro Scottsdale area to our location?"

"We rarely have a chance at monster small talk. I usually just exsanguinate them and go."

"Hmm."

That stupid noise, which meant nothing and everything, was biting-into-a-bit-of-aluminum-foil level irritation to me. Which Liv darn well knew.

She fake relaxed into the chair. "Ball's in your court. Please feel free to clarify the point of this call."

I pulled on old pre-vampire training. This was what Liv and I excelled at. I could brainstorm with Liv like no one else, and vice versa. We got each other's shorthand. We came up with most of our best ideas by volleying back and forth, and the give and take of "What if's" and "What about X instead of Y?".

"There were signs the cryptid community was changing, before. I warned you then. Now I can verify that I was right."

A faint scuffing and swearing filtered through the feed. Liv wasn't alone, although the others—my brother, my sister, Bruce—were out of sight. My family. This was the reason I'd trained twelve straight hours at a time, body recklessly using up blood, learning to fight through the need to feed, to blank desires out, fight starved, train until sunrise forced me to stop. The reason I eventually beat out the sun's hold on me and the reason I drank blood from monsters. The reason I got up every night and started the fight all over again.

I dropped the last of the pettiness and one-upmanship. "You're seeing it too. Last night, with thirty vampires in an area that can't support a quarter of that number. The step-up in mission call-outs. This insane growth in windigo numbers, plus windigos and ghouls sharing the same territory. Reports of only a quarter of the usual migration numbers from the Canadian and Alaskan Regions. The chatter about Britain's sentient cryptids suddenly being MIA, and how do they even get *off* an island?"

I picked the laptop up and paced, thinking best aloud and on my feet. "We don't know what it means yet, but something is brewing. Some sort of a shift in the power dynamics in the cryptid world."

"And you're right in the middle of it." My sister dropped the detached act. "Things are going FUBAR at the same time we find out you, an ex high-level Company commanding officer, are now one of the infected. I don't believe in coincidence."

"This all started long before my change, and you know it. If I can put my pride aside here so can you."

"The difference being, I have responsibilities and other people to consider."

Inside, I flinched. On the surface, I kept composure. Meeting Stavros' exacting standards. "We need help, and your team, Terrence's team—the Company, whether they've realized it yet or not—needs help."

"And somehow at this exact time, you've reappeared to save the day." Noises burst from behind Liv. She bent so her face filled the screen, and the professional disapproval fell, replaced by a sister's sense of betrayal and hurt. "Why are you a vampire? Why should I trust an agent that broke the most important vow we can make, to die before being compromised?"

Her intensity blazed across the distance, hot and angry, like we were in the same room.

I'd had a careful speech prepared. Instead, the truth slipped out. "It wasn't my choice." I caught myself, before I went places I might not come back from, or hurt Stavros. "You're wrong though. Dying before becoming infected and turning isn't the most important vow. Our most sacred is that we protect humans from cryptids at all costs. That is what Stavros and I are doing, every single day. It's all we do."

"You are one of the monsters."

For a split second I wanted to punch through the screen. Rip those words out of her mouth and take her lips with them. I shut the cold rage down before Stavros' soft but implacable *"disciplina"* echoed. The virus-created anger and aggression had nearly drowned me the first months of my existence.

I sat and adjusted the laptop. "I'm a monster who kills other monsters. I am very, very good at it. Together, Stavros and I aren't like anything you've ever seen." I didn't squash the tiny trickle of pride that flowed through me. I'd been proud of my job and my team. Then, I'd lost it all. Now, I had something else to be proud of, even if pride was all I had to keep me warm.

The noise erupted again on Liv's end.

The screen slid sideways flashing over Kimi and Josh and the clock on the side wall. Then Bruce's livid face jammed in taking up her space. "So that twisted vamp turned you as his toy, because after the fuck knows how many years he can't get it up any other way. And now you're living out some jacked up vampire Bonnie and Clyde fantasy. That's your mess, not ours."

Bruce was such a jerk, eyes fierce, spitting accusations. Furious, and passionate, and perfect, and not mine anymore.

"Bruce, put Liv or Kimi back on."

His face went from stroke red to bloodless, shock in his eyes.

The view shifted to Liv, with Kimi hovering over her shoulder, and I spoke to them. I couldn't look at Bruce and be what I needed to be. "Stavros has spent centuries killing vampires that overstep, without ever getting caught and without ever leaving a trace. The Company built me. Now, Stavros has added after market modifications. We are unique. We can go places the Company can't, hear things you can't. Vamp populations are exploding, and all these fresh vamps are social media savvy. The newest hunting grounds are dating and hook-up apps. Ride shares. It's easier for vampires to hunt humans, and easier to create new vamps. Neither of us alone are enough."

All facts. As for the rest—fresh vamps with no nest Master, nests with Masters who should know better than to flaunt their kills but no longer tried for discretion, victims that bore not only marks of vampires but also of other cryptids, more oddities Stavros hadn't added up yet—those puzzles were only for us.

I also had a private project of my own. I hadn't forgotten the mystery of the anangoa, a cryptid killing machine that shouldn't exist in the Americas, and shouldn't have gotten from Southeast Asia to these shores without leaving a swath of murders visible from space. The creature that had been my and Bruce's introduction. Nor had I given up on studying the windigos' new habits I'd started on before I changed.

I'd lied to Liv earlier, because sometimes I did take time for a quick and painful chat before I finished off my targets. Stavros only hunted vampires, at least, he had before he got stuck raising Vee-the-vampire. He hadn't noticed the changes in other cryptid species, or understood the significance if he had. We—the Company—policed anything cryptid, and that hadn't changed for me. I felt it in my bones, all of it, the vampire, the 'digos, the other higher cryptids, they were all parts of the same puzzle. When I had a cogent explanation to present, I would.

"Are you seriously proposing the Company partner with vampires?"

Liv's question jerked me back to the moment. "I'm proposing you, and Josh, and Kimi, who have worked with me, team with me and Stavros. We have a mission lined up tonight. Intel is there's a shipment of humans meant for both the human and cryptid markets."

"I haven't heard any chatter." Denial aside, Liv's attention took on a laser focus, like she was attempting to pry the information from my brain.

"You will. Call this a test exercise."

"There's the Company. And everything that isn't. No." Liv cut our call, the screen going black.

ruce

BRUCE DUMPED the salmon meant for lunch in the trash, coughing on the smoke from scorched fish. Then in one sweep knocked the rest of the mise-en-place on the prep counter into the trash behind it, and grabbed scorched pans.

Josh glanced at the charred mess. "Not like anybody has an appetite today anyway."

Bruce grunted and slammed the dishwasher on the dirty utensils. What he wanted was to shove that supercilious fossil of a vampire into a compactor. His urge grew with every glimpse of the asshole as Vee paced around, accidentally showing flashes of a fucking couch, and fucking lamps, and her fucking new life.

"Fucking vampires." Out of condiments and kitchen gear, he stopped in the middle of the kitchen, pulling out the coffee press and then searching for the beans Liv kept stashed out of Josh's sight. Bruce would take anything to keep his hands busy.

Kimi pushed the machine out of his reach and held out a mug, steam rising from its contents. He sniffed. "Lavender and chamomile?"

She signed, "The last thing you need is a stimulant."

He glared at her. "The last thing *any of us* need is a vampire with access to this compound. That thing has taken over Vee's mind, manipulated her, and probably coerced her into sharing every detail about the Company. We should be chewing coffee beans and planning non-stop, not fucking relaxing."

Kimi chose a bar stool, levered up, and criss-crossed her legs, settling in for the duration.

Perfectly aware of where his sister taking that position led, Josh groaned. "Now? In here? There's knives at hand. This is not a strategic plan, Kimi."

She ignored her brother, fingers flying. "The compound's access codes change constantly, as you're well aware. My drones are up. The fence is electrified, same as every minute of every day, and the chem content in the mesh extending underneath us hasn't suddenly changed."

"What the hell is your point?" He crossed his arms, glaring harder.

"Vampires storming the compound isn't the reason you're raging. That Vee is a vampire isn't even the majority of your issue."

"Bull. Fucking. Shit," he enunciated clearly.

Implacable, she bulldozed ahead just like her damn sisters. "Your rage-inducing fact isn't simply that Vee is a vampire or that she has been MIA for over a year. Your trigger is how she drops *we* and *us* in the conversation and doesn't even realize she's doing it, because it's become ingrained habit."

His pulse drummed in his ears.

Josh shifted, scooting further away, even though there was a massive oak table between them. "She isn't wrong. That look you've got right now? Every time Vee mentioned her and the vampire guy in the same sentence, you got that expression. Like you wanted to hack somebody up the way you butcher a side of beef."

Bruce took a step forward, and Josh raised his hands in surrender. "Don't shoot the messenger."

Bruce got words out around his teeth grinding. "So you're telling me it didn't bother you? That when Vee finally pulls some miraculous risen from the dead return, she's not just infected, but she's playing house with some fucking walking leech? That she's probably on that blood-sucking parasite's leash? Don't fucking lie to me."

Josh shifted in his seat, fingers beating a rhythmic tap-tap on his thigh. "Yeah, okay. That was a hella lot to swallow."

"How about that corpses show more emotion than she does now?" Because he was that much of a dick, Bruce poured more salt on their open wounds. "How was it, huh? 'Hey Vee, here's the brother and sisters you haven't seen in a year, did you miss them? How about some enthusiasm?'. Hell, that should've merited a tear or two, at least."

Circling through Bruce's head in a never-ending loop was the rest of the question. How about *him*—the person Vee swore she loved. Vee, who had begged him not to give up during the worst of his treatment, when pain was his constant companion and she was the only one who couldn't accept he was dying. Vee, who swore she treasured any time with him, under any circumstances. Him, now the person she'd dismissed. Waved off. Only addressed twice. Two fucking times, total.

When she had spoken, she'd called him Bruce. Not B, but Bruce, the name she hadn't used since before they'd slept together the first time. When they'd both had to admit whatever was between them wasn't a simple fun fling, but real and involved both their hearts.

'Bruce, put Liv or Kimi on.' No asking how he was. No emotion on her face. He didn't even register on her radar anymore. What they'd been to each other, what they'd been together, didn't register any more. Not a flicker of happiness or relief or love in her eyes.

No asking to talk, zero response to his demand, where before she'd never have passed up the opportunity to verbally spar. Then make up, their way. How long did it take to forget about someone?

A hell of a lot longer than fifteen months. Unless Vee had had a head start.

His thoughts went to the same place it had all night. Kimi pulling up the tracker on Vee's truck the night Vee hadn't come home. Liv frowning at how far out of their regular patrol area the truck was. Liv quickly exiting the program, trying to hide from him how many trips the program showed Vee had made to the abandoned base.

Vee wouldn't cheat, ever. Loyalty to the people she loved was coded into her DNA. Although there was a time he wouldn't have blamed her if she had looked for a way to release the stress and hopelessness, temporarily escaping into someone who didn't reek of disease and mortality.

Vee hadn't cheated, but by her own admission she'd been with that thing, alone, at least three times a week. Alone with the sly old monster for months and months. Maybe long enough to fall under its control. Then let the thing hatch a plan and set her up, just to turn her.

He hated Vee for taking that chance. She'd saved him, but they'd all lost her in the process. He'd lost her, and the life they'd had, and the one they'd planned. He'd been ready to go at the end, after the treatments failed. He'd made his peace.

He could've died, the way normal humans did every day, then Liv and Josh and Kimi would have gotten Vee through the grief. She and the team would have carried on. She'd still be Vee—alive and loving her family, still kind and shining as bright as the summer sun.

The blare of cell phones knocked him out of his bitterness. All three phones erupted, the programed HQ call-out notice chiming the opening chords of *Bad Karma*, thanks to Kimi's damn sense of humor.

Liv strode in. "Weapon up. We have a confirmed target."

Josh rose, but hesitated instead of peeling out for the armory like usual. "Vee was right about a hit tonight."

"We have a pinpoint on human traffickers," Liv not-answered.

Josh pressed, his relentless streak showing. "Vee's intel checked out then."

Liv's face stayed impassive. Locked down, the way she did to hide her feelings. The mask she'd worn more and more often since Vee's disappearance. "Alternately, she's setting us up for an ambush. We are now going in assuming there are potential hostiles on at least two fronts."

Hostiles, meaning whatever trash cryptids had the humans, and Vee too if Liv designated her a threat. Bruce's stomach pitched.

Kimi and Josh exchanged one of their private looks, and glanced at him then away too fast.

When Liv tipped her chin toward the armory they all went though, including Bruce. To suit up, and consider the possibility of losing Vee for the second time.

CHAPTER 31

ee

"WE CAN WAIT NO LONGER." Stavros' voice in my ear was as certain and unavoidable as the grave.

He was right though. Dawn was too close. We could fight in the sun but our reserves were already low. Daylight also added to the danger of bystanders being drawn into the conflict.

We'd pushed the start of the fight as far as possible, waiting until the innocuous U-Haul truck arrived with the other half of the trafficking ring inside. The more we eliminated the better for future vics and for us. We had to stay ghosts, which meant eliminating every vampire involved, and quickly enough none had a chance to report what was happening, or that their attackers were other vampires.

We were in position. The vics were here. The entire trafficking crew was here.

The team wasn't.

I'd held out the olive branch. They either weren't ready to accept us and our offer yet, or would never be ready. Liv's hesitation, I got. She'd always been more about order and the sanctity of rules. Now as C.O. all the responsibility for team safety fell on her. She'd never screw around with that.

Kimi and Josh…they could go either way, although ultimately, they'd follow Liv the way they'd once trusted and followed me.

Bruce—he could bitch, and yell, and hold grudges with the best. Some tiny part of me had been sure he'd come through tonight. That he'd turn all that bulldog determination toward convincing Liv to take this chance and try a joint mission. I couldn't be with him, but I had a stupid half-formed idea of at least working beside him. Being able to protect him and not just from a distance as I had been.

That was a dream, this was reality.

I breathed in and held it, sorting the smell-tastes of suburban backyards—sand and rock, scrubby backyards, the coolness of tar shingles under my knees and one palm. The faint dampness of the sprinkler systems a street down sacrificing precious water to feed spring lawns. The sharp stink of new paint and drywall from the latest home under construction in the model home development.

The pong of diesel from the truck waiting beneath us to transport the eight humans chained in the completed three bed, two bath house, to buyers—human for sex or domestic work, cryptid for worse.

I loosened the stone lid to the bottomless cenote, the thing I saw as a dark well inside me my humanity had been sacrificed in, and felt for the thing I'd trapped in it. I couldn't let the virus-warped version of me out of the pit it lived in. Dipping my hand in and scooping up enough to fuel the speed and reflexes I needed, that was easy as breathing now.

The landscape took on a silver-edged glow. The bright pink heat signature of humans came clear, moving in a huddle from the house basement upstairs toward the truck. So did the lighter red of the two vamps with the prisoners. The monsters had miscalculated in their greed. The rental-style box truck was too large to fit in the suburban two-car garage, and they'd had to park it just outside in the drive. We had to hit while the humans were in between.

At Stavros' soft *"now"*, we dropped in tandem, even our heartbeats synched. Landing at the same instant behind the three vamps stationed by the garage's roll up doors.

Slapping one hand over the fanged mouth of the nearest vampire, I drove my blade straight through its fabric and flesh. Then grabbed the heart and crushed the muscle between my claws. I braced my knee and pushed, shoving it off my arm to crumple to the blacktop.

Stavros reappeared beside me. Older, stronger, that much faster, his two targets were already dead and tossed inside the truck. He scooped my kill up to join his, back before I'd wiped my hands clean.

We flowed into the garage, then split up to opposite sides of the door leading from the laundry room to us. The door opened, releasing the sweaty stink of human terror. Releasing soft sniffles, and the salt of tears, old and new.

Stavros was in before the door finished opening, after the one vamp in the rear.

I spun, grabbed the one in the front of the group and kept going. Long hair scented with lilac shampoo washed over my face—I had the female. One leap sent us inside the dark truck, out of sight. My knife bit through vertebra, separating her head, her mouth pulled in an 'O' of surprise. The blade kept going, jamming into the metal of the floor. I jerked the machete free and resheathed, as Stavros landed beside me, depositing his dead load.

He stashed his blades and I followed suit, scrubbing hands clean on my dead vampire's shirt—she was in a designer athletic shirt and trendy leggings, the cute suburban mom persona hiding the predator inside.

Satisfied we wouldn't further terrify the vics, I rummaged through the other vamp's pockets. I hopped to the clean concrete of the drive, leaving Stavros to roll down the truck door on the grisly load.

I met the tiny group as they stepped out. All kids, one still in that shorts-under-a-skirt combo moms put on the little girls who liked to run and tumble. The group stopped, several looking around for the captors that had been herding them like cattle through an auction chute.

I made my voice clear but soft. "Hi. We're here to help you guys."

They all shoved in tight around a woman, really only an older teen, trying to hide. Tears streaked her cheeks and a bruise colored half her face. But still she pushed the others behind her, the look on her face calling bullshit on my greeting.

"Where're the others—Clara and Mike?" her voice wavered.

"They're gone, and they won't hurt you again. No one will, okay?"

She eyed me. "Who are you?"

'Agent Ramirez' almost slipped out. But that wasn't me anymore, and I didn't have a badge to reassure them I was one of the good guys. "That isn't important. I am here to see you all get someplace safe."

No dice. She sidled away, taking the others with her.

If they got back in the house and locked the door, I'd have to do some stunt a regular human couldn't, tipping this observant girl off that I wasn't human, and hugely complicating the situation.

"Look, I can't tell you more than that I'm here to get you guys safe." Slowly, I unzipped my jacket. I fished inside, her wary eyes on me the whole time, then held out the two packs of doughnuts. "Here. I doubt they really fed you."

The smallest girl, the one in the skirt set, tugged at the teen's hand. "I'm hungry."

I held up the doughnuts and sat down on the concrete, cold under my butt, and folded my legs. Then tossed the food underhand. She caught them on reflex. After a minute of hesitation, she opened the packs and handed them around.

"Now what happens?" She asked as the kids devoured the snack, chocolate and tears mixing.

I studied her, layering information from sound and smell they way Stavros taught me. She smelled of fear but her heart rate wasn't wild. No adrenalin dump coursed through her veins. "Do you know how to drive?"

She nodded.

"Do you feel up to driving? Can you handle all these kids in a car?"

She straightened, and pushed curly bangs to the side. "Yes. They listen to me. We just want to go home."

"Good. Where's home?"

"Reno, but on campus this semester. I'm a sophomore. The kids are mostly local, I think."

I rose and she tensed but didn't bolt. I held up the ring of keys I'd taken from the male vampire, presumably Mike the Asshole Trafficker. The fob matched the logo on the sedan in the garage bay. I tossed her the keys, then pulled out a phone, a cheap burner, and held it up for her inspection. "The address in here is for a shelter. They specialize in abuse and trafficking cases. They're open twenty-four hours and supply food, clothes, basic medical, and a counselor. They'll take care of injuries, and calling police and families for you and the kids."

She was nodding along as I spoke, relief lightening her expression. She'd been the adult here, clearly, keeping it together for the younger kids, but was more than ready for someone else to take over.

"Promise me you will go straight there." I channeled an Instructor, which seemed basically the same as a college professor, someone she'd already learned to trust and take orders from.

"Yes! Yes, definitely. We will."

Since she made no move to get closer, I pitched her the phone, too, and made a wide arc around, opening car doors as I went, ending with the vehicle between us. "There aren't any car seat things, so no speeding. No one will be following you or trying to grab you, I give you my word. No. Speeding. Got me?"

She was already pushing kids inside, the available seat-belts clicking. "Got it."

Almost cryptid-fast, she had kids inside, doors shut, and was in the driver's seat. The engine turned over, car backing out carefully. It stopped and her window whirred half-way down. "Who are you? What do I tell the shelter and police?"

"Say that you think someone scared your captors enough that they ditched their plans and ran. Then you grabbed the kids and one of the abandoned cars." I crouched so that we were almost on the same level. "That's all you need to repeat, okay? You didn't see me. Please."

Clear eyes studied me for a second. "You're undercover police or something?"

"Yeah, and blowing my cover—"

"Could get you hurt," she finished for me. "Ok, bye, thanks." Her response ran together and the window closed, car in motion again.

As the taillights blinked, vehicle turning out of the subdivision, Stavros reappeared beside me. "We are no longer alone. There are humans in a vehicle to the east, and one on a roof three houses to the west. They are all armed."

The team was here after all. I just didn't know if they were here to help us, or eliminate us.

ruce

BRUCE HAD LOST feeling in his hands half an hour earlier, when Josh had exited the truck, taking his sniper set-up to a roof position and getting the trafficker's house in his scope sight.

The trafficker's and Vee.

Bruce's knuckles had locked around the wheel, white and bloodless. The world narrowed to the house down the street and to Liv's breathing beside him. Waiting to see if she would give the kill order.

The entire team had night vision goggles on, but it was still impossible to catch details. His view was clear enough to see the two vamps drop out of nowhere and disappear the guards between blinks. And for Vee to step out, confronting the kids that walked out of the house.

Pretty sure his heart quit fucking beating, waiting for Vee to attack, or for her to sneak even a sip, all Liv would need to drop the hammer. His body went from terrified to numb and back as he mentally bounced from scenario to scenario. One with Vee jumping a kid, him sitting here while Josh put a bullet in her head. One where he knocked Liv out before she could issue an order. One of him driving the truck straight into Josh's path, giving Vee a getaway distraction. One of driving into Vee. He'd almost settled on that one, roaring through the yards to the house and jerking Vee into the truck and…

As his foot flexed on the gas, Vee folded into one of the heart-achingly familiar boneless poses she'd take on the bed with him, talking about her day, or on the floor with her sisters after a workout. Now, she unzipped her jacket and pulled something out.

"Report, Josh." Liv's voice snapped bullet fast, tension giving it sharp edges.

"It's—she's giving them food. Doughnuts? Damn, those are our doughnuts."

Bruce breathed around the knot choking him. Those fucking cheap-assed pieces of over-processed dough covered in wax and chocolate that Vee and Josh, hell, the entire damn crew, thought were the height of snacking until he came along. Yet they still clung to sneaking them in every time his back was turned.

Jesus. If she was luring kids in with them…

Vee rose to her feet and the air in the truck vibrated, Liv opening her mouth to issue the order.

Then Vee tossed the tallest kid the packs.

"What is she *doing*?" Liv keyed the tablet in her lap, bringing up audio she'd had off, too wary of vampire hearing to risk giving themselves away with the electronic's hum.

Vee's voice came in, tinny but real, sending the kids to a safe house, to the shelter downtown. Not a Company safe house but still a good one, legit and all human.

"That's it. That's Vee." Josh lost all semblance of a cool sniper. Bruce caught the click of Josh's rig being folded. "I'm coming in. That's our Vee."

Bruce still half-expected Liv to order Josh not to. As the front of the truck remained silent, he glanced over. Liv's face wasn't any more responsive than before, except for the skin tightening around her eyes.

The truck door opened and closed and he jumped, rapping his head against the roof. He'd forgotten about Kimi, doing foot surveillance, his reflexes and training fucked and useless tonight.

Liv finally moved, turning to Kimi who signed a simple, "It's done."

Before Bruce could grill the pair over what the fuck that cryptic exchange meant, the side door behind him opened and Josh slid in. He stowed the bag with his sniper setup between the seats, words tumbling out. "You saw what I saw. Vee never touched those vics. Neither did the other guy."

"Vampire," Bruce barked on instinct. "It's a fucking vampire, not a guy."

Josh's habitual easy-going expression altered, the cold analytical killer that could stare through a scope at a living being then choose the perfect moment to end its life coming out. Firming his jaw. "Shit's getting crazy left and right. Vee just saved a load of trafficked kids from a gruesome end. The male, whatever he is, helped her do that. According to Vee, he's the reason she's walking and talking and sending kids back to their parents."

Josh turned his hard gaze on Liv, then Bruce. "So I'm not pulling down on either of them yet. You want to murder our sister, you'll be doing it yourself."

Liv turned her back on her brother. She flicked open her phone, which lit with a green dot, the speck moving as they watched. "Start the truck."

A tracking device. Kimi's recon had included locating and planting a bug on whatever ride Vee had. Liv hadn't been any more sure than he was about Vee's termination. Part of him wanted to chew her ass out for not following Company mandate, and the rules set for keeping agents alive, because if he lost one more person he loved, he was done. The bigger part wanted to hug her until she couldn't breath for holding onto the same starving shred of optimism he'd tried to bury and couldn't.

Kimi gave him and Josh one of those shrugs and smug *you're so adorable* winks, and settled back in her seat.

He threw the truck in gear and roared out to confront a pair of vampires in their home nest.

ee

I smoothed my shirt down. Not that there was much to do one way or another with a basic black turtleneck and black tactical pants. I played with the idea of grabbing the jacket I'd hung on the rolling rack behind the screen that created my room and the semblance of privacy. Wear the jacket because it was at least kind of cute? Or leave it, because black leather didn't really read as welcoming?

Stavros raised his eyes from his book, some dry, antique history of a saint, and watched me for a moment, gaze sharpening. "You are unusually restless. Are you—"

"Swear to god, I don't feel the need to torture and kill anything,or drink anyone dry, okay?" I cut him off before he went back down that road, with the same truthful answer I always gave. I wasn't on the verge of losing any of my hard won control. I had to concentrate and reach for the hunting urge. Same with feeding. I didn't actually feel hungry-hungry, the biggest triumph out of all of Stavros' training.

A heavy frown pulled his brows in. "Do not blaspheme, niña."

"Sorry," I said for at least the fifth time today. Mastering my vampire instincts had been easier than following his no theological-swearing rules.

"Perhaps a training session to defuse your residual excitement?"

"No," I spit out too fast.

Stavros closed his book over his finger, giving me his full attention at the slip-up. I never turned down a chance to train, to spar, to get better at being what I was now.

Thinking fast I changed the subject to one of the few guaranteed to shut down the conversation. "We need curtains."

He recoiled like I'd tossed a windigo doused in chem at him. "We do *not*. There are no windows."

"They're a design decision. Not everything has to serve a purely practical purpose." I prowled the space, trying to see it the way someone first walking in might.

Bare brick walls. Exposed steel beams. A single open room, except for a corner that had a small bath, and kinda echo-y since we were on the second floor of a two-story building. It had served as a firehouse, from when there had been horse drawn fire wagons instead of trucks.

A small, worn loveseat, a comfortable-ish chair, and a tall floor lamp, all rescued from the curb, clustered in the center of the space. A low coffee-slash-computer table made of milk crates sat between chair and loveseat. A long, taller wooden table salvaged from junk already here ran along one wall. My last bottle of water, an apple, and sheathed knife barely took up a tenth of the top.

A folding screen I'd cobbled together from canvas and

half of another dismantled table hid my narrow cot, the other half hiding Stavros' cot. More of the machetes Stavros taught me to use, knives, and chains plus extra thigh and shoulder rigs hung on hooks Stavros had driven into the mortar between the bricks. A short workbench underneath held stun grenades, wire, chemicals, training equipment and targets, explosives, and cleaning and sharpening equipment.

It kinda screamed single-minded assassins. Not exactly a reassuring setting.

Stavros' head whipped toward the door and staircase. "Someone is approaching."

I leaped, scaling the loveseat and table, barely making it between him and the doorway in the heartbeat it took him to leave his book and move. I braced a hand on his chest. "I know. It's the team."

"¿Cómo? I detected no pursuers or hostiles on our return trip."

Time to woman up. "They didn't need to tail us because they bugged the car. Put an electronic tracker on it," I translated. Specifically, Kimi had fit it underneath the back wheel well. I'd swept the car, a new thing I'd been able to teach him. I always did, part of my personal security protocol. Which Stavros knew.

His eyes closed for a moment. That too-familiar trace of pity I hated crossed his face.

I tried out my reasoning on him. "Allowing them to locate us and see our place is a sound tactic to build trust."

"It's also a good move if you're lulling prey into a false sense of security," Liv said from the doorway. The one that, yeah, I'd purposely left open when we unloaded post-mission.

I hadn't been so generous with the first floor door. That was too cavalier even for me. Plus, we—they, the team— mastered lock picking before Josh's voice ever changed.

Since we didn't exist, Stavros saw no need for an electronic alarm system. Meaning that getting into this place was embarrassingly easy for any agent. Basically, I left enough security to hopefully reassure the team that this wasn't an ambush where they needed to come in hot, but not enough to alert Stavros well before I heard them, either.

I kept a hand on his chest, although if he decided to go through me I couldn't stop him, and turned my head to Liv. She had her second favorite blade on her right thigh and her preferred Glock with chemical rounds trained on us.

She stood square in the middle of the doorway, not minimizing herself as a target. Liv didn't make that kind of mistake. I breathed around the lump in my throat, at our version of a peace gesture. "I figured we know where you sleep, so it's only fair you know where we sleep."

"I doubt this is your only bolt-hole."

"No more than Scottsdale is the team's only base. This is our primary space though. I can give you the locations of the others."

Stavros' sigh traveled through my arm and he tilted his head back to stare at the ceiling.

Liv tensed, only visible in the way her weight shifted to her dominant foot. "What's he doing?"

"Dios, dame fuerza," Stavros answered for me and crossed himself. "I now find myself asking the Savior for patience far more frequently than at any previous period of my existence."

I shrugged since it was probably true, and let him go, turning to Liv. "I don't have anything to hide. *We* don't have anything to hide. Other than being outed to other vampires. If you really hate me, you can drop an anonymous tip to any true Master in the country, and they'll do the wet work for you."

"You two don't seem soft targets."

"We aren't." I didn't see any point in false modesty. "We are reason enough for vampires to band together temporarily, long enough to take us out."

Liv tensed again when I moved, although her gun stayed trained on Stavros. I crossed to the table and picked up the knife sheath. Hoping I was right, I took the few steps to offer it to Liv.

She studied me, head to toe. Slow and thorough. Then held out her left hand, motioning for the knife. I unsnapped the guard and I laid the sheath in her palm.

She did the judge-y single eyebrow thing Kimi and I had never mastered. "I have a blade."

"Your second favorite. Thought you might want your favorite back."

She bent her wrist enough to check, frowning and turning it back and forth. "It has a nick."

"Picky much? I cleaned and oiled it after I took it out of that dead vampire." I crossed my arms.

I saw it, the millisecond she made her decision. I put myself between her and Staroves, but Liv only holstered the Glock in a practiced move and added the knife to the rig on her left thigh. "What am I supposed to do with this, Vee?"

We both knew she wasn't talking about her newly sharpened knife.

"Do what we do best. Think outside the box."

Liv leveled a flat look at me, hiding something darker behind the calm. "Outside the box was all you. And look where it's gotten all of us."

Vampire reconditioning training came to my rescue. Only Stavros felt me flinch, hurt and despair trying to rise from the grave I'd dumped them in.

"Calm, niña." I latched onto the measured voice that had become my lifeline over the last year. Now, conditioning reminded me that all that was really left was a dry dusty echo, like a weathered and picked clean carcass left in the desert too long. Only a leftover memory from my human life.

I only got to depend on Stavros for so long. Mastering myself was the whole point of this experiment.

I walked to the sturdy workbench catchall and propped my butt on it. "Then I'll innovate again. There's no arguing the vampire population is on the rise, and has been for a few years. Apps and social media? Text for a ride, and the meal comes right to you. There's certainly no denying vampires are the most significant cryptid-adjacent threat." I held onto Stavros' detached calm and said it. I claimed what I was. "We're strong, but more importantly, intimately understand human institutions and reasoning. We are capable of co-opting innovations and organizing."

"As we've seen, your version of innovation leads to disaster."

Well, at least I knew where I stood with Liv. I talked over her and her challenge. "You've seen what Stavros and I can do. Our unique situation also lets us go places humans can't, and thus we catch chatter even the Company doesn't."

I returned the favor, looking her up and down. "Or at least not soon enough to be effective." I took a tiny, snotty measure of satisfaction from the way she bit down, teeth grinding, nothing to be seen from the outside, but easy enough for me to hear now. "Plainly, we need to find a way to work together."

"No."

"Yes. If you really meant that no, you'd have already reported us. Since we're alive and you're here, you obviously didn't. Let's be real. On some level, you know I'm right and you're already playing scenarios in your head." I raised my voice, addressing the pair of heartbeats just outside the door. "So are you two."

Kimi and Josh stepped in from either side of the doorway.

Kimi took in everything in the room, part agent, part her artist soul.

"Getting turned isn't happening." Josh had his hands on both guns.

"Our sharing that with anyone else isn't on the table," I said, voice as cold and decisive as I could make it, before Stavros lost his shit. We'd already discussed this, at length, but if he had a hot button, turning humans was it.

I felt him at my back, his aura touching my much flimsier one. I also felt a whiff of his stress, for want of a better word. A huge measure of his concern because he knew how powerful having my family here, in arm's reach, once was for me. Most of his stress was personal though. Having lived hundreds of years alone except for hunts, sequestered from others vampires or humans, our messy, loud emotions felt like being caught in a wave of pure chaos and being pulled under for him.

This was one of the few areas where I was the senior partner. Without looking, I reached behind me, laying a reassuring hand on his rigid arm.

The steps rattled, shaking under the force of angry boots and Bruce stormed into the room, most dramatic entrance possible, classic Bruce.

My grip on Stavros tightened, and his hand covered mine.

Like it was magnetized, Bruce's gaze went to our hands. If possible, more blood climbed his neck to his scarlet face. "You can't fucking be serious about this shit."

I wasn't sure if he was talking to me or Liv.

The sharp pop of Kimi snapping her fingers, jerked everyone's attention her way. She signed, "My calculations show that they have a one-hundred-percent success rate and that they go on two-point-three times more missions than we launch. My data is incomplete but that's a significant dent in the cryptid danger."

Bruce's attention bounced between my sisters, ending on Liv, who only tipped her head in acknowledgement. "The data—you aren't buying this bullshit?"

"You saw what they can do." Josh ducked his head at Bruce's accusing glare, but didn't back down, and turned to me. "We can discuss you coming home."

He switched back to Bruce. "We lost part of our team, man. Maybe we can get that back. Open your eyes—that's Vee, right there in front of us."

"It's not just Vee," Bruce snapped. Then a gun was in his hands, sighted expertly at me. "But I can take care of that."

"What are you doing, Bruce?" I funneled calm, patience, into my tone, for his and Stavros' benefit. Stavros was perfectly capable of hauling me out the door, into the car, and headed for a different state before Bruce drew another breath.

"I'm doing what you should be doing—protecting this family." Bruce's grip altered a hair. Targeting Stavros. "Once that *thing* is gone, then we discuss you hauling your ass home."

I moved, the same time Bruce's finger flexed against the trigger. I tapped his wrist right where nerve ran over bone. The barrel dipped as his hand spasmed open, the fired bullet slamming into my shoulder as I nudged Bruce. Not hard, only enough to put some distance between him and Stavros, Bruce stumbling and his back hitting the wall.

He stared at me, shock leeching color out of his face. Appalled either that I'd touched him, or that I'd taken the hit.

"Victoria."

I didn't need Stavros' soft heads-up. I'd heard the rasp of weapons clearing three different holsters. I turned my back to Bruce. Keeping my tears under wraps—and wow, would I be glad when the memory of how to cry faded—I ignored the burn of chemicals and held Bruce's confiscated gun, butt first, out to Josh.

Josh's gaze darted from my face to my wound and back. He straightened, his gun disappearing, and took Bruce's weapon. "What happens now?"

"That's up to you guys." I glanced at Stavros to double-check, who only dipped his chin in permission. With the security of Stavros having my back, I addressed Liv. "Assuming you can control your team enough to have a civilized discussion."

"How are you not burning?" She stared at my wound, blood still trickling and creating a wet spot on my shirt. "How are you still standing?"

"The blood. It's because of your diet." Kimi made the connection before Liv did. "The tolerance to sunlight and our compounds is because you feed on other vampires. There's some property in virus-mutated blood boosting your immune system. Or stem cells repairing damage in real time. Potentially a cumulative effect."

Her theories at the science behind our physiology were undoubtedly closer to the truth than Stavros' religious convictions about our subsisting on our kind being divine justice. I shrugged, forgetting the bullet, and hissed at the resulting bright burst of pain.

Kimi had a blade out quick as a thought, and came at me, implacable as when we were sparring in our Academy days. I held one arm out to fend her off, the other to halt Stavros as he surged forward. Leaving me caught between old and new relationships.

"I cannot allow them to harm you. That isn't part of our testing." Stavros eyes were all human, plain brown and brimming with sadness.

Kimi snapped her fingers in his face. His sadness turned to shock. Eyes widening again as her hands danced and I translated. "The chem has a two-minute dissolution window. The longer you whine and get in my way, the more Vee absorbs." I didn't need to translate the single middle finger she held up at the end.

I angled my wounded shoulder to her, and held still as she slid the tip of the thin, lethal stiletto blade, one she'd plunged between skull and spine on numerous creatures, into me. With a practiced flick, she flipped the bullet remnant and last of the un-dissolved solution out.

I exhaled in relief. "Thanks."

She gave Stavros a *look.* Then turned it on Bruce. Neither man said a word, gazes skittering away from hers.

I bit the inside of my cheek to keep the laugh in. Then faced Liv, amusement gone. Kimi had tried to help me, where Liv hadn't budged. "We're useful. We can take hits. We aren't impulsive or out of control. Call me when you're ready to coordinate." I fished a slip of paper out of my hip pocket and handed my number to Kimi. "Bye."

"You're throwing us out?" Josh blurted, still processing our three-way sister byplay, a beat behind us as always.

Stavros finally had enough. "Victoria is asking you, far more politely than your behavior warrants, to return to your home and allow us to repair the damage you've done. You are —" he gave a half-pause "—welcome here again, though I hope you recall your manners by that time."

A dusky tint colored Liv's cheeks. She dipped her head to Stavros. Then nodded to Josh, who'd locked onto a still stunned Bruce's elbow, sending them out first, Liv and Kimi on their heels.

Not daring to look at Bruce again, I finally let out a breath as Kimi closed the door.

"I hadn't anticipated the blatant, continued violence when I offered up this proposal." Stavros handed me a wad of gauze. "Your restraint was commendable."

"By our family standards, this was a total success." Only half the team wanted to slam the door in my face. Namely, Liv, my ex-right hand and confidant and best friend, who considered my continued existence a disaster. And Bruce, the person I'd loved most, who now hated me the most.

"I don't know if there are enough prey in all this state to heal you of more such successes." Stavros' voice came from the other side of the screen as I ducked in, pulling off the ruined shirt, laying a loose barrier of gauze over my aching wound, skin around it already turning gray, and pulling on another black turtleneck. I grabbed my jacket and headed for the door, and a hunt for monsters to feed on in order to undo the damage my family had done.

CHAPTER 34

ruce

THE SHRILL BUZZING of the compound's alarm set Bruce's already fucked nerves on edge. Without looking at him, Kimi raised one finger in a *"hang on"* gesture, then tackled the system keypad. The noise cut off, whatever she'd done overriding the warning that their arriving guests weren't part of the compound database and weren't cleared for admittance.

The damn computer didn't recognize Vee anymore.

Neither did he.

Twenty-four hours after tracing Vee to her new hideout —he wasn't calling that barren pit a home, the hovel less personal than a secondary compound that only saw action once a year—and he still hadn't made his peace. He couldn't wrap his head around any of this. Maybe the Company had a manual detailing how long it took to process your world getting fucked over, again. Three times in two years had to be a record.

They should also cover how to let go. Because he'd honestly thought Vee would at least take him up on the challenge of returning here to—visit. Argue. Give the two of them a chance to discuss this shit in private.

He gave a humorless laugh, one that had Josh pausing in checking ammo rounds and side-eyeing Bruce. "You up for this?"

"Are any of us up for this?" Which was the most either had said since Josh hauled Bruce's ass to the truck and shoved him inside, locking the rear from the driver's seat so Bruce couldn't get out, post-Vee shooting. They hadn't even had the usual monosyllabic, one-sided conversation in the gym as Bruce beat the hell out of the bag.

So, Josh was pissed that Bruce was cock-blocking his reunion with his sister.

Even Kimi had resorted to pointed looks and not much else since they'd gotten HQ's notice of a cryptid gathering, and Liv had used the number Kimi had programmed into all their phones to call Vee.

The team was going on a mission with a pair of vampires.

Bruce only realized he'd muttered the last out loud when Liv stopped beside him.

Her grip on his shoulder was firm, acknowledgement, not a warning. "This is a risk and we're treating it has such. If at any point, any of you feel Vee or this Stavros entity have set us up or are a threat, take them out." She stared at first Josh and then Kimi.

"Since when do we rely on feelings for kill orders?" Josh slammed a magazine into a rifle, arranged it on the table beside the rest of his arsenal.

Bruce knew he was displacing even as he rose and leaned over the bigger man. Hands braced on the table, face to face with Josh. "Since Vee disappeared for a year and a fucking half.

Then reappeared just when we're ass deep in alligators. You can bitch and whine and point fingers at me, and at Liv, all you want for protecting your asses because you know what Vee, the *real* Vee, would hate most? Dying wouldn't even make her list. It *would* fucking devastate her that some monster version of her killed you. You don't have the market cornered on hating this situation and these choices. So, shut the fuck up."

"He isn't wrong." Vee strode in like she owned the place. With the vamp beside her, both in that all black, head to toe bullshit, huge machete handles rising from knee high boots. Ghosting in without a sound, like some fucking comic book vigilantes.

She spoke again. "At least, he isn't wrong about my not wanting to hurt any of you. The part about you not being allowed to express an opinion is a different matter. I meant what I said about transparency. I'll answer any questions you have, now or later."

The vampire beside her frowned, but didn't interfere.

"Did you set this up? Did you somehow feed this information to HQ to create an in for the pair of you?" Liv positioned herself between the team and Vee.

Vee faced her, probably neither realizing they were mirror images of each other, down to the crossed arms and challenging jut of their chins. Kimi and Josh exchanged a glance, heavy on subtext. Even when they were on opposite ends of a debate on mission tactics, Vee and Liv had never been this outright aggressive.

"I didn't. We caught—" Vee hesitated "—information on this hot spot shortly before you did, and we were already prepping when you called. We'd have hit the gathering whether you joined in or not."

Bruce sure as fuck hadn't missed her hesitation. "How did you find out about it? And don't try that vague shit."

Vee answered Liv instead of him. "From a scrub—a nestless vampire."

"You didn't think it's a setup? How did you verify this intel?"

Strained lines cut Vee's forehead for a second. Slowly, silver limned her eyes, an unholy ring around the brown. She opened her mouth and fucking dainty fangs showed, her face thinning until the bones were pronounced, skin stretched over a skeleton. Lips a bloodless blue. She stood, letting them see, not starting at Josh's short *"fuuuck."*

The fangs vanished, her eyes human. "That's how I verified. Hard for anything to lie to us when we're drinking their last heartbeat."

"Fucking hell," Josh repeated.

"It was necessary." Stavros' voice intruded, unfamiliar and out of place. "Distasteful as you may find it, such lengths are required to heal wounds. If you don't care for Victoria's methods, perhaps reconsider before attacking her again."

A growl rumbled across the room. Coming from Bruce, not from the vampire.

"It's time to go if we're working together," Vee said.

Bruce grabbed his gear. Vee finally, fucking finally, looked at him. "We don't need you now. With us, the team is at full capacity again. Stay here."

Hurt battled with anger, both of which had become familiar and comfortable as a favorite well-worn shirt. He shoved past Vee, who stepped back fast, making sure they didn't touch. "First, you aren't commander here, Liv is. Second, fuck you."

CHAPTER 35

ee

JOSH'S SNIPER fire came in the form of audible *thumps* and vampire heads exploding, showering us in a near constant mist of blood and brains. First, from him opening us a path through the mob of vamps and windigos. Now, from him keeping the stragglers from ambushing us or cutting off our path back to the truck and daylight.

I hooked claws into the back of a fleeing vamp's shirt and hauled it around, the machete blade in my other hand neatly lopping its head off.

A grunt from my right marked Liv and Kimi tag-teaming another, bleeding the huge vampire from multiple cuts. Kimi's knives flashed like a chem-edged threshing machine. Liv's larger blade hit the creature's thick neck on a backstroke. Two more cuts, and the headless body slumped to the sawdust-covered floor.

Disgust evident by his curled lip, Stavros backhanded a

windigo my way, the mostly hairless creature's stench mixing with the vampire gunk.

My snort-laugh broke free as I caught the creature midair and snapped its spine, dropping it and wading into the thrashing mass of 'digos still snarling and snapping at each other. I stomped on vaguely canine heads, crushing the vicious predators. Leaving Stavros to finish off the last of the vampires. The jerks had been watching and betting on the cryptid version of a dog fight before we and the team ruined their night.

Stavros punched through a vamp in biker leathers and chain and came out with a claw full of mangled heart. 'Digos done, I pulled the body free of his arm for him, pausing for Stavros to wipe the blood and bits on the vamp's vest. Despite his being clad in a set of our never-ending supply of fighting gear, I'd still have an hour of his complaining over the viscera and windigo goo splattered on his clothes.

At least he'd finally agreed to hunt cryptids, after my months of nagging exhausted him.

Normally, we'd handle this our way, from a distance, utilizing contained explosions and fire. That was the best way to be rid of vampires, with the lowest risk to us. However, this bunch had chosen a spot in the midst of a human-heavy area. I wasn't sure humans who fought dogs and roosters and staged bare-fist cage fights counted as deserving mercy but...still human. Which left us doing the hand-to-hand combat thing.

Stavros scowled at his crusty knuckles and bent, giving his hands a more vigorous scrubbing on the dead vampire's jeans. After, Stavros tilted the thing's neck my way. "The blood is fresh enough."

"I'm good."

His lips thinned. "Your wound hasn't fully knit. Wasting

blood, weak as it may be, is unwise. Why must I continually remind you?"

I didn't think the team was ready to watch me drain a corpse. Hearing I did it was one thing. Watching it live, that was something else.

I shook my head and Stavros kinda glared, but straightened. After infecting me, it had been a rough path for both of us but he eventually overrode his instincts, and always respected my choices as long as they didn't put humans in danger.

At least we finished our disagreement before Liv and Kimi approached. Liv gave Stavros a nod and added, "That's the last of them."

Stavros and I already knew that, no non-team heartbeats left in the arena. I kept my mouth shut, Bruce's harsh reminder of what I wasn't still stinging.

This joint mission had gone off flawlessly. No one on the team tried to take me or Stavros out when our backs were turned, or when we were mid-fight. So far. And Stavros had kept a close eye on me as we fought. Hopefully, I got brownie points for ignoring Bruce's barbs and cooperating with Liv and Kimi instead of challenging them over perceived prey and territory.

"That leaves cleanup," Kimi signed and made a face, toeing the closest windigo.

Stavros didn't need me to translate, in full agreement with my sister's wrinkled nose. "I'll dispose of carcasses while you regroup."

Which was his way of making sure I didn't waste more energy, burning through blood on a menial task like lugging around dead windigos. Stavros disappeared, taking the biker and a couple of 'digos with him.

Liv and Kimi both twitched at the too fast exit, but recovered quick. "Handy," Liv said.

"True, that. Stavros had ways to disappear cryptids we hadn't even thought of." Which, probably not a topic to bring up with people who still considered us borderline enemies.

Kimi perked up, interest in data and details totally eclipsing the agent vs vampires thing. Or she was doing her job, gathering more intel, this time on us. "Like?"

I nudged at my aura, trying to pick up emotion from her. With zero result.

Torn, I started to chew a thumb hangnail, remembered it was coated in windigo ook, and stopped. But…what the hell. They'd already seen me fight, part of my battle-face on display. I concentrated, and my short, utilitarian nails lengthened into claws. "Dismemberment and shredding, then either dumping or burying is always on the menu. For bigger body counts, usually acid or fire. Today, it's dumping though." There was a deep pit covered in layers of dead cryptids, human pets, what might've been a couple of human remains, and lime. Stavros was adding another layer.

"You aren't helping?" Liv asked from her crouch, wiping blades on the vampire I'd killed. She examined one, and put it away. Kimi and I knelt and joined her, Kimi especially fastidious about her blades. Like, as bad as Stavros.

"I'm not as strong or as fast. Difference between four-hundred-plus years and a year-plus." Machete clean enough for now, I strapped it out of the way. For a second, it felt like I was home. In synch with my sisters, wrapping up after a successful mission.

With us face to face, Liv paused, tip of her blade pointed down, looking me in the eye. Challenge clear. "Be straight with me. No human blood? Ever? You're telling me you aren't tempted right now?" She fit two fingers into a rip in her left sleeve, and spread the fabric, exposing her forearm and a gash, shallow but dotted with blood

So much for my stupid, content illusion.

Kimi froze, head still bent over her knives, waiting.

"I swear to both of you, never. Not one drop."

Liv's voice went softer. "Vee, we've seen new vampires. Cryptid behavior one-o-one freshman year, standard curriculum for all of us. Freshly mutated vampires are all instinct, all hunger."

The Company captured baby vamps every year and brought cadets to observe, making sure we understood how vicious and brutal a vampire really was under the human trappings. Pounding in why the Company vow was death before being infected.

I squatted there and waited until Kimi looked up. "I woke up locked in a cage, under cubic tons of rock and dirt. Stavros provoked and starved and goaded me for months. Making sure I never slipped, over and over and over, before I was ever allowed to walk out of that cage. He was looking for any weakness, a reason to end me."

"Why? You made a vow. We all did. I mean, why—"

I did the one thing we'd vowed never to do—I cut Kimi off. "I goaded him, too. I tried to make him angry enough that he'd slip and kill me. But he never did. Instead, he trained me until I won't either. I'm the only person he's ever turned."

Kimi and Liv exchanged a look, not sold. Liv looked back at me. "Him infecting you was a very vampire move."

I traced random patterns in the sand and sawdust, searching for the words to explain. "Stavros only did it— infected and turned me instead of letting me die—because I'm Company. He told me point-blank their eighteen-year indoctrination and training regime meant I might have a shot. How we were raised was the only reason he thought I might have a tiny hope of beating the virus." Not that he called it a virus or beatable. Not that I'd thanked him, either.

Kimi cut to the truth. "We were raised to be aggressive

and competitive but never to go too far in training sims, and to evaluate all options. We internalize when to compete and when to kill."

I lifted a shoulder. "Yeah. I kinda had coping mechanisms. Who knew the Company prepared me to be a vampire?"

Kimi's hand locked around my wrist, at the same time Liv spoke. "Never say that, not even here, to us. If Oversight even thought—"

"I know. They'd burn us to the ground." I slumped. "I shouldn't have outed us to you and involved you guys. There's something building though. All this crap with ghoul behavior, windigo altered migration routes, and that freaky anangoa thing, and the increase in—"

Kimi's grip tightened, enough it hurt, before she let go to talk. "You were right. You said something was wrong, before. We shouldn't have laughed about conspiracy theories and joked it off and ignored you."

I wanted to reassure Kimi that we were cool. Lie and act like I hadn't run what-if scenarios a million times as I huddled in the dark, hating myself a lot, and hating the Company, and Terrence, the closest other regional C.O. and our friend, who'd listened but only to humor me, and the team—my brother and sisters who rolled their eyes when I brought up oddities—just a little.

Instead of looking Kimi in the eye, I double-checked holster snaps while addressing Liv, in our shorthand. "Useful vampires. Possibly accurate-ish cryptid conspiracy theories. Decisions on contacting HQ."

"We've been brainstorming," she admitted. "Pitching best case scenarios. HQ hasn't scheduled the Assessor visit and inspection, to officially sign off on Bruce's permanent status. That was put on hold."

Hope flared, taking me by surprise before I could lock the emotional memory down.

"Finding some way for you to return would be a lot easier without Stavros," she said. "You'd be a lot more palatable alone."

"We're a package deal." I didn't have to think. Even as that illogical spark of hope blew out like a candle in a draft.

"Are you guys—" Kimi made a not-so-vague obscene gesture.

"No!" I shook the image off. "Warn me the next time you want to try anything else that'll require me to bleach my brain."

"You're very close." Liv drew on C.O.-level diplomacy. "You're extremely protective of each other. Help us understand."

I double-checked Stavros was out of earshot, and still lowered my voice and motioned them in.

They both tightened our circle, the same as we'd done thousands of time when sharing secrets. "It's partly a vampire thing? He infected me, and I suspect there's some sort of DNA sharing attached to the virus. Like with beehives and ant colonies and their queens, maybe. But theory only, so whatever. There's legit a bond like—" I sketched a wide, wishy–washy circle "—I sort of feel where he is. Super vaguely, I feel his frame of mind too. He definitely has the same with me, although, he can control his filter and is much more sensitive."

I inhaled, and blurted the part they might take the most issue with, and the part Stavros would definitely have a way huge issue with. "We're a team. I also still have a lot to learn from him, about our history, vampire social structure, and being a vampire and what's next just for starters. He's... important to me. He healed Bruce. I told Stavros why I captured him, and knowing I'd kill him at the end, he still willingly gave his blood every week. Even when he was starving. And he saved me. It wasn't the way I would've chosen, but he did."

"That's pure Vee," Kimi signed, meaning my alleged soft spot for pop culture heroism and all things romantic. Which, true, but she could still bite me.

Not done, she plowed ahead. "He's put up with all this—" Kimi indicated us as stand in for the whole situation "—out of some highly suspect vampire biological imperative?"

My sister's dismissal, like what Starves had done, and was continuing to do, was frivolous or some ploy, cracked my good-sense filter. "He hates vampires. *Hates* them. I mean all other vampires. He's held himself away from humans since he was infected. Oh my god, he'd die if he knew we were discussing this, but he is lonely. It's the saddest thing I've ever seen." That got blank looks from my sisters. Because they had no clue what truly alone meant, or what my being thrown into Stavros' life had done. Resentment stirred, definitely a vampire emotion.

I tried again. "You would not believe the stuff he lets me get away with because he wants me to be the vampire-ish version of happy. Oh—he doesn't actually call it happy, but, just go with it. Anyway, we went trash picking for a loveseat. To put that in perspective? The guy who slept on bare rocks for hundreds of years and used candles and considers concrete floors and halogen lanterns a luxury, helped me load a floor lamp from the curb on trash day."

Liv rolled her eyes. The tiniest smile sneaking out. "You and your strays. First a belligerent chef, now an orphaned vampire. Jesus, Vee."

She didn't grasp the sadness and crushing loneliness Stavros' existence had been until a year ago. She couldn't. I could. I saw clearly what it meant to lose the company of people who loved you. Without Stavros, that was me. I wasn't abandoning him, ever, both for my selfish sake and because he deserved more, and I couldn't tell him I loved him and he was my family now, since vampires didn't love or have family, but I'd dang well show him what love and family had felt like as a human.

Thinking of love and loss led me where it always did. To Bruce. I didn't know how to bring him up.

Kimi and Josh were feeling me out. They were willing to give me the chance to prove I was mostly me, so they'd have some part of their sister back. An emotionless virus-mutated me was better than no me. Probably.

I was on probation with Liv. No matter we'd loved each other as much as Josh and Kimi loved us, she had to be the voice of reason. It was on her to keep the team safe. I got that. I'd have worried she'd been compromised if she hadn't acted exactly the way she had, as a C.O. first, sister second.

Bruce though… I didn't know. We couldn't be what we were. Stavros had been hella clear about that. I hadn't expected Bruce to be the one who blocked every overture though. So...angry, about everything.

"Bruce," Liv said, like she'd plucked the topic straight from my brain.

This was what I'd wanted. An opening to ask about him.

But asking meant potentially hearing how much he despised me. His opinion, any emotional attachment associated with it, shouldn't have an impact on me. Except being in the same room with him took all my willpower not to react. Shutting down the emotional memories that involved him and us used even more energy than dealing with my sisters or Josh.

"He is red-lining," Kimi signed into the charged silence. "He's lost all of his lifelines, and all his support networks— his family, his industry peers, you."

"I was running out of things to tell his mom and Kenny when they called," Liv said. Her eyes narrowed when I didn't respond. "Oh, why am I talking to them, you ask? I'm talking to them because Bruce won't. He dodges their calls. Even the girls'. They are rightfully upset."

"He is still in remission. They shouldn't be." That, I knew.

Kimi's eyes narrowed, like she'd found a clue and was about to dig in.

Liv so wasn't done yet, though. "Are you being serious? All he does is live in the gym, wait for missions, and keep opening and wallowing in that file he—" no missing the guilty way she changed topics "—in the report from the night you died. I love Bruce, too. We all do. You though, you're acting like…I have no clue."

I got stuck, between Liv still conflating my being infected with my dying, and Bruce's change. Her mention of Bruce reading documents must've meant Liv's report on the night I disappeared.

Liv's reports were always meticulously detailed. I didn't remember everything from the attack, but I knew we'd left a destroyed truck and a bloody scene. Something like horror coiled around me at the idea of Bruce having to learn what happened—

"Say something." Liv leaned in, violating my personal space. "Does he look at all okay to you? Do any of us?"

The challenging body language, or her glossing over the whole part where I'd just told her I'd been infected against my will, spent months in a freaking cage, and basically tried to get killed touched off the anger that was a real, current emotion.

The cruddy sawdust fighting ring took on a silvery cast, meaning my eyes were glowing, and I kind of didn't care. "You? Yeah, you look pretty pleased with your position and your life. You *all* look like you are carrying on just *fine*."

Kimi sucked in a breath. Shocked I was right or that I was willing to go there.

"Someone had to deal with the fallout from what it turns out was your decision to willfully trash Company rules, and keep us all alive. You don't get to pass judgment on how we all managed to survive." Liv's hand tightened around the knife hilt.

"And neither do you on how I survived, which you clearly wish I hadn't."

Kimi put herself between us, signing fast and aggressive, like it was that or smack both of us. "You can't truly believe that?"

Stavros swooping in and out removing more bodies stopped us all from saying anything even more unfortunate. Kimi shivered at the wash of air, Liv's eyes widening as she realized who'd caused it. Only bloody sawdust was left, where a body and head had been a second before.

"That is..." Kimi's fingers stilled, mid-sign as she thought.

I grabbed onto safe, emotionless facts—why Stavros and I were here, my duty, that this was only a training exercise I had to conquer. "Useful. Useful and generous. He'll have the site scrubbed equally fast," I put out there. As close to a peace offering as I was capable of. I had to get away from the anger before it turned into my harming everyone here.

"We can?" I dipped my chin to outside and Josh. And Bruce, who watched Josh's back while Josh watched ours.

I headed out, already two steps away before Liv and Kimi rose. Blinking hard, I adjusted to the light, sun already rising over the far-off desert hills, pink and gold hazing the horizon.

Josh squatted, folding away his gear into the rear of their truck. Bruce stood by him, attention on the pit and entryway. His gaze met mine, and it felt like a weight lifted. Then he whirled and took the few paces to the front, and jerked his driver's side door open.

Shapes exploded from the shadows on the opposite side of the truck hood.

I sucked in a sharp breath the way Stavros taught me, filtering scents. The old-blood stink of vamps swamped me.

A pod who'd either arrived late to the cryptid games, and been caught outside between the pit and our fire fight, or who had fled as we rolled in, and then been trapped. With the sun rising, they sped for the relative safety of our truck. Via the open door Bruce stood by.

Liv barked a warning from behind me. One of Kimi's throwing knives breezed by my cheek, hitting a vamp in the thigh. Not stopping it, in its desperation to avoid the sun.

I launched, knocking the wounded one away in a spin. Met the other face to face, its claws slashing at my head. Whirling a beat too slow, a claw pierced my scalp. I lashed out, and my claws scored along its ribs, at least tearing it away from Bruce.

The vampire, a female under the goth makeup, hissed and lurched at me. I grabbed for her and brought my claws together, and kept going, scissoring her head free. I tossed the already smoldering carcass toward the empty parking lot.

The smoke obscured the second vamp's location, and I paused, listening. Weight hit my back. The bigger creature's charge knocked me to my knees. I heaved, half throwing it off. We rolled, slashing at any body part available, legs tangled, jaws snapping.

I braced one knee and flipped us, landing on top. Blood running into my eyes and screwing up my vision, I punched down and hoped. Hitting flesh, I kept going, shoving my fist through its face. I put all my weight into it until the skull cracked and my hand buried in the sandy dirt. Trapping me against a slowly flaming carcass.

Someone grabbed my shoulders and hauled me back.

Jerking me free, just as sparks fountained and the body caught fire in a whoosh of used oxygen.

I stumbled and landed on my ass between Kimi and Josh. I coughed, choking on smoke, eyes watering. Then remembered Bruce, and scrabbled on all fours, head swinging like a windigo's, searching for him.

He lay crumpled against the side of the truck, face slack. I made it to the truck in a spurt of sand and blood, kneeling over him close enough I felt his breath on my face. I quashed the panic, followed Company trauma protocols, feeling for broken bones, damaged spine. Nothing shifting under my exploring fingers, I laid him on his back, careful of his head.

"Here." Josh offered me his jacket. I bunched it under Bruce's head. Then kept going, patting him down, compulsively searching for wounds or fractures I'd missed.

Beside me, Josh tensed.

Stavros appeared in front of me. "I can't—" I turned panicked eyes on him.

"Victoria." His stern semi-reprimand steadied me. "Trust what your senses are telling you. You hear his heartbeat, his pulse's speed, his breathing. He's stunned, but otherwise unharmed."

"Fine, yes." I concentrated and counted beats. "I'll believe he's okay when he wakes up and bitches and stomps off, okay?"

Liv knelt beside me, repeating my pat-down more slowly, as Bruce finally grunted. "Come on. There we go," she coaxed, and he shoved upright using her shoulder as a brace.

"How many fingers?" I held four up. Realizing too late there was blood on them.

Bruce blinked, expression soft. That look he had every morning when he first woke, before the bluster was in place for the day. The one where when he found me already up and watching, he rolled to his side and just—stayed. Being us. The familiarity set up a weird ache in my middle.

Bruce blinked again. "Vee?" His tone matched his expression, and he held a hand out to me.

I jerked out of Bruce's reach, heart hammering. Because I wanted to take his hand, get lost in the emotions. Which wouldn't end in a way safe for Bruce or my siblings.

I put on the detached, professional mask I'd once used with rattled civilians. "Anything hurt?" I tilted my head at his chest, stand in for new injuries and old ones. Where he'd had the minor surgery and where the awful port for the chemo treatments had been.

Bruce's locks and wards slid back into place, vicious scowl back. At the scuff of boots milling around us, his expression sharpened. "Get the fuck off me. All of you."

He used the truck and pushed the rest of the way up, and grabbed for the door handle.

Josh cut him off. "You know the rules, my brother. No driving after a black out."

"I wasn't knocked out," he bitched, but pivoted and jerked the second row side door open, climbing in and slamming it on all of us.

I stood, suddenly tired. The pink and gold landscape wavered. My knees wobbled, turning noodle-y. Then Stavros had me, not letting me face plant. He lifted me into his arms.

"Vee?" Josh pushed in, apparently got a good look at me, and said a string of blasphemous things that were *sooo* going to piss Stavros off.

Voices washed over me, then seemed to pull back like an ocean wave leaving shore, volume receding.

"She needs—"

"Hell, no!"

Kimi's face hovered over mine a beat, until the darkness crowding in blotted everything out.

ruce

"WHAT THE FUCK?"

If Josh repeated that phrase one more damn time, Bruce was going to mow Josh's beloved basketball hoop down with the truck, *while* Josh was shooting hoops. Bruce swiveled in his seat, and swallowed against the vertigo he wasn't admitting to. It wasn't as painful as the stupid wash of bliss he'd experienced, that had done more to lay him out then getting his skull vamp-knocked against a truck, when he'd gotten his rattled senses going and felt Vee's hands on him.

No matter how long they'd been apart, he'd always know her touch. Fingers brushing over his face, down his chest. He'd had dreams exactly like this. With her there, so real and alive.

Then he'd woke up enough to unstick his tongue, ready to touch her, reassure her he was all right and ask if she was. Instead, he got to see her jerk away like his touch was poison.

Vee looking to that damn vampire for guidance and reassurance instead of to her sisters or him. Her new preference.

The truck rocked, increasing his nausea and he hit the window buttons, trying for fresh air. Instead, he got the stink of charring pork from burning vamps. That, and to watch Vee fold up like a broken doll. Stavros caught her, and her face went from ashy to copper. The same painful hue as when they'd all ended up too drunk one Christmas at the beach, basically passed out outside all day without shade or sunscreen, and even Josh had ended smeared with aloe gel.

Burning. Vee was burning.

"What the fuck?"

He'd bitch at Josh later, because the guy's statement summed up the problem.

"We must go." Stavros waited for the crowd to open, scanning for a hole.

Instead, they pressed closer, Kimi signing, Josh translating. "Why is this happening? She shook off the chem solution."

"This is the price for burning through the blood. She was not fully healed, yet insisted on this mission, and then used the last of her reserves in this fight under the sun. We must go. Immediately."

"If she needs blood, then get it from this one." Liv heaved at the headless vampire body, not yet on fire thanks to falling in the shade cast by the truck. "Put her down here."

The old vamp didn't move. "That will not suffice nor can she consume it."

"It'll do in a pinch, and I've seen half dead vampires bite into anything close by." Liv faced down the fucking arrogant prick.

"Victoria isn't one of your savage creatures."

"What kind of game is this, asshole?" Bruce elbowed in,

joining the conversation. "Fucking feed her or I'll gut you and let you be her lunch."

Kimi pressed between them, head tilted and studying the asshole. Two seconds before Bruce officially lost his shit over the vamp's grandstanding, Kimi slowly mouthed, "She can't, can she?"

Stavros went still and expressionless. Like a fucking statue, completely hollow of life, the new most unnatural thing Bruce had seen in three years of wading neck deep in cryptids, fights, and gore. Bruce didn't get whatever it was that Kimi had hit on, or the vampire's reaction. Pissing Bruce off past all limits.

Of-fucking-course Liv grasped the meaning, some mix of that sister shorthand and C.O. ability to think three steps ahead of everyone else. Voice tight, but horror shading her words, she said, "You trained her too well. Her first instinct isn't survival or self-preservation."

Stiffly, Stavros dipped his head. "She has…overcome…her innate vampire responses, to a degree I hadn't anticipated. Your army's emphasis on prioritizing other's lives and well-being over your own combined with my training in an unexpected way."

The pieces finally clicked together and hairs stood up on Bruce's arms. Whatever psychological torture the guy inflicted on Vee had fucked her up to the point her mind or body or both had no damn idea what she needed to even live.

"Then how are you going to get blood into her?"

"She will wake eventually. At which time, her needs can be taken care of. Her healing will be slower, but manageable."

Bruce's chest squeezed like he was having a heart attack. Vee didn't look asleep. She looked comatose. Barely alive. Too close to the way he'd seen her in his nightmares again and again.

Kimi pushed at Bruce, surprising a grunt out of him,

knocking against him to open a path. Then she waved at Stavros, and pointed inside the truck, intent clear.

"Kimi, take a beat," Liv intruded.

Josh picked up what Kimi meant. "There's blood at the compound. We keep our types on hand. She might not be able to feed herself, but we've got bags, IV kits, all that. Like, the same principle as hooking up a dehydrated person to a bag of fluids."

"We need privacy and quiet." Stavros acted like he hadn't heard Kimi or Josh. "Our site is closer."

Fury and fear blazed through Bruce. "Need, my ass. What you mean is that privacy is what *you* want. This is about Vee, and she needs blood and right the hell now. Get your fucking fossil ass in the truck."

An actual emotion filtered across the old vampire's face, but not anything Bruce could interpret.

If this was a ploy, the creature using Vee as an excuse to get into the compound…it didn't matter. Bruce would get Vee home, get her what she needed, then he and Josh would eliminate the vampire before it pulled whatever evil it had on tap, infiltrated the team or Company.

"Stop." Liv's voice did more to quell the palpable anger than a bucket of cold water.

Kimi got in her sister's face. Signing fast enough Bruce missed part of it. But he caught the way Liv closed her eyes for a second. The action as good as a yes, agreeing to what-ever Kimi demanded. "Are we all in agreement? We're allowing Vee and Stavros in our compound?"

Josh's harsh verbal agreement and Kimi's signed, "Yes" overlapped with Bruce's, "Get in the truck."

Vee might not give a shit about him and the future they should've had, and might've chosen this vamp over her family. But he'd burn everything down—the compound, the

Company, this town—before he'd watch her slip away from them again.

"Victoria will not touch human blood." Stavros' tone was frozen-too-the-bone chilling. The pure hopelessness of a grave untended and forgotten marched over Bruce's skin. Pulling up tangible ghosts—Bruce's diagnosis when the chemo failed, when he thought it was the end, dying in Vee's arms. His grandparents' death beds.

Josh staggered, hands rubbing down his arms. Kimi's hands went to her throat and the nearly invisible white scar.

Metal shimmered in the morning light and when Bruce blinked, Liv's blade rested against Stavros' jugular. Words squeezed out of her throat like they were fighting to stay put. "Drop it. Drop this psychic attack."

Like waking from a true nightmare, the despair faded. "Ram that through his throat," Bruce got out.

Stavros' gaze swept them. "Victoria will not touch human blood, under any circumstances. That's her law as well as mine. I disregarded her explicit wishes once, one of many sins I'll answer for on judgment day. I'll not force my wishes upon her ever again, nor will I allow anyone else to."

Josh swore, jerked out his knife, and dropped beside the dead vamp. "Somebody get me a container."

Bruce scrabbled between the seats. He found his prize, pulled out bottles of water from the portable cooler, and cracked one open. Dumping the water, he pitched the bottle to Josh. Kimi grabbed another from Bruce and followed suit.

"Will this option work?" Liv's knife didn't waver despite the oily sweat on her upper lip. A remnant of whatever she'd seen when hit with the glamour that'd debilitated the rest of them.

"It is sufficient for now."

They got busy draining vamp blood, to save one of their own.

 ee

I TWITCHED, floating and unconnected. Needing to fight, grab an enemy's heart and jerk it out, to protect...someone. To train so I could finally do the one thing left to me. I could be free to do...

I couldn't remember who I had to help, or how, and rising panic pushed me further into consciousness.

When I shifted, the surface under me dipped. Whatever I was on, it wasn't the concrete and stone of the old underground bunker, or ever the lumpy relief of the air mattress I'd liberated from a military surplus store.

I stopped, distanced myself from the uselessness of emotion, and fell back on my new training. Inhaling, I taste-smelled in a way humans couldn't. Then listened, blocking out my heartbeat.

The comforting scent of old parchment and C-4 met me,

the smells that meant Stavros. The slow, calm tap of his pulse, signaling we were safe, wherever here was, came next.

I hadn't been this fuzzy and confused on waking since I'd learned to hold off sleep and wake myself, night or day. At least not since Taos and the battle with a nest holding humans on a wellness retreat as shields, where I'd burned through all my reserves under the desert sun.

Somehow, I'd done that again.

Crap. Stavros would be disappointed. Learning my limits, staying just inside them was as important as keeping control and remembering to fight with vampire tactics instead my old human ones. I was disgusted at myself. When I screwed up, it put Stavros in danger, too.

I angled my elbow under me to sit and a dull pinch pulled at the back of my hand.

"Be easy." Stavros' voice was warm as a fuzzy shirt and socks after a cold mission.

Meaning he was using aura tricks. Meaning, we weren't as secure as he wanted me to believe.

I was on my feet, crouched and balanced before my eyes even opened. "What's wrong?"

Pushing, I scooped up some of the me that lived in the dark well, listening again, senses refined by the addition.

The combined impact knocked me to my butt—the coconut of Liv's moisturizer, the thick wax and astringent of Kimi's oil paints and thinner, the rubbery sweat of Josh's basketball. Over it all hung the green-vinegar tang of the natural dish detergent Bruce insisted on.

Something weird tried welling up my throat. Not hunger or rage. Something I didn't completely remember and didn't want to.

Stavros' aura draped over me, helping me press the not-emotions flat. I exhaled. Inhaled again, held it, let it out, able to separate from the emotion. "I'm fine." I blinked, bringing the room into focus.

Stavros sat beside the bed, the way he had when I'd first turned. Except, in the crazy-heavy old barrel chair from the corner of the office—my old office—not on a cavern floor by my cage. I reached sideways, muscle memory in play, and flicked on the lamp beside the table. Right where it should be in the room off mine and Bruce's, with the solid antique furniture and metal locker at the foot of the bed.

The room I'd given Bruce when I scooped him up after our second meeting, hiding him from a rampaging lizard cryptid that had marked him as her prey.

Somehow, I was back in the main compound. But not in the room Bruce and I had moved into together. This was the extra, used for visitors.

Liv never would've let us in here unless there was a crisis.

"The team—were there more vampires after I blacked out?" *Bruce.* Bruce had been down, laying beside the truck. Had I been wrong, did he have a bleed I hadn't sensed? Some even more devastating injury?

Hands caught my shoulders. I blinked up at Stavros, both of us now by the door, feet from the bed. His grip kept me from charging through the exit. Heat flooded my face. I hadn't meant to move, and hadn't realized I had.

"You dispatched the last vampires, and the team is well."

"Then...why are we here?"

"You were the emergency." He paused, seemed to consider what he wanted to say, even more precise than usual. "Your sisters and brother are formidable. They refused to take my word as to your eventual well-being."

Embarrassment and the weight of failure filled me at screwing up so badly. Enough that *agents* worried I'd bite it. But the bitterness mixed with a shard of...hope. I was pretty sure this was what hope had felt like. Pride, too.

Kimi and Josh had voted. They'd convinced Liv to bring me in instead of leaving me to desiccate in a pit fighting ring.

I flexed my hands, the sharp pulling of my skin interrupting again. I rolled my hand over. Medical tape stretched over the back, exactly where an IV would go.

"They didn't. Kimi didn't—" I couldn't finish the damning thought. This was why we were alone. Kimi had thought she was helping by giving me blood. Instead, she'd accidentally broken my rule. Stavros' rule. There was only one outcome for this disaster. "Do it in the desert. Not here where they'll see and blame themselves."

Kimi couldn't know the blood was a death sentence. My last act was making sure she never did.

Stavros squeezed my shoulder, then recalled he didn't do PDAs, even private ones, and dropped his hand. "They respected our law. Your brother siphoned from the outcast's carcass. Your sister gave you the blood of only our kind." He frowned. "I've never known it to be done in such a fashion, but I felt when your needs were met."

"Yeah, IV's and transfusions." Big deal. I was interested in the important part of his statement. "You called them my brother and sister, not ex-team."

He'd hammered it in, that words had power, and I had to take in and incorporate that I was a vampire now, not a person. I had no ties except to Stavros, others dead when I lost my humanity. Monsters—I used to call vampires 'predatory mutations'—until I became one. We were monsters, and monsters didn't have family or friends or teams.

I'd hated him every time he forced me to repeat it. Night after night until I quit screaming it in his face, and recognized it as truth.

Stavros sighed. "They see you as their sister. It's not simply a thoughtless habit—I feel their belief." He touched the center of his forehead.

The motion highlighted the fine lines that rarely appeared, Stavros far too composed and practiced to stress. The same lines that I'd caused the first six months, when my raw emotions pummeled him. They had sent him out into the sun for relief multiple times, wasting blood that was hard to come by because he was stuck with me instead of hunting. What the emotions of four people, all wired after a mission, plus processing my stupid emergency drama were doing to him…

I scanned the room for our gear. No jacket, no machetes. Whatever. Those could be replaced. "Let's go." I jerked the door open.

Liv and Kimi stood outside it, Liv with her fist raised to knock. Her brow did that thing, calling you out on your shit with one simple move.

Kimi got to it first though. She signed, "You're better?"

"Yes." I peeled the tape off and balled it up. "This was kind of brilliant. Thanks."

Liv propped against the door frame, arms crossed, basically barricading the exit. "Were you planning on thanking us in person, or just bailing without a word?"

"A text later counts as a word."

Kimi could still swear more creatively in ASL than most people could verbally.

I reached for her elbow, then stopped myself. Contact only heightened emotions, and that I didn't need. If I'd been paying more attention outside the fighting pit, the straggler vamps would've pinged my radar. Instead, I'd been focused on Bruce, and this dumpster fire was the result.

Because bad situations could always get worse, Josh and Bruce spilled into the hall. Even I felt it, like static in the air, the extra emotions heavy and turbulent as an incoming lightning strike.

I glanced at Stavros. The lines on his forehead and

around his lips added years to his appearance. I turned back to the crowd. "Thank you. I mean that. But it's time for us to go."

"Just like that?" Josh pressed in with Kimi.

Behind me, Stavros went rigid. The bond between us hummed, some of Stavros' insulating control breached. Josh and Kimi's energy sparked against me from the front. The mix of the two realities meeting made my skin crawl.

I caved and took the half step back, until my shoulder touched Stavros, hiding in his aura and kinda hating myself for my weakness. Hating that I wasn't fueled enough to withstand simple interactions. IV aside, the vampires hadn't been powerful and I was still...not hungry. More hollow-ish, like part of my mass was missing. That was how I knew when I needed to feed, when I felt physically too light, too easily unbalanced.

If *I* had burned through blood, Stavros had done far more. I pushed his rule, catching his hand. Trying to strengthen the bond and read-read him the way he could with me. "Did you...?"

A hint of emotion played over his face, softening him. "There was sufficient amount for you alone. I'm well enough though."

I hated this. With the same steady hatred that fired me to fight vampires. I'd gone from looking out for a team, taking care of them, to being the one that needed help. I was the weak link.

Bruce's growl came through loud and clear, even from the back of the pack, hidden by Josh's height. "This is how the fuck you say thank you?"

I met his anger with my own version. "Let's cut the crap. None of you can really want us here. This was an emergency situation and you felt you had no choice. Now, the emergency is over."

Liv straightened, jumping to the logical but wrong conclusion as to why we needed out. "You can't control yourselves in such close, extended proximity to humans."

I didn't see a weapon but she was armed, and debating using it.

"Our control isn't an issue," Stavros said.

Liv glanced between us.

I shrugged. "What he said. None of you trip my trigger at all."

I realized what I'd said, and how it came across, at the same time a wave of pure fury came off Bruce.

The look Liv gave me was cold as one of Bruce's kitchen blast-freezers.

"You can't want us here," I blurted.

"Like you give a shit about what any of us do or don't want," Bruce answered.

Liv held up her hand…and he shut up. Another change since I'd been gone.

"You want us to trust you." Liv looked at me from under her brows. "Fine. Give me a reason. Stay here, where we can see what you do. Let us see what your reactions are now, and how we might—*might*—be able to integrate my team with your team in the field long term."

"We have to go back."

"What, like that crap-hole is better?" Josh shoved into the conversation again.

"It's livable."

"Victoria." Stavros joined the conversation. Just not the way I expected. "This idea has merit."

I wheeled around on him. "What? No. This, all of this, the noise and the people and—and the general peopling can't be comfortable for you. I won't ask you to do that." No matter how much the part of me I hadn't finished shedding wanted to.

Clearly there had been more than hygienically question-able vampire blood transfusions taking place while I was out of it.

"We agreed the situation must change, at least for the foreseeable future. No matter how uncomfortable change may be. This is an acceptable extension of our lessons." He switched his attention to Liv. "Are there more private quarters?"

"These are as private as it gets."

Stavros' tactful reference to lessons meant my last test. He'd decided my staying here was an even better way to train, and assure I was reliable. Adding a significant layer of extra work for me, and a larger opportunity for me to screw up. Instead of leaving it at 'sorry, no room', heading back to our base, and making it easier for myself, my mouth took over, ignoring my brain. "The annex."

The annex, the extra area attached to the gym, used for the ultra-rare creatures that HQ might need for experiments, or that we needed to extract information from.

"Those aren't living quarters," Kimi signed.

"They have everything we need—space and privacy."

Liv straightened and turned for the main area. "If you want furniture, you two are hauling it out there yourselves."

I didn't know if the invitation was the best possible outcome, or the worst.

CHAPTER 38

ruce

"*All we need is privacy.*"

Vee's voice telling them—him—how little they appealed to her and how little they meant, repeated in Bruce's head on an endless loop. The audio was accompanied by 3D images of her pressed against the damn vampire. His hand wrapped in hers and her blatant concern. Vee had been prepared to leave them, without a word, her new go-to response. She had a new family, and they weren't included.

Bruce was the worst kind of hypocrite. After telling Josh that Vee didn't belong here, hell, after telling *Vee* she didn't belong, he hadn't been able to stay the fuck away. Especially not when the vampire had laid Vee on the med bay table, already looking dead, or when Kimi hooked up the shitty IV after figuring out how to use congealed vamp blood.

As soon as the last of the blood left the tube, the hovering vamp scooped her up and disappeared to the empty room Liv offered. If the vampire had willingly remained, then the situation wasn't as routine as he acted. Bruce had been ready to take a fire axe to the guest room door after Vee had been in there for most of a day, out of his sight and with no update.

"I don't think Vee meant it that way." Josh's tone was subdued, nearly lost in the evening breeze rustling across the rooftop, wrestling with his own version of processing Vee's dismissal.

Bruce didn't look up from his study of the potted thyme, one of a dozen herbs scattered over the roof deck. "She meant it."

Jamming his foot against the floor, Josh stopped the meditative back and forth creak of the platform swing. "Man, I don't get a sex vibe off them. They're not—you know."

"Jesus Fucking Christ." The curse lacked bite though. "I know that, asshole." As bad as the situation was, at least Vee wasn't banging some antique. That age difference would've been another level of skeevy and wrong on top of this whole crisis.

"I'm saying, she was still off. Not completely healed, or whatever the equivalent is now, and you know how prickly she always was after an injury. She's not as flat-out mean as Liv, but she hasn't ever been a fun patient. The worse the recuperation, the worse her attitude is."

Bruce had to agree. He got where the whole vamps as undead myth came from. He'd stared at her chest the entire drive in watching for the next breath, each agonizingly far apart. The monitors Kimi attached freaked right the fuck out over injured vamp BP and heart rate, too.

So had he, pacing the hallway outside the room until Liv couldn't take him anymore. She'd gone to check, despite the vamp's high-handed, "I will inform you when

Victoria is ready," grand pronouncement as he left the med bay.

Liv arrived just in time to catch Vee ghosting them. Barely steady on her feet, face ashy-pale under the brown, but not able to wait to get away from them.

Josh kept going, as relentless as his sisters. "C'mon. We have to cut her some slack."

"She left us. Her choice. She doesn't want to be here now and as far as she's concerned, she doesn't need anything from us. Vee's never had any trouble communicating and she was pretty damn clear tonight."

Kimi popped up, scaling the ladder like gravity didn't apply to her. "She's a crappy patient and kind of a snot. She is so not okay and does need us though. We only have to remind her. We also need her." Kimi flicked her finger at Josh, using the initials for their favorite game. "CoW marathon with Jace in five minutes. You in?"

The last gaming invite was directed at Liv, still on the stair connecting rooftop to the hallway.

"Pass." Once the other two left, Liv joined him, letting the hatch close on Josh's animated gaming battle plan rundown.

Liv watched Bruce, while he watched the sun vanish behind the mesa. The pushy crows that usually lined the tree gave way to the tiny bats that swooped around the security lights, picking off mosquitos and moths.

When she finally spoke, her tone blended with the darkness. "I can tell them to move back to whatever hole-in-the-wall suits them."

"Do you want her gone?"

Liv tilted her head back, joining him in watching the bats, taking her time. "My reasoning for observing them is tactically sound."

Which meant she wanted to see if any of her sister remained, as badly as Josh and Kimi did, but wouldn't ever admit it. Maybe not even to herself, going by how she and Vee were suddenly sniping at each other every other word.

The hell of it was, so did he. In the face of Vee's rejection, he still lived from one breath to the next, praying his Vee existed inside the cold, driven vampire shell she was wearing. Purpose sparking to life, he pinched a handful of thyme from a pot.

Liv twisted to face him as he flipped the roof hatch open. "What are you up to?"

Liv wasn't giving up, and neither was he, no matter how much hurt and anger was simmering on either side.

"Reminding Vee of who she is." Food had been the bridge between them the first time they learned to communicate, when a barely socialized soldier, and a relationship phobic jerk were forced to coexist.

Food was his love language, according to Vee. Meaning the kitchen was his best hope for getting through to her again, prying her out from the remote shell she was hiding under. It was the only avenue left to try to bring her back to them.

CHAPTER 39

ee

I PULLED in the last of the blood and felt when the unnerving emptiness in me filled enough. That one last drop needed, like leveling off a measuring cup, except my version was like my center of gravity had steadied. I dropped the vampire, booting its body closer to the incinerator, Stavros' meal already burning to ash inside while I refueled. Done, I stretched, fingers reaching, and turned to check on Stavros' opinion of our second inter-group mission.

The entire team stood in the center of the morgue-turned-vampire-disposal center, watching me.

They'd watched me drain a vampire after my taking it down. It hadn't been dead when I latched on to drink, and I'd been so off, I hadn't realized we had an audience. Something too much like guilt and panic fluttered in my stomach.

I pulled on Stavros' training, and crushed the emotion.

This was me. I'd been a well-disciplined predator long before becoming a vampire. "Perimeter secure?"

My back turned on them again, I told myself it wasn't because I was afraid of their reaction, and hauled the body to the incinerator, stuffing it in and slamming the scorching door.

Liv matched my brusque tone. "We're clear on this end."

I brushed past her. "I'll double check with Stavros for stragglers or surveillance, then we'll meet you at the truck."

I pulled a vampire disappearing act, little point in walking and pretending to be human now.

Stavros crouched on the peak of the roof, surveying the area. He rose at my appearance, in as animated a mood as he ever got. "This foray went well. We—" He stopped, catching sight of my face.

"They saw me feed," came out, instead of the question of whether we were all clear I'd *meant* to ask. "They saw it."

"Did they attempt to harm you?" Stavros was beside me in a blink. He tilted my chin up, and inhaled, checking me out.

"No." I started shaking my head, and couldn't stop. Shivers hit. Except I hadn't been cold-cold since being infected. "They saw me." The entire show, complete with fangs and drinking blood from a living creature.

"You yourself stated that was a possibility, when we ran scenarios before deciding to approach this experiment."

"I know." I didn't know why I was reacting this way now.

"Do you believe they will attack us once we reappear?"

"Maybe? I don't think so?" I settled on, "No." Liv wouldn't have wasted the opportunity, if she intended to eliminate me.

"Don't be ashamed." Stavros applied pressure, raising my head and forcing me to meet his eyes. His aura lapped at the edge of mine. "Never be ashamed. What you are was forced on you, yet you've used our curse for a good and righteous cause."

I opened all the way, not embarrassed of needing his surety and deep calm. Steadied, I stepped away. "I'm not ashamed of you, or of what we do."

We dropped to the cluttered dirt yard, and my bravado aside, walked sedately to the truck instead of the usual *whoosh* and appearing.

Everyone but Josh was already inside, my brother half in and standing facing us on the passenger side running board, elbows folded on top of the roof and completely relaxed. "Speed it up. Liv's got a report to fudge, and we've got a team to beat."

Stavros frowned, checking with me, and I translated. "Company online gaming competition. It's hardcore, with bragging rights bestowed on the winner and deep shame upon the losers."

"You want to learn?" Josh squinted, evaluating Stavros. "Dude. Vampire reflexes could put us over the top."

I nudged Stavros, practically stuffing him in the back seat, and inappropriately silly. "Absolutely not. Your rivalry is vicious and way out of his league."

Two hours later, all evidence of gore and blood meals washed away, I prowled from one side of our cobbled together suite to the other. Then from one corner to the other, from the real bed that I'd damned well hauled out, now hidden by the screen I created with sheets woven around the bars of the cage, the room's central feature. Then to the opposite cage and bed, the one I guilted Stavros into dragging out for himself.

If he could insist on things for my own good, I could turn that table on him.

I circled the bank of interrogation equipment, index finger bumping along the solution-coated chains.

Stavros materialized, and lifted my hand away. "Go"

"To spar? Okay." Anything to dispel this twitchy thing just

under my skin. It had to be restlessness. I was all juiced up, or as much as we allowed ourselves, and antsy for another mission.

"Go inside to...your sisters." Stavros frowned like he couldn't believe the words were his.

"Why? Has Liv gotten a HQ callout?"

We'd moved enough equipment here to be mission-ready, extra blades, explosives, and clothes. I went for my closet and the tactical pants and jackets hung neatly on the cage bars.

"Not that I'm aware."

I left off gearing up. "Then why am I needed inside?"

Stavros went into lecture mode, hands behind his back. Gaze to the front, which meant an uncomfortable subject. "Aside from proving you have mastered the discipline required to survive, we're residing here in order to allow the team to become accustomed to us, and alleviate any suspicions that would impede the ability to hunt together effectively."

"Missions," I corrected him automatically. "We go on missions, not hunts."

"Just so. Yet another reason you're the bridge between us and this team. You cannot bridge that gap staying sequestered here, away from the team."

"*We're* bridging it."

Stavros sighed and met my eyes. "Perhaps in time. For now, that duty falls to you."

"They're still emotionally-loud, huh? Even with acres and walls between you and them," I said.

"I'm—what's your word? Acclimated. I'm becoming acclimated. However—"

"However, you already had a road trip today, and me leaking emotional goo all over you."

"Your control in general is exceptional, niña."

Fine them. I ninja-hugged him, a quick hard hug around

his middle, and then let myself out while he re-starched his rumpled dignity. I was calling this a vampire-on-vampire interaction and so, outside of the rules about emotional triggers and humans. A freebie.

The yard was empty. I followed my all-human perceptions, up the metal steps and into the hall, between the den and library. Which was also the furthest point from the kitchen and Bruce's room. Maybe the team's extreme emotional projecting was wearing on me too, and no one projected like Bruce. Not even Liv, though she was a close second. I hadn't dared look at Bruce post-feeding debacle. He made sure he was in the driver's seat facing forward, sunglasses on for the drive home, and waited until I'd left the car before he'd even unbuckled.

I hung on the doorjamb, and poked my head into the den, waiting until Josh quit crowing and shared a high-five with Kimi.

"Kicked Jace and Matteo's butts again?" The remainders of their two separate massacred teams, the guys had bonded during their recoveries.

Josh started, but quickly recovered and flipped his mic out of the way. "Do I own my brother's ass? Why yes, yes I do."

From her spot on the good chair, Kimi leaned enough to flick Josh's ear, then signed, "False. I own all of you amateurs."

"Only the two of you?" Liv and Bruce weren't hardcore gamers, but occasionally joined in. Kimi and Bruce even played some PG level game with his three nieces.

"They don't play anymore." ASL could have sub-text, and Kimi's was loaded, her face full of hidden hints, gestures hitting certain words harder.

Josh played peacekeeper. "They've gone to pick up supplies."

I.E., the farmer's market. Unless that'd changed too while I was gone. I checked my inner clock—not even close to dusk, but…

"They can take care of themselves." More loaded Kimi-guilt as she read me. Although I wasn't sure if she was irritated with me, them, or all of us when she added, "Bruce needed some air."

"The town's clean. Kimi checked informants and drones for them. They're good." Josh stretched and ditched the head-phone. He ambled out, a *creak-pop* marking his door opening and closing.

When he came back, he tossed Kimi a packet and ripped into the other himself. I sniffed—Kimi had peanut butter cookies, Josh the pork rinds. With Bruce out of the compound they'd broken out the contraband. I blinked, that stupid itchy-twitchy *something* underneath my skin back again.

When Kimi set the package down, I helped myself to a cookie and plopped on the arm of the least popular chair. Cookies were almost as good as a doughnut for drowning… not sorrows, since vampires didn't have those. I settled on drowning residual stress. Stress was physiological, not emotional, so again, okay under Stavros' rules.

Kimi and Josh both froze, him with cheeks full of pork rinds. Which he promptly blew all over the gaming console, yelling, "The fuck, Vee? You can eat?"

I stopped mid-chew. Then chewed faster and swallowed. "Yes?"

Kimi shoved me, nearly unseating me and rocking the chair precariously. She signed, "Don't be all surprise yes-ing. You've totally eaten before. Do not even try to lie."

"I wasn't!"

"So, you and Stavros eat?"

"Sorta?" I ducked out of Kimi's retaliatory reach. "I mean,

we don't have to. But, it helps. Well, it helps me anyway. I've kinda reintroduced Stavros to the simple joy of occasionally dining." Once a week, mandatory dinner, but this wasn't the time to get into that. I had a stroke of inspiration. Stavros deserved pampering a little, since he was enduring extra stress by living here, and for him an indulgence meant books or wine. "Can you text Liv and ask her to pick up a couple of bottles of decent wine? Maybe don't tell her the request is from me, though."

"You two need to work your crap out," Kimi signed, not hiding both her exasperation and that she was deadly serious.

Which was usually how Liv and I ended any protracted arguments—Kimi calling us on our nonsense. Plus, neither of us wanted to truly get on her bad side. This was hella different than who borrowed whose favorite skirt though, or accusing the other of fudging the half point that put one of us ahead of the other on a test.

Kimi stared through me like she saw into my heart. "Bruce talked about hope being more than he could manage while he was sick, and I understand why you didn't tell him about Stavros. But you should have brought your plan to us. We're a team. We would have been right there with you, chasing any potential miracle for him. You don't think Liv is especially hurt that you didn't at least try out a theoretical run-through on capturing a vampire with her, the way you guys make all complicated decisions?"

"I wanted to protect you guys from the potential repercussions of my choice."

"What affects one of us affects all of us. We were all pretty unstable by that point, I grant you. Still. To fix this, you have to do your part."

Since I wasn't supposed to care, about old ties or new feelings, I wasn't equipped to fix what was wrong.

Josh finished choking on his rinds, washing them down with an equally outlawed neon sports drink, and going for a more neutral topic. "Eating. You two haven't had one meal here. I repeat, the hell, Vee?"

"Those are team meals." My hands had curled into fists and I made myself loosen up before bones popped. I hadn't been able to miss the scents from the house the night before, and today. Bruce had gone all out, baking my favorite bread, the one he'd first made after seeing what we faced on missions. Then there was the breakfast pizza he'd done the morning after he announced, not *asked* but *announced*, he was staying with the team, and me, permanently. At lunch, he'd doubled down, making a version of the decadent chocolate, cinnamon, and cayenne cake Kimi and Liv bought for the celebration when his test came back clear.

That one had almost broken my resolve to stay outside. Then firmed it up like concrete. Bruce had an asshole streak and was doing this to punish me, because I couldn't be what he wanted me to be. Because I'd basically rejected him since I'd returned. I wasn't human, I wasn't part of the team, and I wouldn't be doing things like keeping up with his nieces. If I couldn't be here under his terms, he didn't want me here at all.

I'd reminded myself his antics had no power over me as a vampire.

Smart enough to pivot, Josh grunted. "You and mister wine snob gonna cook fancy shit and what, have wine over your five course dinner?"

I rolled my eyes hard enough to risk getting an eyeball stuck. "I'm a vampire, Josh. Not a magical unicorn. I still can't cook anything that doesn't go in a microwave and then directly on a plate."

"What does Stavros like?" Kimi leaned closer.

Thanks to Bruce's influence, we'd all learned the nuances

of dining.

"He doesn't know. Like, seriously doesn't. He hadn't eaten real food since he was infected." At Josh's, "Oh, damn," I bounced in place. "Right? I'm slowly educating him. Nothing seriously spicy or highly seasoned, though."

"That uber-senses vampire thing is for real?" Josh leaned in too, curiosity stoked.

"It's more like a super refined taste-smell combo." I didn't see any reason to freak them out with the whole truth, that things with lots of garlic were an issue. Anything with capsaicin. Even onions, if they were in quantity. While fighting not to sleep, I'd researched. Garlic caused anemia in animals. Theoretically, we could have a similar reaction. It wouldn't kill us, but wasn't pleasant either according to Stavros.

Josh's eyes widened. "Wine. Like, because it's close to blood? That whole Christian church thing with wine turning to blood."

That earned him another ear flick and Kimi's, "What have I told you about mixing B-movie plots with real science?"

I snort-choked, but the accusation was valid. "Nothing so arcane. Stavros has a soft spot from before he was turned. His hacienda grew a vineyard. He let it slip before."

"Before we knew about him." Kimi's amusement fled, anger taking its place again. "The vampire you were keeping and experimenting on, and dosing Bruce with. For months upon months."

I met Kimi's gaze, then Josh's. "I won't apologize for that. I wasn't sure the blood would work. All the research I accessed had focused on applications aimed at wound heal-ing, not disease treatment or eradication, and even those results weren't reproducible. And whether it did or not, if none of you knew, none of you were culpable in an Over-sight inquiry. My choice, my consequences."

"Like any good C.O." Kimi's face was weirdly neutral.

Josh directed his attention to fiddling with the rind package, the plastic crinkling. "Liv's good. She's a good C.O."

"Of course she is. That's why she was lieutenant." The person who'd step in and keep a mission running or a team going if the C.O. fell. I was glad she'd done exactly that. Really.

Josh cleared his throat. "You and Stavros should come to meals. Not do this aloof thing. Bruce is still king of the kitchen."

I ignored the Bruce comment. "It's tough for Stavros. He's old and strong but conditioned to solitude and silence. He's just recently gotten mostly immunized to me."

"That his excuse for keeping you away all this time? What he wanted mattered more than us?" Josh left off messing with the packet, challenge clear.

"He wasn't. He was teaching me to overcome all the ugly that comes along with being a new vampire, to get back out and protect people. Not telling any of you was my choice, too. Even he didn't know if I could accomplish what I wanted to, and I wasn't putting you or myself through hoping then having it crushed. I'm also not the sister you once had, and I can't change that. If I have to choose, you guys have each other. Stavros only has me. I only have him."

"C'mon, Vee." Josh crushed the packet, tossing it at the trash can across the room, frustration evident. "That's bullshit. Kimi and I are right the hell here, and so damn happy you are too. Then there's Bruce. You two are epic. You haven't even given him the time or chance to see if you two are still good. I mean, you and Bruce—"

"There is no me and Bruce. That part of me isn't there anymore." I rose, ignoring Josh's curse and Kimi's soft gasp. "Message me if Liv brings in the wine, please. 'Night."

ruce

BRUCE STOMPED DOWN THE BALCONY, each metal stop *bonging* at the impact, an incriminating scrap of plastic crushed in his hand.

Kimi sat on the bench by her birdbath, camera out. Probably taking shots to use on another art project.

"You didn't clean up the evidence." He dangled the fucking pork rind packet in front of her nose. She only *"hmd?"* and kept flicking through shots on the camera. The junk food was *an* issue, not *the* issue, but it would damn well stand in for him and Vee, and Vee draining a still-kicking vampire, then disappearing again. Fuck. He hadn't processed the blood thing aside from not being a quarter as disturbed as he should be.

His temper notched up. "Do not pretend you're innocent. If one of you was eating this chemical-bathed, cancer-causing trash, so was the other."

On cue, Josh stepped into the yard, the annex door closing behind him with a solid *thunk*.

The annex where Vee was playing house, having dragged shit out of storage all day one day, emptying the storage locker and carrying heavy oak beds like it was nothing.

She'd set up house and ignored his every message this week, each attempt at communicating carried on the breeze, because he'd propped the outer door open as he cooked. Hell, he'd left the door open even when he wasn't cooking. An open invitation for her.

Vee couldn't eat what he prepared, but she damn well could smell it with her super senses. She could understand what he was trying to say. Hell, he couldn't always distill their relationship into words. He had always been able to do it with food, and Vee had always understood, right from the beginning.

So, he'd done his best, and gone all out. Telling her their story, the high points and how they'd found each other, how they'd gotten through every disaster and roadblock. How he thought that in the end they'd won.

She'd either forgotten his language, or flat out didn't care anymore. Anger and hurt not having any other outlet, he turned it on Josh. The guy had put up with more than his share already, but would again anyway, because that's what family did. "Explain this shit, you conniving overgrown asshole."

Josh turned to Kimi for an assist that didn't come as she stayed absorbed in her camera. "Uh, it was a one-off?"

"Bullshit. What have I told you about this garbage? How the hell are you going to stay sharp with this crap in your diet?"

Josh took a slow step back, apparently under the assumption Bruce wouldn't notice his retreat, and tried again. "It was only a snack."

"Bullshit again. I know there was more than this, because you can't be bothered to clean up your trail of crumbs."

"Kimi and Vee ate it too."

Kimi froze mid-camera tap. Josh caught his fatal fuck up and swallowed, loud in the raging silence.

"Vee ate. This. This junk?"

Josh hadn't ever been able to lie to him about anything substantial, now no exception. "Yeah, as a post-gaming celebration."

Bruce's thoughts bounced wildly, finally landing on one. "You grabbed the bottles of pinot. Where did they go?"

Kimi touched Bruce's leg, offering him comfort he couldn't deal with right now.

Josh flinched but answered. "Vee asked us to have you guys pick those up. I took them to her a minute ago."

To her and Stavros.

Vee had been able to eat this entire time. Not with him though. At least he had his answer to why she hadn't responded to his attempts to reconnect—she didn't care any longer.

Kimi tapped his hip, demanding his attention. He ignored her.

Josh plowed ahead. "Look, we all said some things when Vee first came back, about her not belonging, her not being an agent anymore. So now she thinks the meals are team-only, and hasn't wanted to crash them. That's all, no other reason, no conspiracy. She's being polite and doing what she thinks we want."

The fuck she was.

Reading Bruce's face, Josh talked faster. "Seriously, swear on my Harden jersey that's the truth. I'll tell her it's cool and she'll be here in a heartbeat. Tonight. She'd love to eat with us tonight. Bruce, man, this is what we all need, sitting down together for a reason other than planning a mission. Really talking, and starting to heal, all of us."

Bruce inhaled and held it. Let the breath out. Not knowing which way to explode. "Fine. Tonight."

Josh's face lit up. "I'll let them know." He jogged away to deliver the news to them.

Them, but not them as in him and Vee.

Josh slowed and called, "Oh, hey. Nothing crazy seasoned. They don't do spicy or some shit."

They'd fucking eat what he fixed or starve. If Vee didn't care enough to come be with her family and him unless she was nagged and guilted into it, he damn well wasn't catering to delicate vampire dining whims.

CHAPTER 41

ee

I HESITATED on the house balcony and smoothed my turtleneck for the third time since I'd left the annex and crossed the yard. Then tightened the band holding my high ponytail, hair long enough to tickle my neck even when pulled up on the top of my head. I couldn't cut hair for crap, a salon visit was right out, and Stavros...he might've tried playing hairdresser if I'd asked. I liked my hair too much and wasn't that desperate yet.

At the clatter of flatware from inside, I quit wasting time. I had black turtlenecks and tactical pants and plain hair because my purpose was killing, and killers didn't need civilian clothing or favorite make-up brands, or split-end serum and flatirons. This dinner was only about solidifying our bond with the team, in order for all of us to do our jobs.

Any weirdness itching away under my skin and causing second thoughts and concerns about appropriate dress all had to be from the team's human emotions splashing over me, not my actual feelings.

I opened the outer door and walked into the chaos of humans and dinner prep.

Kimi was setting the table, the only one of us who ever met or exceeded Bruce's strict placement outline. Liv worked beside Bruce, handing him plates. Josh hovered between kitchen and hall, clearly the lookout. He caught sight of me and relief washed over his face.

He'd been the one to come pitch this dinner idea. Half swearing the team wanted a celebratory first-job-together meal since I'd been out of it after our first job, and half begging. I'd always sucked at turning him down when his heart was invested in an idea.

"Hey, in here." He motioned like I didn't know where to go.

"Need a hand?"

"We're good." Liv handed Bruce a last plate, doing what had once been my job.

Josh pulled out a seat for me at the end of the table closest to Bruce, my old spot.

Bruce finally turned and gave his teammate *the look*. The one where Bruce had hit his limit and was done playing.

This time, Josh only glared back.

"I can sit there," I motioned to the seat furthest away.

"That's mine." Josh abandoned me and lunged for the other spot, the poor chair sliding under the impact and adding another scratch to the floor.

I'd won a position as team leader once, then lost that position.

I had also nearly succeeded in fully taming my vampire nature, doing so in record time. Making a new place for myself here was the final step. I could dang well sit through one awkward dinner. I took my seat. "This smells amazing."

Bruce twitched but didn't answer. Dinner did smell wonderful. He'd gone Italian, one half of his comfort food zone. I tried not to read anything into his choice of preparing something personal. The air was rich with fresh parmesan, tomato gravy that had simmered all day, oregano from the herb pots he kept all over the roof, and fresh onion and garlic.

Discreetly, I sampled the air. Okay, lots of garlic and thyme and oregano. I caught myself, lowering my hand before I chewed at a nail, another leftover habit. I'd eat around whatever Bruce had sauced so heavily, Stavros' warning in mind.

That plan died a swift death as Liv handed me a plate filled with ribolita. The hearty stew was Bruce's take, made in a bread bowl instead of with pieces of bread. Leaving no way to pick around the gravy.

Everything tasted sharper and more intense now, something I'd discovered the first time I'd eaten food after being infected. Overwhelmingly so in the case of a street tortilla I'd picked, not knowing better.

The chair on my left scraped. Bruce sat, whole body rigid, his shoulders too tight. The tension matched the glare he'd given Josh.

Kimi and Josh had been wrong about rekindling any romance. But I'd shown up out of nowhere just when Bruce had gotten over me and moved on, as evidenced by the efficient way the kitchen prep ran, and the smooth way the team ran. Liv had to be wrong about Bruce not being in a good place, because aside from the tension between Bruce and I, this was just another day.

There were apologies owed though. Bruce had every right to hate me and to find my presence here an intrusion. I had basically experimented on and drugged him, without his consent and knowledge. I needed to own my actions, because no matter how big a jerk Bruce was, I wasn't blameless. Maybe he'd have been more willing to forgive if it meant us back together as a couple, but that wasn't possible. Him finding my presence intrusive was valid.

His growling and autocracy aside, he loved Josh, Kimi, and Liv as much as I had, and they'd asked for this thing, to include me, and he was going way outside his comfort zone for them. The least I could do was woman up and try to make this easier, or take the hits in place of the team if he needed to vent.

The heat from Bruce brushed all along my left side, the feel of him as familiar as breathing. If either of us shifted an inch, our knees would connect. The line of tattoos, the earliest one he'd gotten and the first one I'd ever touched, circled his thick forearm. Visually, I traced the lines, then kept going across his chest, memory filling in what was underneath his shirt. My gaze stopped on the left, where my tattoo was.

It was only the remembered comfort, and a familiar scene, that made me want to stay here beside him. The longing to physically trace over the ink was an emotional muscle memory, not anything current.

Stavros had hammered in that it would take time to recognize the dusty relics of past emotions, then separate them from what was real, and longer still to eliminate them. Which meant my weird itchiness only felt like sorrow and guilt and loss. The withered bits of love, and regret. So, catching the fresh lemongrass of his organic small batch soap, and residual spice of the herbs he'd handpicked, always his scent, didn't make my chest catch the way it would when we'd come home from a mission and he'd be sitting at the table with his hundredth hand of solitaire, and green tea.

Nor was the flutter that came when I'd catch a glimpse of him working, sleeves rolled up, showing off muscled arms and the full sleeves of tattoos, forehead creased in concentration. Or leaning against the basketball hoop's post, shirt plastered to his thick chest after a game of horse with me and Josh.

"Bow your damn heads." Only Bruce would start a prayer by swearing. He'd been religious in his own way before, but this was new.

Every other head around the table bent.

Okay, not new to them. I tried to watch everyone while Bruce's deep voice spoke a blessing, but ended up watching him. New lines traced his forehead and created grooves around his mouth. Too-early silver scattered here and there in his beard, hairs that came in when his grew back after the chemo, probably only noticeable to cryptid or vampire vision. The combination should've made him look older, haggard. Instead, it suited him. Like his grump, his appearance held more authority.

My fingers ached to smooth the worry lines away. Nothing had ever seemed quite so dire when we were touching.

His eyes opened, catching me staring, as everyone else dug into the meal. I was glad for my current inability to blush as his gaze locked with mine. His frustration and anger were easy to read. Beneath those surface emotions sat something else. Hurt. Hope.

The chair didn't move but Bruce did, a fraction, angling his body my way.

Mine mimicked his, still tuned in the way we'd been in and out of bed. That link had been forged even before we'd slept together. His hand hovered, his spoon not touching the bowl, like he'd forgotten about it, or something more important had stopped him, mid-action.

When I didn't turn away to my dinner, he laid his spoon

down. His empty hand inching across the table toward mine. A question in his eyes.

A part of me struggled, drawn to it and to him. Wanting to complete that connection, weave my fingers through his, the way we'd done hundreds of times. The desire wasn't a memory. It was sharp and bright and of the *now*. The electric jolt that set my skin tingling, heart beating faster.

Nauseating panic stopped me. I couldn't feel those things, because they only led to one place for vampires. Everyone at this table dead, while I savored their last breaths.

I grabbed for my spoon and broke our intimate bubble, scooping up too much ribolta, sauce spattering the table.

"He too good to eat with us?" Bruce snapped, grabbing his spoon and stabbing it into his bowl.

Josh and Kimi hadn't passed on what they'd pried out of me. More realistically, they had and Bruce chose not to believe it.

I played clueless, not taking his verbal bait, and definitely not engaging in the sparring Liv swore was our foreplay. "This is all new to Stavros. Socializing will take an adjustment."

"Like this isn't new to us?"

I shoved food in, hoping it still worked to pacify Bruce. He'd always been fifty-percent less growly when people were enjoying his art. I chewed, then fought not to gag at the sudden onslaught. The flavors too much, overloading my taste buds and my sense of smell, leaving me as nose blind as a human.

"We have lots to discuss."

I grabbed onto Liv's matter of fact tone as something to focus on besides the food.

"Can't business wait, one fucking time?" Josh's hand flexed around the spoon, threatening to bend it.

Kimi shook her head and signed, "This is too important."

"The Assessor." I didn't need to guess.

Liv's eyes narrowed and she paused, spoon hallway to her mouth. "Have you hacked HQ?"

"You guys have a bizarrely unrealistic idea of what turning cryptid-adjacent can do. It didn't give me magical sous-chef abilities, and it definitely didn't bestow some cinematic *Ocean's Eight* level hacker powers. I don't need to see HQ files to know what's hanging over the team. The assessment was postponed when—" I drew in a breath, the memory of the moment I realized science wasn't going to save Bruce still holding the power to suck the oxygen out of my lungs, and dared look at him—"When you were so sick. When it was so bad."

He was fine. I *had* hacked every one of his doctor's visit notes and lab reports, the medical practice's firewalls a joke. I'd seen him alive and whole on missions. Yet I still needed the reassurance of seeing him sitting here, healthy.

His attention on me, not just my face but taking in my body language the way I was his, his shoulders relaxed a notch. As soon as I spoke again they went ridged. "Things were postponed again for the customary bereavement hiatus."

On the theory that eating might forestall him erupting and that continuing would numb my mouth the same way it had my sense of smell, I took another bite, and focused on the discussion.

"HQ called yesterday. Our time is up and since I can't find a way to delay that doesn't involve a strike team burning this compound down with us in it, we have a problem." Liv left off eating and steepled her fingers. Her not happy, but still willing to listen pose. "Not to mention the impossibility of explaining certain oddities in our mission reports, eventually."

I grabbed the water glass by my plate and washed down

soup. The lemon in the glass burned across my already sensitive tongue. "Plus, the whole point in Stavros and I approaching you was to be involved and work out a way to inform HQ, and then Oversight, of what's coming down the pipeline. That's our priority."

Bruce stiffened beside me at the reminder.

I scooped more food, anything to help appease him.

Kimi signed, "You have a plan." Not a question.

"We have to convince the Assessor that Stavros and I are human." I drained my glass in the heavy silence. Acidic water wasn't as painful as more sauce.

Liv finally spoke. "I assume you have some plan other than mentally whammying the Assessor. Which would postpone our getting burned down for a few hours, if that, then when the disparities in their memory show, result in an airstrike on us instead of a plain old strike team."

I breathed around the line of fire burning from my mouth down to my stomach and picked up the glass, forgetting it was empty. "Is there any milk?"

"I got it." Josh frowned at my plate, then grabbed my cup and went for the fridge.

I pitched my voice loud enough he could hear. "HQ has noticed increased oddities by now, whether they're admitting to it yet or not. They've also marked your uptick in missions and volume of species in each attack, despite Stavros and I pre-policing as much as feasible."

I accepted the refill from Josh, taking a gulp, nodding my thanks as the milk washed a measure of the sting away. "With all the chaos, it won't come as an out of the blue surprise when you report you rescued me and one other human from an underground cryptid-run fight club."

As the burn turned to fire ants chewing their way from my lips to my stomach, I downed the rest of the milk and cleared my throat.

Josh jumped to refill it, not asking this time, frowning at me or Bruce. When I checked, Bruce had stopped eating, watching me.

Crud. I picked up the spoon I'd abandoned, scooping up another bite.

Bruce's hand flexed my way, then stopped.

I swallowed, finally not tasting anything and turned back to Liv and Kimi.

Liv's fingers drummed against the old table, in time with her thoughts, and Kimi absently swirled her spoon through the soup, mentally running possibilities and scenarios.

I leaned in. "You are the only people who know sun-tolerant vampires aren't a myth. The Assessor is always only a formality, making sure you all are okay, have what you need, and remember HQ is there if you don't. As long as Stavros and I do what we need to beforehand, we can stand in the sun—I can pull out a beach chair and bikini—or juggle chem-coated knives the entire time the Assessor is here." I cleared my throat again. "They can sit down and watch us demolish a pizza and a gallon of milk." I sipped from Josh's second refill. Despite the pain in my throat, it was difficult to swallow, so I sat the cup down.

Kimi tapped the table, and gaining our attention, signed, "They'll have your last physical on file. They'll expect new scars and wounds."

"You'd have to have enough to sell the disappearance plus additional damage from fights." Liv added onto Kimi's dose of reality.

I steeled myself for this part and pushed away from the table enough to untuck my shirt. I bit the inside of my cheek, because I couldn't angle to only show Liv and Kimi, then regretted the tic, a harsh jolt of pain sparking from the bite and jerking a gasp from me. Josh and Bruce both tensed.

There wasn't anything I could do to soften this reveal. I

pulled my shirt up to my collarbone, making sure the neck was covered and glad of the sports bra. Ridges inflicted by claws ran from one shoulder down my chest. A missing chunk and divots that couldn't be disguised as anything other than bite wounds patterned my stomach, all pinker than they should be. Stavros and I needed to drink again, although the morgue vampire I snacked on should've taken care of this, at least enough that the wounds looked faded.

Kimi was there before I could drop my shirt, kneeling by me, her fingers warm on the lines of scars. I hissed as she touched—more rammed, it felt like—on the raised marks running under my bra. She jerked her hand away, startled as much as I was.

She signed agitated-fast. "When I did the IV, I felt the old marks on your arm from that ghoul in the border town. These, though. You didn't have these before."

"These are from—" I took a minute, the tickle-burn in my throat turning into a cough "—from the night when Stavros and I were attacked. Those don't disappear the way post-infection injuries can."

"They're the reason you have damn turtlenecks instead of tees." Horror tinged Bruce's voice.

I shrugged. "Vampires and necks, right?"

Kimi signed, "You said injuries *can* disappear. Meaning they don't always? But vampires can heal wounds. At least, that's what we're taught."

"If an older, stronger vamp injuries a younger one, then those scar. Assuming the younger vamp survives, which most don't. Some other things can leave permanent damage too."

Bruce swore and I reached for the food, hoping it would stop whatever he was pissed about. He snatched my plate away, then circled the table, grabbing Josh's. My brother lunged up and grabbed the rest despite no one having finished and announced, "Everyone's done."

The tickle in my throat changed to an ache and moved into my chest. I covered my mouth and cleared my throat. Dampness splattered my palm. When I glanced, blood dotted it. I hid my hand under the table and scrubbed my palm on my pants. Something was wrong and I had to get out of here soon. I talked faster. "Anyway, we'll both have scars to show an Assessor, old, older, and new."

"ID?" Kimi signed. "That'll be harder to come by for Stavros."

Yeah, creating a paper and cyber trail for a four-hundred-year-old vampire who didn't exist wasn't exactly cake.

"Hard but not impossible." My voice was turning hoarse. "If *you* create an identity and history of him teaching combat skills to explain how he was able to last in the fighting pits, and a setup for his being kidnapped by vampires in league with human crime syndicates? That's also a trail a skilled enough Company tech agent could follow if questions arose, and culpability if we're exposed by the Assessor. There's no plausible deniability and no claiming you guys didn't know."

Josh came back, balancing dessert plates. The squares looked like tiramisu, but I had no sense of smell left to verify. "I told you, we're in," Josh said, thumping a plate down in front of me.

I felt another cough coming. Things inside my chest rattled, wet and loose. Not eating would piss Bruce off, because rejecting his food always did on an elemental level, and as someone who knew that about him, and did it anyway would read as me rejecting him. But I needed out, now.

"Talk this over and really think about the ramifications." I stood, then wobbled, Bruce catching my elbow. I pulled it free. "I have to go."

When I reached for it, I couldn't access the unlimited boost that should have been pooled in the well inside me, only a scant sliver. Barely enough to get me out the door and downstairs before it gave out and I had to bolt at a human pace across the yard.

I tapped the keypad on our door, and the cough broke loose, violent and impossible to stop. Blood splattered the keys. My fingers slipped, screwing up the code.

Stavros flung the door wide and for the first time I'd ever heard, swore. He grabbed me, lifting me inside.

ruce

JOSH BEAT BRUCE OUTSIDE, already to the annex door by the time Bruce made it down the stairs. Josh tapped the keypad, then drew back, shaking his fingers like he was trying to shake something off. Bruce sprinted and got there in time to watch Josh scrub his hand on his pants. "The fuck?"

Bruce grabbed the taller agent's hand, jerking it into the light. Pink stained Josh's cuticles. When Bruce reached for the touch pad, Josh slapped his hand away. "It's—shit, it's blood."

Bruce's gut clenched. He'd seen the moment Vee hesitated over the stew, then bit her cheek, that shit she did when she was about to do something she damned well knew was stupid. He watched her down the water, then the glass of milk Josh brought. The only time she'd ever willingly drank milk was the occasion another team's C.O. had dared them with Ghost Peppers. She'd been the first to gulp down half a jug trying to kill the burn from the capsaicin.

"Fuck, fuck, fuck." His swearing blended with Josh hammering on the locked door, her brother unwilling to try to punch in the code through Vee's blood. Blood she'd coughed up over Bruce's food, because he'd inadvertently poisoned her.

Liv and Kimi arrived a beat later, Liv's gun out but by her thigh. "What was that?" Her gaze swept Bruce and Josh. "You two know something."

"Vee said that she and Stavros didn't like spiced-up food but this was a stupid bowl of soup." Josh pounded harder.

Kimi pressed in, dug in a pocket, and came out with a square of gauze from her never-ending supply and swabbed it over the pad. She held it out to Liv, the white now stained the dirty rust-red of blood.

"That is more than a dislike of seasoning." Liv holstered the gun.

Kimi shoved the sample into Liv's open hand and then signed, "She said their senses were heightened. I think she must have meant she couldn't physically tolerate spices, probably some other natural and synthetic items as well, not that she didn't care for them."

Her eyes, so like her sister's, widened. "Garlic. Vampires and garlic?"

"That's fantasy bullshit." Liv glanced from Kimi to them. "Or maybe not."

Josh's unrelenting pounding finally produced results. The door opened, the older vamp blocking the entrance. He didn't say anything, the fucking neutral mask he wore firmly in place.

This time, Bruce caught real emotion seething under the facade. Bile rose in Bruce's throat. He had to quit blocking out what the virus had done, admit that Vee was different on levels he hadn't looked at head-on. If he'd accidentally injured Vee due to his ignorance and hurt feelings—

The vamp's attention snapped to Bruce. "You."

Liv eased between them. "Could one of us speak to Vee?"

"No."

"She's obviously not well. Could I check on her? Please?"

Stavros evaluated their group, eyes staying brown yet polar-vortex cold even without vampire add-ons. "She will speak with you when she feels the need. That won't be tonight."

"There's been a misunderstanding." Kimi signed and Liv spoke. "We didn't realize how sensitive she was to certain foods. I promise you, it wasn't intentional. She's our sister, we wouldn't—"

Stavros held up his hand, halting them. "Whatever you may believe to be the truth, I smell only guilt." His gaze nailed Bruce to the sandy ground. The vamp half-turned toward the annex interior, archaic Spanish tumbling out rapid-fire, speaking to Vee.

A cough came from inside. Bruce caught a sliver of chalky face behind Stavros. "Guys." Vee's voice was a whisper and he surged forward to catch it all, to apologize, to demand to see that she wasn't bleeding out. He was jerked to a shoulder wrenching halt, Josh locked onto his elbow, cranking it hard, bringing Bruce up on his toes.

"This isn't a good time, okay? I'll see you in the morning," Vee whispered.

Liv chewed the inside of her lip. "Is there anything we can do? Girls' sick day—ice cream and rom-coms? A couple of new ones dropped on a streaming service this month."

After a hesitation, Vee whispered, "Raincheck?"

"Absolutely. We—"

Stavros closed the door on anything else they had to say.

"Damn it." Liv gave in and swore, then pressed over her

eyebrows, pressing at a headache. "Okay, that did not go well. However, accidents happen. We'll find out what does and doesn't work for Vee and be more careful moving forward." She nodded at Bruce, fucking trying to make him feel better.

Liv motioned to the house. "Vee was right though. We have issues to discuss in more depth and then a decision to make."

Kimi huffed, since they all knew the decision was already made, and calling Liv's bluff.

"Yes, fine. Project Dupe the Assessor is a go. We need to get on with creating a paper trail that doesn't scream *fake* for a freaking vampire," Liv admitted.

Josh waited until his sisters had moved out of earshot, Bruce still in the shoulder lock. "Tell me this was an accident with the food. Fucking tell me it wasn't intentional."

They both knew better. It didn't matter that Bruce had only intended to offend Vee, not harm her. "I fucked up."

Josh let go, shoving Bruce away. "I should let Stavros turn you into his dinner." He got in Bruce's face, bunching the neck of Bruce's shirt in one fist. "Fix this and fix it now. If Vee leaves, we are done. You may think Liv's on your side but she won't forgive you for this either."

CHAPTER 43

ruce

AN HOUR and a feverish burst of inspiration later, Bruce hovered outside the annex door and passed a warm bowl hand to hand. Somebody, probably the old vamp, had scrubbed the keypad clean of Vee's blood. Bruce had punched on the compound's internal video surveillance as he worked in the kitchen, in some vague hope of seeing Vee. Instead, as the sun faded, he'd seen the guy leave for the backside of the compound.

Bruce wouldn't have to go through the vamp to get to Vee. Although, he deserved whatever shit Stavros would've rained on him.

Fuck. Time to quit being a coward.

He slid the main panel aside and keyed in the code to open the intercom. Then almost stalled out because how the fuck did you start to apologize for giving someone the food equivalent of Ebola?

The intercom came on with a soft buzz. "Yes?"

Vee's voice was louder than a whisper now. But the roughness and that painful rasp were laid squarely at his feet.

He cleared his throat. "It's me. Bruce." His pulse ramped up as seconds ticked by. "Can I come in?"

Silence rode the air for another agonizing moment, then he got a tentative, "Sure."

He keyed in his code and the locks clicked. He nudged inside then broke every compound protocol, kicking one of Kimi's decorative painted rocks over to keep the door standing open—for Vee's comfort, not his.

When his eyes adjusted, indoors darker than the early evening dusk, he wasn't the only rule breaker. The god-awful halogens had been hot-wired, none of the usual automatic lighting blasting down to bath the cavernous room in harsh white.

A pool of warm yellow light shone out of the goddamned cage, the chemical-enhanced one they used for hostiles. The bars had been hidden under the blue paisley of sheets from the guest room locker. A string of the fairy lights Vee and Kimi always pulled out for Christmas looped along the top of the sheets.

Vee had turned the cage into a room.

He closed his eyes, drowning in the absolute wrongness of what their lives had come to. He'd hidden enough though. He opened his eyes and stepped to the cage doorway.

Vee sat in the middle of a nest of crumpled sheets and blankets, obviously a hasty bed making job. His gaze traveled the shit room. Her few clothes hung on the bars, the pool of light coming from the gooseneck lamp that'd been in a utility closet as long as he'd been here. A barrel chair that'd been in the office, then the extra guest room up until an hour ago, sat beside the bed. His investigation landed on Vee's pillow, decorated with a faint spray of blood flecks. "Motherfucker," slipped out.

Vee tensed and flipped the pillow over to the unstained side, then shoved it completely behind her. "Is something wrong?"

It didn't take a genius to figure out she meant had the team voted, decided the plan to fool the Assessor was too much effort, and he'd been sent to tell her to get the hell out. Because that was the kind of bastard he'd turned into.

"Kimi's working on I.D." Which wasn't what he wanted to say. To tell her that of course she was staying and that wouldn't ever change. Even the front Liv put up was all for show and he'd damn well known it the second Liv tried to lure Vee into the main house with freaking rom-com's, their and Josh's ridiculous, nearly sacred, make-everything-better go to.

He wanted to tell her he'd nearly lost his mind when he'd seen the roadmap of scars all over her. The ones she'd been willing to show. Which meant there were more, and worse, covered by that turtleneck she had on even now. He wanted to tell her how he'd been thrown back to the night they'd lost her. Shredded seats. Torn metal. Blood soaking the sand. And no Vee, and how that had been the worst moment of his life. Until he'd seen the savage bite marks over her torso and half-assed understood what she'd gone through, and he'd do anything, give back the remission, his career, everything—for her never to have suffered that way.

Vee watched him, wary as one of the feral cats that hung around restaurant kitchens, while she braided her too-long hair into a loose weave. The braid was the one she'd twist together every damn time after they had sex and got to the hunting for clothes stage.

That everyday action punched straight through his chest.

Vee's fingers stilled. She scooted almost imperceptibly

into the headboard, away from him. Feeling like the world's biggest fucker, he held out the dessert bowl and spoon. They had seemed like a sound idea until he stood in front of an exhausted, wary Vee.

Her gaze went from the bowl to him and she nibbled at a hangnail. She caught herself and dropped her hand. "Thanks. Seriously, but—"

"This won't—" *fucking poison you* hung unsaid. "It's milk, egg, sugar, and nothing else. I didn't even add vanilla or salt, in case."

Vee leaned forward. Precariously close to the edge of the bed, and if he hadn't thought it would freak her the fuck out, he'd have grabbed to keep her safe. But right now, he was a bigger threat.

She studied the bowl. "Pudding?"

He caught her nostrils pinching in as she sampled the scent.

"Plain egg custard pudding." The kind his grandmother had made for him when he was hurt or sick. He'd shared the story with Vee, long before they were anything to each other but a polite agent and an annoyed civilian. She'd been so damn enthralled at the novelty of a parent figure providing comfort when hurt, instead of a reprimand and lesson on being a more effective future cog in the killer wheel.

He cleared his throat. "It's still warm. Probably." He held it out again. "It might help. Be soothing or some shit. Fuck, I don't know." He didn't have the first clue how to help her now.

She accepted his shitty offering, cradling it in both hands. Vee held it closer and inhaled. Probably his imagination that it was only the normal inhale of savoring food, not an inhale checking for a trap and poison. "Thank you."

Guilt wrapped tighter and he shoved his hands in his pockets, out of temptation's way, before he committed some sin Vee couldn't overlook, like touching her. Pushing the thick braid behind her shoulder. Pulling the dreary shirt off her and checking the wounds she wouldn't let anyone see.

"So, yeah." He gathered his sorry ass up to leave her in relative peace.

She didn't look up from the pudding, as if this fragile detente might not survive direct eye contact and said, "You don't have to go."

He sank into the chair like his strings had been cut, elbows on his knees. Doing a shit job of blocking out the chair was only there because Stavros had hauled the monstrosity down a steep flight of stairs and across the yard to use as a perch to watch over Vee as she coughed her stomach lining up.

"Fuck." he dropped his head into his hands and scrubbed through his hair.

The clink of spoon on the china stopped. "Fuck, Vee. I'm sorry," he blurted to the concrete floor. "I swear to God, I'll be more careful from now on. I'll measure ingredients with a gram scale."

The bed creaked and the ragged tip of caramel brown braid swung in front of his down-turned face. He looked up into Vee's face where she'd bent double with that unearthly flexibility she'd always possessed, trying to see him from a half-upside-down crunch. This close, the sweetness of the pudding and traces of plain white soap caught him. He dragged in a breath, dragging Vee in, through lungs that felt like they were being crushed in a giant fist.

Her expression was soft, the old C.O. authority she used to wear as naturally as breathing gone, and the new, aloof vamp coolness vanished. Her face held the same open realness as when they used to talk for hours, caught up in each other, the rest of the world forgotten, drunk on being in the same space.

"It's okay. You didn't know vampires reacted this way to certain foods." Her breath whispered across his cheek, caress-soft.

He pressed his eyes closed, and because he didn't deserve absolution, told her the hard truth. "I did."

When he opened his eyes, Vee was across the room, out of her cobbled together bedroom, standing by the exit. Staring at him like she didn't recognize him.

He swiped a rough palm over his face, eyes damp. "I didn't know this, that the food would physically hurt you." He jerked his chin at the pillow. "But Josh told me in passing that spices overwhelmed vampire senses and that you didn't like them. What I did was petty and spiteful and I swear to God, I'll never do anything like this again. Vee, I'm sorry."

She sat the bowl on the bench holding rubber boots and pliers, delicately, with more restraint that he ever possessed. "There's something going on in the cryptid world, and the vampire population is not only out of control, but tied to the other oddities. The team can't handle the increase alone, or find the root cause. Stavros and I can find the source, but not if we have to investigate and handle all the nests at the same time. We have no choice but to work together for the duration. You and I are more than capable of avoiding each other until the situation resolves. Pretend I never came back if that's easier. I get that things aren't the way you'd prefer between us, and so you liked me better when you thought I was dead and rotting in some ghoul's stomach, then alive and not your version of perfect." Her voice was emotionless, each word hitting like hailstones. "Close the door behind you."

She didn't move as he rose and stepped outside. The door *shushed* closed behind him but the click as Vee engaged the deadbolt that had never been used in the team's tenure carried clearly.

Vee

I ZIPPED the foldout pockets in my boots, the left boot shaft holding my smaller coated knife, the right holding extra det cord, and stood. My throat only felt scratchy rough now, and when I put the tight sports bra on, my chest didn't hurt at the pressure around my ribs. However, I'd used up too much reserve in healing. I needed to hunt. Stavros had been right, again. We weren't agents and we didn't execute missions. We were unnatural predators, and we hunted.

I stepped into the morning sun and flipped out my sunglasses. Fuck looking approachable. Fuck wasting energy filtering out the sun.

A lighter shadow separated from the receding shade cast by the compound balcony. Stavros stopped, head cocked and not even subtle about checking me out. This was the first I'd seen of him since he left the evening before, pre-Bruce revelation.

"I'm going after those stupid chupacabra for breakfast." Saying it upped my level of pissed-off-ishness. Chupacabra meant excavating a den, and their blood always carried a nasty, goatish aftertaste.

Without a word, he dug in a bag slung over his shoulder, and held out a gallon sized milk jug. I twisted off the top and instead of dairy, the familiar goat's ass scent shot out. I looked closer, at Stavros' dusty boots and the dirt on his sleeves.

He'd spent the night digging out the chup' nest. For me. So I didn't have to. My eyes burned. I held the equally stupid tears in through sheer willpower, and fuck whoever might be watching, drained the jug.

When I recapped it, swiping at my lips to remove the inevitable blood mustache, Stavros dug in his bag again and shoved a bulging plastic sack at me. I kept my hands to myself and peeked inside, at a laptop—our laptop—plus packages of tiny doughnuts. "I don't know what to ask first."

He plucked the jug away and thrust the other stuff into my hands. "The machine has films for you."

No way had Stavros loaded anything on the laptop. He didn't even know how to turn it on. "Your sister Kimora added movies with tales of love and romance."

"Before or after she raided Josh's snack stash?"

Stavros trained his eyes on the horizon over my head. "Kimora accompanied me into town where I...restocked. These food items are safe for you."

He had gone shopping. He had ridden with my sister. My sister had chauffeured a vampire on a grocery run, alone. Together, they'd created a portable version of rom-coms and ice cream. I kept the weepies at bay, but couldn't stop the sniffle.

Stavros' eyes widened. He snatched my haul and vanished into the annex in a burst of speed and cowardice.

I made a circuit of the yard, trailing fingers through the luke-warm water in Kimi's birdbath, over the back of the bench near it, along the succulents, potted hedge style near the perimeter.

I ended up on the narrow walkway running the back of the building, as the team spilled into the yard. Liv had had them out on one of her morning runs.

They moved in unison, as graceful and coordinated as they'd ever been. When Liv stopped, Josh and Kimi halted a micro-second later. Josh must have snarked at Kimi. She dropped and leg swept him, putting him on his butt. Liv held out a hand to help him up, her laughter carrying.

They didn't need me. A fact I'd known deep inside, from watching them on missions. They'd been flawless. As good, as solid, as when I'd been the C.O. I admitted it to myself now. They had never needed me. I'd hung onto a wisp of a dream, of coming back, uniting us, them accepting Stavros, and me leading my team, to get me through my transition. It'd all been an impossible daydream I'd used to keep me going, not a realistic goal.

Stavros appeared beside me. "You are well?"

Meaning, was I going to leak and snot all over him.

"What happened? After you were turned, and went home to your hacienda?"

"I never tried to return. I wasn't as brave as you."

I snorted, an ugly sound. "You mean you were smarter. There really is no going home again."

"Your family…" Stavros stopped, because he'd known all along, that reuniting was never real but psychological training wheels I used to deal with the transition and what I needed to do to accept my training and my new life.

"Kimi and Josh are trying. Liv may *want* to, underneath all that logic and rule quoting. As C.O. she has to put personal desires dead last though. She doesn't completely trust us and probably never will—exactly how I'd act if the situation was reversed. Since we can't be together, Bruce wants me gone. That's what last night was."

A trickle of anger, cold, calculated, and precise came through our bond. Another first. All Stavros had ever sent me was calm or control, and always on purpose.

Startled, I turned to him.

His face was a study in starkness. "I'm aware." He looked down at me. "We need not reside here. The team has observed us and we have watched them. We know our techniques mesh. You can converse with them by your computer, we will each do our separate sweeps, and meet only for agreed upon hunts."

"My test—"

"You have fulfilled it. Your automatic choice to remove yourself and heal last night instead of punishing those your body perceived as attackers responsible for your pain was above and beyond my expectations."

"Oh." Feeling more numb than victorious had to be a vampire reaction. I ran my thumbnail over the metal pipe rail, back and forth, a dozen layers of paint flaking free to drift away. "Once we've gotten to the bottom of this weirdness, once the cryptid world is back to reliably murderous behavior…"

"We have many options," Stavros said.

I nodded. "Pick someplace new to go. Anywhere you think we'd like, that isn't here. Can we travel? Like, really travel?" Because if I stayed on this continent, I'd keep coming back to the team, watching from afar like I'd done before, and keep reopening that wound.

"The world is yours, niña." He touched my head, a there-and-gone benediction. "I'll start arrangements." With that, he vanished.

The team clattered up the steps, metal ringing. They slowed as one on catching me up here.

"Morning." Even as I greeted them, I studied Liv, wondering if she'd known what Bruce was doing. He'd said that Josh told him about the sensitivity.

Liv only nodded, her ponytail swinging. Josh wiggled between Liv and me, checking me out. "You feel better?"

"I'm good."

He frowned and something darker passed over his face. "Bruce threw out the rest of the ribolita. That shit won't happen again."

"It's no big." I wouldn't be eating with them again anyway.

Liv's phone chirped, a snippet of conversation from the two grumpy old dudes from the Muppets, the new tone courtesy of Kimi, no doubt. "Back in a sec." Liv stepped to the far end of the walkway to take the call.

Kimi slouched beside me, butt against the rail and signed, "How about cashing the movie marathon rain check tonight? I loaded the classics for you, but we haven't delved into the new romantic goodness that is *The Kissing Booth* and *To All The Boys I've Loved Before.*"

I couldn't get no, the smart answer, out. Saying yes to this, with her and Josh, would make it so much harder when there was no brother and sister to watch movies with and recite the cheesiest, most romantic lines with.

I could stay in touch with them, except that was splitting up the team. Kimi and Josh on one side. Liv and Bruce on the other. Any dissonance, no matter how minor, could compromise team performance. Missing one step could end with one of them never coming home.

So, I did the right thing, even as my chest kicked up a new ache. "Thanks for the laptop upgrade, and for doughnut shopping with Stavros. I can only get him to hit vending machines."

She frowned at my evasive answer. "The shopping was his idea. He came and found me, not the other way around."

"Seriously?"

"He's totally a cinnamon roll."

That surprised a laugh out of me. "Not really. Okay, maybe he has a hidden sweet-hero cinnamon roll center. Don't call him that to this face though. I don't want to have to try to explain cinnamon roll boi to him. His dignity couldn't handle it."

"He learns fast."

"Ooookay?" This was my morning to be confused.

"I showed him the alphabet, and he got it after one demo. He picks up every sign that way."

"You two talked?"

Kimi looked entirely too smug. "He'll be conversant fast."

"Hmm." No, he wouldn't.

She pinned me with a suspicious stare.

Josh glanced from her to me, then back, taking his cues from Kimi.

I needed to tell them that I was leaving. They deserved to hear it first, and from me. "Look, guys—"

"That was HQ." Liv rejoined us, cutting off my moment, tapping her phone against her hip. A tick that showed whenever she was thrown a curveball. "The Assessor is coming."

Even more reason to bail ASAP. We could be gone before they knew Stavros and I existed, and let them finalize Bruce's inevitable official Company approval.

"When?" Josh straightened, all agent now.

"Forty-eight hours." She turned back to me. "They really want to eval you and meet Stavros. I'm sure they've already put you both on the roster to spend a few days at HQ and see the therapists. All normal actions for potentially traumatized agents and dealing with PTSD and survivor's guilt."

The chupacabra blood curdled in my stomach. "You already told them about us?"

"I submitted the report yesterday."

"I'll let Bruce know," Kimi signed, heading for the door, an equally excited Josh close behind.

"Holy crap, Liv. That was fast." Way faster than I'd expected.

Her tap-tapping stopped cold. "Be honest. You planned your miraculous reappearance now because of the sixteen-month rule."

Sixteen months was the rule, when a body wasn't found, before an agent was declared legally demised and temporary team fill-ins and promotions become permanent.

We were having *that* conversation. The one we'd both avoided because deep down, we both wanted the same prize. The one I'd once had. The one Liv held now.

I answered in the same vein. "I had a bet going as to whether you'd ever report that I was alive."

We could revert to over-competitive thirteen-year-olds in record time, knowing what we were doing, and still not able to stop. Except this was no momentary dust-up over who had the best hand-to-hand score that week. A spat we'd both forget about within twenty-four hours.

Liv leaned her forearms on the rail, surveying the mountains. I mirrored her position. "Bruce made me promise to hold you together and keep the team on track after he died," she said. "Instead, I've held him together, more or less, and kept the team on track after *you* died."

"Yeah. Hella inconvenient, my being alive. You and Bruce seem to agree on that, even if it is for different reasons."

She gave me a serious look, all traces of teenage squabbling gone. "Don't even. Don't you dare go there. I may be furious you were reckless, devastated you didn't bring us into the loop, and angry that you are blowing Bruce off like it's nothing, but I was never happy about your death. If you honestly think I am, you are more fucked up than Bruce is."

She deserved better than my attitude. She'd done what we'd all been trained to do—step in and keep the people we were responsible for safe. Teams who lost a member, who couldn't recalibrate, those were teams that ended wiped out.

Matching her gravity, I dipped my head to her. "You're doing an incredible job. You're an excellent C.O."

"I know. We're in a good place, finally." Meaning, they'd recalibrated just fine, my absence successfully compensated for. Also meaning my being here again was a potential liability, risking screwing up that teamwork.

She pushed off the rail and went inside, leaving me to wonder for the first time whether my sister or my ex-lover would out me as a vampire to the Company, leading to a death I wouldn't be coming back from. Okay, not death. But only because I'd be valuable as a research subject for the Company.

"This alters our plan." Stavros reappeared. He'd heard the whole thing, even if he'd tried not to.

"It alters *my* plan. I can't disappear now after just reappearing. The Company will either assume I'm infected, or I'm still human but working with vampires. There's only one solution to either problem, as far as they're concerned."

"We must convince this Assessor of our humanity, as well as my worth."

Frustration made me sharp. "I. Me. Get it? This idiot plan was my idea. You don't have to be on the hook. We can convince them you didn't survive. You can leave, right now, and…and continue your work. Go and pack."

"That shall not happen."

I raised my voice, shoving into his aura, sick on adrenaline and disappointment and some worse emotion. "You don't get it. The Assessor will be rooting for us, but they are also freakishly observant. They're meant to be, to find any cracks in a team's foundation, so the flaw can be repaired. Except, we are the kind of crack that *can't* be fixed."

"We have discussed this and—"

"I'm not finished. We talked about jumping through hoops, but we didn't discuss being stabbed in the back," I yelled. Far too loud for his sensitive ears. Too loud for mine.

The quiet was overwhelming. As was Stavros' disapproval, radiating through our bond.

I took a breath and re-centered. He dipped his head in both approval, and command to continue.

"Bruce may wait until the Assessor arrives and expose us, because he hates me now. Unless Liv does it first, not because she hates me but because she's protecting her commission and the team." The admission tasted liked the spoiled blood I'd had to consume once when things were lean. Awful and disgusting but still necessary.

I whispered the rest. "I can't not show up for the Assessor. They'll hunt us to the ends of the earth. They might also eliminate the team, just to be sure. They wouldn't want to, but it's protocol to protect the rest of the Region and HQ."

"Victoria." Compassion colored the simple word.

"No. Uh-uh. Do not *Victoria* me. I'm not done yet. The *'et tu, Brutus?'* risk from Liv and Bruce is on top of us fueling up enough to eat horrid, potentially tainted food and pretend we don't hear things no human should be capable of, or overreact to scents, or I don't even know what. It's also on top of performing in daylight for who knows how many days. The kind of vampires we'll need to feed on...oh my god. Old, old ones. We can't blow them up from a safe distance, and that's the only way we've ever faced any that old and powerful and scary and probably damned well prepared."

"Do not blaspheme."

I paused mid-rant.

Stavros crossed his arms, stern teacher face on.

"Seriously? We're discussing life and almost certain death, and your take-away is my language choice? Only one word from your restricted list, at that? Damned doesn't even always have a religious connotation."

He started to speak, but I wasn't done now either. "I'm the one who pushed and pushed for us trying for Company acceptance. Honestly, my family's acceptance. It's always been about them accepting the new me. The odds of us surviving fighting the caliber vampires we need to drain, then convincing the Assessor, are less than fifty-fifty. Walk away. Please."

He dropped his arms from the stern fold, and some indefinable otherness with them. Left himself real and bare. Even his voice held a different cadence. "Niña, I couldn't save my naturally born children. I *will* do better by you, my created daughter. Come what may of these tests, you'll never be without family so long as I exist."

"But—" my voice wobbled "—but you said we're demons. Vampires are demons and we don't have emotions or families or need real doughnuts. And something about luxuries and our only purpose being hunting. And if I had emotions, I flunked our last test because I wasn't safe to be around."

He sighed, one that held none of the usual exasperation. "You are the most pure-hearted person I have known. When I watch you, I can believe your claim that we are not demons or the damned. Demons can't love and you love your brother and sisters unconditionally." He took a breath that visibly rattled him. "As I love you. I didn't dream I was still capable of loving. God wouldn't grant a demon a second chance and a second family."

He spread his arms wide in a helpless shrug. "Tú eres mi hija."

I walked into his hug, and hid my face in the scratchy fabric covering his chest. I could hardly understand myself between my sobs. "If this is what it feels like to have a parent? It's amazing."

Stavros wrapped his arms around me, my head tucked under his chin, rocking me like I was a kid. His kid. He said I was his daughter and Stavros never lied. "Whatever may come, we face it together," he whispered into my hair. "I am sorry your family rejects you, but I won't."

ruce

As Vee and the other vamp walked in, Bruce bolted from the stool at the tiny two-person bar. This was the spot he'd staked out a few hours before. Right after hearing Vee and the vampire—shit, Stavros—he had to accept who the guy was to Vee. Right after hearing fragments, enough of their argument to stop his damn heart.

Vee honestly thought her sister would stand back and let Vee die. Hell, would facilitate Vee's end. Vee thought *he* would let her be hurt or die.

Once he'd waded through that shit, he'd processed what she'd said about feeding on some old, powerful vampire and come to the conclusion that there was no way in hell he was letting her, her and Stavros, face that nightmare alone. They'd take care of the Assessor preparation, then he'd somehow reassure her that while Liv was right about both of them being messed up, that in no way equated with him ever harming her or wanting her gone.

Thus, plastering his now numb ass to the bar stool, because it was by the only exit to the garage and Stavros' and Vee's ride.

Vee didn't even look at him, her gaze sliding over him, as she started for the hall. "We have a private mission."

"Yeah, we know." Josh, Kimi, and Liv emerged from the hall holding their rooms, weaponed up. They'd heard at least a portion of the same chilling fight he had and had come to the same conclusions.

Vee and Stavros whirled, putting themselves back to back. Waiting for a fight. Vee facing Liv, Stavros facing Josh and Kimi, but most of his attention on Liv and Bruce. The two vampires expecting the worst from them and immediately thinking this was an ambush.

He and Liv needed their asses kicked for assuming Vee was the old Vee, the pre-viciously-attacked-fucking-bleeding-in-the-night Vee. Worse, for assuming she was impervious.

Before Vee had reappeared, he'd been fucked up and heading for an ugly end. He'd lost half of his soul, and everything else, the people and things still existing in his life...none of it eased the torment.

Vee though—she'd lost him, and he'd never doubted she felt for him as intensely as he felt for her. On top of that mind fuck though, she had lost her entire family. She'd lost her career, except being an agent wasn't a career in any of the team's eyes but rather their whole identity. Who and what they were. Yes, he had held friends and family at arm's length, not accepting their help. Vee hadn't had that chance to choose—she'd lost her entire support network, all at once. And Vee was fucking made of connections with the people she cared about.

Worse, she'd become something she'd been taught to despise.

He'd been caught up in his own pain at Vee's rejection of him, or at least, of the role he'd once played in her life. Hurt and confused over being fucking demoted, and not stopping to think about Vee's pain, much less how she had to be emotionally and psychologically broken. Her coping skills and decision process shot to hell. Of course her actions and decision making was fucked. And he'd acted like that was her fault, when in reality she didn't have a damn bit of control.

And he'd failed Liv, too. Not thinking about the impact of her losing her sister, then having to take over being the person who kept the rest of the team together so they didn't end up like their lost sibling. He'd taken it at face value that Liv was okay, when he damned well *knew* she wore a steel-plated veneer over her real feelings.

When he had been damaged, his body and his mindset from the cancer, Vee had been there, giving him the strength to put himself back together.

In return, he'd abandoned her when she'd needed support the most. He'd topped off his self-centered performance by wallowing and ignoring her sister, now *his* sister and one of his closest friends. Liv had damned well watched out for him even as he failed her.

Liv stepped up, hands loose at her sides and making it clear she wasn't going for a weapon. "We assumed you had a lead on this vampire or already had one in mind who suited your needs. We're ready to roll on it when you are."

Vee and Stavros did that thing, Vee pressing into him, not touching, but sharing some message. Whatever the message was, Vee didn't relax. "This isn't a mission. This is a hunt, and it will be dirty and bloody, and basically? It's none of your business."

"Policing cryptids is our business."

"The vampires will be dead before nightfall. There, end of your business."

"Jesus fucking—*vampires*, plural?" Came out of his mouth before he could stop it. The plan was ball shriveling enough when he believed they were taking on a single ancient powerhouse.

Vee didn't speak to him, but to Liv, "Plural. Bye."

Josh took a turn, after Kimi elbowed him in the stomach, sure as shit a reminder they'd been up to something too. "Look, we overheard. You're going after big game. You need a support-team, and here we are."

"We need a support-team we can trust, not another enemy at our back." Vee was obviously done pulling her punches. "Is this a shortcut? You talked it over with HQ? Lull us into a false sense of security, get us in the field, and take us out while we're preoccupied? Nice and neat, and bonus HQ points."

Kimi closed her eyes as if she was in pain.

"Vee, damn it." Liv waded back in. "What I said earlier was out of line. What you said earlier was out of line. None of us want you gone. Yes, I'm C.O., and yes, that used to be your role and isn't any longer, and resentment is normal and we'll deal with it later. Let us help, if for no other reason than you were right about Oversight burning all of us down if they find out about you. You've been here with us long enough to call our loyalty into question."

It killed part of his soul when Vee straightened, shoulders relaxing. That, she believed. That it was about Liv being pragmatic and protecting the team, not about Vee being part of this family and that they cared if Vee lived or died. "Fine, we can strategize. Your office."

She shoved past Liv, headed for the office and the maps, once Vee's, now Liv's. "Let's get this over with. I'd like to have a meal that I'm reasonably certain isn't doctored with the intent to kill me."

"It's a vamp, Vee. It's gonna try to kill you." Josh joined the exodus to strategize.

"Yes, but I expect it to." Vee shoved the office door open.

Bruce angled to go after the crew, and hit a barrier, in the form of a vampire. One regarding Bruce like he was something found on the bottom of a shoe. "Leave them be. You and I are due for a conversation."

Bruce bit down on the automatic "Fuck off." The old vampire had saved Vee as well as been watching out for her this entire time, when Bruce hadn't been able to. He was important to Vee. She'd lost enough—Bruce wasn't adding to that stress again.

For once he chose his words carefully, keeping his pride and ego out of the equation. "I owe you an apology. I owe Vee...hell, there's no way to quantify what I owe her."

"I do not comprehend what my daughter values about you. I have seen wounded, cornered ghouls behave less viciously and with more compassion than you have." Silver haloed the vamp's brown eyes, effect shining brighter with each word.

"I was an asshole." Bruce owned it. He'd never had a problem claiming what he excelled at, or what he fucked up. "I let my shitty attitude take over and took my hurt out on everyone else, Vee included. I will make it up to her, though. You and I don't have to be drinking buddies, but we do have to find a way to coexist. We have caring about Vee in common, and that's a solid start. Tell me what I need to do to help her. Tell me what she needs from us."

The vampire's eyes flickered brighter, like a candle flaming higher. "Your words mean nothing. You're craven and petty. In all my centuries on this earth, you are the one human I have considered killing. Only Victoria eliminating you from her life saves yours. She's seen to it that you won't have another chance to harm her, since I'll ensure she'll be a continent away from your deviltry."

Bruce hadn't thought the knot in his gut could get any bigger, but it inflated by a magnitude of ten. "Another…what the hell are you—"

The team spilled into the kitchen before he could form a coherent thought. Josh and Kimi both gave him a hard stare.

Yeah, fine. They'd tried to bring Vee back where she belonged, and he'd undermined them. This clusterfuck was on him. He nodded at them, accepting his guilt.

Kimi tapped the vampire's elbow and signed directly to him. She was going over their plan and linking Stavros in. Stavros was more of a team player than Bruce had been since Vee came back.

The vampire walked out with the pair, intent on Kimi's conversation. Bruce ran his hands over his face and into his hair, clinching hard enough pain shot over his scalp. He had to get his shit together.

He ducked into the side hall to take a breath and get his head in the right place. Lock his jealousy and being butt hurt away before it caused more damage. At its core, that's what this whole damn thing had been about. His jealousy over Stavros getting to be the one Vee relied on, getting to share this honest-to-fuck transformative experience with Vee.

Bruce knew, *knew*, that it had to have been unimagin-ably hard on her. She also had to have been in as much pain being separated from her whole family and her life as he'd been in while thinking she was gone. Vee would've returned sooner if there had been any way under heaven she could have. He didn't know what went into being a newly transformed vampire. He didn't need to know to grasp she'd had some kind of overwhelming shit to conquer.

He slumped against the wall. Vee and Liv's voices echoed, the freaky acoustics of the y-shaped hall at work.

"We'll work the perimeter. Josh will pick off singles," Liv said, like she was confirming something they'd already discussed.

Bruce stood. He'd take this, a private minute, to apologize again. He had a hell of a lot of apologizing to do in order to begin re-earning Vee's trust.

Vee's voice rode the air, intimate, but weird. "You really have done an incredible job with the team."

"Thank you." Liv's tone was just as off. "It's past time to be honest. Are you going to make a play to take it back?"

He froze. This… he should've seen this. Jesus, he'd been blind.

Liv and Vee had always been competitive. Before Vee disappeared it had been positive, each pushing the other to be better. The easy competition serving as their version of cheerleading, all about building each other up. Now, he felt the change in their dynamic.

"You were right about the timing. I didn't consciously admit it but I pushed my training hard, keeping this deadline as my incentive," Vee answered her sister. "It was this barely-there wisp of a daydream at first."

"And now?"

"I want it. All of it. My team, my position. None of it really matters though. Even if I wasn't infected, and my brain's response wasn't suspect, the team isn't mine anymore."

The scuff of heels on wood stopped, the sisters halting. Vee spoke again. "We're leaving. As soon as we figure out who or what is behind this vamp population shift, and re-level the playing field, we're gone. Stavros and I will stage a believable, fiery death in one last raid. After, there'll be heart-felt speeches and accolades all around, and HQ lavishing brownie points for you guys carrying on so bravely. We're leaving the Americas and you'll never have to see us again."

"Vee."

"Tell me to my face you don't want the C.O. position."

"Of course I want it. I want to keep my team, the family I love, safe. I can't hand them over to this version of you, the vampire."

"Exactly. Let's be clear, here. What I'm saying is, if our mission today is really only about Stavros and I eliminating a nest the team isn't equipped to? And you have the urge to take a shot on us after we do your job for you? You don't need to bother. I'll be gone, you'll be C.O., and your hands can stay clean."

"Do you truly, deep down, believe I would do that?"

"My emotions, which I thought I didn't even have, say no. But we've established they aren't trustworthy. And my head? My head says you are and always will be about the rules. They're the thing that you believe protects teams and keeps civilians safe. Like, your magical talisman."

"You're going to vanish again, just like that?" Suspicion and frustration turned Liv's tone sharp.

"I'll tell Kimi and Josh. But not yet. If you can fake being cool with me being here for a bit longer, I can fake being happy to be here. Deal?"

Liv's sigh carried clearly. "This is so completely fucked up."

Which wasn't a disagreement. It wasn't Liv leaping in to tell Vee she was wrong.

"What about Bruce?

"He'll have to wait to have his *'Yay, Vee's gone'* celebration a while longer."

The knot in his stomach grew to fatal proportions as Vee swept past, Liv following.

He thought he had time and proximity to rebuild trust. A

breather to prove he was truly sorry, and find a real means to show Vee how much he loved her, that he always had, and always would. He'd banked on making up for turning her homecoming into an ordeal instead of the joyous reunion it should have been.

Now, Stavros' cryptic remark made sense. Bruce was on the clock and time might run out before he proved to Vee that this was her true home.

ee

"You sure your intel is solid?" Josh crouched beside me, surveying the estate.

The house and grounds probably hadn't changed much from when they'd been built in the eighteen-hundreds, except for the addition of electricity and paving. The place was all about wealth, but the solid, low-key kind. Something passed down through the generations, not flashy and modern and meant only to draw attention and announce the owner's status.

A flutter of eucalyptus leaves, the grove surrounding the thick adobe and wrought iron walls enclosing the compound on the edge between city and desert, marked Stavros finishing his surveillance and joining us.

"The hacienda has been in the same family since its beginning. That family is also a Master and his nest."

Josh twitched at Stavros suddenly occupying the empty space on my left. "Dude. A little warning."

Stavros leveled his attention on Josh, and I held in a snicker, but not my grin. My brother was about to be the recipient of one of Stavros' teaching moments.

"Vampires of this age give no warnings," he said, severe as a drill sergeant. "This nest has survived by embracing discretion. The Master is old and wise, refuting modern vices and teaching his get to embrace the same restraints."

"No swiping-right, no partying, no social media, or digital footprint." Kimi signed, looking smug as Stavros nodded his approval at her quick grasp of the situation.

"You've known they were here though."

"Sí. Castillo maintains human retainers who also allow discreet feeding, but even through these long centuries he's lived, no deaths and no increasing his nest numbers."

"But now they get hit," Josh said.

"They were always going to die." I shrugged. "Stavros just held them 'til last since they obeyed old laws. *Last* happens to be right now."

"We are the Lord's scourge." Stavros' pronouncement held a frigid, final weight of authority and inevitability.

Kimi shivered, gooseflesh visible, and Josh rubbed up and down his arms. "Sweet dancing baby J—"

I saw the words forming on Josh's lips and caught his eyes, shaking my head hard enough I gave myself a temporary headache. We so did not need a lecture on blasphemy right now.

"You get the human servants. The rest are ours," I reminded them. "Don't hesitate, don't cut any slack. Any humans here are well aware of who they work for, are loyal of their own free will, and thus complicit."

"Yeah, yeah," Josh grumbled, clearly feeling like being

tasked watching humans was beneath him. I glared at Josh. I wasn't sure he or Kimi were taking it seriously enough.

As the morning sun rose, the in-ground security lights blinking off, I dug deep. Grabbing the slippery shadow hiding in the well deep inside, and hauling it out, pulling that power in. When I opened my eyes, the landscape sharpened and brightened. The breeze whispered all the land's and the nest's secrets over my skin.

Purposely I looked at my brother and sister, showing them what I was. I'd seen my face when I dug the power out, skin drawn tight, face thinner, eyes flat silver portals. Josh swallowed, adam's apple working. Kimi's grip on her knives tightened.

Then Josh gave me a quick thumbs up and Kimi signed, "Be careful."

"You too," I whispered.

Stavros and I were gone, streaking over the wall while the rest of the team scaled it, Liv and Bruce on the main gate.

The C-4 blew the huge iron gate in a blast that I felt through my bones. The rev of an engine and squeal of tires followed, Bruce gunning the truck down the drive. The truck was our distraction as Josh and Kimi dropped down on the sand inside.

Stavros and I passed through the barns, horses snorting and shying. We halted at the concrete wash pad. Stavros hooked his claws under the lip and slid it sideways, silent on well-maintained runners.

The scent of resting vampires filled my nose—the always-present taint of human blood, tobacco because someone enjoyed a cigar, and the dusty lavender of modern fabric softener. I followed Stavros down the wide stone steps carved into the basement that didn't appear on any building blueprints, far older than things like courthouses and zoning law.

The affronted hiss of disturbed vampires hit us like a sonic wall. The five in the sitting room erupted from chairs, books and goblets crashing to the floor. The intoxicating perfume of vampire blood grabbed my attention, snapping my head around, fixating on a female vampire. She'd stepped over a broken decanter but had nicked her ankle.

I launched at her. She met me in a leap, claws clicking out. My knife took her hand, claws and all. She shrieked in shock and pain.

The room devolved into the dance of blades, the sting of claws raking through fabric to skin, and the promise of blood. Flashes of color and bone and skeletal faces like mine. Hisses and growls that all ended the same way, life fading from silver eyes.

I whirled in a circle, finally finding nothing else to fight.

I opened our link, locating Stavros. He stood in a side room in front of another vampire. Despite the shredded remnants of Stavros' jacket and the gashes in the other vampire's overly-formal looking clothing, both stood almost at attention in the gore-painted room. Heads high, backs straight. Royal, or regal at least.

When the other vampire spoke, his power laced his voice. Shimmering. Like I should be able to *see* the words, written in gold, appear on the air between us. "I had not thought any of your kind in the new world."

"You were wise to flee your catacombs centuries ago." Stavros' voice was stark, raw steel compared to the other vampire's gilded power. Both old and powerful but in different ways. "You cannot ever escape God's judgment, only delay the reckoning."

"The Lord's judgment or another vampire's addiction to our blood?" He arched a salt and pepper brow. He was tall and sturdy, but hadn't been young when he was infected.

The soft clatter of boots beat down the stairs. I listened

enough to identify heartbeats—Liv's and Kimi's—then went back to the display in front of me. We'd hunted Masters before, none in this sort of close-quarters, hand-to-hand style though. Other than Stavros, this was as close as I'd ever been to a living Master of any significant age.

Like he heard my thoughts, the Master turned to survey me. "She is already almost overcome by the lure of our blood. Bringing a decades-old child along was unwise."

"She has only months, not years, of changed life," Stavros said, no inflection, just a plain fact.

The other vampire's surprise tasted...decadent. As tempting as a Belgian chocolate-on-chocolate mousse torte Bruce had made for Kimi's birthday one year.

The nest Master looked closer, the inspection pressing over my skin. "Extraordinary. Most especially so for one of your *adictos*." He turned back to Stavros. "Why now?"

"We have need." Stavros didn't elaborate.

My attention kept jumping between the team on the landing watching our strange vampire social display, and Stavros and the Master. My stomach growled, and my skin felt too tight, too hot, then too cold. The banked fire too bright. The blood from the female vampire heightening everything.

The other Master glanced at me and made a meditative clicking noise, with his tongue. It had the same feel as when Stavros used my name in the context of *'aha, you're busted'*.

"You would be smart to do as I've attempted. Stay far from this upstart's insanity, and even further from the recruitment efforts. No good will come of altering the balance of power or attempting to jumpstart creation." The Master frowned, his aura brushing and turning pensive against my skin. "Even we cannot hold such power. No one is meant to, human, vampire, or other."

Hairs on my neck and arms rose, a product of basic fear, not vampire powers. *Recruitment.*

He knew something. This Master, and he definitely deserved a capital M, also knew about the weirdness in the cryptid world. We had to talk to him, discover exactly what he meant by upstarts and recruitments. Because both sounded horrifyingly close to organized, in the sense we—the Company—was organized. An entity greater than a mere vampire's nest, no matter how ancient the nest.

The mechanical *click-snap* of a spent magazine being replaced intruded.

One of the team. They weren't ever supposed to be here for this part, and whoever reloaded wasn't waiting for Stavros and me, or thinking of vampire discussions.

The Master's eyes blazed silver at the betraying noise. "If you wish to claim my essence, you will earn it, not cheat with human weapons."

I felt the air shiver with raw power turned loose. He launched for the stairs and the team.

I smashed the female vampire's essence, the virus-created energy in her blood, straight into mine and streaked, landing in front of Stavros. I shoved him back, his stumble also taking the team with him. And kicked the door closed between all of them and this room.

Yelling and swearing erupted, Bruce's distinctive, colorful stream the loudest. Not Stavros though. Through our link, I read both his lack of real surprise and his worry. I knew he'd intended to be in here with me, to finish the fight if I failed, or to stop me if I won and couldn't handle the power. This was as much a test as living near and interacting with my family was, even if it wasn't one we had originally included in the curriculum.

I understood Stavros' plan for me. This was like training at the Academy and winning my position. I had to earn this power, too, and prove I was qualified. If I wasn't smart and determined enough to kill the Master, then I wasn't strong enough to handle the power of his blood. I flipped out the machete and circled him. I'd either come out with the juice and restraint to save us all or I wouldn't come out at all.

* * *

THE MASTER'S blood burned through me. Urging me to drink faster, empty him, and claim the spoils of victory. To take his place. Be done with orders from others and force Stavros to bow before me. For the humans outside to serve me, until their lives one day fed me.

Except…I didn't like human blood.

And the humans outside this room, they were mine, but mine to protect, not to use as food. And at least one of them wasn't healthy, the pulse too fast, another's too slow.

My dislike of human blood had broken the essence's hold over me, and killed off the Master's desires. Mine were the only urges I felt now, dropping me hard back into *my* reality.

I pulled my fangs out of the deceased Master's carotid and focused on my people. Liv and her intensity were first, easy to isolate, her pulse way too fast, upset and in pain. The slow pulse was Josh's, getting slower with every heartbeat. I hooked claws in the door, the wood and iron tearing like rain-soaked cardboard.

I was on my knees by the team in a blink, the sand crunching underneath us, glistening glass-bright, warm air dancing over my head. Everything hyper-real, and painfully beautiful.

The humans finally realized I'd materialized, Kimi reaching for her gun even as the draft my arrival created pulled curls loose from her knot.

Stavros stood between us, hands out like he was asking both sides to take a beat. To think first, not act.

He turned to me, feeling my question slamming through our bond. "Two of the human servants had been out on errands. They had weapons and surprised the team."

Crumpled bodies lay under a portico, one torn mostly in half. Stavros' work. All I cared about were my brother and sisters. Liv had an arm wrapped around her middle. As she breathed, her broken ribs crunched, easily audible to me.

Josh lay too still and blood pooled underneath him. An exit wound tearing the fabric of his tee—the work of a shotgun blast.

"Try to heal them the way the nest Master in Flagstaff did his servant." I caught Stavros' wrist, the contact heightening my plea.

"An offer will not be received well," he said, too carefully.

I stopped and paid attention to more than wounds. Kimi and Liv both had guns aimed at us, even Kimi's face a determined mask. Bruce knelt over Josh, applying pressure and swearing, one long stream of profanity and terror, each word overlapping.

"Let us help. We can do a little to heal him, at least enough to get back to base and the med bay, or call in the med flight." I let go of grudges and competition, begging my sister.

"You don't look like you have our best interests at heart," Liv got out between clenched teeth. "I'm going to need you both to back away. Especially you."

I checked with Stavros and caught my reflection in his eyes. Mine were silver fire. More silver limned my body, an unearthly haze rippling over my skin. My hair blew in a non-existent breeze.

"Niña," Stavros said, equally careful, like a wrong breath would set off a live bomb. "The power rides you. Make it yours. Control it before you're lost to the addiction." His claws slid out, twice as long and deadly as mine. This was the point where I finally put all my training into practice, not giving in to the viruses' changes that tried altering my brain, or failed and Stavros decapitated me.

I balled my fists, going deep inside myself, the grit of sand shifting under my knees and sun beating down on the top of my head fading. The new power looked like mine but where mine was a small, contained thing, a campfire to huddle around, one needing to be watched so that it didn't burn out, the Master's was volcanic. Huge and elemental, capable of destruction I couldn't comprehend, and equally able to create, if directed properly.

I couldn't make the power less, but I could make the container to hold it larger. I touched the cenote I'd created inside me, where the rest of my virus-vampire huddled. Pushing and molding, the well grew, the dark pit opening and becoming bottomless. Finally, the blaze calmed, only the faint hiss of fire meeting water and a haze of steam escaping the well marking my struggle.

I cracked one eyelid cautiously. Then the other. The sun dimmed to early morning normal, the sand just well-maintained landscaping.

"Better?" I chewed at my lip, waiting for Stavros' okay. If this wasn't right, I didn't know what else to do.

"Well done." The pride he hadn't felt when the Master commented on my being so young came out now, personal and soft like a congratulatory hug.

"Liv?" I tried again, daring to look at her.

"Josh was explicit. He doesn't want turned," she said, grief already weighing her voice flat.

"I know and I would never. Stavros would kill me first if I even *thought* to. But we can help you both. Like with Bruce, and he had Stavros' blood for months, and he's definitely still all human. I swear I'm not trying to turn Josh, any of you, or make you into my new vampire team." I said what she was thinking.

She and Kimi shared a look.

Kimi signed, directed at Stavros, "Are you sure it will work the way you intend? You've done this before?"

"I have not." Stavros hadn't wanted to pursue the topic. It skirted too close to turning a human, his biggest taboo.

Liv's gaze speared me. "You?"

"We saw it work." I'd caught the servant and grilled him long enough to discover what I needed to know. It was my and Stavros' second major disagreement.

I rushed on. "We had a nest under surveillance. A ghoul attacked a human, and his nest Master healed a shredded stomach. I know what the Oversight research said, but they were using old samples, and I don't think the virus, or what's important in its DNA, lasts for more than a few hours. With Bruce, he always looked better after I slipped him fresh, not the stuff I had left over for the next day."

"Goddamn, I'm losing him here," Bruce yelled. "Let her try it."

"If he goes too close to death, the blood will only work to turn him vampire," I warned my heart thudding at a sickening rate. This fear of losing my family because I was too far away to help had been one of my living nightmares.

Liv blew out a breath. "Do it. If you can save Josh, do it."

"Stavros has to. I can't yet."

"You remember your promise." Stavros reminded me of the compromise we'd reached after that disagreement.

"I do." That if the blood infected instead of healed, I would end the victim's life on the spot.

He bowed his head to Liv, acknowledging her position. "With your leave?"

Her lips pressed together hard enough they were white,

Liv looked at Kimi, who signed a vehement yes, then me. When I nodded, she said, "I agree."

I flipped Stavros my knife. The chemically-treated edge would keep the wound open longer. He slashed his wrist to the bone and crouched by my brother. I sliced Josh's shirt and tore it away, exposing the extent of the damage. His heart was already missing beats, lips going blue.

Stavros pumped his fist, blood streaming into the wound. I sliced my finger, my blood joining his and pressed Stavros' hand into Josh's ravaged chest.

I twitched at Bruce's increased swearing and Kimi's gasp, while Stavros ignored the drama. His sole concentration rested on Josh, and that delicately balanced point between healing and turning, that I couldn't control yet.

When my brother's heart rhythm steadied Stavros stood, tearing a bit of fabric from his shirt and catching the last of his blood. I got my finger out of the way but left my hand on Josh's bare chest, honoring my agreement with Stavros, holding my breath and praying I was watching healing, not transformation.

Liv's gaze didn't leave me. Despite my promise not to try to take over, create a vampire team, and her agreement, she was in fight mode. The gun in her good hand. At least it was still pointed at the ground, not me.

Kimi scooted over, pressing fingers at the joining of jaw and neck, checking Josh's pulse.

They all started as his lips visibly pinked. The minor damage healed in fast-forward, shallow wounds filling in and scabs forming. The more severe areas knit far slower.

I exhaled, the terror of losing my brother dissipating with my breath. "We should still get him to the med bay because this isn't an exact science. The benefits only last so long. And a second try so soon probably will result in turning. At least, that was the captured servant's claim."

"Fluids," Kimi mouthed. "He's stable enough to move now."

I was in the truck and had it cranked before they realized I'd moved, relief hyping me up more than any virus ever could. I pulled in beside the barn and jumped out. A plastic part in the seats popped and cracked as I laid the last row flat a little too vigorously.

Stavros lifted Josh, carrying him and walking at a normal human pace that allowed Kimi to stay beside Josh, his wrist under her fingertips.

Liv came up beside us, her color ashy but face calm. "Thank you."

"Agents don't thank agents for having each other's backs." The motto we'd internalized popped out before I thought.

Bruce passed by us, hesitating a second before claiming the driver's seat, leaving me and Liv.

"I can, if you want." I held my wrist up and tipped my chin at her ribs. "I can't heal serious damage and save lives like Stavros, but I'm pretty sure I can heal simple breaks. Like, vampires as medics one-o-one?"

Liv studied me like she could see under my skin. "How do we do this?"

I spotted one of the ever-present water bottles in the truck door and grabbed it, then turned my back so no one had to watch me reopen the cut on my finger.

Liv caught my elbow. "If you're slicing yourself open for my benefit, the least I can do is honor that."

I tipped a couple of ounces of water out then cut and dripped blood into the bottle until the water was pink.

When I offered her the bottle, Liv downed it in one go. She capped the empty and tossed it in the floorboard, flinching at either the movement or hopefully, my weak DNA doing its job. Her brow crinkled and she switched from her arm wrapped around herself to minimize movement, to putting her palm against her side and sliding it back and forth over a spot. "That feels…holy crap." She inhaled tentatively. Her pinched expression eased and she took a deep breath. "Wow."

"Yeah, it's weird how you feel the bones moving, right? It totally freaked me out the first time mine healed."

"No kidding. I'm going to say it's worth the weirdness any day."

Bruce laid on the horn and we both jumped, hopping into the truck. He took off in a spray of gravel before our doors closed.

ruce

"Man, this is amazing. Or maybe coming back from the almost dead makes anything taste great." Josh finished off the sea bass, running a finger around the edge of the plate to get the last of the reduction.

"Of course it's fucking amazing. I made it," Bruce grumbled, more out of habit, not giving his friend his whole attention.

Instead, Bruce watched Stavros and Kimi. The old vamp had insisted, in a fucking too-polite to argue with way, on checking Kimi to see if she'd been injured in the fucked up raid, going so far as to come inside of his own volition. Kimi, who usually rolled her eyes and slapped gaming headphones on, thus effectively ignoring anyone who got on her nerves, meaning anyone who dared try coddling her, had let the guy.

Despite Stavros mentioning a training session with Vee,

he still sat with Kimi. Apparently enthralled as she taught him new signs, her mix of ASL and Company.

It was past time that Bruce took a page from Josh and Kimi's book, and worked to reassure and draw Vee back in. He snapped his dishtowel at Josh. "Go see what Kimi's doing."

Josh wiped his mouth and slouched back in the chair. "I can see exactly what she's doing from here."

"Go watch more closely. After you put those dishes in the dishwasher. I'm still not your domestic help."

"You'd think getting shot would buy a guy a day off." Josh rose and cleaned up. He touched his chest where there was a very tender new scar, same as he'd been doing since waking in the med bay and sitting up with only nearly healed wounds and bruises.

"It doesn't. Where's your phone?"

Josh patted the side pocket of his basketball shorts.

"Good. Message me if Stavros decides to leave." Bruce grabbed his phone, shoving it in his pocket.

Josh held an arm out nearly clotheslining Bruce. His voice dropped. "Not until you tell me what you're up to." He glanced at the outer door, and by default, where Vee was.

"I fucked up. Now I'm trying to fix it, so move."

Josh studied him for a minute. "Vee's up to something and Liv's in on it. Which doesn't bode well."

"Yeah, I know. We're working under more than one deadline." Every beat of his heart felt like a tick of the clock, getting closer to losing Vee again.

"If she needs you to grovel, man—"

"I'll be on my knees," he finished for Josh. He owed Josh and Kimi some groveling too. Vee was their sister and his actions had affected their relationship with her. "I'm checking my bone-headed pride at the door."

By the end of Bruce's promise, Josh was nodding along. If Vee were as easy to win over as her brother…but she wasn't.

"I got your back. If Stavros gets through the ASL encyclopedia, I'll convince him talking it out over a beer after a rough mission is a thing," Josh improvised. "Plus, toasting him for his part. There's wine in here somewhere."

"You're going to bond with a vampire?"

The seriousness crept back in. "He didn't have to try to heal me. He could've let me die or try to infect me instead. If I turned, that would've been one more vote for his cause if he was up to something. But he didn't hesitate, according to Liv. The guy is solid."

Before, Josh and Kimi conditionally accepted Stavros as the price to get Vee back. Now it was clear that the rest of the team accepted the guy on his own merits. Bruce would figure out how to tolerate him too, for Vee's sake.

Josh shifted, blocking Kimi and Stavros' view from the den into the kitchen, and Bruce slipped around Josh and outside. He sprinted for the gym. At the door he took a second to pray—that Vee was in there, that he found the right words, that she'd be gracious enough to take pity on his sorry ass.

When he eased in, Vee was mid-form, her eyes closed, flowing through fight movements, her go-to stress release. For the first time he got a look at Vee.

Not a stomach-churning glance mid-fire fight. Not a corner-of-the-eye glimpse in the middle of a busy kitchen, or stolen via the rearview mirror. They were finally in the same room, nothing and no one between them.

On the surface, this was like any one of hundreds of days he'd ended up out here as Vee practiced while he worked on new concepts or his social media accounts before they went inside at the end of the day. Half the time they ended in the gym shower together, practicing another type of physical expression. Assuming they made it as far as the shower, which wasn't always the case.

He caught the instant when Vee realized the person in the gym with her wasn't Stavros. She froze mid-lunge, then whirled. "I'm waiting for Stavros. Nobody else was scheduled for PT today."

"He's busy talking to Kimi. Probably Josh too, by now." As he stepped fully into the gym, Vee stepped back, her gaze darting from him to the door.

"Why are you here?" She eased right. Further away from him, which was a punch in the nuts. "Is this some last-ditch play, since the food didn't work? Are you going to claim I tried to attack you, and hey, no witnesses, so your word against mine, and use that to get Josh and Kimi on your side of the burn-the-vampires crusade?"

"Jesus, no. I'm not—" He shoved both hands through his hair, clinching the roots. "I swear I didn't intend that to be anything other than a meal you hated, like serving Josh anything tartar. Because—fuck, because I'm a dick some-times." He took another step forward.

Vee matched him, stepping back, wary and keeping as much of the room between them as possible. She was slowly circling closer to the door. "Mission accomplished. I don't enjoy choking on my own internal organs."

She took a bigger step sideways.

Bruce shoved backward, his arms spread wide and blocking the door, which yeah. Another dick move. Even before she turned, Vee could put him on his knees, so he told himself he wasn't really preventing her from leaving.

She tensed like he was a dangerous asshole.

"Just hear me out, all right?"

"Unless I physically move you, what choice do I have? Especially since my touching you is probably exactly what you're after."

It was. Not the way Vee thought. Time to talk fast. "You and Liv are up to something and whatever it is, you damn well know Josh and Kimi won't go for it."

Guilt flashed over her face, not able to hide her emotions and one-hundred-percent Vee.

He pointed at her. "You may be a vampire, but you're still a shit liar."

"Here's something else familiar. The issue Liv and I discussed is need to know. You don't need to know. Although, I assure you, you'll like it just fine."

Time to try another tactic to get her to admit what she'd planned, so they could really talk. "All I'm asking is that you not do anything irreversible, and no, I don't have any right to, but I've never been shy about big asks, so why the fuck start now." He crossed his arms, glaring at her to keep from begging. "Whatever batshit idea you two have cooked up, don't do it."

Vee crossed her arms, glaring back. This had always been their version of foreplay, and for the first time it felt like them—real Vee and real Bruce. On the same wavelength, even if that wavelength was one more on their list of hundreds of face-offs.

"Fine. I'll tell you if it'll get you out of my way." The sense of familiarity hit a wall, crashed, and burned as soon as Vee spoke again. "After we convince the Assessor we're clean, and isolate and neutralize whoever or whatever has screwed up the cryptid world, Stavros and I are gone. Coming back was clearly a horrible miscalculation on my part. I'm in the process of correcting that mistake."

He'd overheard her with Liv. Somehow though, hearing this disappearing forever plan directly from Vee settled around his throat in a choke-hold. "No. N.O. Fuck no. We weren't—we aren't a mistake. Fuck, Vee. Take that bullshit back right now." His voice rose the longer he talked until it bounced off the walls. "Do not call us a mistake!"

Vee's eyes brightened, pure human anger and still that fucking perfect brown that got to him every time he looked into them. "There is no *us*. You proved that. Go, you. You always did have to be right."

Her every word hit with the finality of dirt falling on an open grave and terror flooded him. He lunged and grabbed Vee's shoulders, heart hammering hard enough to crack through his chest and leave a bigger wound than Josh's shotgun blast. "This, all this since you got back? It's only a fight. I mean, hell, it's a big one, but we do everything huge—fight, make up, be in love. We are in love. You can't tell me you've forgotten that. It can't be poof, gone, game over."

A moment of hesitation crossed through her eyes. Then her jaw firmed up, whatever the feeling was gone. Vee's eyes turned paler, the alien effect encroaching from the outer edges of her iris until her eyes shown like pits of molten quicksilver. Hot. Lethal.

She lifted her arm and peeled his right hand from her shoulder, easy as breaking a toddler's grip, no matter how tight he clenched. She repeated the maneuver on his left.

He grabbed for her and tried tugging her against him, anything to keep them close and try to get through the barrier she'd built.

With a rip of cotton, his shirt a casualty of his screw-up, Vee broke free. She was across the gym before he could swallow, poised, regarding him like he was some kid in need of a lesson. "You don't know me. Not this me. I guess that's fair though because I don't know you or when you turned so cruel."

He took a beat, looking at her, into her. Past the new reflexes and eyes. She was still all Vee. His Vee, who was as excited as a kid on their birthday simply from wandering a farmer's market, fascinated by the most mundane shit. Who had more reality shows lined up than she'd ever have time to watch. Who couldn't sing a note and rolled down the truck window and serenaded the wildlife anyway. Who was the epitome of loyal, and sacrificed without ever thinking twice when it meant helping someone or saving her family from hurt. His Vee, who he loved with his whole heart and soul.

He readjusted his glasses and walked up to her. "Fuck that. What we had didn't go away." He spread his arms wide. "We had this talk three years ago, when you told me signing on was for life. I signed on, permanently for you and me, and that'll never change. If we have to make some adjustments, and you need more time to heal, that's fine and normal. We will figure it out together."

She chewed on her thumbnail. One small crack in her cool, poised shell. He nudged harder. "This is us. Messy as fuck, but worth it."

"Messy? Are you for real?" Her hand curled into a fist. "Messy. That's what you call it when you were all for Josh taking the sniper shot on me. *You basically told him to.* Then when that didn't work, you tried getting rid of me your way." Dampness pooled in her eyes, not falling, but there.

This shit was his fault. Vee was hurting and it was his fault and Bruce lost the fight to be reasonable and collected. Reasonable had never been their thing anyway. Voice rising to a roar, he let go. "How the fuck could you? How could you stay gone that fucking long? How could you keep us apart that long?"

"I couldn't. I had to—"

He pushed deep into her personal space. "You could've come back for me. Just me, no involving and compromising the team. I'd have gone with you in a damn heartbeat. I don't give one flying fuck about some jumped up virus! Like that could ever change how I felt."

He jerked out of her face, pacing in front of her. The anger, and hurt, and fear all rolling out like a dam had been breached. Blown all to rubble, no patching possible, unleashed and the potentially fatal flood crashing through the breach. "I thought that last round of chemo was rock bottom, the worst time of my life. I was failing you, I was in pain constantly and a burden. Laying there every day knowing that I was splitting your concentration, that you were out on missions and not at a hundred-percent because of me. And if you got hurt or killed...I laid there knowing you might die before me, *because* of me."

He spun back. "Holy shit was I wrong about rock bottom though. You abandoned me. *You abandoned us.* You demanded I keep fighting when I was at my sickest and I did, because hell, you said it. Any time we had left together was something to treasure. I fucking earned the right to be with you and help you fight this damn virus the same way you demanded I fight for you." He punched the training bag, too much hurt to hold in.

The whole room wavered, and his tears only stoked his anger. He did it. Asked the one question he'd avoided, been too damn terrified to ask ever since they learned Vee was still alive. Ever since she had looked through him like he didn't matter, what they'd had didn't matter, and she didn't need anything from him. "For once, tell the truth. Did you ever think of me? Ever? Did I cross your mind once in all those months?" He hated himself for asking, for caring enough that if Vee said no...it would ruin him.

CHAPTER 48

ee

BRUCE'S ACCUSATIONS lit up the gym. The sharp metallic tang of his anger tinting his words bright red, where I could see them for an instant before they faded out of the air.

Had I even thought of him? His question was the key that fit some lock inside of me.

I could walk away and be past him and outside before he realized I'd moved, no matter what he thought of his door barricade technique. I could do as Stavros trained me and ignore my emotions. Ignore everything that wasn't our reason for existing. Do what made sense, think, then act if reward outweighed risk, and fit into our purpose.

Bruce and I had never made sense. But we fit, because parts interlocked, the things the other had filling the empty slots in our own. Now his anger hit me and found the last ember in my soul, when I'd thought I ground them all out over months of starving, fighting, and raw determination.

379

The ember exploded into a fire.

"Fuck you. Really. Fuck you, Bruce." I whirled in front of him, blocking his relentless pacing.

He opened his mouth.

No way. He'd had his chance to talk. I jabbed my finger at him the way he hated. "Did I think of you? All I *did* was think about you and worry. I worried how you'd freak at finding the truck. I thought about how I hadn't gotten to say a last I love you and the stupid, stupid last conversation we had was yelling to each other about not being late for the friggin' dinner. Dinner. Who does that? Oh, and I was terrified the stress would throw you out of remission and that I didn't have any way of knowing. I get that I didn't ask your permission before making my plan and dosing you with Stavros' blood. So, okay, yes, you should be angry about that. I deserve that. But the rest? I was a mutated, parasitic monster, the thing I'd been raised and trained to hate and devoted my life to eradicating. You know, the thing you'd signed on to eradicate too. All I thought about was how I could never trust myself to be near you again and that if I had a soul, which Stavros said we didn't, that would've eaten away at it."

And there it was. The real reason I'd stayed away, then when I was back, kept distance between us. I had hated what I was. I'd finally gotten past that and accepted the new me, because I had no other option.

Bruce and my family had options open. They *didn't* have to accept me. No matter what I'd said to Stavros and Liv, that acceptance was the most important thing to me, and coming back and not finding a place in my family's hearts? I hadn't been—still wasn't—sure I could survive that last blow.

The cresting emotions pushed at me to do something. Move. Yell. Anything. Taking a page from him, I paced. Not yelling but not not-yelling exactly. "Did you know new vampires have to sleep as the sun rises? Like, physically have to, a vamp version of a valium knock out. I had eight hours of nightmares, every day."

Bruce's eyes were huge behind his glasses. Focused on me, maybe seeing me for the first time. This me. The new me. All the things I'd never meant to admit spilled out. "I dreamed of you being sick again because of me. Hurting, dying, and thinking with your last breath that I'd left you willingly. New vampires can't wake up, and we can't stop the falling asleep thing. I knew those eight hours were coming. I tried to piss Stavros off every night. Push him too far in every sparring match, so he'd kill me and it'd stop."

I spun, pacing the opposite way, from the wall of weapons to the heavy bag and back again. Wishing my mouth would stop, but it seemed to be making up for the months of silence. "When pushing him didn't work, I tried to teach my body to wake sooner. Get faster every night. Like we learned to trick our bodies into thinking icy water tests weren't cold and muscles wouldn't lock up. Then, I tried to teach myself to resist the day sleep." Something tickled my face and I swiped my cheeks, drying my hands on my pants. "The whole time I pressed Stavros harder. First to kill me, but when that didn't work, to train harder, be better, learn everything I needed to know faster. Because he said if I could control the virus, I could get out and hunt with him. But really, getting out meant I could see you. I mean, it was from a distance, but I watched you so often.

"Stalker often." I made another wall to bag and back circuit. "I watched you at the markets. Outside training with Josh. Sitting with Kimi and Liv and honing blades."

Instinctively, I dodged at the movement from Bruce's direction, and paced a wider arc past him. "We pre-patrolled the team territory and took out as many threats as I could hunt down." At the bag, I pivoted again, and catching Bruce just standing there, all the supposedly-erased crap boiled over.

The room came into hyper-focus like after beating the Master, my eyes blazing and throwing off enough light that our shadows danced along the walls. I lunged in front of Bruce. "What the hell, B? Were you trying to get yourself killed? Are you suddenly clinically suicidal?" I yelled it, right in his face, my heart thundering in my ears so loud I couldn't have heard him if he tried to answer.

He only stood there, lips parted, which made me madder. "Driving? Fighting? You *do not* fight. What the hell? And that time you drove the truck through the wall and right into the ghoul den? Stavros and I barely got the den alpha that had been hiding in the back before its claws hit you!" I shoved his shoulder.

He staggered. Then fire lit in his eyes and he was in my face. "Yes! Yes, to all your damn accusations. Fuck, yes. You were gone and I was taking out as many of those fuckers as I could until one got me, because you were gone."

He jerked off his glasses, gesturing and arms going. "I went to Temple. Constantly, in every city we hit because you know what? If these unholy things exist, then God has to exist too. Which meant there was a chance we'd be together again after I died."

He swiped at his eyes, but wasn't even close to done. "I'm a son of a bitch ninety-percent of the time, and have enough ego to not only want to be the best chef who has ever picked up a paring knife, but for everyone to know I'm the best. I swear every other word, judge people and pick fights, and I'm an asshole to perfect strangers. But God will forgive a few broken rules, because there's no way he would be cruel enough to keep us apart forever. No God would do that. Not to us."

He finally wound down, his face red, chest heaving like

he'd finished a session with Josh. He closed his eyes for a second, and the fight, his ever-present defensiveness, dropped. "Vee." My name came out as a plea. He leaned in, leaving only a breath of space between us.

I tilted the last fraction of an inch. Our foreheads touched. Feverishly warm skin against mine. The faint char of pablanos from the omelets he'd prepared for the team that morning, and the herbalness of his favorite green tea washed over me.

"I'm sorry," he whispered, voice cracking. "I am so damned sorry. I'm an arrogant, jealous, too-proud bastard. You were all I could think about, every second I was awake, and then in my dreams when I could finally fall asleep for an hour or two."

A sigh whispered over my face, lost and carrying a murky hit of desperation. "Then you came back. Holy shit, Vee. *You came back.* Except you were with someone else, and shit, I know it wasn't sexual, but that almost made it worse. You'd trusted them instead of me. You'd rather turn to them for help and support and had replaced me. My damn pride and ego, and insecurity, that too, they got in the way."

"B?" Insecurity wasn't what I associated with him, or a way I'd ever want to make him feel. His fuck it all and take no prisoners confidence was what I'd first loved about him.

"I wanted you to do some bullshit swearing-you'd-screwed-up and would I please take you back, biggest mistake of your life, grand gesture. Huge and theatrical, like out of one of your damn movies. But deep down, I never, ever thought it'd end up any way but with us together. We'd fight, then be together in the end, tied up with some glittery-assed happy ever after bow. Fuck."

He broke our contact, tilting his head back, eyes on the ceiling and his throat worked, voice hoarse now. "Hearing that petty shit out loud... no wonder all you want is to get away from me. I'm a shit excuse for a human being. None of what I've done and how I've behaved is how you treat the person you love more than anything in the world and that you need more than you need to breathe."

He turned his head away, swiping at his face with both hands. The saltiness of saline rode the cold gym air.

I checked my automatic urge to nibble a cuticle. It felt like we were on a parapet. One wrong move, one misstep, and one or both of us would plummet. This once, fear of what was at the bottom outweighed the usual exhilaration of free-falling.

I didn't know if I wanted to fall as far away from Bruce as possible, or fall into him. Fall into being us again.

Bruce had been...awful. All the horrible things he'd just admitted to. I'd expected yelling and noise when I returned, and having to explain. The louder he yelled and growled the more passionate he was about the topic. The most passionate thing in both our lives had been us.

I hadn't worked out how to deal with seeing him again and there being no us, outside of teammates. I'd purposely stuck my head in the sand. I chewed on the inside of my cheek. Maybe thinking I'd died, and the way I'd died, had damaged Bruce. It hadn't caused cancer, at least not of the body, but maybe of the spirit.

I thought about the way I had returned. If the situation had been reversed...Okay, I still wouldn't have behaved the way he had. We'd been raised and conditioned differently. I would've been hurt that he hadn't felt as though he could trust me though. So maybe his hurt, and yelling, had turned more serious. Darker, and wounded him in a different, awful way.

Being honest with myself for the second time today, I hadn't looked head-on at how I could be only a teammate with Bruce, because I wasn't capable of being *just* anything.

Bruce and I both committed completely, in every aspect of our lives.

I loved my family, my team, my career, and I loved Bruce. We hadn't been like this since before I was attacked. Breathing each other's air. Touching.

We were touching. Without either of us consciously moving, Bruce's hand was over mine. Mine laid on his chest. I dared a look, raising only my eyes, afraid to move anything else.

I had my hand on bare skin, his shirt ripped from his neck to mid-chest, a result of him holding on while I tried to run. His heart beat under my palm, the rhythm I'd recognize anywhere, anytime. The one I'd unknowingly been listening to every night when I tried to sleep, listening until I isolated that familiar thump of Bruce's heart.

My fingertips rested against the sunflower inked over his heart. The one he'd designed, same as the other features flowing from one wrist, over his chest, and down to the opposite wrist. They told the story of his life—the grandparents he'd loved and who had influenced his craft, his career, from refusing to go into law school in favor of a culinary institute, to his promotions and eventual accolades. And me.

I was inked into his skin, too. A sunflower represented me because it loved the sun, the same way Bruce swore I was made for the limelight. All me, even though it was a common flower, a match to my interest in everything civilian and pop-culture that he also swore was mundane but that I couldn't get enough of.

The yellow-gold top of the design and the intricate petals peeked out from the rip. The oval petals my finger was now tracing over, seemingly of it's own volition. Shivers raced over his skin where I touched him, and his harsh inhale followed.

The shivers and noise weren't because he was afraid of

me or hated me. They meant the opposite. This, us pressed together, felt right because he still wanted me.

Something in me cracked. It was the thing that'd begun bubbling when we saw each other in that warehouse weeks before. Then again when I crouched over him after the stupid stray vampire knocked him out and I thought my heart had stopped. It bubbled higher when he admitted he'd tried to hurt me, but had brought pudding because he was sorry.

It, the awful-wonderful mix of emotions, was too much.

I had subsisted on determination and anger and need to survive for so long, ridding myself of all other feelings. Except the feelings hadn't died and been buried any more than I had. Now they were everywhere. As alien and over-whelming as the first time Stavros decreed I should go outside. When I did, the noise in my ears, the air flooding my nose and palate, the moonlight dancing on skin and nerves swamped me.

I couldn't breathe, just like that night. I panicked, needing the anchor of Stavros' aura. I looked up, searching for help. Instead, I saw Bruce with the image of my ashy face and too big pupils showing back from his eyes.

"I don't—" I couldn't squeeze more out. My throat was weird and too constricted. Bruce didn't move his hand off mine. Instead he pressed more firmly over mine, pressing mine against his skin.

One-handed, he undid the last buttons on his shirt, and shrugged it off his shoulders, baring the rest of his torso. "Look. Please, Vee. Look." He dragged my hand lower.

My fingertips trailed over new ink. It was a whole new tattoo. I'd studied every hair, every pore, when I'd hidden and watched him go about his life without me. He'd never been shirtless outside, where I could see him though.

A fresh design interlocked with the vibrant sunflower. An

exact rendering of Bruce's favorite knife, except it wasn't pristine and cared for like the real one. In this version the blade was pitted, edge dulled and nicked. The handle cracked and the metal worn down and rusted. The stem and leaflets of the sunflower wove around the ruined knife, cradling it.

Bruce swore knives picked up part of the chef's soul. He believed they were an extension of the chef, the way legend said a sword was for samurai. A physical reflection of the wielder.

The tattoo was horrible and beautiful and heart breaking. I ran my finger along the tang and stopped where the metal fractured right over his heart. "That's…"

"That's me. And the two of us. This was the only way left in this lifetime for us to be together, for me to physically be close to you," he whispered. "It was all I had left of you."

I finally raised my eyes from the achingly perfect art to his. Everything Bruce felt was written on his face and in his gaze. That he loved me. Even now.

My "Oh" slipped out.

Then his hand was in my hair, sliding the band off and freeing my ponytail. My hair fell in a soft rush, like a shield cocooning us. Bruce dug into my hair with one hand, massaging my scalp and urging me closer. The other hand cupped my jaw, thumb running back and forth over my cheek. The familiar slickness of the old burn that tracked from his palm to the first joint contrasted with the rough, jagged knife scar bisecting the tip of his thumb.

Each stroke coaxed the ember under my naval to flare higher. This was a different fire from the earlier angry explosion. Images sprang to life in my head like a string of Christmas bulbs popping, one after another.

The fierce desire on Bruce's face the first time we got naked. The feel of his solid arms locked around me when I came. The way his nipples hardened when I ran my hand over him. The scruff of his beard against my inner thighs when he knelt in front of me, lips locked around my core.

His lips were on mine now, warm and real. Skilled fingers tangled in my hair, sending jolts of sensation down my spine. The familiar scent of beard conditioner and kitchen herbs filled me as I inhaled. His tongue teased the crease of my lips and I parted them, inviting him in. The sweetness of the agave he used in his tea transferred to my tongue.

Want shot through me, from where our tongues danced to straight between my legs, waking up every nerve and inch of skin along the way. All the emotions I'd only just rediscovered grabbed me, whirling me until I was drowning in a vortex.

I grabbed Bruce as my anchor. He grunted and shifted, slamming us together from chest to thigh, pressing me into the wall hard enough our teeth clacked. A lip hit tooth, mine or Bruce's I couldn't tell, and a hint of blood joined the agave on my tongue.

The raw, primal lust and need met the blood.

Sixteen months of Stavros' warnings erupted, obliterating every image of Bruce and I, painting a macabre canvas of chewed up throats, torn wrists, and blood spattered walls. Scenes we had walked in on during hunts replaced passionate rooftop sex with a pile of mis-matched body parts, drained and tossed aside, and slow, intimate early morning lovemaking was erased by nude victims left where they'd fallen, bites covering every inch of skin.

I froze. There were rules. As much as I hated them, those rules had gotten me out of a cage, given me purpose again, and the control to be with the people I cherished.

Losing control meant death for those around me. Bruce and I lost control in bed, lost in each other and oblivious to rules. The metallic tang still on my lips was the first step on a road I couldn't come back from.

Stavros had admitted emotions were real, and not always bad. No matter what, my losing control was though, whether it was brought on by anger or by lust. Testing wasn't done, and now I'd fail and Stavros would be forced to kill me, even though I suspected it would break his heart to do so.

I pushed against Bruce's chest, and he hesitated. He put an inch of space between us. "Vee? Talk to me."

I slid out of his embrace and away, my back scraping the wall.

He stared at me, eyes focusing, lips swollen. One kiss, and we'd ended up half naked in public. The sensation of drowning hit again. Bruce reached for me, his lips moving.

I couldn't hear over the roar in my ears. One of us had nipped the other, and I wanted more. I couldn't separate sensations and tell if I wanted more contact or more blood, not for food, but for the violence. I had no control around Bruce. None.

The one thing Stavros had beat into me, the thing that kept me from turning into the monster hidden deep in that well inside me was the one thing I lost as soon as I was near Bruce.

I shoved away from him before the monster came out. If it ever did, any human near me was prey. Dead.

ruce

"Vee!" He grabbed for her hand, but caught only air. "Wait." The crash of the gym door hitting and sticking was his answer.

Vee was out of sight before he took a step.

"Damn it!" He'd fucked up, somehow. The horror and confusion painting Vee's face punched him in the gut. He'd screwed up, again, and she had freaked and run. He paced the length of the gym, mentally arranging and rearranging his actions, his words, and her reactions, down to the smallest sweep of her lashes, like clues to solve the puzzle of what this Vee needed. If he could see the bigger picture, he might learn how he could help her.

He played with the possibility she was pissed because she'd responded to him while she was also still furious with him. He couldn't get that puzzle piece to fit. They'd fought, and made up this way constantly. For fuck's sake, Kimi even snarked that it was their brand of foreplay.

He slowed, going back to the nest Master mission and the way Vee instantly assumed the team was ambushing her and Stavros. She'd been quicker to believe they only offered help in order to keep Oversight off the team, than she was to believe her family wanted to have her back on a dangerous job.

Then replayed the conversation he'd overheard between Vee and Liv, Vee asking her damn sister not to take a kill shot on her. He'd wondered then about PTSD, and God only knew what other traumas. This, though...

Vee had physically altered thanks to the virus. As a vampire she was stronger and healed most wounds. That didn't mean her psyche was as resilient as her body.

They'd enjoyed playing dominance games in bed, and sex that left mutually consensual marks. They'd both gotten off on it, because each trusted the other implicitly. At least, they had a year and a half ago. The physical assault Vee had been through since then...he'd already fucking seen she had lost part of her ability to trust.

Jesus. Without that level of trust and intimacy, he could see where he might have thrown her back into a place where getting physical sent her right the hell back to the night she'd been savaged. He'd blocked the door, and put hands on her. He'd all but ground her through the wall, not even asking if he could kiss her.

That felt like part of the truth. But not all of it.

When she'd bolted, she'd run like she was unarmed and a pack of ghouls were after her. That withdrawal had only happened...he freeze framed back through the last twenty minutes. The kiss. That had been the turning point. She'd said she *had* loved him, not that she still did. He'd pushed and bullied and assumed, not giving her the option of saying no.

She hadn't said she wanted him, period. Had the kiss been a test to see if she was still attracted to him?

Unconsciously, he rubbed over the raised scar tissue below his collarbone. The scar was the last visible reminder of his diagnosis, the spot where the port had been. His thoughts went to a string of bad places, and landed on a worry he hadn't had to face since Vee disappeared.

Yeah, Vee had been there right beside him through that medical hell. She had trapped and bled a vampire for him. She had wholeheartedly joined in the drunk celebration after his clean labs, her relief and joy palpable.

Vee was all heart though. Fucking textbook good and kind, and fanatically devoted. She didn't hesitate to do the hard thing. She would have acted in the exact same way if it had been Josh that was sick.

Bruce hadn't brought up marriage. He'd just bought a ring and run with his plans. Vee had talked about the two of them and the future. He'd had a few years of seeing how society's idea of normal and the Company's idea of normal didn't fucking translate though. There were too many things he took for granted that were alien to the team.

So Vee had talked about them, but that didn't necessarily mean them as in a couple and that her feelings hadn't already mellowed to just friends. Shit, or friends with occasional benefits, which sure as hell was a Company norm.

He forced himself to tackle head-first the suspicion that had nagged at him the entire time he was recovering—that the illness had altered how Vee saw him, even after he'd gotten the all-clear. He couldn't shake the insidious voice in his head that whispered that the surgeries, treatments, scars, and nursing had taken a toll on her attraction to him. She'd had to be caretaker not lover

Since her return, she'd glanced at his chest more than she'd looked him in the eye. At his chest, right where the damn port had been. She had just admitted she monitored him once she was free from the cage—he couldn't even wrap his head around the cage part, and that was sure as hell something Liv and the team needed to know about. Vee had fixated on damn medical visits and results this whole time. She'd also said her nightmares were of him ill.

Today, Vee hadn't really freaked until...until he'd stood there half naked, and she had touched him. His brain finally fit the puzzle pieces together. Vee hadn't been mad, or even having some sort of PTSD flashback. Her emotions and reactions had been all over the place but she'd slammed on the brakes after the kiss.

If Vee had been on the fence about her attraction and trying to rebuild their intimacy, the callous way he'd acted and the crap he'd put her through might be the final nail in the coffin of their relationship. His knees gave and he ended up on his ass.

If Vee didn't want him anymore, he had no one to blame but himself.

ee

I KICKED open the sleeping bag and dumped my hastily packed duffel, then sneezed at the puff of dust that greeted me. This was a second-tier safe house, and we hadn't used it before. The cave was at the edge of the team's territory though, and the further away the better now.

I knelt to unzip the bag, zipper tab cold under my fingers, and hesitated. What point was there in unpacking and pretending this was a home? We'd tried that and it had nearly blown up in all our faces.

More neatly, Stavros sat his bag and weapons pack beside his pallet. When he'd felt my need—I'd been projecting as hard as possible—he'd arrived seconds after me by the dug up 'chup nest I'd hidden out at.

He'd taken one look at my face and fangs and silently left to gather our crap. He had returned only minutes later, burning way too much power. His speed silently confirming what I'd suspected. I wasn't in full-on hunting mode but I wasn't completely in control, and couldn't stay in the compound. Due to my failure, our experiment was finished.

Now, Stavros methodically went through the cave, checking the stores we'd left a year before, examining the weapon's cache for tampering.

When the scuff of bags and crates opening ceased, I cut a sideways glance. He stood a respectful distance behind me. Because he understood the dangers of pushing a baby vampire, where Bruce didn't, nor how close he'd come to being another murder statistic for the Company to track.

Stavros finishing signaled the end of my reprieve.

"Is—I think I did fail. Everything is about control, and I didn't lose it-lose it, but I was close. If I hadn't run and if you hadn't been there, I could have." This isolated base would be an ideal spot to execute me.

His nostrils flared, picking up scents or emotions, or both, from me. "No."

"But I—"

"What did he do to you?" Darkness curled around Stavros' words like a toxic vapor cloud. This was the anger of an old vampire.

"We were—" No. I wasn't putting any part of this on Bruce. He hadn't known better. I had. "What happens when you get aroused sexually? What happens when you orgasm?"

If silence had a flavor, and it did, this one was one-hundred-percent appalled.

Stavros finally answered. "We will not discuss this topic."

Umm, yes, we would.

I jumped to my feet, rounding on him. "We should've already discussed this! We discussed—and by discussed, I mean you've lectured in excruciating detail and at great length—on every other situation I needed to anticipate and master reactions to. How could you not have mentioned this one very crucial scenario? All you said was we don't have emotions and relationships and, duh, of course I couldn't with any other vampire, because we're Team Mysterious Vampire Killers. That one-line answer is unacceptably vague." I was displacing on him, and I knew it.

"¡Por Dios! I am your—your father. Enough."

"Parents are supposed to explain sex and sex education to their children." Probably. The Company had classes from early puberty on, but I'd watched enough movies to get that wasn't how the civilian world handled it.

Stavros' response was to become fascinated by the roll of det cord he held. I snatched it out of his hands.

"This is vital information. If you can't get over your uptight Jesuit conditioning, use broad strokes. What happens? Did you lose control at first?" If it was a matter of more training, I'd lock myself back in the cage until I mastered this skill, same as all the others. The ghost thump of Bruce's heart against mine was as real as if it had just occurred. I already missed it. Except *missed* was too shallow a description for the ache inside me.

A mask settled over Stavros' face, and my frustration spiked. If he even tried walking away and pulling that inscrutable bs…

His gaze focused at a point over my shoulder. "I can't answer your question."

"You can. Pretend I'm some random vampire in need of a lesson or that I'm not even here. Talk to yourself. Vampires are social animals and have sex all. The. Time."

His jaw set. "I cannot supply you that information."

I threw the cord down. A loss of control, but it could go on today's tab, along with preparing to physically shake the facts out of Stavros.

He finally looked at me, not at the horizon. Allowing me to see the regret and sadness in his eyes. This was way, way more than his distaste for discussing what he deemed socially embarrassing topics.

I stumbled to a halt as facts connected—his composure, the weariness, and his word choice. *Cannot,* not *will not.* "You haven't...ever? Not in four hundred-ish years? Not once? With yourself even?" Fine, I hadn't masturbated this entire time, but I'd been obsessed with crushing the new part of myself that wanted to fight and kill anything and anyone. Four centuries of absolute celibacy was outside my comprehension.

"Never."

We were *so* very messed up. I'd tackle Stavros' romantic life next, after my crisis. "Other vampires have sex. Hello? We've killed a lot mid-intercourse."

"What did you observe during these glimpses?"

At the shift from normal conversation to lecture mode, I automatically fell into my role as student. I concentrated, meticulous Company schooling, now augmented by the excellent recall courtesy of my new DNA. We really had caught plenty of vampires unaware and engaged in every conceivable position and parings, including a few I still hadn't figured out how to replicate.

I thought out loud, the way Stavros preferred, verbally showing my work. "Vampires have high sex drives. There was lots of variety, but all of it seemed vigorous. Definitely physically demanding."

"Continue. Pay attention to all the details," came his stern response.

I sort of zoomed in on each memory, like zooming in with a camera. As soon as I did, I understood the common denominator. "There was always sharing blood. Blood-play, I guess, since some of the partners were getting bled instead of sharing." Fresh blood perfumed the air at every scene, sometimes the participants wearing it like body paint. Sometimes the entire room was painted crimson and rust.

"Feeding, not sharing," he admonished.

He was right. The blood was never equally sprayed or worn. Awful as it sounded, I thought I'd understood when the victim was human. Of course they were the losers in the pairing.

But looking at the scenes from this new view, at least one vampire was always bleeding for another's enjoyment. Going deeper—it was always older or higher status vampires feeding off of and using weaker vamps.

The worst part was that I never got any hint of intimacy. All I'd ever seen or sensed was hunger, violence, and at least one participants' pain.

It took two tries, but I managed to ask. "So to get off or even get aroused, vampires—us—we tear into each other or into victims? There has to be pain?"

"Crude but accurate."

I licked dry lips. "What happens with humans and vampires?"

"You've observed that as well."

"That can't be all that happens. I mean, not every encounter ends with the human dead." My memories realigned themselves with my new insight, and all but shouted the truth. "Does it?"

"All do, whether it's immediate or after multiple...uses. Perhaps the death was the intention from the start, the sexual acts merely vampires playing with their food and not—"

"Not an accidental loss of control," I finished for him. "Not a loss of control at the moment of orgasm."

"Correct."

"But you aren't positive, are you? You don't know as an

unequivocal fact that the deaths were always intentional, do you?" It hurt to get the words out, especially since I could feel Stavros' belief through our link. He considered orgasm as another intense emotion that triggered our prey drive and was trying to spare me the pain as best he could.

His tone gentled. "No, I'm not certain. Death may be the accidental yet inevitable part of sexual response as a vampire. Perhaps only another vampire can survive the experience." He took a visible deep breath. "Though many vampires also don't survive those encounters. You've observed the high rate of turnover in the nests."

"Pick a human you think is hot, then turn them, have great vampire sex ending in the newbies death, rinse and repeat. That's it. You think that's the reason why there's so much turnover. Not from Company missions, or territorial disputes, other cryptid predators, but stronger vampires using up new recruits. We're parasites."

His head dropped a fraction, acknowledging I'd nailed the lesson. This once I hadn't wanted to.

It wasn't just religious hang-ups, and not existing on other vampires' radar that kept Stavros celibate. If sex meant a stronger, dominant vampire controlling and abusing a younger, weaker one, he'd never stoop to that low.

I studied the feeling, turning it back and forth, examining its form. Then incorporated the truth of what we really were and let the numbness spread through me. "Thank you for always being honest with me."

"Your ability to face unpleasant realities and carry out required actions was the reason I believed you strong enough to infect."

He meant I couldn't erase the murderous necessities rewritten in our DNA by the virus, ensuring we could never be with anyone who we truly loved. But I could survive the training to eradicate my emotions, to erase the thing that would make me want contact with another person. Because for vampires, contact was only another word for death.

Stavros had been right after all. We were damned creatures.

CHAPTER 51

ruce

L IV WALKED INTO THE YARD, Kimi beside her. She flipped her phone around, screen to him. "This message from Vee makes no sense."

Bruce didn't bother checking the screen. He already had a good idea of what it said. Keep him the fuck away from Vee, please and thank you. Maybe asking Liv to explain the breakup facts of life to him.

"Tell her—tell her it's safe to come back from whatever desert walk she took." He hadn't seen her in hours. "I'll make myself scarce. I'll keep my distance." He made weary muscles work, rising from the bench. Feeling tired and used up in a way he hadn't since he'd been sick. "Tell her I'm heading into town and you can have your movie night."

He paused. "Tell her I won't make this weird. That I'd like to apologize if an apology will mean anything to her." He'd use the hours to get his shit together. There was no epic fight and epic declaration of love coming, so he'd take Vee any way she'd accept. If it was teammate only, fine.

"That's going to be fucking hard to do with her not living here anymore." Josh strode in from the direction of the annex, boots hitting the ground hard. He covered the last few feet in a lunge. His fist smashed into Bruce's face and Bruce stumbled back, pain rocketing thorough his cheekbone. Josh hauled back for another punch then hit an invisible wall, choking, Liv's arm snaked around his throat, other hand locked around her wrist. Her knee slammed into the back of Josh's, robbing him of balance.

Kimi's arm now around Bruce's neck, Bruce cough-gasped, fighting for oxygen as she held him in place.

Josh bucked and fought but couldn't shake Liv. His face turned red.

Blood pooled in Bruce's head and he held one hand out, clear he wasn't fighting back and rapped Kimi's elbow with the other, tapping out.

Josh finally rapped knuckles on the ground, conceding defeat.

Liv and Kimi eased up, but didn't let go. Liv's slicing tone cut through Josh's harsh breathing. "Explain yourselves. Josh first."

Josh coughed. From his spot on his knees, he glared up at Bruce. "Vee and Stavros are gone. All their gear is cleared out. The gym door looks like a rabid ghoul bulldozed it. Or like some asshole drew down on Vee and she had to run, again." Josh dug heels in, clearly amping for another round, and Liv tightened her hold.

Brown eyes, so damn like her sister's fastened on him. "Your turn. Explain why this would be an *'again'* situation while you're at it."

Josh didn't give him a chance. "He tried—"

Bruce owned his fuck ups. "I over seasoned dinner on

purpose the other evening. Josh said Vee and Stavros didn't like spicy, and I interpreted that as finicky palates and being divas. I intended to piss both of them off." Horror crept into Liv's expression as he kept going. "I didn't realize it would physically hurt her."

Like that mattered or was an excuse. He hadn't intended to harm her but he had. The result was the same no matter what his intentions.

The one thing he'd never thought he'd see on Liv's face when she talked to him edged the horror out. Pure mistrust. He'd lost Liv's trust. His actions were the cause. Lost Kimi's trust too. She shoved, pushing him away and joined her brother and sister.

"I tried to apologize to Vee after." Tired, he let it all go. "It was a shit attempt and she didn't accept."

"So, you took another shot and took your spite out on her again," Josh growled.

"No! That's—"

"I saw that door. And you out here talking about it's safe for her to come back and keeping your distance." He didn't try to get out of Liv's hold but the look he gave Bruce promised they weren't finished. "I told you we were done if you didn't fix what you'd made a mess of. Instead, Vee's gone."

Liv let Josh go and offered him a hand, pulling him to his feet. She did put her arm out, keeping him corralled away from Bruce. She bent and rescued her phone. Woke the screen and read. "We need privacy for the duration. We'll return two hours before the Assessor's arrival, to brief on last minute details, perform as discussed, then return to one of our bases. Liaising by video is more efficient in the future."

Kimi's hands flew. "What happened in that gym?"

She made the gestures bigger. "Do. Not. Lie to me."

He'd earned the humiliation and more. He spilled the

whole story. "I kissed Vee. I didn't ask and I didn't give her a chance to say no."

Kimi and Liv shared one of those coded sister moments. Kimi signed, "She's fully capable of evading your advances before you finish thinking of them." She paused then added "You are still a raging asshole though. Consent. Learn it."

Liv tapped her phone on her leg. "Elaborate, with actual details, please. Because Vee could disarm and immobilize you before her change, so either something else was in play here or…I don't know yet."

He admitted everything. "I think it was a test. I initiated it, not Vee, but then she needed to see if—" he had to clear his throat "—if there was still anything between us. If she still felt any attraction to me. She doesn't." He took his glasses off, buying a minute cleaning them off on his shirt, squeezing his eyes to keep the tears in because he wasn't doing that out here. That was for when he had the privacy to melt the fuck down.

He replaced his glasses. "That's why I said tell her I get it. Message received. I respect her decision." Even if it carved him hollow. Heart and soul gone.

"Bullshit." Josh's bark carried across the yard.

"Leaving is pretty clear," Bruce growled back. "Let her know I meant the apology. This is her damn home too, and I swear to God I'll respect her boundaries going forward. I don't want her to vanish again, either, you dumb fuck."

"That's not why he's calling bs." Liv held up her hand, silencing them. "Vee's—okay, a vampire, so there's that."

"Learning curve," Kimi added, shrugging. "Almost mastered."

"Good for you," slipped out, snarky and automatic. "Shit, forget, I said that. I mean it—I'll figure it out, too."

"We mean we both could've sworn she still cares for you." Liv put the phone away.

"Yeah, that," Josh seconded his sisters. "Jackass."

And fuck if that didn't make it worse. "She does. Hell, it's Vee. Of course she cares about people. However, that's as far as it goes with us. It started before she—before the vampire thing."

"When you were sick?" Josh's eyes widened. He'd seen the engagement ring. He'd known what Bruce had planned the night Vee disappeared.

Bruce didn't deserve leniency but he silently begged Josh not to say it. Not to whip out that last bit of history. Another chunk of Bruce's soul, laid out for Liv and Kimi's pity.

The guy gave him an almost imperceptible nod. "But—" Josh brightened, grabbing onto some imaginary hope.

"Look, I'm only gonna say this once, then we're not talking about it again." He pointed at each of them. Got various degrees of agreement in the form of a shrug and dubious head tilt. "I have been a jealous bastard ever since Vee rejoined us, wallowing because she didn't swoop in here the second after she woke up as a vampire, turn to me as her hero, and us ride off into the sunset. I've bailed on every chance to have a rational conversation."

"Why would you not want to talk and—"

He held up a hand, stopping Liv. "There's more to it. I worried that having to be a nurse, being the caretaker, seeing all that went with being ill changed how Vee saw me." His hand crept up to his shoulder and the fucking scar. Kimi tracked his movement. "Then after, I tried being romantic the night we got the clean labs and we all partied and ended up half-lit. Then again the next morning. Vee brushed me off both times. She couldn't see me as desirable or what the fuck ever then. Hell, she may not have even been at a point then to realize or articulate it. But she confirmed her results today in the gym. So, there you go."

Understanding softened Kimi's face. "You'll always be fragile to her. Broken."

If it was anyone else, he'd have put them on their ass for the remark. Kimi got it in a way Josh and Liv, even Vee herself, didn't. Sometimes, the people who loved you the most wanted to protect you the most, even if *protect* turned into *restrict.*

"Yes, and none of that's Vee's fault. It is what it is. You aren't going to attempt some fairytale romance bullshit to try to change her mind. We—" he indicated all of them "—are accepting this as the new normal. And making this shit hole a *better* shit hole than the one she's been forced to use or that annex cage. We're making a place she'll be comfortable again. A place she wants to be. We'll make it the Vee version of fucking Disneyland, her happiest place on earth. Despite how it's looked, the last damn thing I want is for her to be unhappy or leave. You got me?"

Nobody disagreed. Kimi had said it—it was still Vee and when she came to a decision, end of story. At least the end of his and Vee's story together.

He wasn't letting his adopted family fall apart, and sure as hell wasn't losing Vee again. He'd clawed his way from a Jewish-Italian kid sneaking around high school Home Ec kitchens because his parents had forbidden anything but AP classes, to a fucking world class chef who wrote his own ticket. He'd beat back the Big C. He wasn't afraid of a challenge.

ee

"We moved the beds back in here, and cleared out the annex," Josh said, hovering like a mother hen. Trying to be helpful, but his emotions marched across my skin like gnats —not painful, but distracting.

I doubted he had the same problem, but Stavros shifted an inch, enough that his aura fell over me. My itchy-twitchiness backed off. It sucked out loud that he still had to do crap like that for me.

"We would've moved them," I said a beat too late.

"We don't mind." Josh hurried past my and Stavros' spot, the two stools at the short bar, while the team sat at the giant table. It probably looked like our position was a statement, that we weren't part of the group.

We weren't, so…

Josh futzed at the counter, then turned and held a mug out, steam wafting from the top. "Coffee, extra cream. It's decaf. We weren't sure if caffeine—" he missed a beat, probably looking for a less divisive word than *poisoned* and settled on "—if it was a problem for you guys and went with decaf out of caution."

He looked to Stavros. "I wasn't sure if you were a coffee person. We have green tea, juice, water."

"I require nothing," Stavros said, the perfect model of professional detachment.

"Neither do I."

"I didn't touch it. Liv made the pot, Josh poured it," Bruce said, like he was reporting a plain everyday fact, where he should've had his boxers in a serious twist over the implication he'd tamper with food or allow Josh command of Bruce's domain.

I couldn't read him. He had nodded to both of us when we arrived, unsettlingly civil and polite. Now he sat midway down the table, not at his usual head of the table slot, but not as far as he could get from us either.

I'd braced for full-on, hulk out furious Bruce, or icy-disapproving Bruce over my bailing when we'd been mid-talk. Mid-kissing. Whatever. Then, this turning into more of his Outburst, Part Two. Instead, he seemed almost bored. Like the gym and our emotional cyclone—and the kiss, that kiss, that had shaken my foundations, proven it was all a flimsy house of cards to begin with—had never happened.

Some things Bruce approached methodically. Thought out in depth, planned, and obsessed over the minutest detail. Most of his decisions were impulse though. That *'What the hell, let's see what happens'* brashness and sense of adventure had been one of the things that had drawn me in.

Which left me considering whether the kiss had been pure impulse. It wasn't only the being a vampire part that was new and different. Before, I had been C.O., clear on my duties, sure of my place, and aware of my actions. I wasn't any of those things any longer. I couldn't guarantee my reactions. Sometimes I wasn't even sure *why* I was acting or reacting to a situation the way I did now. Bruce had called us messy, but maybe there was a limit to his enjoyment of relationship-chaos.

I'd so overestimated what a capable, super-special vampire I was that I'd totally misread his outburst and advance in the first place.

If he was having second thoughts, I should be glad. That made this, and my inevitable leaving, easier. If I kept repeating that mantra, maybe I could force myself to believe it.

"The coffee might help sell the Vee's-a-human idea." Liv stood and poured herself a mug from the carafe—Liv, who considered decaf an abomination—and walked to the bar instead of back to the table, hitching up on the bar top to sit beside me. Sipping the fake coffee.

"We meal planned." Kimi tagged in. "Oatmeal for breakfast. Grilled chicken, clam chowder, white flour bread for the other meals. The Assessor may decide we don't have taste buds, but there shouldn't be anything in the meals that'll hurt you to consume in front of them."

Josh piped up. "We have doughnuts and wine, since we know those are a go."

This was…weird. Wonderful, but weird. I knew Kimi and Josh were pro-Vee. I'd been positive Liv wasn't though, and after the gym yesterday and low key welcome today, probably not Bruce. Definitely not to the extent of producing bland food. That was a sin worse than decaf coffee and our junk food combined—and Bruce executed search and destroy missions on Josh's doughnut and squeeze cheese stashes on the regular.

The weirdness only escalated when Bruce cleared his

throat and spoke. "You can double check every course to be sure." He wasn't talking to me but to Stavros.

I pulled up the vamp-ness from its lonely well and tasted the air, watched Bruce, the way his muscles tensed or relaxed, looking for subtle signs with my hyper-vision. All I got was sincerity. Bruce meant it. He was serving blah food willingly and asking for Stavros' opinion. I had zero clue what to do with that.

Stavros had plenty of ideas, however. Silver circled his iris, and his face thinned, skull showing through nearly translucent skin, lips blackening. A very intentional display of our otherness. A ghost of the display he used on me after I captured him, when he feared I was going soft.

Now he fixed all that unnerving attention on Bruce. Predatory. Chilling. Even second-hand, hairs rose on my arms. "I do not trust you near my daughter. Had I any other recourse, you would never breathe the same air or occupy the same land. You have shown your true nature, as I am now showing you mine."

I braced for an explosion. Bruce didn't take well to challenges or threats on a good day.

Wood squeaked against the worn kitchen tile, Kimi rising and joining us.

She spoke to Stavros. "I checked and tripled checked that no ingredient was in the same family as garlic or any related subspecies, working on the theory there's some compound in it that's incompatible with your physiology, the way our chemical compound is incompatible with cryptid biology. I taste tested that they really were what they're labeled as. I made a list of ingredients and amounts, too." She handed him a paper filled with her sparse, neat writing.

Then she caught his hand, wrapping it in both hers.

The scariest vampire I'd ever met—froze. At a loss, his perfect calm wavering. After a moment, he retrieved his hand. Only to touch Kimi's chin, the way he did mine. "You, I will believe. You are as Victoria—estás del lado de los ángeles."

No one had ever compared me or Kimi to angels.

Stavros turned to Josh. "As are you. You share your sister's bravery and nobility."

The center of my chest ached. A happy ache. My sorta father had adopted my brother and sister, too.

Except emotions still weren't something I could indulge in, despite Stavros signing off on them, because I couldn't trust my judgment. I was zero for two in eliminating them today. I stood fast enough the stool skidded and Liv tensed. "We need to change clothes. Josh you're close enough to Stavros' size, and the Assessor will be expecting borrowed stuff."

My worry about him and Josh side by side had evaporated.

"Can I hit your closet?" I turned to Kimi. She was between my and Liv's height. Close enough.

"Wear your own BDUs." Liv took another sip of fake-coffee. Then made a face and sat the mug the length of her arm away.

"You kept my stuff?" Slipped out, more proof I was far from a master of my emotions or actions.

"Duh. We may have a clichéd sibling rivalry, but I love you and your favorite-skirt-stealing self." Liv looked me square in the eye. Liv, my sister, not Liv the agent or Liv the lieutenant or Liv the C.O.. "I wouldn't let anyone get rid of your stuff, even if they'd wanted to, which no one did."

I couldn't—flat out could not—give in to emotions and hug her. Let the tears burning behind my lids free. "Fine. Where's it stored?"

She frowned at my terseness. "Where do you think?"

As Bruce rose, so did Stavros' power, like ozone before a

lightning strike. Peaking when Bruce said, "It's in ou—my room."

I touched Stavros' shoulder, bringing his attention to me and his power down a notch. "It makes sense. They'll expect Bruce and I to still be a couple." Something I should've thought of. Twenty-four hours. I could perform for twenty-four hours, pretend we shared a bed and life.

Bruce was already heading down the short hallway. The one that only contained one regular room, and the suite, the C.O. quarters. Liv hadn't ousted him despite taking over.

"I set up the extra room as yours, made it look lived in." Josh jumped in, talking to Stavros. "They're nice rooms. Real electricity instead of pirated, king size bed, WiFi. A group shower, but there's endless hot water."

I hated and loved that Josh was trying to sell Stavros on compound living. My stomach twisted into a tighter knot. I had to sit down with Josh and Kimi and explain, once the Assessor left. I shot Liv a look, thanking her for not telling them, instead giving me the chance. Her face was still too open. She glanced down the hall, then to me, and back to the hall that ended in my old room. Josh wasn't the only one trying to sell a vampire on Company living.

Unless it was a trap. Lulling us, waiting for the Assessor and, possibly strike team, maybe already under orders to hold off until then. For the combined backup, to assure we'd be taken alive to experiment on. Especially if she'd shared our daylight tolerance with Oversight. A huge bonus for her, bagging us. I hated the thought.

And hated that I couldn't shake it. Liv's expression shifted, frown winning. I couldn't tell if it was because I wasn't excited or because she read my suspicions.

Josh was still talking, overwhelming Stavros with words and his enthusiasm. "Your room's the only other one on this hall. It's right beside Vee's. You'll be close to her. Able to hear if she needs you." He shot a glare at the back of Bruce's head.

It wasn't my imagination that Bruce hunched, shoulders rounding as he spoke to the guys. "Vee will be safe here. I swear, and I'll keep proving it, as long as it takes."

"Your words hold no value."

"I'll make sure he keeps to it." Josh's tone darkened and he stood shoulder to shoulder with Stavros, the two bonding. Josh was a horrible liar, and worse actor. If Liv had called in Oversight, he didn't know about it. Neither did Kimi. Unless she had hacked Liv's email, for funzies, and now was hatching some too-risky, intricate counter plot to foil Liv.

I rushed after Bruce's retreating form. Better his polite disinterest then this, all the jerking on my heartstrings. Worrying if I'd need to defend two siblings from the third. All because of me, and my selfish need to thrust myself back into their lives.

Bruce already had the door open and had gone in the room. The one I refused to think of in terms of *ours*. I took a deep breath, held more firmly to the hard-won detachment and walked into the heart of my old life.

My preparations were useless. The room was exactly the same. Kimi's swirling abstract rendering of Bruce and I taking up one wall. My framed movie posters everywhere. Not consciously choosing to move, I was circling the room. Fingers trailing over the dresser, my dozens of necklaces draped on the stands taking up all the space. My hairbrush tossed in the center, where I'd hastily pulled my hair up the night I went out to free Stavros, rushing before anyone had time to catch me and ask where I was going.

The unopened bottle of champagne and two flutes on the bedside table, where we had brought them the night before my leaving. And a buzzed Bruce, who'd lost all tolerance for alcohol, falling asleep against me before we could open it for our own celebration.

The shirt I'd had on that evening, a raucous neon tee with *Party Time* printed on the front draped over the locker at the foot of the bed. The shirt I had grabbed from my closet, loving the boldness and cheerfulness, a match to our spirits, delirious with relief and happiness. The room wasn't just the same—it was a shrine. Maintained precisely the way I'd left it.

I wrapped my arms around my middle, holding myself together. When I tore my attention away from the memory lane trip, Bruce stood across the room, bed between us. Looking as lost as I felt.

"Everything you need is in here," he said, voice almost absorbed in the mess of clothes and furnishings, all of our past life. The bed, perfectly made and drowning under all the pop-character pillows, like a giant tangible question between us.

The only new element was the sleeping bag at Bruce's feet. One pulled from storage, completely Company-issue.

I grabbed for the out. "Bed's yours. I'll take the bag."

"Take the bed, Vee. Not a damn bag on the floor."

"I've slept in worse."

"You don't have to anymore. That's the point." Pure frustration laced his voice, volume rising. "Jesus, there's more to life than sleeping bags and squatting in abandoned buildings. We've had this exact conversation before, only this is a hell of a lot lower-rent version." His knee flexed. Precursor to him kicking the snot out of the bag, which would hit the dresser, sending jewelry rattling and bringing Stavros in here, in full-blown over-protective vampire-Dad mode.

I was too young, too slow, and wouldn't be able to intercept Stavros before he had hands and fangs on Bruce. I darted in and snatched the bag before Bruce connected. Which left us far too close together again.

Bruce swallowed, his throat working. "I'm not going to try to crawl in bed with you. I meant the apology last night. I'm sorry as hell about what happened in the gym, and I swear I'll never do that again—back you into a corner, try to touch you, any of that."

His stupid post-gym text, via Liv, basically saying the kiss hadn't meant anything to him. Now though, he sounded as if the promise was the last thing he wanted. Like it hurt him to say he wouldn't touch me.

"I don't…look. I'm getting so many mixed signals, and I'm having a hard time with what's real and what's not." I hugged the bag to my chest. "The vampire thing, I'm not as good at it as I should be, as I thought I was. Not my interpretations or reactions. I don't trust my reactions and you guys really shouldn't either," I admitted.

Not something I'd planned to say. In the moment, it felt like I owed him that honesty, though.

"Vee, fuck." Bruce started toward me then halted, and jerked his glasses off, polishing them. His tic, his way of slowing the action. He replaced them. "You've been a vampire for less than a year-and-a-half. You're a walking miracle as it is. Nobody, expects perfection. I get—" he bunched his hands into fists.

"No, I don't. That's some arrogant bullshit on my part. I *don't* get what it's like. What you've been through, what you're still going through. I don't have any frame of refer-ence. This is what I do know—I want you to be comfortable here. Not just today, but permanently. So, I'm telling you I've got my head out of my ass. As much as I'm capable, at any rate. As soon as this test is over, I'll move into a room in the main hallway. Or you can if you'd rather. Hell, if you and Stavros need to share this room, we'll make that work."

I shredded a hangnail. Weighing Bruce's words. Factoring in his reaction the day before. The kiss. Today, with the special menu and involving Stavros.

Neither of us had ever been into games, or holding off on tough conversations. Except we'd kind of done exactly that since I came back, first because I wasn't supposed to have emotions and being that close to Bruce, and pretending I was fine with it, was too much. Now, because I didn't trust my own read on my emotions, seconding-guessing myself, and because I didn't want to admit we couldn't be together, because getting naked would end in my hurting him. We both also seemed to have forgotten how to communicate. "After yesterday, what do you want? I mean really want?"

Bruce turned to the bedside table on his side of the bed and grabbed a jar. The cuticle cream I always used, battling my bad habit. Now mine healed without outside aid. When he held out his empty hand, asking, I still stepped in and gave him mine.

He scooped the gel into his palm, then massaged it over my hand, spending time on each finger. Callused hands gentle. The sort of gentleness he kept hidden unless someone he loved was in need, or in those rare moments of perfect peace between us.

Head bent he finally answered. "I want you to be happy. There are a lot of selfish items on my list, but what it all comes down to in the end is that one thing. You being happy."

Bruce said I should stay. We'd be in separate rooms. If I had the luxury of time...Stavros admitted he'd been wrong about our ability to care, to love. What if he was wrong about sex too? I didn't need to bite Bruce to get aroused—watching him work, sitting beside him, his hands on mine right now, that was all it took.

I might be able to convince Stavros that staying was the

best way to perfect my control. He would be right beside me, completing training me. With time, there was a chance I could master that part of my nature, all the awful things the virus had altered in my brain chemistry. Stavros could make sure I didn't accidentally harm my family or Bruce in the process, assuming Bruce still wanted an us, not just a platonic, flaky roommate.

"What—" I cleared my suddenly tight throat. "What if I'm not sure what makes me happy now, or how to go about having those—items?"

"Then this will be a safe environment for you while you learn."

I wanted to believe him. More than I'd wanted a C.O. position, more than I had ever wanted almost anything. That exception being him healthy and not in pain again.

The warmth of his hands massaging away my imagined hurts loosened the real question between us. "Once, you asked me where I saw me, us, I guess, in five years."

His hands stilled. "I remember."

"Now it's your turn. Where do you see yourself? Where do you see us? Do we give this a real try, if I tell you it's going to take time before I can really be with you?"

"I signed on for life. I'll be here, planning pop-ups and doing my best to watch out for the four of you."

"Answer the other question."

Bruce finally raised his head. "I don't know what I'm supposed to say. Tell me what will keep you from bailing on us again, and I'll say it."

A trickle of anger snaked through me. "It doesn't work that way, and you know it. You raised hell about honesty. And, you have grounds to, with my dosing you on vampire blood without your consent—"

His anger flared to match mine, and his hands tightened. "I don't give a fuck about that. I was dying so it couldn't get much worse, and I know like I know my own face that you wouldn't have tried anything that would've turned me into a damned vampire."

Realizing what he'd just said, his face lost all color. "Fuck me. That's not—"

"Wow. So much for vampire-me being your thing."

Confusion chased away his anger. "What does that even mean?"

"It means maybe—maybe—you are trying to deal. But deep down, where it really counts, you see me as a thing, not a person. Got it." I jerked free and turned for the closet, and the reason I'd come in here.

"That's bullshit! How the hell can you even think that? Yes, I was a complete bastard before. But have I done one thing, even one, since we talked yesterday to give any credence to that damn idea? Instead, I spent the night putting together safe meals, to get this Assessor bullshit done as quickly as possible, and get *you* back here with me as quickly as possible." Bruce caught my elbow. "That should answer how I feel about you now."

It felt like he was sincere. Like I tasted his truth on the back of my tongue. I half-turned, wanting to see his face, and nearly tripped on the small trash can we kept by the bed. It rattled and fell on its side, and fabric spilled out.

A gray shirt. The one I always slept in, because Bruce decreed it was special, since I'd been wearing it the first time we said our I-Love-Yous. The one that he'd insisted stay here safe, not be risked on jobs, or even regular wear. "Did you do it?"

"What?"

I twisted enough to see his face and pointed at the shirt. "Did you throw it away?"

His jaw worked, but he answered. "Yes, but—"

"Did you mean it when you tossed it? Did you mean to throw it away?"

"Jesus, fuck. Let me explain."

The door banged open. Kimi leaned in and signed fast, "The Assessor is pulling some super-efficient Assessor moves. She called, following procedure, except she's less than five minutes out. Why aren't you dressed? Go!"

"Tell Stavros."

She nodded and vanished.

Leaving Bruce and I alone again.

"Vee."

"Did you mean it?"

Bruce's voice was rough. "Yes. But I didn't do it yesterday. I didn't do it today. It doesn't count."

"Yet here it is, still in the trash. It so counts." I reclaimed my elbow and finished my trip, grabbing BDUs and shutting myself in the bathroom.

I admitted I was a mess. Bruce was equally screwed up and wouldn't admit it. Mess plus mess equaled disaster. The kind my heart definitely wouldn't survive, and that the humans around me might not walk away from alive. Maybe good intentions, Bruce's and mine, didn't amount to enough to withstand reality.

ee

WE POURED out of the house garage and into the yard, stopping only feet in front of the compound gate, the growl of a Company engine already audible even to human hearing.

The Assessors were basically always on an agent or team's side, their inspections meant to cheer a new team on, or if there were issues, isolate them and provide resources the team could use to get back to optimum performance.

Each Assessor was also able to work unilaterally, and their decision was final, though. Plus, there was the whole *hey, now a vampire* thing to conceal. Acceptance today wasn't a given, if Bruce and I couldn't get our crap together enough to be in the same room for more than five minutes.

There was also the Liv issue. I was reasonably certain she hadn't done any sort of deal, selling us out to Oversight. However, if things went badly and the Assessor became suspicious? I could see Liv going on the offensive, outing us in order to save the team. She wouldn't want to, but analytically, trading in me and a vampire she had no real history with, in order to save the entire team, was the logical, correct move.

At least Liv and I had agreed on going on the offensive and taking the high ground, being transparent and welcoming, hopefully insuring the tone for the visit.

In this case, that translated as all of us standing in the bright morning sunlight, temperature already hovering near eighty. Starting out as clearly helpful, and totally non-vampire-ish, and hopefully subconsciously making the Assessor even more open than usual.

Stavros had spent the evening before memorizing his new identity. The hardest part was his archaic diction, better now thanks to non-stop online tutorial videos.

Kimi had set him up as Bolivian Special Forces, the military service accounting for his ability to survive, the location explaining his accent. The upheaval in the country made it difficult for even the Company to easily access records, another layer of protection for us.

The Hummer, used in place of common SUVs and only by the Assessor division, rolled through the gate and stopped not quite inside, back of the vehicle just past the gate. Tinted windows obscured the occupant.

"Form up," Liv and I said at the same time.

I drew a breath and stepped back, an inch behind her. We couldn't add leadership tension to this exam or we were sunk before it began.

The team came to parade rest. Stavros on my end. Bruce and Josh in the middle, Kimi on Liv's end. I had a moment of shining pride. This was my family, proud and strong. Even with only the minimal weapons, sidearm and knife, they projected lethal competency.

Liv met my eyes and I saw the same pride in hers. She gave me the tiniest smile, more a slight crinkle of her eyes. It hurt my heart, worse than an actual claw or bullet to the chest would, to think she might want me dead or in a Lab cage. I begged her, a one-sided wordless plea, not to turn on us.

The click of locks disengaging broke my and Liv's silent back-and-forth conversation. Like they were synchronized, vehicle doors opened in unison. Doors, plural. Standard procedure was one Assessor. Two meant this so wasn't the usual easy-peasy, supportive interview.

For whatever reason, Oversight already viewed us as a threat. That was why they hadn't given us more than a few minutes notice. They were suspicious enough that they hadn't even fully entered the compound on seeing the team lined up and waiting.

Josh swore.

"Steady." Liv's low command didn't carry past our group. "An additional Assessor changes nothing."

Theoretically. Assessors weren't simply desk agents. They were also the best of the best. Our elite. Perfect scores in classrooms, evals, and labs, on the range and in the gym.

In sleek, high-tech looking jackets and multi-pocket pants instead of standard team BDUs, their attire was closer to what Stavros and I fought in. Theirs was probably the newest version of Kevlar though, fang and claw resistant. Assessors had access to tech and weapons even the teams didn't.

The taller of the two, a woman maybe a decade older than us, stepped forward. "Commander Muñez."

"Ma'am."

A team wasn't supplied beforehand with the name of the Assessor assigned to visit.

That the one staring out at us still elected not to introduce herself or her partner sent a chill of recognition through me. Without names, they were the Company's version of Stavros and I. The ghosts that policed their own.

I wanted to reach for Stavros' aura, his reassurance and calm. Doing that might put everyone at risk. If anyone had created a means to detect a vampire's psychic powers, it was Oversight.

At the crook of her finger, the Assessor AIC, Agent-In-Charge, signaled her partner to join her. He stepped beside her, face as expressionless as hers.

"Sir." Liv gave him the same deference.

She'd always been better at deftly handling the politics. Now, Liv dipped her chin, seemingly asking, but in reality taking control of the situation when she said, "I'm sure you'd prefer to get started as opposed to wasting time. May I?"

The Assessors watched Liv long enough for the pause to turn awkward. Finally, the woman answered. "Report, Commander."

Liv had already sent detailed reports. Meaning this was pure cross-examination. I had completely miscalculated today's purpose. Far from being here to aid us, this visit was meant to trip us up, get us flustered if possible, and open us to contradicting our previous reports.

All our neat little standing-in-the-sun tactics and special meals were useless. There was no innocent until proven guilty with our Assessors. Today it was guilty until proven otherwise.

Stavros and I had memorized Liv's detailed accounts. I tuned out Liv's voice and risked it, stretching my too-new, too-weak aura as far as it would go. Then pushed harder.

I felt Stavros shift. He'd caught me, but didn't reprimand or attempt to shut me down. He tacitly agreed with my take —we now had enemies in front of us, and potential betrayal behind us.

I didn't feel duplicity coming off Liv or Bruce, didn't hear her pulse or heartbeat speed up. Liv was naturally that cool under pressure. Bruce's pulse was always fast, full of life and passion.

Of course, I'd already made the mistake of believing I was some perfect vampire princess-prodigy, and been spectacularly wrong. Liv and Bruce had sworn they were on our side and wanted us here. But the shirt in the trash? That might be closer to the truth, after all.

I scooped, drawing from the thing inside of me, even as a measure of inner balance left at my recklessly using up power. I concentrated, searching for that first hint, Liv's scent changing as she decided turning us over to the AIC was the more strategic move. Searching, to give me even a split-second advantage. A second to get Josh and Kimi out, make sure they weren't drawn into our fight, losing their position or worse. A second to tag Stavros, and run.

Liv's recital drew to a close. The AIC gave a tiny nod and Liv motioned.

Stavros stepped forward, hands behind his back, at parade rest.

"Husiy Villca, Bolivian Special Forces, ma'am." Stavros gave his name and rank, coming to full attention, every inch a soldier, down to the tone of a lower ranking officer addressing a superior.

My turn. I took two paces to put me even with him. "Victoria Ramirez, Region Two Company agent one-one-seven-four-three, ma'am." It burned up my throat worse than Bruce's ribolita, but I added, "Former Commanding Officer, Southwest Region Two, Division Two."

The AIC's gaze, eyes the hard blue of marbles, drilled into us, then settled on me. "And what are you currently, Former Commanding Officer Ramirez?"

The answer rolled out, an integral part of me, and the rest

of my name, my inner identity.

"I am an agent and arm of the Company, loyal to my team, serving as my superiors direct me, the protection of civilians from cryptid threats my first purpose." I prayed she didn't sense the weakness in my answer. I *wanted* to be Company, an agent, a shield against all threats non-human. But if my team and sister didn't accept that, then what was I really?

From her tone, the Assessor held the same questions. Her gaze went from me to Stavros and back. "We are to believe you both engaged in, and survived unscathed, a mixed vampire and cryptid fighting pit."

Definitely not a question.

I caught the hem of my plain black turtleneck, untucking it and pulling it over my head, left in only a regulation sports bra. Beside me, Stavros did the same, leaving him bare from the waist up.

Waves of fury and grief buffeted me, Bruce's clearest.

Mounds of scars ringed Stavros' neck and arms, especially at the bend and across his stomach, easily identifiable as bites. He was old enough to have healed the chunks and claw marks from the windigos gutting us, and the wounds from the vampires' bullets and knives during the desert ambush. He stood unashamed, giving me the strength to do the same.

I came back to parade rest. New and weaker, I had more souvenirs of that night. I wasn't trying to hide anything. Not the mound of scars over my shoulder where one freakishly huge, out-of-control windigo had latched on, shaking me like a terrier with a rat, cracking my shoulder joint. Not the long, jagged lines running from one side of my neck, over my throat and continuing down my torso from claws attempting to disembowel and shred me. Not the bites on the other side of my chest, as vampires had jockeyed for a spot to strike.

Not the crisscrossed mess of claw marks across my back. "We survived, ma'am."

Dirt scuffed behind me, Bruce flinching, but his fury cresting. He might no longer see me as human and an equal, but his heart was also as large as his ego. I hated that this display was hurting him.

I didn't get any emotion off either Assessor. Only a clinical, "Arms out" command.

The male Assessor, the AIC's lieutenant, sat a small case on the hood of the truck. He came out with a medical tourniquet and syringes. Twin vials and a palm-sized device took up the bottom of the box.

Vials full of our chemical solution. The device pre-loaded with a sample of my DNA, from our files, information input either at birth or the moment we were brought in as infants. They were preparing to check for anything other than my base DNA sequence, anything other than human, for me and Stavros.

If things went horribly sideways, this was where it would happen.

Kimi had pulled out a new personal project. Refining synthetic membranes that mimicked human skin. The Company used a less realistic version, laced with chem, when an agent went undercover. It was meant to entice a creature to bite, thus poisoning it.

Kimi had repurposed the concept. Her creation was one piece over our skin, a few CC's of blood next, then another piece of membrane sealing the pocket closed. Stavros had them at neck, elbows and wrists. My throat was too thick with scar tissue to allow for a membrane, so I only had elbows and wrists.

The blood in my decoy was from the last of my pre-vampire med kit, blood each agent donated, stored for emergencies in the base's med bay. Stavros had generic male human blood. He'd stooped to hitting campus during a blood drive, and distracting a healthy looking guy long enough for Kimi to steal a sample.

The syringes were small and the tubes smaller still, the analyzer only requiring a drop to sequence. The synthetic skin blended perfectly with ours.

I presented my arm. The tourniquet tightened, above the bend of my elbow. The Assessor lieutenant worked quickly, needle puncturing faux skin.

As blood filled the syringe, a wave hit my aura. A ripple growing to a tsunami. A shockwave, carrying the same hints as the Master I'd consumed.

"Incoming vampires!" My warning still hung in the dry air as Stavros' aura fanned out, searching for more information, for a direction. Liv didn't argue, hand going into her pocket for the gate-control fob.

Streaks erupted from either side of the gate. Vampires, auras older and tasting of the Master. They sprang from where they had burrowed under dirt and sand, just outside our wards and alarms.

My aura shivered as theirs shot closer, familiar but not.

They weren't as ancient as their Master, but they were far older than any others I had fought. They felt like but not like us. And...full. They had fed from other vampires, recently and recklessly, as much as they could stomach.

Stavros threw open our bond, showing me what the combination heralded. The vampires would burn, but way slower than normal. They could fight in the sun. Long enough to take the team with them as they died.

Liv's thumb tapped the fob. The gate activated and rolled on perfectly maintained tracks.

Feet from closing, keeping vampires out and the team in, the gate hit the Hummer. The truck's rear panel not fully inside our lines. Motor screaming, as it tried closing. The gate rocked the truck a precious few inches before grinding to a stop. Every alarm in the compound sprang on, flashing lights, the ear-piercing wail of breached or malfunctioning protections.

The Hummer roof dented, one vamp landing on top, two others flowing by on either side.

"They're here for revenge. They will not stop." Stavros' voice rose over the siren.

The vampire on the truck crouched, silver fire lighting his eyes, face spectral. "We are justice for our Master and nest, vulture."

"Only death awaits you here." Stavros speech fell into his archaic pattern, all trace of the modern gone, eerie growl under the words.

The other vampire laughed, tone bitter and hopeless. "We choose to die free, not fall to the abomination that is coming for all of us. We aren't those weak fools willing to be recruited, sacrificing their nest mates in hopes of escape,yet met with death and ruin anyway."

Sun shone off the speaker's cufflinks, hanging onto a shirt stained with old blood, rips in what were bespoke dress pants. The other two vampires circling him non-stop thanks to too much blood, the vampire version of too much caffeine, were equally beat up. They'd tangled with someone or something already.

All the action happened between human heartbeats.

The Velcro-rip of weapons torn from holsters hit the same time as the lead vampire's last words.

A bullet jetted past my head, shot originating from behind me. From the shitty small caliber H and K's, all we were allowed during an Assessor's visit.

The new Master flexed his hand in command, and the two circling vamps whipped around. Speeding toward the team.

The Master launched, as his siblings tried penning us, like wolves on a hunt.

"Go!" Stavros aimed at the Master, intercepting him mid-leap, claws lashing, blood spraying like rain.

The Assessors' sidearms, larger caliber, cracked in response. I spun, racing for my family.

I dropped, sliding and sand scouring bare skin, kicking out, taking the female vampire aimed at Bruce and Josh. It twisted, viper-fast, swiping a new row of furrows down my shoulder. My backswing took half its face. Silver eyes, madness shining through, fixed on me, even as Bruce and Josh emptied rounds into her.

She got a claw-hold under my ribs, flexing hard. I slammed my linked hands into her, shattering her hold. We rolled over and over, fighting like animals, a tangle of snarls, claws and teeth. Smoke rose off her, the stink of slowly heating flesh coating us.

My rib gave, in a loud snap. I pulled on Company training instead of relying on vampire tactics alone. Digging my shoulder into her, flipping her. Slamming a knee in her stomach, pinning her. I slashed across her neck, Josh's blade sprouting from her eye a second later. I scissored claws together and her neck bones cracked, head rolling free.

I swiped my face on my shoulder, scrubbing blood off, searching for my brother and Bruce. They stood protectively over me, Bruce in a shooter's stance, practically straddling me. Josh bent to jerk his blade free, his attention going past me. "They're pinned."

I rolled to my feet, rib grating, and came up facing Kimi and Liv. The third vampire, the one that looked more like a mountain range with legs, circled them. Slow for a vampire, but faster than humans anyway, darting in and out, testing their defenses.

Bullet holes decorated his chest and back, blood dripping

and mixing with the sand, where Liv emptied her clip into him. The hem of his torn shirt smoldering as his skin reddened. He fought the way the other had—oblivious to pain and survival. On a suicide mission.

As the smolder turned to flame, he laughed, held his arms wide and sprang at my sisters. Aiming to take them in a mockery of a bear hug, trapping them against him as he burned.

"Separate. Down low," I yelled.

Liv and Kimi split at the team shorthand.

Kimi dropped, knives out, twin blades lodging in one of the giant's knee, then rolled free. Liv whirled in a deadly dance, putting herself inside the vampire's arms, but ducking low and slicing his hamstring on her way out. Martyr-like recklessness or not, hamstringing was basic physics.

The giant lurched, his support gone. Liv and Kimi hit him from the side. The vampire listed, and they closed in on the other side and kicked the back of his damaged leg. Finishing shattering the kneecap.

Liv tore free as the vampire swayed.

I leaped, landing on his back. Riding him as he went down, rearing back and then smashing my claws down between his shoulder blades. Breaking through his back, through ribs to his heart. My momentum kept me moving, punching through his heart, and imbedding my claws deep into the dirt underneath.

Smoke boiled off the dead monster, and I choked, coughing. Hands closed around my upper arm.

"Easy," Josh barked, saving himself from an instinctive defensive slash.

Another strong pair of hands grabbed my wounded arm. Bruce, his heart rate increased to stroke levels. Him and Josh getting me off the dead, flaming vampire. My claws and arms came free with a sucking noise.

Pain screamed along the exposed skin of my hands and arms, already blistering. I sucked in enough air to snap, "Form up!"

Josh and Bruce went back to back with Liv and Kimi.

I whirled, searching for Stavros. He was locked against the last vampire, the leader. It wasn't as old as Stavros, but it fought with the mindlessness of a fanatic. I recognized the look. Heedless of its survival, living its last breath, using it to kill as many of us as possible. Like an agent taking a last doomed stand.

Bullets peppered the sand around the death-duel. The Assessors, their chem rounds splashing on impact, spraying both vampires. One round in the strange vampire's side, torn flesh blackening.

A matching spot on Stavros' stomach. Not poisoning him yet. But pulling more of his reserves, trying to heal him. Sapping bits of his speed and sun proofing.

All his focus on the fight, his aura was open. I felt prickling, like the start of a sunburn, along his bare shoulders. Leaving him and the other vampire too evenly matched.

The pair spun by, close to the Assessors, who flowed apart, jumping to each side, saving themselves by leaving a cleared path to my team. Then the two came back side-by-side, smooth as glass. Facing us and poised to take everything in front of them out, vampire and human.

Smoke spirals lifted in the air. Thickened, wreathing the vampires in a dirty fog. The pair of spinning vampires heading right at Bruce and my family.

Stavros stumbled, losing his grip. Arm now freed, the vampire slashed at Stavros. Who bent backward, nearly doubling over in an effort to evade, but his footing slipping. The new Master closed in, fire licking around his form, the stench of his burning hair lodging in my sinuses. He'd turn them both into a funeral pyre if he got Stavros in his grip.

Stavros felt enough of my intent, his alarm spiking the air. Calling my name as I launched at the attacking vampire. I hit bone and muscle, but at an angle, too far sideways for a killing blow. Claws wrapped around my ribcage, digging through on either side.

Pain blossomed and the old Master's stolen power exploded out, trying to heal me. Robbing me of mass. I wobbled, too light, unbalanced.

Stavros whipped upright, behind my attacker. Too far away still. The vampire was already pulling its claws out of me, inch by inch, considering me done for while over my shoulder, its mad gaze locked on Bruce and my brother and sisters.

I grabbed the vampire's elbows. Used the last of the strength its Master had lent me, ramming its claws deep into me, hitting bone. Pain blackening the edges of my vision. Keeping it stuck to me, as blood ran down my sides, my legs wobbling.

Bone claws, twice the size of mine appeared on the other side of the vampire's head. Stavros locked onto its skull. Twisted hard, bone crackle-popping, lifting me along with the vampire. Blood splashed my face as its head tore free.

Stavros' hands shot out, grabbing me, pulling me loose and off, leaving bits of me on the dead vampire's claws. We fell, hitting the ground in a sprawl of pain and heat. Our harsh breathing roared in my ears.

I still recognized the familiar click, and thump, of a spent magazine dropping, followed by the solid snap of a new one fitting in place. I shook my head, flinging blood and gunk out of my eyes.

The AIC stood square, gun trained on Stavros. Her lieutenant on one knee, scope sighted on me. Their faces were pale, but determined. "Sun tolerant vampires."

If they fired, and the bullets tore through me to the team behind me…

I laced my hands on top of my head, but rose. Painfully slowly, giving the team a bit more cover and talking the entire time. "They didn't know. I lied to the team and I messed with the blood tests and scanners to show we were human. Liv, the team, none of them knew what I was."

"What we are." I amended my statement as Stavros mirrored me, rising with his hands on his head. Guilt replaced some of the blood and power I'd lost, centering and weighing me down.

Stavros was in this position because of me. "They're innocent. Run their blood, their DNA. Hit them with the chem solution and you'll see, they won't react."

I nodded at the testing case, or at least where it had been on the truck. "The team will pass. Do the hypnosis thing and a psych eval. They're all Company, and not compromised."

I pushed my aura, thin and weak. Pushing at Stavros to go, run, be safe, burrow in the empty chupacabra den until dark. Not to die because of me and my needs.

Instead he took the half step to put himself even with me. "We are no threat to humans."

Red flashed from the lieutenant's weapon. Laser sights. If I could see myself, there would be a red dot on my forehead, same as on Stavros'.

Sand squeaked. I stumbled, a body ramming my back, pushing and making a space between me and Stavros. Liv elbowed through, facing the AIC. She shucked her tee, leaving her in a sports bra, a match to mine. Showing unblemished skin, showing she hadn't been bitten. "The Company motto is human safety first, at any cost to ourselves. Which Vee and Stavros have done, again and again. I've watched them save people, save kids, get torn up in the process. Look what they've done here today."

"They were saving themselves, due to some vampire war they started." The AIC wasn't backing off.

For the first time, Liv didn't play ideal soldier. "Open your damn eyes. They could have bolted before we blinked. Instead, they're willingly standing here. Be real—you can tell he's an old, unbelievably powerful vampire. He could've gotten into our heads in a heartbeat. Instead, they're torn up, literally burning up, yet still standing here." Liv held her tee out to me.

The last of my doubt turned to dust. My chest ached but because it was cracking open, draining out the last of the jealousy and fear, obliterating the last of the emotionless wall I'd cultivated. The last hurt gone.

This was my family. My team. I had their backs and they had mine. I pulled the shirt on, cutting some of the sun damage.

Liv shoved her abraded, bloody arm in my face. "See? Amped on adrenalin, badly injured, yet they are in full control. This is Victoria Ramirez, my sister, and a loyal agent. She is doing exactly what a true Company agent, a C.O., does, protecting her team."

"You have one chance for yourself and this team." The AIC's words lashed out, full of revulsion. "Be a Commanding Officer. Do not allow emotion to ruin your judgment, and fail your team."

The creak of Liv grinding her teeth reached me. "Vee is a good soldier. She is loyal. So is Stavros. You saw them fight. They can do things no agent is capable of. They are assets and they don't touch human blood, ever."

The AIC cut Liv off. "She *was* an agent. The other is a stranger and vampire, undoubtedly the one responsible for her infection, and intent on infecting the rest of you next."

I saw the tightening of the AIC's shoulders. The determination firming her jaw, set on taking out Liv. After her, Josh, Kimi, and Bruce.

The world came into that alien hyper focus. My hair lifted, power I thought was all gone rising. I'd kill the Assessors before they touched anyone here. They were worth breaking Company and Stavros' laws. He could kill me after, fast and clean. Liv could spin the story, blame their deaths and mine on the dead vampires, keeping the team safe in the end.

Stavros' voice rose, regal and authoritative. "It's as you say. I am a stranger."

He eased in front of Liv and I as he spoke. "I am an asset though. In my arrogance, I believed my role was to kill the demons, those such as what I became. To be the warrior of God, his scourge on earth. But that belief was only my ego daring to claim I was His weapon. Perhaps God in his infinite wisdom allowed my creation to serve another purpose. I had forgotten humility, giving myself a grander purpose than I was worthy of, until now. I am older than you can imagine. In my centuries I've encountered every creature of this continent. You see that I am able to live under the sun. I will give you all my secrets. You will use me to further your research, giving you advantages it would take you years to divine otherwise, if ever. You will use this to kill the demons. I only ask that you spare Victoria and her family." He never glanced at Bruce. Not giving away what I'd done, how he had saved Bruce. Not putting Bruce in the Assessors' cross-hairs.

The AIC's gaze landed on me, fury underlying the disgust now. "You betrayed your training and every oath as a commander, telling a monster about research aimed at saving untold agents' lives."

"She did not." Stavros frowned. "Your secret research is less secret than you know."

The AIC's finger flexed on the trigger.

A compact, angry human tornado blasted past us. "Jesus fucking Christ, get your uptight tunnel-vision head out of your clenched asses." Bruce, in all his swearing glory. Arms spread wide like he could shield all of us.

"Are you joining in pleading a useless case?" Disdain dripped from her words.

"Fuck that self-sacrificing, martyr bullshit."

Kimi and Josh flanked us, creating a wall of support. My eyes burned, and not from the sun. This was us, in synch, my team again.

Bruce glared. "Let's talk more about secret labs, unregulated experiments, diverting government funding, and collusion with big pharma. And that's only what I know about personally. There's sure as hell worse skeletons that I don't. Yet."

"I warned Oversight. We should never have expected a civilian to understand, or to prove trustworthy. You have no concept of loyalty or sacrifice."

"You know what civilian celebrity chefs *do* have? A cult following and a fuck load of well-connected friends in the media." Bruce crossed his arms, legs spread, standing his ground. He was magnificent.

He also wasn't done. "Might want to hold off on your kill order. Yeah, I know how the Company thinks. Kill first, write a report later. This situation won't go away that easily. I've compiled a packet—names, dates, locations, photos. A shit load of videos. It's just waiting to be set in motion. Lift one fucking finger to harm Vee or these people, including Stavros, and that bomb goes out to news editors, TV anchors, bloggers, and every social media platform. Oh, and my fans. I lost a few over the last year's hiatus, but there are still three-point-one million, as of today's count. Because if I don't check in? It automatically sends."

Kimi snapped her fingers, a sharp pop in the loaded

silence. Everyone's attention achieved, she signed, "Chase as many potential avenues as possible to block the information leak, but the story *will* get out. Then there will be an investigation. One that asks what happened to the whistleblower."

I flexed my hand, calling claws out. Ready if they turned a red dot on Kimi after realizing her self-care fun included deep-diving in files she shouldn't be able to access.

She was in her element though. She elbowed Liv, and Liv picked up the conversation. "The Company coming to public attention will be problematic, but only a short-term inconvenience. We both know that."

As C.O., Liv had access to the same briefings I'd had, was privy to the fact that there was a contingency plan, an elaborate, meticulously orchestrated one, in place for the time either cryptids or the Company were outed.

Bruce snorted. "Whatever PR plan you've got? There will be an entirely different kind of shit storm if your reveal goes down this way. Painted as a cut-throat cult, murdering civilians and suppressing information vital to public safety, to protect yourselves. Your asses will go from being humanity's heroes to its villains." Bruce's speech had the ring of truth because he hated what we did. He saw it as them using us, not valuing agent life, and always would.

Liv's tone was calm, matter of fact. "If that happens, we risk no longer being the government's golden child. There are already factions that resent our autonomy, as well as our bottomless funding. We will lose our ability to set our own rules and act outside of government and military authority. If we aren't dismantled altogether, we will end up under the thumb of bureaucrats with no clue what cryptids are and can do, or what agents need to effectively counter them."

I wanted to cheer as my sister's clinical rundown lit up the AIC's decision. Instead I tucked claws away, tamped my aura down, and pulled myself into parade rest again. Reasonable. In control, as I addressed the group. "The Company's policy is humans first. A Commanding Officer's is humanity, and her team, first. I have to conclude that as an autonomous unit within the Company, the Assessor's mandate is similar, except to Company and Oversight first. Acting rashly today will undermine that mandate. It skirts treason."

The AIC was destined for TMJ and veneers if she didn't stop grinding her teeth. Liv gave me a side-eye. Apparently, I was doing well enough though.

I put my good-C.O. face back on. "What Stavros just offered, the secrets of vampire culture, their potential for healing, our ability to move about during the day—I truly believe those are invaluable. I also support Oversights research initiative. There are older, stronger vampires than even Stavros out there. Only Stavros and I have the ability necessary to identify and isolate them. We can go places human agents can't. We will bring in the specimens and intel the Company needs. We are already integrated seamlessly with the team. This team can be a new clandestine tactical strike team, a specialized unit for Oversight's needs, while also fulfilling its duty as Region Two's team." A shadow team within a shadow organization.

"You are a vampire. You can't possibly believe you have a place in the Company or that we are foolish enough to think you wouldn't put your needs first."

I was, but that wasn't my only identity. Not anymore. It was just one more title to add—sister, agent, C.O., bad karaoke singer, and significant other, hopefully. "I was born Company and I will die Company. Stavros wasn't born into our order but he is also a solider. His only objective for four-hundred-years has been killing every vampire possible. I didn't choose to become a vampire. But I can choose how I use the changes that happened to me. I choose to continue protecting the people under Company protection, ma'am."

"As do I." Stavros gave a respectful nod to both agents. "I will swear whatever oaths you require, and fulfill them to the best of my ability. So long as they do not violate the oaths I made to God."

I couldn't read the AIC. My aura too thin, her control too good.

Liv cleared her throat. "If you dispose of Commanding Officer Ramirez, and Stavros, you will have to dispose of me as well." The clear, resolute gaze she trained on them was impossible to misinterpret or doubt.

Josh and Kimi moved shoulder to shoulder, Kimi's even with Liv's, Josh's with me. Bruce at the end. A wall of trust and acceptance.

"You'll be forced to eliminate the entire team," Liv amended.

I made a last try. "If you ever want us gone, all you'd have to do is drop a word within the vampire community as to what we do."

The male Assessor, the lieutenant, was frowning, furrows between his dark brows. Maybe open to hearing what we were saying.

I took a deep breath. Stavros said to keep it secret. I had hoped to use it as a bargaining chip. Instead it was our last-ditch play. "Once word gets out that we feed on other vampires, and only other vampires, that it gives us heightened abilities, our execution notice is signed. Only a few Masters know it's possible and they don't share that information. It's the one pact they all came together on, overcoming territory and power plays."

For the first time, something other than anger gleamed in the AIC's eyes. Speculation, and hope, maybe. She mentally re-shuffled the deck, slotting in this new information, what it might mean. How to use it and us to Company benefit. "You feed on your own kind. That's how you're standing here, impervious to the sun. You aren't some mythical new being, the virus mutating to a more lethal form."

Not really. Heat already prickled along my scalp and uncovered arms, another layer of pain added to the burns from wrestling with our attackers. Stavros had locked down on his aura again, but simply looking at him, the reddening along his forehead, was enough.

The lieutenant spoke up. "You are telling us you feed from your own kind?"

"They aren't my kind." That sharp protest slipped out before I thought. It echoed across the desert.

I took a deep breath. "Stavros taught me. I've never had human blood. Neither has he. We never will."

Liv added, "We've watched them. They've feed solely off vamp targets, and other cryptids in a pinch. If they were lying they couldn't keep up that façade for this length of time without starving."

"It's true," Kimi signed.

The lieutenant's finger relaxed a fraction against the trigger. He kept eyes on us, but spoke to his superior. "Oversight is still deep in plotting out potential new approaches. Perhaps now is the time to finally implement new techniques. This could be a field trial."

She actually took her attention off us for a heartbeat. "By recruiting monsters into our ranks?"

"By allowing an agent with an exemplary record to attempt to reintegrate with her team in an effort to combat new threats." Sadness wafted off him, his grief bringing a second-hand lump to my throat. "We've lost ninety-percent of two teams, and half of another. Why not let vampires take the hits instead of our brothers and sisters? If the vampires fail, it doesn't matter. Either way, Oversight will gain more real world data."

Half a team gone. I'd known about the one with Jace, our

brother and Josh's twin, and then Matteo's shortly after, another year-mate. The other had to be new, within the last week. My stomach lurched, wondering whose team it was. Who didn't make it.

"You're entertaining this idea?" The AIC's demeanor lost a portion of its aggression. The guy might not be leader, but she valued his input.

"This Region's mission rate is one of the best in North America, and its improved in the last month despite an increase in missions." He shrugged, a hint of weariness in the line of his shoulders. "Logistically, if we bury this team, there's no one to replace them. The newest cadet grads…" He shook his head.

The grads trained with a team for months, or longer, and had to have that supervising team's C.O.'s approval before the grads being assigned their own Region Division. Kids fresh out of Academy would be slaughtered.

Liv and I exchanged a loaded glance. We'd both done turns as Instructors. Kids were so not getting killed on our watch.

"Poppers." I addressed the Assessor. "Fit Stavros and I with poppers as insurance."

Bruce swore, low and creative. I picked up fury from him, but over it the sour tang of terror.

Poppers were chips inserted in captured lower cryptids, who were then released in hopes of them leading a team to their burrow or nest. They also provided basic readings on the subject's body chemistry and condition. All Company lab rats had an expiration date though. When the subject's usefulness ended, the chips were detonated in a mini blast either at the heart or brain stem, depending on where it had been inserted.

Thus, why they were dubbed poppers by everyone but the Lab crew.

If the blast didn't kill the creature, the targeted load of toxin it dumped in the subject's system would. If the creature tried clawing, chewing or cutting them out, same outcome.

"Fit me too." Josh stared the AIC down. "Vee might gamble with her own life, but she'd never do it with mine."

"Josh, no," I whispered.

"You'd do the same if I was the one with a target on my forehead."

The soft swoosh of skin against composite was the guy lifting his finger from the trigger to rest against the guard. "This is the loyalty the Company strives for. Maybe I am crazy, but vampires have no loyalty to anyone but themselves, and no restraint once blood hits the air."

The AIC watched us. Layers of calculations going on behind her blank mask.

The crows that hung out here and were the bane of Bruce's existence came back, doing their harsh call-and-response.

The sun picked up intensity, a patch of sweat dotting the back of Bruce's neck.

Across the bridge of my nose already hurt like a bad sunburn.

"Put your damn shirt on," Bruce growled. Glaring first at the AIC, then at Stavros, who did as he was told.

Proof he was hurting worse than I was. Even with my power almost drained, tangible emotions swirled thick around me. Company-bred determination from by siblings. Anxiety and resolve from Bruce. A mix of amazement, weariness, and caution from our unexpected ally. Finally, comfort and the good kind of warmth, directed at me from my team.

The minutes ticked, sun brighter, Bruce amping up by the second. Soon he'd explode into action.

I reached hard for Stavros. If the vote went against us, I

could grab Bruce and Liv. Stavros could take Kimi and Josh. Except we had nowhere safe to go and couldn't make it far if we did, with our ability evaporating with each heartbeat.

"You'll be monitored."

I jumped at the AIC's curt announcement.

"You, personally, will be monitored." Her hard gaze pinned first me, then Stavros. "Your team will be as well. You will do your usual status reports, as well as detailed weekly reports to Oversight. You will do detailed reports no later than two hours after each mission, as well. Your phones, base computers, and other devices will be monitored."

She paused, attempting to stare Bruce down. "You'll all submit to random bio-testing. Ramirez, you will be held responsible for him, and his actions."

Him being Stavros. Better than *it* or *vampire*.

She continued her checklist. "Any deviation from reports and testing, or refusal to submit DNA as well as any other samples the Lab may deem necessary, will result in termination. Any increase in your locale's population, unless eliminated within twenty-four-hours, will result in termination. Any increase in suspicious human disappearances, deaths, or deaths by vampire attack in your locale will result in termination. Any leak of what you are or who you report to will result in termination."

Now, she scanned the team, pausing at each person, lingering on Bruce again. "If anyone else on this team or any other team is turned into a vampire, there will be nothing left of you, the compound, or any living thing within a mile strike radius of your location. We. Will. Not. Have an army of Company trained vampires. There are no lengths Oversight won't go to, up to and including civilian casualties, to see that doesn't happen. Those deaths would be on your head. Am I clear?"

As one, we all chorused, "Yes Ma'am."

Hopefully, only a vampire could detect that *'Ma'am'* meant *'fuck you'* when coming from Bruce.

"Your probation begins now." She kept her gun out, while our sorta-ally jogged to the Hummer, popped open a door revealing a compartment equipped with standard Company issue field weapons, accessories and kits, plus multiple devices and cases we didn't carry. He came out with a case and two pair of plated handcuffs used to transport live specimens.

Anger vibrated off Bruce, like ants marching over my skin. Josh's fury was almost as potent. I touched his elbow. "We agreed. It's okay."

He blew out a breath, and gripped Bruce's shoulder, half warning, half commiseration. I heard knuckles pop as Bruce clinched his fists.

"Four paces forward and face west." The AIC gave us our orders. Getting us away from the crowd. Facing us out so no one was behind the lieutenant's back as he worked.

Stavros and I did as commanded, Josh a beat later.

"You two put these on, then hands behind your head." The guy tossed first Stavros then me the cuffs.

We fastened the cuffs, a line of fire circling each wrist as the chem compound they were laced with met skin.

"Kneel."

I dropped to my knees, knowing what came next. Soft thumps marking Josh and Stavros doing the same.

"You can still leave," I whispered, for Stavros' hearing.

"Never," Stavros answered, equally soft, lost under the click of the Assistant's case opening.

As he stopped behind me, comprehension colored Bruce's face, going stroke-red, then draining to white.

I caught his eye and shook my head. Tried to tell him that this was it, my only chance of staying, my only way to protect the team. My only option to protect him.

He kept his gaze locked on mine as the lieutenant swept my hair out of the way, putting pressure on the back of my skull so I'd bend my head a degree, leaving the nape of my neck bare. They weren't taking chances, putting poppers at our brain stems. The syringe hissed and then bit into my skin, a cold pinch. Injecting the tiny lethal chip as moisture gleamed in Bruce's eyes, him blinking fast to hold tears in.

Pain radiated from my wrists up to my shoulders, skin feeling tight and puffy on my face and scalp, the chem poison traveling through my system. I stayed put as the assistant repeated the ritual with Stavros. Only breaking my almost palpable connection with Bruce when the lieutenant stopped in front of Josh.

I turned my head to the AIC. "Please. You have an immediate kill switch on me and Stavros. Don't do this to my brother."

In response she leveled her gun at me.

"C'mon, Vee. I agreed. Plus, it's the least I can do." Josh gave Stavros a quick nod. Acknowledging what Stavros had done, saving Josh's life.

Stavros tipped his head in response. "Agents don't thank other agents."

"Shirt up." The lieutenant gave the order, ignoring his partner's frown.

Josh pulled his tee off and stood in one motion, then laced his hands behind his head again. The guy used one hand, feeling along Josh's sternum, and moving left. Finding the spot, he wanted over Josh's heart. Placing the popper by the heart instead of the brain stem wasn't much of an improvement, but it was a show of respect, one agent to another.

The guy nodded and stepped away, fitting the last injector back into the case.

"Now, get those damn things off them," Bruce ground out.

The AIC didn't answer.

The other did, from his spot back beside the Hummer, leaning in long enough to switch one box with another. "After this."

He at least hurried. I rubbed my arm against the side of my head hard enough that the patch with our fake blood pulled loose, then offered him my arm straight out, rolled so soft skin was facing up, making the job of hitting a vein easier. He stared at the swatch of red skin reaching from my fingertips, all the way up, and disappearing under the tee's sleeve.

He got back to business, drawing twin tubes of blood, quickly labeling and stashing them in the box before the sun exposure degraded them. Same with cheek swabs he offered. I awkwardly scrubbed along the inside of my cheeks, gathering DNA. When he flipped out a scalpel and prep jar, Bruce swore.

The guy hesitated, realizing how close my fangs potentially were.

I turned my head politely, able to catch Bruce's eyes again. "It'll heal. No big," I soothed, while the blade sliced off a swatch from my inner arm. It would heal, but not while I was slowly being poisoned by chem, wrists beginning to smoke from the combination of it and sun, blisters appearing. I lowered them, doing my best to hide the problem as Stavros got the same treatment.

I caught my bottom lip, chewing at flaky skin, a stand-in for cuticles.

More power used up on his battle with the Master, smoke lifted from Stavros' wrists straight up, without a breeze. The faint, stomach-emptying scent of roasting meat scented the dry air.

The guy stepped out of our reach, science experiment done. His part, anyway.

The AIC watched us, distant, clinical. Probably waiting to

see at what point pain would win and we'd turn on the humans, thus giving her permission to end us.

Josh made a move, his tee still in hand. Trying to decide which of our wrists to toss it over.

"At attention, Agent Silva," I barked.

He reacted out of habit, stopping with shoulders back, facing forward.

Sand squeaked again. Not checking, I barked the same order at Liv and Kimi, pre-empting their intervention. "Team at attention. That includes you," I added for Bruce's benefit.

The lieutenant cleared his throat. The AIC still gave it another span of heartbeats, the stink of us burning obliterating the pong of diesel and the burnt oil stink from the gate motor. "Keys."

Her lieutenant wasted no time, tossing them to Josh, who snatched them out of the air.

"Stavros first."

Josh didn't hesitate, getting them off Stavros.

My brother winced at the bloodied, blistered band, then whirled to me. When he finished I held out my hand for keys, then gathered both pair of cuffs. I offered it all to the lieutenant. Ignoring the new burn across my palm, match to the fluid-filled blisters decorating me wrists to elbows now.

He stared, then took them, giving me a formal nod, the same as he'd given Josh.

"Your fucking show is over." Bruce stomped forward.

I eased between him and the AIC, too aware of the rifle still in her expert grip. "Ma'am."

"It isn't over until I know you won't mesmerize and feed off this team."

I got out, "Permission, ma'am" even as my stomach clenched. She wanted to see us feed. My siblings sort of had.

Bruce too. But not like this. Not the whole show, us draining bodies and as quickly as possible.

"Go," she said.

I offered a clumsy mental prayer. Not sure if it was for the AIC not to freak and fry my and Stavros' brains, or for my family not to freak and it change how they saw me. To lose their overwhelming feeling of love and acceptance.

So, I pretended, confident game face on, tipping my chin at Stavros. "Master for you." I headed in the direction of one of the slowly charring lesser vampires.

Stavros caught my shoulders, gently turning me toward the Master instead.

I dug my heels in. "No, you used up all your reserves, you're burning and—"

He laid his finger over his lips, borrowing Kimi's sign for shut it. "You are wounded far, far worse, though you don't know it. I'll do well with the two. Go now. Do not be ashamed of who you are or what you need to do to survive, because it is all in service to helping others."

Taking strength from him and his obvious pride, instead of his aura, I flipped the Master around and went to one knee. Kneeling because I felt like one of the dried cornhusks we decorated with in the fall, without substance, about to blow away, and I didn't have the strength to haul the carcass up and stand to feed.

A shadow fell over me. Liv and Kimi, purposely angling to give me shade. "We've got you," Kimi signed. "Both of you."

Josh and Bruce stood by Stavros, throwing another shadow over him. Bruce's glare daring the Assessors to say one word.

A stupid smile tugged at my lips. I copied Bruce's fuck-them-all attitude and drank.

CHAPTER 54

ee

LIV EYED the neat stack of dead vamps in the shade of the annex, then eyed me.

"I'm thinking drop them beside the 'chup den." I answered her wordless question. We didn't know to stand upwind the first time we had more than one to dispose of on a mission. We'd had to toss clothes, down to the skin. No getting the rank, spoiled barbeque smell out.

"Works for me." She stretched, then winced at the pull of sore muscles. "Need any help?"

"We've got it."

"You sure? You've still got a primary report to lie your way through. Somehow, I doubt the vampire virus power-up extends to improving your typing accuracy."

"Primaries are the C.O.'s job."

"Exactly," Liv agreed. Like this wasn't monumental. Like

she hadn't just dropped the thing we both coveted between us, like a bone between two dogs.

Proving his wisdom, Stavros hefted the carcass on top of the pile and vanished in a burst of *I'm avoiding this drama* speed.

"Liv—"

"You are C.O.."

I worried a cuticle. "I know we were being mouthy and boasting about skills and qualifications and who deserved what. You've led this team as well as I did. Maybe better, because you were dealing with a crisis and losing a member. HQ acknowledged you as C.O.."

"This is your team. It's always been your team." Liv sighed. "It has. I only had to be sure you wouldn't put them in danger. That you were still you. Now, I am. No one will bat an eye at you stepping back into your command."

She hugged me for the first time since I'd reappeared. I shuffled and hugged back. She added in my ear, "I'm still using the private shower, though."

With that she pulled loose, acting like her eyes weren't red and damp as mine.

She mock-saluted and headed in, where Kimi was already writing new code, tweaking our drones to monitor the two that had appeared less than half an hour after the Assessors drove away. Josh was out, welding the damaged main gate. Humming as he worked, despite having fought off a vampire nest and being tagged like wildlife.

I toed at the remaining corpses. I should help. But processing all this, the last few hours… Assessors, shadow ops work I'd sold us into. Poppers. Josh and his open hearted, terrifying decision. Not wanting to harm a human, but being willing to as a last resort. Leadership, and the new weight of it.

Bruce, who was doing a crap job of hiding that he was

hovering between the steps leading to the compound, and the bench. Starting to pace, then recalling he was trying to be invisible, only to repeat the action a minute later.

"Hey," I said softly. Not sure of what he wanted, or of what I wanted.

His answer was more subdued than I'd ever heard him. "Am I bothering you?"

"No."

"Did you get enough? Blood," he clarified, voice gruff. "Josh and I could—shit, I don't know. At least find a chupacabra, or something stop-gap from the butcher shop."

"I'm fueled up." I went back to not-disposing of cadavers.

Bruce went back to not-pacing. Sort of. He glared at the drone dropping low over the annex. Then blurted, "You and Liv knew they'd agree to this plan, and that there was a contingency for turned agents."

Out of sight, I crossed my fingers. "*Knew* might be an overstatement. C.O.'s do a separate, private course after they are chosen, where we're briefed on protocol should cryptids or the Company be irrevocably exposed."

He stopped in front of me, arms crossed. Catching that I hadn't answered all of his question.

"As far as we're aware, there isn't a contingency for infected agents, aside from humane elimination. But we'd seen a few things that logically lead to some theoretical attempt at putting a turned agent into play short term. Not like this obviously, but the idea was there and I punted. So, like fifty-percent sure? fifty-ish?"

"Jesus Fucking Christ." His voice rose. "You two took that insane fucking risk, and then another with those damn kill chips."

"You really want to go there?" My volume rose to match his. "Blackmailing the Company?" I narrowed my eyes. "Is there really a dead drop of names and videos?"

His anger dropped along with his volume, serious in a way I'd rarely seen, no bluster or threats. "Yes. I created it three years ago. A day after my decision to join the team. In case you—any of you, or hell, better yet all of you—ever wanted out. It was leverage. I figured I should do it while I was relatively in the clear, before I was under Company scrutiny. I updated it a few weeks ago." He cleared his throat and shrugged like this wasn't huge. He couldn't meet my eyes.

If he'd tweaked it… that was when I'd returned. Before I'd moved into the compound. Half-formed thoughts rolled through my brain.

Bruce didn't make any move to go. Patiently leaving me sorting through a chaotic array of thoughts and feelings, and landing back on the same one no matter the path I took.

I already knew in general that human blood held no temptation. Now I knew it didn't when wounded or fighting either.

Today, emotions were added to the mix of fight-fueled adrenalin, the excruciating pain of semi-torture from sun and chem and sheer terror for my family, who I loved, being hurt or taken from me.

I'd been ready to defend the team. Ready to kill both Assessors if that's what it took to save family. The idea of attacking people, much less fellow Company agents, made me sick even while I'd forced myself to plan how. But it was duty, not want. And I'd been able to walk away. Hadn't needed or wanted to kill after resolving to if needed. There'd been no fight against instinct.

So, if terror and desperation and love hadn't turned me into a monster, maybe other extreme emotions didn't, either.

"Fuck, Vee, I—"

"There's something—"

Our conversations crashed into each other. Bruce pulled

his glasses off, although he didn't have anything clean to polish them with. "Go ahead. I swore I'd quit shoving my wants down your throat, making what I wanted feel paramount."

I felt the brush of Stavros' aura arriving moments before he did.

He would stop me if I was horribly wrong, before anyone was injured. He'd take me out if I went full hunting mode. This was as ideal a situation as I'd get. "Can I sort of test a theory on you? It's, okay, it's a huge one and—"

"Yes." Determination firmed his jaw. "Whatever it is, yes. I owe you that much."

"This can't be about repayment for some imaginary debt. You being a jerk, or healing you, or whatever." My stomach pitched at the possibility I was wrong and that he was forcing himself to be near enough to touch me. Then pitched again at the possibility of being right about his attraction, but my screwing it up. He'd said what we'd started in the gym was real, and that his feelings hadn't changed.

Bruce shoved his hands in his pockets, as if he didn't know what to do with them. "You have to hear me when I say this, all right?"

When it became clear he was seriously waiting for my answer I got out, "I'm listening."

"Good. This isn't repayment. There's no debt between us. What I'm saying is that I know you don't feel about me the way you used to." He cleared his throat, like words were getting stuck. "I'm not going to lie or wave it off—it hurts like hell. I'm also not going to pretend I don't love you. I do. I always will."

Seeing something in my expression, he held up his hand, asking for more time.

"But, that's okay. My feelings, your feelings, we're allowed to feel how we feel. Having said that, whatever you need right now? I'm here for it."

His brows drew in, body language verging on angry. "That shit the Assessors were spewing, and then forcing you to drain bodies in front of us like you were animals, was emotional and mental abuse. If you need to test out that they're wrong, and prove that you're safe to be around us? Even if you only need to prove it to yourself, or that watching what they forced you to do doesn't change one damn thing as far as how we all view you, I'll do it." He stared at me like he was trying to push the truth into me.

I caught myself chewing the inside of my cheek to keep from blurting out how I felt about him. If this test didn't work, and I once more wasn't as in control as I thought— telling Bruce how I felt then jerking it out from under him would devastate him. Me, too.

Attention on Bruce's patient face, I reached without looking, unsheathing the machetes. We'd rearmed as the Assessors left, too twitchy to go weaponless. Now I handed mine behind me. Stavros took them.

Or tried to. I couldn't seem to convince my fingers to unlock from the hilts. So much, too much, was at stake if I was wrong.

Stavros spoke, tone proud. "I will also do as you need. Niña, you have been a revelation to me. We have not lost the ability to feel the full range of emotions. You have reminded me of kindness, happiness, laughter. Emotion itself isn't our enemy, nor are ties to others a weakness. They can be the same source of strength, giving us purpose, as when we were human."

My fingers loosened, giving up the blades. I closed the space between me and Bruce. "Stavros will make sure that I don't hurt you."

Bruce's hands, still in his pockets, clenched, the popping

of knuckles clear. "There's no damn way you'd hurt me. Ever."

I gave in to what I'd wanted to do since I woke up underground in a cage without him—touch Bruce again. I traced the set line of his jaw, short beard, wiry-soft under my fingertips. Over his eyebrows, back down. Touching lips as familiar to me as mine. More familiar maybe. Smiling, grumping, issuing orders or insults, pursed while he came up with brilliant food and career breakthroughs, swollen when we kissed.

I leaned, careful that only our lips touched, a barely-there brush. My pulse too loud in my ears. Bruce's louder still. Tentative, I increased the pressure, and Bruce's desire scented the air. No clue if it was because of new vampire skills or joy at being with him again, but it tasted like his agave habit. Sweet and pure.

He shifted, hips bumping mine. Then stilled, blatantly afraid of offending me. He wanted this. I wanted this, and to banish that awful hesitation, to show him he was right. We were right together.

I nibbled at his lower lip, a move that used to drive him crazy. His lips parted, inviting me in, still letting me take the lead and set the pace. I wanted him to understand that he didn't have to hesitate or hold back or ever worry I didn't want him. I tried putting all that truth in a kiss, hands finding their way to his shoulders, and familiar muscles.

I finally broke the kiss, daring to check Bruce's expression. His face was too pale, not the flushed we-are-getting-naked look I expected.

His eyes closed, lashes dark against equally dark circles under his eyes. Not opening them, he said, "Just now—was that what you needed?"

"Yes." I rubbed my thumbs along the skin of his neck. Tendons stood out like cables under my touch.

Another muscle worked in his jaw. "This is the part where I should walk away. You're in control, not some fucked up virus. You do understand that?"

"Yes."

"Can—ah, fuck." He scrubbed a hand through already wildly mussed hair.

I tugged on his arm, pulling his other hand out of his pocket. Then repeated the maneuver with the one now balled into a fist. "Listen, I—"

"Can I kiss you?"

"Yes."

His hands cupped my face, lips gentle on mine. Sweet instead of demanding. I pressed against him, telling him this was perfect. That we were together, that we had time now to learn about the new versions of us.

In response one hand slid behind my head, firmly molding lips together. Making it impossible to tell who was exhaling, who was inhaling.

His other arm locked around my waist, corded forearm melding us tight together. The sweet kiss ignited, turning urgent. His tongue traced the crease of my lips, and when they parted, darted in.

He added firm nips, the pressure of his teeth against my skin sending electric pulses through me. Threatening to melt me, but waking my body up like it had been in some kind of hibernation at the same time.

I caught his tee, jerking and untucking it, then sliding both hands underneath, flat against his stomach.

Muscles contracted hard under my palms, and Bruce surged forward. Then hesitated again.

I snagged a belt loop, jerking him against me, pelvis to pelvis. When he complied, I gave in to the need to get my hands back on him. I ran them up from his waistband. The new tattoo still fresh in my head, I slowed enough to understand what else might be new, learning the planes of his stomach and chest. Finally branching out over the width of the shoulders I'd dug nails into so often, and down his biceps, those still covered in familiar ink.

Who knew how long later, he eased us apart, but with my lower lip still caught between his teeth until the last moment. The move that drove *me* crazy.

His chest heaved and he only went far enough to rest his forehead against mine. Voice rough and broken like shattered glass, his words whispered over my cheek. "Your shirt —I was a mess that night, right after your 'I'm alive but a vampire and here's my new person who replaced you' reveal. That jealous knee-jerk response was weeks ago. I have emptied the trash for recycling a dozen times in the last three weeks. But I never emptied that can. I never had any intention of emptying it. Ever, Vee."

He took a deep breath like he was diving, going somewhere the next breath wasn't guaranteed and he might never make it back. "So whatever all of this is, this kiss—which is fucking wrecking me—whatever it means? Know that one truth. I was never touching that can and letting go of that dream."

"Bruce—"

He gave a harsh bark-laugh that hurt me to hear, and sounded like it'd been dragged over razor wire for him. "I told myself I couldn't do friends with occasional benefits, assuming you'd even consider touching me. But I was deluding myself. Whatever you need from me, whenever you need it, I'm here."

I tried to break in. "Bruce—"

He kept going, like once he began talking he couldn't stop himself. "Fuck pride, as long as I have you even for a little while. I'll never say no to you."

I resorted to laying a finger over his lips. I had zero right to silence him, but I couldn't stand him hurting for even one more heartbeat. "Don't—do not—doubt that I love you."

I should've known a measly finger was no deterrent. His lips moved against my skin, even as I pressed harder, looking for a second's break to tell him how wrong he was. "I know. I do. That's how you're built. That you don't love me the way I want, in the way you used to, is my problem to deal with, not yours. I'm not dropping that responsibility on you."

Clearly, it was going to taker stronger measures to out-talk Bruce. I put all my exasperation into it, and, okay, a little enhanced volume, too. "*Oh. My. God, B*. Will you knock it off for one minute? Thirty seconds even? I'd take thirty seconds."

His attention snapped to my face. His lips still parted mid-argument. "What did you call me?"

"Um, impossible? At least, I was inside my head, because you weren't giving me a chance to use actual spoken words."

"I—"

"*B*. Seriously?" Somehow my hands had found their way to my hips.

He shut his mouth. Fast.

"Right. Bend forward for me?"

He obliged, but his expression remained wary.

I worked his shirt the rest of the way over his head, dropping the fabric on the ground, because we had an endless supply of regulation tees. Plus, I was making dang sure he wasn't ever going to have cause to wear one again. No more missions, and guns, and tactical gear.

I laid a reverent hand on the sunflower and broken knife, right over his heart. "I don't have any outward markers like this one to show how I feel. So, verbal is going to have to stand in." I splayed my hand to cover as much of the heart-rending design as possible. "I love you this way."

Slowly, he let go where he still held my waist, and

moved his hand to cover mine. When I didn't shy away or start lecturing again, he wove our fingers together. Cautious, but hope erasing some of the lines grooving his face.

I squeezed his hand lightly, hopefully letting him know I wasn't leaving-leaving. Monitoring his expression in case I'd read him wrong, I slid my hand down his perfect ink, past his stomach, and stopped over the bulge in his tactical pants. "I love you this way, too."

He studied me, his body stiff. Holding himself together maybe, and definitely away from me even though we were touching. His tone was equally reserved, putting effort in to distance us that way too. "Be honest. Look me in the eye and tell me you aren't saying what you think I want to hear in order to keep peace within the team. Tell me this isn't you doing that self-sacrificing Company C.O. bullshit they trained into you, trying to be everything to everyone but yourself."

My hair lifted enough that the ends tickled my neck. The me reflected back in Bruce's eyes was outlined in the faintest silvery glow, subtle enough to be sun reflecting back if you didn't know what our power manifested as. Heck, maybe only visible to other vampires even then.

Okay, extreme frustration brought out a drop of vampishness. Then the power flickered, the tiniest of whirlwinds looping around our connected bodies in a merry swirl.

Bruce didn't recognize it as power or even notice.

But I did.

The power, the genetic modification, whatever it truly was—it reacted to my moods and will, not the other way around. The alien virus DNA wasn't a thing outside me to be fought against anymore. It was simply mine, another part of me, to do with as I saw fit.

A weight I'd carried for a year and a half, time that felt

more like eons, drifted away and broke apart, like the whirlwind had.

"Why are you smiling?" Bruce frowned at me, a chunk of the real Bruce, my Bruce, pushing through.

"Because we are crazy close to the gym. And it's empty."

Bruce's heart rate jumped, then jumped again. His face was schooled enough not to give away his eagerness at the mention of our favorite out of bed sex spot though. "Are you sure about this? Completely, with no reservations you're ignoring in the hopes they go away?"

Which translated as 'Are you going to freak out halfway through and run?'.

I glanced toward the gym. Late afternoon sun glinted off honed steel. Stavros, ultra disciplined, analytical, and demanding Stavros, had propped my machetes against the farthest annex wall. It was his blessing. He believed I was no danger to Bruce. I had passed it all, the tests we had planned, those we hadn't, and now, the strongest personal temptation I'd faced.

Despite chips and new rules, I had control of my life again—not a virus, not people who thought they knew how I thought and reacted or what I should be or do better than I did. I worked our fingers back together, backing up a step. Trying to look totally confident while biting the heck out of the inside of my cheek.

Bruce moved a step my way, silently agreeing to my plan. Except as we walked, he watched me out of the corner of his eye. Wariness mixed with hope, the same possibility of wanting and being wrong that kind of fluttered right under my breastbone.

The gym was unsettlingly cool and dark after being under the sun and cloudless sky.

Bruce held his hand over the inner I.D. panel, head tilted

in question. I swallowed and nodded and he punched in the rarely used code to lock the door behind us.

Leaving us alone together.

Staring silently at each other, possibly both of us afraid to find out what came next.

For the first time, I purposely touched the newest part of me for something other than a boost when fighting. Taking time to really feel it instead of automatically squashing it, which had really equaled me only stuffing a chunk of myself away. It—I— felt the same exhilarated-nervous. Because it really was me. It had been for a long time, but I'd purposely misunderstood and punished myself because I'd thought it was all I deserved.

I put a little muscle behind it and opened up. Nudging until my hair visibly lifted, no random breeze as the excuse. Working a bit harder, the room brightening a few shades to me, meaning the silver I couldn't see tinted my eyes. "This is okay?"

Bruce caught the hand not wrapped in his. Stopping my automatic, unconscious cuticle shredding. "Yes." His thumb rubbed back and forth over my hand. Soothing me the same way he'd done hundreds of times.

I wanted to wrap myself in that comfort. But there was still that nagging last worry. I reclaimed both hands, and jerked the tee off before I lost my nerve. Logically, I knew he had seen me already. At least, a lot of me.

That had been in the midst of a fraught, adrenalin charged life and death situation. I still heard his horrified response whispering in my head.

Shirt squashed in my fist, I gave him an unobstructed view. "Is this really okay too?"

"I fucking hate that you were hurt." He pried the shirt from my stiff fingers and tossed the tee. "I also hate that you feel you have to ask me that question. May I?"

Whatever it was he was asking for, I nodded. Kind of a wobbly nod, but still.

Callused fingers brushed my cheek. Followed the line of my jaw, and kept going, inevitably hitting the ugly, scarred ridges of claw marks cutting down the side of my neck.

Instead of flinching or hesitating, he traced along them, the same as he'd done with my unmarred face. A shiver pebbled along my shin.

"These mean you survived. You fucking won and came back to me. You are so damn perfect it hurts to look at you." He trailed the very tips of his fingers from my neck down my chest. Then switched and skimmed along my arm with the back of his hand, the hairs raising in a ripple of goose bumps.

At the end, he caught my fingers and laid them on his chest. Not over the tattoo, but above it. Right on the raised scar from his treatment. His heart banged under my palm. "Be straight with me. Does this, and everything that it stands for, affect how you see me?"

It took me a second to understand what he was asking. The pieces clicked together in a burst of clarity. I smoothed my hand over the spot, lavishing it with the same attention as I had his lips and chest. "Survivor goes both ways. Your scars aren't any different than mine in the end. You fight. You always, always go all in, like at this super hero level. Life was painful and excruciating but you kept fighting for me and us, and that's the sexiest and most amazingly romantic thing ever."

A sigh shook him. Like mine when I'd accepted that I was still me.

I gave myself free rein to indulge, tracing over the old ink that was as familiar and incredible as his face and voice. Moving on to the new design next, greedy to memorize its lines and graceful whorls. They really were his love and devotion given shape and color, permanently worked into his skin.

Chills the same as mine raced over his skin. "Jesus, Vee. I dreamed this exact scene so many nights. I can't tell anymore if this is real, or another dream and I'm going to wake up hugging nothing but your shirt, and—"

"And alone," I whispered and shivered, the ghost of that shared desolation still clinging, somewhere inside me. Almost as real as the here and now, too easy to catapult back to a barren cage and the despair.

We both needed to banish that ghost, and the best way was one we'd made uniquely ours, naked and together.

I grabbed at my bra. It only came loose in patches, dried blood and gunk flaking from parts, others damp and stubbornly adhering to my skin. Stuck on me with my blood, the attackers' blood, probably Liv's and Stavros' too. And nasty fluid from the popped blisters.

I let go fast, scrubbing my contaminated hands against my thighs, but my pants were equally awful.

The enormity of it, of my life—the fighting and maybe dying and the cages and blood—all hit at once. "I don't—" I turned to Bruce, my breath coming too fast. I shoved my hands behind my back, out of sight, but cold, clammy blood was all over them, under my nails. "It's everywhere and you shouldn't—it will get on you too and—"

Bruce caught my shoulders. "Breathe with me. In. Out."

Once I tried, he nodded and pulled me against him, murmuring encouragement. "There. Just like that."

"I don't know what's wrong with me," I whispered. "Everything is fine now. I don't know why this is happening."

"Only you would live through the chaos and pain of the last few years and call it *fine*." He rested his cheek against my hair, cradling me. "You went through a year of hell with me, while keeping the team together and still fighting at peak performance, and hadn't had time to process that experience before you were brutalized and your life completely altered against your wishes. That trauma has caught up with you. It's your turn to let the people who love you support you for a while."

He switched to stroking my hair. "Let go however you need to. I've got you."

His breath warm on my scalp, and the quiet of the room made it seem like we were in our own, protected universe. Little by little my breathing slowed, my heart rate synching with his.

"Better?" His soft question barely disturbed the peace, like he felt what I did, how important this moment was.

I nodded, and whispered, "I want to touch you, but I can't because there's blood all over me."

"We both need that. Here." Keeping me close, he turned us toward the back of the gym, and the showers I'd somehow forgotten about.

"Wait right here." Once we were inside, he leaned into the shower, turning water on and playing with the temperature until steam rose around us. He left long enough to grab a pile of towels. The super fluffy ones reserved for use after incredibly cruddy missions when we'd gotten beat up enough to warrant the hot tub on the other side of the room.

He stacked the pile on the counter and turned to me. Making me the center of his focus, he eased the disgusting bra over my head, then undid my belt. I obeyed his short instructions, holding arms out and lifting legs when he told me to, until I was naked.

"In." He settled me under the heated waterfall, shed his clothes, and joined me. He positioned me where he wanted me, my back to the water. Satisfied, he slid behind me and fit my back against him.

I squinched closer and let him do whatever he wanted.

For now, that was lifting my hair and running fingers through it. The green, fresh scent of his shampoo was sharp and welcome.

With impossible patience he teased the knotted, gunky spots out, working up to my scalp, fingers sure but gentle. He tipped my head against his shoulder, carefully rinsing suds out.

By the time he started with body wash along my back, the nightmare flashbacks and fears faded.

This, a shower, our compound, Bruce's touch, felt solid and real. Now his hands on me reminded me that we were together. Naked. In one of our most frequented sex-is-fun spots. Something we hadn't done in far too long, even before I'd been taken.

I squeezed out my hair and flipped it over my shoulder, squirming out of Bruce's grasp.

"Talk to me, Vee. What's wrong?"

I turned, catching the worry tightening his expression. He swiped water out of his eyes, plastering his hair down in the process. Droplets sparkled along his lashes and beard. Water slicked his skin leaving his tattoos bright and gleaming.

"It's your turn." I needed to touch him. Now.

Like he heard me, he felt for the bottle, never taking his gaze off me. He swallowed hard, throat working. For whatever reason, this felt like one of those pivotal moments, about far more than sex.

When I motioned, he bent his head, letting me massage short, rough-soft strands and scalp. Quickly tilting his head back, he rinsed soap out to get back to watching me. Like looking away was physically painful. His gaze devouring me.

The way he looked at me—I was just Vee. We were *us*. And nothing else mattered.

Lathering body wash on both of my hands, I slid behind him, starting at his shoulders. Massaging along his spine, swirling soap down his unmarked back to his ass. His sharp inhale felt like permission and a request all rolled together, and made me bolder.

I drew blunt nails over his hips, his muscles clenching, then flexing and clenching again when I worked upward along the same path.

He braced both arms against the shower wall. I pressed my breasts against his back, my hands busy traveling around his ribs, dipping lower, skirting tight, dark curls.

I ducked under his arm and turned my attention to his front. I kissed scarred knuckles, and started with his first tattoo, a band along that wrist. Following the story inked into his skin. The tale of his rebellion, choosing his own path. His inspirations and his family.

I continued across his opposite shoulder and arm to his achievements, and kissed those beat up knuckles too. I'd been saving his chest. Now I concentrated on our story. Tracing in reverent brushes, my kisses dotted between strokes. Ending at his heart, where the two of us were visibly united.

I caught a hint of salt on the steamy air. His tears or mine, the shower spray concealed them, freeing us to release feelings and hurt.

My palms splayed on his chest, I dragged them down his stomach. Going lower until I reached curls, and burrowed in. My thumbs outlining but not quite touching yet. Teasing, I kept going along the inside of his thighs, nails skimming.

His cock stood out, hard and ready. I grasped it, stroking from base to tip, then back. My grasp firm and just this side of too much, the way he craved. The grip that had him throwing his head back and driving hard into my hand.

"Jesus, Vee."

"Prove this isn't a dream." We both needed real and gritty.

He caught me around the waist, switching places in a blur

and spinning me to face the wall. One scuffed hand cupped my breast, tweaking the nipple, first one, then moving to the other.

His other hand was between my legs. Proving he was still a master at getting me wet and writhing. His fingers circled, finding the perfect spot and teasing me near the brink.

I arched into him, his cock rubbing against me from behind. "B."

Understanding, already falling back into our personal shorthand, he moved the fraction that let him slide inside me.

I mimicked his technique, bracing one arm against the tile for both of us. As Bruce wrapped an arm around my waist, the other still busy teasing my clit, I reached back, grabbing his hip. Urging him faster and harder, to drive out everything but the sensation of our bodies sliding against each other.

Shadows flickered on the wall in front of me. My power lighting us up, and throwing a shadow version of us on the tile.

Shadow Bruce and Vee, joined the way we were meant to be. The sparks of pleasure, wild and heady from Bruce's fingers and pounding thrusts, joined together. The entire room lit in silver as I came.

Bruce held on tight enough to mark me, molding us together, his fingers digging into my hips. His release exploded a handful of heartbeats behind me, the syllables of my name running together.

When his shudders tapered off, he wrapped his arms around me. Still keeping me tight against him, skin to skin. I wrapped my hands over his and leaned back, into him and his strength. The steady beat of his heart telling me I was home.

We rested under the spray, relearning each other. Both of us letting go of separation and hurt.

"I don't know if I can make myself move," he whispered against my ear. "I never thought I'd have this again and I'm half-afraid if we move that I will wake up, or some world ending catastrophe will blow through the door."

I played with his fingers, letting them give me the security to dip back into the last eighteen months. "There's something out there. Way more than some vampires making pets of windigos and hosting raves. We—all of us, Company included—have to discover and study whatever is really behind the upheaval, the purpose and end-game. Those vampires today had already been in some kind of major fight. Even revenge shouldn't have had them tackling us until they'd healed and regrouped."

Concentrating on the concrete—Bruce's hands, the warm spray of water—let me keep going, past the edges of my nightmare. "The night Stavros and I were attacked—" Bruce tensed and pulled me in, which, I was totally okay with, "—it was coordinated. They knew where we'd been, and somehow anticipated where I was heading. They had to know, to have fielded that mixed pack waiting in the middle of nowhere for us. I don't remember most of it, but I swear I didn't hallucinate or imagine their preparedness. If it had been any vampire other than Stavros, we wouldn't have fought free. If it had been the team, I don't think we could've either."

"You were right. You told us again and again that something was off, and none of us, not one damn person, listened to you." Grief and guilt shaded his flat statement.

I wriggled around, not breaking his hold, but able to use my hands as blinders, like with horses, on either side of his face and forcing him to look at me. "That's done. Over. We're in the here and now, with here and now concerns and objectives."

"Whatever is coming, we're facing it down together." Bruce tugged me flush with his chest again.

I wrapped my arms around his neck, not allowing either of us to go to that dark place, pulling us out of the spiral he was falling back into. "That sounds perfect. Know what would bump perfection to the next level?"

His chest rose on a deep inhale he held for a beat before letting it go. Meeting my attempt at our kind of normal. "You are missing the entire purpose of the word. Perfection implies the pinnacle."

"Not true. Also, one word—pudding. Like, the biggest bowl you've ever made. Is gallons a legit measurement for pudding? Because it should be."

Bruce's grip increased, either ready to choke or hug me, but his laugh rocked us both.

ruce

"For the last damn time, put the blindfolds on, and quit whining." Via the rearview mirror, Bruce glared at the SUV's inhabitants.

Stavros frowned and gave Bruce one of those sanctimonious, stick up his ass glares over the swearing.

Beside him, Kimi leaned over the console, blindfold dangling from her fingers, and made her opinion known. "I should be exempt. How am I supposed to communicate otherwise?"

"Being blindfolded doesn't prevent you from signing."

"It prevents everyone from listening to me."

"Exactly. You lot can refrain from talking for five damn minutes, and I'll be driving and not taking my eyes off the road."

"What if we can't stay silent for five minutes? What if that unnatural state sets off some catastrophic chain reaction?

Then boom, California falls into the ocean." Taller, Liv didn't bother with the console, instead hanging over the back of Josh's seat. The sense of humor she kept hidden from anyone but family sparkled, lighting her up in her own under the radar way.

"I'll risk it. Pretend you grasp the meaning of *surprise* while you're at it." He pointed at her as the stand-in for the entire team. "You're all shit at keeping secrets *secret*."

Including Josh, who had claimed shotgun, beating his sisters to the front seat. He wore a ridiculous grin and was fidgeting like Bruce's youngest niece, hyped on sugar.

Bruce narrowed his eyes, expression promising their brother no end of vengeance if he said or did anything to tip Vee off. Or Kimi or Liv, who would immediately spill to Vee.

"B, this may be a lot of unnecessary subterfuge." Vee nibbled at a nail, like she was imparting shocking information. "We all know this is a surprise party to celebrate your designation as a new team member. Which, we are all in for celebrating and letting loose, definitely, because this news is amazing," she rushed to add.

"Blindfolds. Now." Ideally ASAP and before they hit the off ramp and realized where they were bound for.

They finally complied, humoring Bruce, with the exception of Stavros, and fuck him. But the guy did mostly stay out of inter-family politics and kept his mouth shut.

Compulsively, Bruce's hand went to his blazer pocket and the ring box tucked in it. The one he'd had for nearly three years. It was past time to pledge to Vee that they were officially together, fuck outside circumstances. And damned if he'd allow any crisis, even Liv's theoretical natural disaster, to derail him this time.

The whole night was to show Vee what she meant to him. To help confirm, after his asshole performance when she first came back, that this was where she belonged, and they were the people she belonged with. That they *all* loved, supported, and needed her.

His family...even Kenny had cried when Bruce told them Vee had been found, and was alive. Bruce fed them the story HQ had crafted for her reappearance, that Vee had been held by the group who had attacked her client, using her skills and finally getting free. They had flown out, his dad demanding to see for himself that Vee was okay, and his mom had hovered, fussed, and cooked for Vee every day until they'd had to return to Westchester.

Plus, it had been three months to the day since Vee reappeared. Probably whimsy on his part but the timing *felt* right. Momentous.

He still woke in the darkest point of the night, terrified and grabbing for Vee. Praying there wouldn't be a barren spot and unused pillow beside him.

Vee was always there though, and almost always curled tight against him, fighting her own nightmares, with a hand on the back of her neck. He suspected her fear was for Josh and Stavros, not herself.

They were getting that damn bomb out of her and Josh. Stavros as well. End of story. That was Bruce's next project.

He pulled the truck into a slot. The empty parking lot provided ample choices, bare on what should be the restaurant's busiest night of the week. He owed his friend a month long pop-up in exchange. The deal was worth it, and it was time for Bruce to get back to his craft. He'd finally had that itch—to create, to bring his passion to the public.

His gut doing somersaults, he opened his door, then Vee's, taking her hand. "Grab hold." Vee with him, Liv latched onto their brother, and Kimi with Stavros.

The owner opened the restaurant's side door, giving Bruce a thumb's up along with the keys so Bruce could lock up later.

Bruce guided the crew through the building and out onto the expansive outdoor patio.

With Vee's fingers curled around his, there was no hiding how his hand was sweating. "All right. Take them off."

The team wasted no time. Bruce watched them take in the space, all the tables gone except one in the center, set with champagne, and truffles and pastry from the patisserie blocks away.

Like they were connected, Kimi and Liv turned in a circle, admiring the tiny golden lights strung around the pergola rafters, looping along the trellis, and outlining the tall wooden privacy fence.

He dared a look at Vee.

Her lips were parted, the light's glow reflecting in her eyes.

"B. Wow." She cupped a platter-sized flower by her head. One of a shit ton he'd ordered, enough to cover the fence and transform the space into a fantasy garden.

He and Josh had worked eight straight hours earlier that day, after Josh had put his rom-com viewing knowledge to use, and drawn up a pattern based on the wedding proposals from all of Vee's favorite movies.

Vee turned to Bruce. "This isn't what we were expecting —we assumed something more along the lines of margaritas, and karaoke, and dancing." She touched a silky magenta petal. "This is gorgeous but you shouldn't have had to do the work for your own party."

"This isn't a welcome to the team party." He shoved his bout of nerves aside.

Liv caught his eye, already getting the real reason for the blindfolds and over the top décor in a flash of the understanding that had made her the leader able to hold them all together, and get them through tragedy in one piece.

Her lifted brow spoke volumes, covering *"Really?"* and *"Like this?"*

He shrugged. He'd already been set on a group proposal after the way they all stood by him when he was sick. He was doubly sure now. "The team does everything together. I accepted that a long time ago."

"B?" Vee let the flower petals whisper over her fingertips in a puff of herbal sweetness, turning all her attention on him.

A giant fist closed around his heart, ready to crush it if he'd judged wrong.

Now or never.

He cleared his throat. "Tonight was something I'd had planned for a couple of years. A lot has changed since then—illness, your time away, a new team." He gave a bare nod, acknowledging Stavros. "I'm hoping one thing has remained constant through all those upheavals."

He dropped to one knee, the patio stones under him as solid as his belief in his new family. He focused on Vee as his pulse turned into a never-ending *please say yes* beat. On the yellow dress swirling around her thighs, the color as vibrant and alive as she was. Those perfect lips he never took for granted, and never got tired of kissing her favorite berry lip stain from. Her eyes, the honey-brown deep enough to drown in, outlined by the thinnest band of quicksilver, like it had always been there, and hell if he didn't love that too.

He pulled the tiny velvet box out. The crack of the lid opening was like thunder, heralding some foretold event or prophesy. The diamond was inset into the band so it was all level, no edges to catch, utilitarian but beautiful. He'd chosen platinum for the setting, partially because the metal was sturdier than gold, partially because of its rarity, like Vee.

In a twist of irony, it now matched her vampire-silver

aura. If he believed in fate, this was the confirmation that they were always meant to be.

With Vee still silent, he went on. "I don't know why getting married feels so important, because I will never leave your side, unless you send me away, and no ceremony can change that. Yet somehow this ring is vital. I can't promise I'll be easy to live with or that I'll make your life smoother or that we won't fight. However, I love you with every damn cell in my body."

He drew in a breath and all of the courage he possessed. Putting it all in the question—the first time they kissed, the first time they made up after a fight, the first time she had walked in post-mission and found him in the kitchen waiting, when she first met and clashed with his family. Their first I-love-you. The way she'd been his touchstone during the worst of his treatments. Then the excruciating pain of them being apart, and the joy of the last three months back together. "Victoria Ramirez, will you do me the honor I probably don't fucking deserve, and marry me?"

He held his breath like some love-struck kid so that he didn't miss any nuance of her answer, his heart doing its damndest to pop out of its bony cage.

Vee looked to Stavros. "Can vampires get married?"

"I have entered many churches and sought the comfort of holy ground. As God has chosen us for His work, I believe the same holds for synagogues and all other places of worship. He can't but approve of your marriage vows." The old vampire looked down his nose at Bruce. "Some acts should only occur once blessed by holy vows."

Bruce met the guy's glare with one of his own. As if Bruce gave a damn that after his and Vee's first enthusiastic night together, Stavros had moved to the main hall next to Josh, while muttering about sins of the flesh. Or that he gave the two of them pointed looks every time they got handsy or headed to their room.

"Right." Vee turned to Liv. "Can agents get married?"

Liv's finger tapped her thigh as she thought. "There's no rule pro or con. I suspect your entering into a civil union will barely register in the face of recruiting a media savvy civilian, then adding a vampire." Her face brightened. "The question of marriage might work as a distraction so Oversight doesn't allocate quite as much time and focus to the whole vampire thing."

"And less attention to you being a vampire. That is actually a very strategic play," Kimi signed.

"Okay, that's true. There is that whole section on assets and conduct though," Vee said.

"Doesn't apply here. Bruce isn't an asset anymore," Kimi signed, Liv nodding along.

"Jesus Fucking Christ." Bruce's voice rose as they prepared to launch into comparing yet more hidebound Company rules. "You are *killing* me here."

"Maybe I should do the asking you to marry me explanation too?" Vee neatly tucked her skirt under her knees and knelt in front of him. "I mean, I'm kind of impulsive, and come with a whole family already, and I really do prefer the vending machine doughnuts." She tipped her chin at her siblings and their guilty as hell expressions. "So do they. Sorry. Plus, vampire."

She smoothed her skirt, only looking at him from the corner of her eye, like she was honest to God nervous. "However, as a plus, I get along great now with your whole family, even your brother. And I think you're a brilliant artist, and I could watch you work all day, every day, except, call-outs and all, and wow, your beard and tattoos are hot, and I love you with all of my heart."

She finally took a gulp of oxygen and met his eyes. "I'll totally marry you. If you're still okay with all of that."

"Fuck yes, I'm in."

Josh whooped, Liv and Kimi cheering and clapping.

Still, the only thing that truly mattered was Vee, and the soft, intimate smile on her face. Just for the two of them. And the way she wrapped her arms around Bruce's neck. With her clinging to him, he stood and whirled her around, like a closing scene from one of her movies. He'd never bitch about her viewing choices or call them unrealistic again.

CHAPTER 56

$\mathcal{E}$PILOGUE—LIV'S TURN

I PROPPED against the edge of our two-person bar, the tile chilly after the warmth of the restaurant patio and dancing until we were sweaty, and watched the team, fresh from Bruce's proposal event. Fueled by copious amounts of champagne, and near-overdose of sugar, the group was loud, bordering on raucous.

Happiness filled every corner of the house. Honest, no holds barred, not waiting for a problem to drop, happiness. The cloud that had hung over them—us—was gone. If I let my gaze unfocus, it was like before Bruce got the cancer diagnosis, and before my sister disappeared, leaving a hole in all of us.

Kimi and Josh were vying over a disputed box of leftover truffles on one end of the kitchen. Bruce and Vee were lip-to-lip on the opposite end of the room, drunk on each other. I wiped a last happy tear off, although my mascara and liner had lost the battle somewhere between Bruce's way-romantic toast and watching him and my sister cling to each other on the improvised dance floor.

Stavros caught my eye from his seat at the table, a concerned frown replacing what we'd finally determined was his contented face. Very low key contentment, but also very real. Vee swore vampires could sometimes read human emotional states. I slapped on a smile, not wanting to ruin the evening or worry him.

Having him here definitely didn't suck. Stavros fit in with the team as if he had always belonged. He respected our skills, never hovered, and never interfered once plans were set, not challenging or undermining Vee's or my authority.

He was an excellent teacher too, on a par with any of our Academy Instructors. He shared a staggeringly long lifetime's worth of combat skills and unorthodox vampire killing tactics. Making us the only team with insider information. Our mission frequencies had spiked, but so had our success rate.

Despite acting so circumspect, I still got the feel that he was watching out for us all, the way he did with Vee. A situation which also didn't suck.

Kimi left off taunting Josh, and as smoothly as she created code, promptly drew Stavros into a conversation. At first I thought she'd taken him on as a project. After time spent with him, and comparing his odd actions to the way Bruce's mother and father acted, I'd had one of those epiphany moments. Stavros acted the same with us. We'd been adopted by a vampire-dad. Kimi was enjoying the novelty of having a parental figure. So was I.

I rubbed my breastbone, the action doing nothing to banish the awful ache there, too much love and relief mixed with an equal amount of...clarity. Some new and awful emotion I'd never had before and wished I could rid myself of now.

It was horribly ironic that just as Stavros filled a spot in the team we hadn't realized was there, some hole I had no control over opened up deep inside me. As Bruce and Vee split off, lost in each other and heading for their suite, my weird restlessness crested.

I intercepted Josh as he headed for the common room, cutting him off before he could fall into gamer mode. "How do you feel about a road trip?"

"What's up?" He stretched, as loose and at ease as ever. Like Stavros, content with the team and his new teammate.

I gave the disappearing couple's backs a look, my brow lifted. "I think they might enjoy some privacy for a few days. Or, you could accompany Kimi on the surprise museum crawl she has planned for Stavros." Stavros probably would enjoy the museums, but mostly Kimi was dying to get details from a source who'd witnessed history first hand.

"Where are we headed?" Josh took a huge step away, distancing himself from the pair, like Kimi would grab him and force him to imbibe the minutia of historical accuracy.

"We could hit HQ, get the monthly samples out of the way, and spend the rest of the time visiting."

Josh's face clouded at the implied mention of his twin brother. "I'm a go."

Jace was theoretically taking his turn at acting as a visiting Instructor. And that was important, something we all did. Except once Jace's term was complete, he would still be in the worst kind of limbo, the only survivor of a massacre that took the rest of his team.

He spent the majority of his down time hanging with Matteo, the victim of a similar, more recent disaster. Theirs was one of the teams the male Assessor had mentioned during our shot to heck assessment visit.

The guys were healed, but at loose ends. I couldn't imagine what they were going through. Both teams had consisted of our year mates, agents we'd grown up with, and thinking of them now clogged my throat with tears.

I cleared it, my grief reflected back in Josh's eyes. "Meet you in the garage?"

Josh nodded and went for his room to change, and grab his travel bag.

I only had to change. My bag had been packed for days. Part of me aware of what needed to happen, even if my heart hadn't been ready to accept the decision at the time. I took a look around the room I'd called home since we'd passed our exams and final externship, gaining our own Region.

The duffel slung over my shoulder, I lifted the envelope from its spot on the dresser.

Deep down, as soon as Vee returned I had known the inevitable outcome. But the letter still hurt—writing it, and holding it now.

As much as it shredded me, it was part of being a good leader. I didn't want the growing pit inside me to poison my family, or change who I was.

The team was fully integrated. Everyone was at their best. Stavros was an invaluable ace up their sleeve. The biggest issue was taken care of—Stavros fit the role about to open up. Meaning Josh and Kimi could stay in the positions they preferred, behind the scenes.

I was so damn proud of all of them.

I propped the letter on the desk, once more Vee's domain —her desk in her office.

* * *

AFTER THE USUAL security profile and clean room decontamination, and our new normal of blood and DNA profiling completed, we dumped our bags into the suites reserved for visiting teams. Josh split off to find Jace, and I wove through the enormous warren of the dedicated executive and diplomatic offices.

When I arrived at the connecting wing, a hub linking admin offices and agent wings, and knocked on the claw-resistant frosted glass door with the discrete Team Controller plaque, it opened immediately. I gave the Controller's aid, a peppy last year cadet I remembered from one of my stints as Instructor, a smile.

He still tripped all over himself, holding the door for me. "Agent Rayez is expecting you, Instructor—I mean, Agent. Ma'am."

"Olivia is fine. You're weeks away from being a full agent yourself."

I let him knock, giving him a beat to regain his bearings. At Ray's brusque, "Enter," I smiled and waved him off.

It wasn't as if she hadn't known we were coming, my call and I.D logged into the HQ system when I texted. Or hadn't had the option of pulling up satellite feed from the moment we turned off the main highway, miles from the Company's primary roadway. As far as the outside world knew, we were a conglomeration of loosely linked research and development companies, large enough to support its own mini-town, complete with a private academy.

In mutual agreement, we waited a beat until the aid's chair caster's squeaked. I dropped into the cushy chair nearly large enough to qualify as a loveseat. She pressed her thumb to a bio reader on her desk's corner and a drawer slid open, revealing its treasures.

"Has the Level One class tried their hands at discovering what's in the drawer?" I asked about the unofficial rite of passage. In our time, it had been learning what was in our hand-to-hand Instructor's office. It wasn't about stealing, something no Company kid would ever even imagine, but about taking the dare and executing the challenge as a team. Pure bragging rights for the kids.

Ray poured us both a shot of mescal and handed one over. "Not yet, but I predict sometime within the next thirty days. I'm thinking of putting a glitter bomb in there."

We said it at the same time. "But glitter cleanup is a beast."

I tapped my glass against hers and the smoky liquid burned its way down like it still held some of the fire that produced it. This was our tradition since we'd done a mixed agent mission ages before.

"I'm surprised to see you here ahead of schedule." She pushed her empty glass to the side, and settled back in her plushy chair, fingers steepled. Morphing from friend to professional.

Josh, Kimi, and I still had standard access to HQ. Partially because the Assessors didn't trust samples not taken by their staff, partially because banning us would have thrown up far too many red flags. We played the visits off as mandatory counseling sessions. Learning to process the trauma of losing our C.O. and sister, Josh almost losing his twin, and all our grief at the loss of two teams, all of them friends.

It was also impossible to conceal our last few missions, since the Cleaners had rolled through the complex with live specimens we'd obtained, destined for the Labs. Vee and Stavros were more than upholding their part of the Assessor's deal.

Now, I kept my expression neutral. Fishing in my deep jacket pocket, I pulled out and handed Ray the form I'd had as much difficulty with as the letter I'd composed for Vee. This pain was threaded with a narrow line of hope.

Ray pulled the paper across her desk. She took her time reading the form, despite recognizing what it was the moment she scanned the title.

Done searching for whatever insight into my head that she was after, she laid the paper face down, and studied me. The clear, probing gaze that destined her for the position of Controller, matching up kids, creating new teams with the highest possible probability of coalescing and succeeding in the field, took me in.

I didn't know if she was mentally accessing the information from my files, strengths, weaknesses, personality and psychological profile, or attempting to wrap her head around her friend's unheard of decision.

"It's not April first, and I'm not going to ask if this is a joke. Can I ask why you came to this conclusion and choice? The real reason, not the carefully thought out and crafted excuse for HQ records." She flicked the form, the paper rattling. "I never imagined this scenario."

I recited the reason I'd written on the request, including Stavros official alias. "With Vee back, Bruce passing his assessment, Husiy Stavros Villca's request getting fast tracked thanks to his military qualifications, the team is at prime capacity."

"There are plenty of teams with six or even seven agents. Some teams coalesce that way and splitting them over an arbitrary numeric suggestion would negatively impact performance and morale."

"You and I are both aware that may not be the case going forward. If the cryptid demographics continue shifting, Oversight will strongly suggest capping teams at five in order to create more teams to spread out as simultaneous incursions increase." That was a key bargaining point to present Oversight, if a CYA façade was ever required.

Her bland, diplomatic face impeccable, she countered my bluff. "Potentially, yes. Which would affect cadet teams still forming, but have no bearing on yours."

When I didn't speak, she kept going. "You are lieutenant

in one of the top teams not just in the Southwest, but in North America. A team that is also popular. You not only kept it together after losing the C.O., you excelled. The team's stats are higher than ever."

She studied me, her forehead creased and confusion trumping professionalism. "They are your *family*, Liv. I'm of the opinion that one of the factors contributing to your success is that your team is so tight-knit. You're all incredibly dedicated to each other in an already dedicated atmosphere."

"There's no rule prohibiting my request, Ray."

"No, and that is because what you're proposing is universally a last-ditch effort when there's no other option for all the parties involved. This is…unprecedented."

"I'm aware." Just as I was aware that with clean bio scans, passing all the lab tests, and the few carefully chosen actions and hints I'd dropped in Oversight's drone reach, it would be easy for Oversight to decide that family ties aside, I didn't care for living and working with Vee and Stavros, unable to overcome my innate, trained aversion. Same with needing more ground covered as the vampire expansion continued.

Kimi and I had calculated odds on the Assessors approaching one of us with the offer of basically spying on Vee and Stavros and reporting back to the Assessors.

They had chosen me. Maybe I gave off the vibe that I wasn't happy without even realizing, and they picked up on it. I'd agreed, of course, prepared to send them information that wouldn't harm my sister and Stavros, yet keep Oversight happy and off our doorstep.

The discussion with Kimi also had effects she'd never intended, fertilizing the seed dormant in my subconscious. With my agreeing to play spy, it opened the way for a new life, without violating the rules and the team being eliminated for voiding the harsh contract.

Oversight would bend the rule on no one else knowing

about what Vee and Stavros were. They'd see the guys I was visiting next as another layer of information on our agent-vampires, even more objective and less personally invested than I was.

Ray completely abandoned the Controller persona. "Hells, Liv. Your frankly iffy run at melding a bare handful of adult agents from not one, but three different teams—all possibly traumatized, two of whom haven't been in the field since watching their siblings die—into a functioning unit is likely taking on a lost cause. You can't really want to trade your team, respected by the entire Company, for a high risk gamble with a narrow probability of succeeding."

"It isn't my team." I hadn't meant to allow the real feelings, the heat in my tone to escape. But, now it was out there.

The reason why I couldn't be that person anymore, the previous version of Olivia Muñez, Lieutenant. It was like a shed skin—it didn't fit anymore. It wouldn't ever.

Finally understanding, unwanted compassion, and even more unwanted pity flashed over Ray's face. "Are you willing to push Kimi into the Lieutenant role? Despite her high scores, she's never shown interest in the position."

"Stavros is ideally suited for second in command, and neither Kimi or Josh will disagree." I altered tactics, redirecting the conversation. "I've given my idea a lot of thought from a tactical perspective. One of my proposed members is a sniper, also leaning heavily into the intelligence gathering range, and with the laidback, personable attitude civilians are drawn to and trust. The other member excels at urban reconnaissance, and rural tracking, with a side specialization in munitions and explosives. Until the missions that wiped out their teams, both were classified in the top five percentile of agents. With my rank, tactical rating, and knife and hand to hand skills, it rounds out a team."

Ray blinked, and might as well have had a thought balloon over her head.

I preempted her next argument. I knew Matteo, with his kind heart and endless loyalty, and Jace was my brother the same as Josh, just as brave, just as loyal. "The probability of any team surviving those two attacks was close to zero, and not a result of either agent holding back or failing. It's amazing that they are even alive after the damage they took fighting to save their team members."

"Completely off the record?"

"Whatever we're about to discuss goes no further than this room. Mescal's honor." My attempt at humor tanked. Probably because I felt anything but light and funny. I didn't know if I'd ever get back to that emotional space again.

Ray shoved form, bottle, and shot glass away, ignoring the glass tipping over and leaking on the paper. She leaned in. "This new team? You'd be on your own. HQ won't send you any cadet teams to do their externship with you. I'm talking bare bones. The opposite of the support and resources you're accustomed to."

"I'm aware of that as well." No matter how good our past teams were, how exemplary our record within our old team, now we weren't anything but leftovers. In a life where teams were also family, and the basis for the entire model, we were lone remnants.

HQ was basically extended family. This oddity with the Assessors aside, the Company would never ignore any agent, throw one of us away, or inadvertently treat or see us as expendable.

However, the odds were heavily on the side of failure through no fault of our own, and no lack of our effort to succeed. They couldn't expend resources on an experiment doomed to failure. Such as sending cadets to train with a team that couldn't operate at full effectiveness, thus putting cadets in increased peril.

I scooted my empty glass over to join hers, and pitch completed, leaned back to wait. I'd done all I could, and exposed the raw holes in my soul for scrutiny.

Ray sighed. Her go-to when she agreed.

The fear I'd been holding at bay, that she, and by extension HQ, would deny my request on the grounds that I was more valuable where I was evaporated.

Ray flipped the new team formation request face up, belatedly patting at the wet edge, and signed it. "Technically, Oversight has to rubber stamp this as well, but that's only a formality."

Mentally, I agreed. In this instance, they would weigh a highly unlikely experiment involving vampires as Company personnel versus a slightly less unlikely experiment in potentially forming a viable team of leftover humans, and come down on the side of at least salvaging three useful agents. In this one thing, the odds worked for us.

Ray tossed the pen and form aside, standing and crossing the invisible line from agent to friend, and held her hand out, the handshake ending in a heartfelt hug. "I will be rooting for you. If there's anything official or unofficial I can do, call, text, email, whatever means of notification you have at hand, and I'll put all my weight behind getting it for you. You and the guys deserve better. Got it?"

"Got it." I let go of one extended family member, and went to find what might turn into my other, future family.

The hall to the barrack's common rooms felt like a miles long trek in full gear, and the shortest walk ever, at the same time.

The bark of video game weapons and trash talk told me I'd picked the right room.

I propped against the doorframe, watching Jace and Matteo yelling at the screen.

Jace glanced my way, giving a dazzling smile and fast chin tilt, acknowledging me. A move so similar to his brother's that I had to look away for a second, to drive off the stab of grief and homesickness.

After another moment of my not moving on, Jace tapped Matteo on the shoulder, figuring out I wasn't simply passing through or even here to join the game.

They left off gaming at the same instant, a good sign that they were still field-savvy—and hopefully, building their own connection and communication shorthand.

Despite Matteo's resemblance to a walking wall of muscle, Jace took point. Another good sign, especially in my future lieutenant. "Yo, Liv. Need anything? Josh headed to the cafeteria a few minutes ago to *accidentally* run into Nandi." He and Matteo both snorted at their sibling's lack of finesse.

Matteo flicked his mic out of the way, silently joining in on whatever action was going down. A pinkish-brown line marred his dark skin, curving around the back of his ear and disappearing into his fade, the only outward evidence of his injuries.

I pulled on all the reasons this was technically a good plan, and all the emotional reasons that we—Matteo, Jace, and I—needed this second chance. "If you have time, I have a proposition I'd like to get your feedback on. How do you two feel about windigo migrations and a change of scenery?"

The guys shared a look.

"We have more time than we know what to do with." Matteo scooted his bulk sideways, patting the empty space on the couch, inviting me to join them.

* * *

THANK you for reading Agent Down!

If you enjoyed the story and have the time, a quick Amazon or Goodreads review is *always* much appreciated. Reviews don't need to be long to help boost a book's visibility. "This is a fun story, I liked it" or "How drunk was the author when she wrote this story?" are short, to the point, and equally valid.

Your feedback also gives me an idea of what y'all want more of in upcoming stories, and what you aren't so crazy about.

ACKNOWLEDGMENTS

A huge thanks to the best critique partners around—Cath, Kat, Jes, Cyn, and Mud—and to the Omegas crew for keeping me honest and inspired.

All my gratitude to the amazing Anne Raven of Black Bird Book Covers who always goes above and beyond, as well as to fabulous and fabulously patient editor Jenny Lane, and the incredible PR team at Psst Promotions and Let's Talk! Promotions.

Thanks to my sis Amy, and other-sis Debbie, for listening to plot woes and schlepping to Cons. Thanks to my MIL Cathy and Favorite Cousin Bill, who keep adding to their bookshelves.

Props to my fabulous ARC team—the Advance Cryptid Recon Agents—for their enthusiasm, creativity, and help. Y'all are the best.

A huge thank you all the readers who have fallen as hard for the Region Two crew as I have.

Finally, all my love to Mr. WW for his support, eye for detail, and patience.

ABOUT THE AUTHOR

Janet Walden-West lives in the Southeast with a pack of show dogs, a couple of kids, and a husband who didn't read the fine print. A Weird Dog Show Chick in her downtime, she's also a 2X PitchWars alum and Mentor, and a Golden Heart® finalist. She writes intersectional sexy-times romance and boss-girl fantasy heroines.

She is represented by Eva Scalzo of Speilburg Literary Agency.

Visit me at Janet Walden-West

ARC Group—Janet Walden-West's Advance Cryptid Recon Agents

facebook.com/janetwaldenwestauthor
twitter.com/JanetWaldenWest
instagram.com/janetwaldenwest
bookbub.com/authors/janet-walden-west
amazon.com/Janet-Walden-West/e/B07DD9FNQ5/ref=dp_byline_cont_pop_ebooks_1
tiktok.com/@janetwaldenwest

www.ingramcontent.com/pod-product-compliance
Lightning Source LLC
Chambersburg PA
CBHW021747190726
48288CB00009B/3187